THE BONE SHRINE

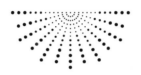

SCOTT MACFARLANE

THE PUBLISHER

NichéEco Imprints
PO Box 381
ClearLake, Washington, 98235

www.nicheeco.com
info@nicheeco.com

THE BONE SHRINE, a novel

First Edition Paperback and eBook,
Copyright by Scott M^{ac}Farlane ©2021
All Rights Reserved
NichéEco Imprints
Member, Independent Book Publishers Association

Cover Art & Design, ©2021
BRENDA MATTSON

Editor
CATE PERRY

This print edition from Barnes & Noble Press.

Library of Congress Control Numbers
Ebook ISBN: 978-1-7368570-0-7
Print Edition ISBN: 978-1-7368570-1-4

✾ Created with Vellum

"Faith sees best in the dark." –Søren Kierkegaard

for
every
Joe & Mary

&
for Grace

TABLE OF CONTENTS

–NichéEco

CHAPTER ONE

I.
GRACE

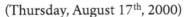

(Thursday, August 17th, 2000)

Joe lurched to a stop and Mary's braid of wildflowers swayed back and forth below the rear view mirror. He watched her brace herself against the glove compartment to keep from falling forward. In her condition, he really needed to go easier on the brakes. Headlights beamed through low sagebrush to reveal several sun-bleached cow skulls in and around a neat and tidy jangle of other skeleton parts.

"The Bone Shrine's even cooler!" Joe said after Mary had tilted upright. He grabbed a flashlight before hopping from the idling old Pathfinder SUV. Soft sand slowed his steps to the ten-foot diameter circle of stones that enclosed far more bones than he remembered from a few years before.

Mary got out of her car and stood behind the open passenger door with arms crossed at her chest. "We're not sleeping here."

"Why not?" he asked and saw her staring at the shrine like it was something tended by extraterrestrials. Mary patted the sides of her bulging baby bump. The dome light illuminated her harsh glare that told him she was dead-set on getting out of here. "I really don't think we should be dropping in on Gunnar at this time of night," he said. "It's your fault we got going so late."

"Who said anything about staying at your cousin's? I offered to pay for a motel room."

"Why spend the money?" Joe had been camping out all summer, and after their baby came, life would get spendy. Two or three more weeks, the doctor had told her.

Mary rubbed her bare upper arms like it was chilly outside. The *aum* of buzzing mosquitoes argued otherwise in the stifling hot August night. "I remember your cousin and his old girlfriend bringing us here," Mary said. "Daylight, Joe. In the daytime. That wasn't at midnight."

Joe knelt to inspect all the new, elaborately positioned bones. "That same cedar's still here, too," he told her, pointing a couple dozen yards behind the Bone Shrine at a silhouette in the moonlight.

"This was a creepy spot then, even creepier now."

Joe reached over his shoulders and scratched, but pulled his arm back to his waist when he figured Mary would be watching him. He'd swallowed his last Vicodin this morning and his skin was starting to talk back.

"Can you check out that pick-up truck first thing in the morning?" Mary asked, patting her belly again.

"Sure. Why not?" His cousin had to have a bit in reserve, not the prescribed crap that barely hinted at what his body was starting to crave.

Joe also knew that Mary was tiring of driving him around in her rig. He lowered the flashlight to see the full overhead moon brightening her face. Pregnancy made her face glow during the day, but this eerie nightlight had her seeming a bit older, not close to as old as his cravings made his insides feel, but definitely more mature than their eighteen years of age.

"Last time I talked to Gunnar, it hadn't been sold. The ride has a shift-on-the-fly 4X4 with a super cab for the baby. The guy owes him.

Said it's pretty tight for being ten-years-old, but most of those Toyota's are if they haven't been off-roading too much." Joe needed to have a solid alibi for coming all the way to Moses Lake. A pick-up indeed. He just hoped Gunnar could hook him up. Joe's source in Portland had dried up. Gunnar had never thanked him much last year for taking the fall, so if he had even a single fix, his cousin owed him. He figured he could hold on till morning. His cravings weren't that bad yet, just threatening like storm clouds, the kind that piled up thick and dark with a coming downpour, but still off on the horizon.

He watched Mary staring with a kind of sadness over the dark, dry landscape. "Are those dog skulls?" Mary asked, glancing at the Shrine and rocking from one foot to the other.

"Pretty sure those are cow skulls on the sand below the altar." Joe highlighted them with his flashlight. "Come check it out!"

"No way. I'm just fine where I'm at."

Other bones were carefully laid out inside the ring of smooth stones––the kind of river rock used for fireplaces in hunting lodges with none as big as a man's head. Only a few stones were as small as a fist.

"I'm not talking about the big cow skulls," she said. "What about those smaller ones along the edge?"

Joe used his beam to circle the perimeter. The shrine was laid out like a big clock. On the north, east, south, and west edges, he checked out the four canine skulls. Each was placed just inside the ring to rest on a tan-gray hide; the nose of each skull pointed towards the center of the circle. Joe knelt and lifted the end of a hide so it was high enough for Mary. "Can you see how wild this tail is?" he asked her. "Pretty sure these are from coyotes," he added. "Don't know who would worship animal bones, though."

Mary rocked from side-to-side. Her palms patted the underside of her nearly full-term womb. "The Fish Indians say that Coyote created the Columbia River." She turned away from the bones and peered across the arid basin again.

"Come closer, Mary. Take a look."

"Maybe in the morning," she answered.

Mary knew plenty about the big river. They both did, really, from teen jobs working at the new museum and spending free time digging into the secrets of the Columbia. Moses Lake had a different geology than where they lived in Oregon. Here, the Columbia Basin snagged plenty of irrigation water from the river since the ground was mostly level with hundreds of weird marshes they called potholes. Huge plowed circles for growing potatoes and other field crops were cultivated where the soil allowed. Joe focused his beam on the altar in the center of the shrine. A crude, low platform had been built with thick crisscrossing femurs that reminded Joe of oversized Lincoln Logs. When he centered his flashlight on the surface of the altar, he noticed a bird skull on top.

"I'm telling you, Joe. Don't plan on camping here." Mary's hands jerked in the headlight beams.

"I've got somewhere else in mind to crash, but that doesn't mean you can't take a quick peek at this little altar that wasn't here last time."

"Jeez, Joe. Just drop it. Let's get going so I can use a real bathroom."

A worn road-sign on the dirt road had pointed to camping in four more miles. Joe didn't expect to find running water there, but a semi-clean Porta-Potty would be nice. He'd drive them to the spot in a few minutes. Man, oh man, he wished he hadn't run dry of Vicodin, or worse yet, the real deal.

Joe could also see that nothing hid Mary's pregnant belly, not her loose, tan, sleeveless blouse with frills at the shoulder that were the color of turquoise, and not that matching wide skirt. He had no clue why she thought she needed to dress so slick for their drive up from Oregon to Moses Lake, but she even wore dangling copper earrings with turquoise beads that contrasted with her tan outfit. The jewelry also went with her thick, jet-black locks and thin, ginger-colored side-braids––her natural hair color. Too stylish for a girl about to drop a kid, but pretty cool for a girlfriend.

"Hey Mary, see how the bird skull stares at you. Reminds me of your new tattoo with those big eye sockets."

"I believe you." Her attention was lost in the lights of Moses Lake. The eastern Washington town shimmered like a dust storm of rust rising in the night. Mary rubbed her upper arms in a way that showed him how short her fuse was getting. He didn't have much time to inspect the new-and-improved Bone Shrine.

Joe pointed his flashlight over carefully scattered ribs, femur shanks, and pelvis shards spread across the sandy area between the coyote and cow skulls. He took care tiptoeing into the circle for a closer look at the dead bird on top of the altar. His flashlight illuminated where someone had inserted a small wooden peg into the plywood altar surface. They had put the skull over the peg and skeleton wings stretched wide with the talons trailing behind. The wings and claws were secured with twine through small drilled holes onto the top of the altar. The bleached bones under moonlight reminded him of a featherless, fleshless raptor in flight.

Joe shuddered when he leaned closer to see that it was a Northern Great Horned Owl. Under his eerie flashlight, he recognized right away the well-arched beak, the size of the bird, and those sharp talons. The night raptor looked as though it had been horizontally crucified, the way he was feeling, like his demon monkey of withdrawal was goading him to carry a cross of his own. Joe guessed the owl had been baking all summer under the high desert sun until only the bleached bones remained. Except for leftover, tiny tufts, he imagined all the feathers windblown across these scablands the way the past year had slowly plucked him clean of any plumage he'd once had.

For the first time, Joe noticed an opening below the back of the altar--there were only three walls of femur bones secured by leather strips at the front corners that held up the platform. Joe got down on a knee to better inspect the odd construction. The backside, away from the road, opened like a niché. Directing his light inside, he saw a mound of bone shards.

A niché was what his mom called the small arch recessed in the wall of the formal dining room in his family's Victorian home, but inside hers there weren't any bones. Instead, she displayed her statuette of the Virgin Mother cradling the Christ child, the one she warned him, under the threat of eternal damnation, never to touch. As far as Joe knew, only Mary Quinn had pulled it from his mother's niché. One night, the previous Fall, his girlfriend spent several minutes holding and rotating the figurine in her hands. Mary was too good to be roasting in hellfire for evermore, but maybe she'd jinxed herself. Maybe that's what caused her to get knocked up.

He read the burnt lettering on the wood surface of the altar, the one that held the owl skeleton. Even seeing the words upside down, he could make out the warning: *Mess With Me, and I Mess You Up.* Really weird, Joe thought, when he knelt down again to check out the niché. Teeth, claws, broken ribs and mandibles were piled several inches thick to cover the sand and fill half of the opening inside. His own ribs itched, his nostrils dripped, and he started in with the scratching again.

One bit of bone seemed strange. He touched what didn't feel right. He wiggled it back and forth. The corner of a small box began to emerge. Joe tapped it with his flashlight. Definitely sheet metal painted in off-white enamel. When he pulled it free, the latched container was a bit longer, but thinner, than the old-style rectangular lunch box he once lugged with him every weekday to elementary school. He pulled the box from the hiding place and read the red lettering on the metal cover: 'FIRST AID KIT.'

Joe unsnapped the two latches and went bug-eyed at the sight. Inside there were no bandages, gauzes, ointments, or scissors. Instead, he saw exactly what he was beginning to desperately crave, except the best you could get. This was the kind Gunnar had first turned him on to when he was slow to recover from the pain of that operation, and his doctor cut him off of his painkillers. He focused his flashlight on the eight, vacuum-sealed plastic bags. A typed label was stuck to each bag that read *China White, 0.25k*. The bundles filled the metal kit.

There had to be two keys of smack here! Unless the dope had already been stepped on, this was the best smackola anyone could score. What if it hadn't been cut? Joe wondered. Looked like powdered bones, but would be worth over a hundred grand per kilo if pure. No wonder they called this a shrine!

His mind raced. There was no need to announce this to Mary. Talk about curing their money woes, newborn baby and all. *Finders keepers, losers weepers*. Joe set the First Aid box at his feet. With his flashlight beam pointed up his chin, Joe lifted his nose to the stars and closed his eyes for a loud, night piercing coyote howl.

His voice carried across the scabland and echoed faintly. When he trained the flashlight away from his chin, Mary's eyes were wide. He'd really startled her. Oh well. Joe pulled out one of the bundles and peeled up an edge of the *China White* label. He took his trusty Swiss

Army knife from his jean's pocket and opened the small pointed blade used for dirty fingernails. Joe poked a hole in one of the sealed pouches just to snort a bit. When he leaned in to inhale the White, his vacuum cleaner nostrils only extracted the tiniest bit of dust and not enough to even feel when Mary yelled as loud as he ever remembered.

"I can't believe it!"

He reared back and dropped the little knife into the niché where it disappeared into the fresh depression where he'd just pulled out the kit. His flashlight showed nothing red, only white, loose bone shards.

"Joe!"

He'd had the pocket knife since his dad gave it to him on his 12th birthday, but there was no time. Not with a find like this. He covered the hole quickly and pressed down the label on the plastic, even though the adhesive side didn't stick over the dope dust.

"Hold up a minute," he yelled back. Joe's withdrawal hadn't gunked up his inner gears quite yet, but the monkey clinging to his shoulder leaned into his ear with a threatening whisper. He ignored his obnoxious buddy. The poppy powder could wait a bit, but not for long.

Joe turned the flashlight towards Mary's face. She glared back as though whatever 'it' was, was his fault. "It's all pretty unbelievably weird," he added, doing his best to hide his rush of anticipation from what lay at his feet.

With this find––when the growling turned snarly––he could calm his personal powder monkey, keep the dynamite from igniting, keep the annoying primate locked up like a stick of explosive inside his inner shed where it belonged. There was also the delicious sugary blast of soon being flush with cash.

From the Pathfinder, Mary sounded disgusted. "What the hell? It's like I just peed myself."

"Do you need a diaper?" he asked, lightly tapping the First Aid kit.

"No diaper, Joe. More like a hospital." Her voice had turned surprisingly calm. "I think my water just broke."

Startled, Joe's body froze erect. He turned his beam on Mary still in the same place with palms up and hands away from her body. She stared into the sky, no doubt questioning the timing.

He wondered about his own demon timing. He'd swallowed that

last painkiller in the morning, but what did it matter now? He'd deal with his addict dick-of-a-self later.

Mary dropped her hands, lifting her skirt away from her thighs and hips. "Let's get out of this place," she told him, turning towards the well-used Pathfinder and climbing inside the still running rig with its vents blasting cold air. She left her passenger door open and urged Joe to speed up whatever he was doing.

Joe lowered the beam towards the Bone Shrine. He clasped the metal case shut with two quick snaps. Tempted to snag the stash right then, he told himself not to be rash, to think this through. No need to carry the box to the SUV and risk Mary seeing it. With a barrel full of questions for him, she'd go all out ape on him.

Joe yanked a coyote hide from beneath one of the canine skulls. Peeking towards the Pathfinder and not seeing or hearing Mary, he wrapped the first aid kit inside. No time to waste. Turning, he accidentally kicked one of the coyote skulls upside down, dropped his flashlight, and left the thing shining over the bones where it landed. With the hide-wrapped metal case under one arm, Joe rushed over to the cedar, a wide, bushy tree at least twice as tall as his six-foot frame.

He pressed into the thick tree limb by pushing through cedar branches, poking his eye, scratching his neck, and gouging his ribs. Twisting sideways with the box under his trailing arm, Joe inched between more punishing branches until he could feel the trunk of the tree. Man, oh man he wanted to sample the goods.

"What in the hell are you waiting for, Joe, our second child?"

"I dropped something," he answered.

"Nothing like I'm about to drop," she bellowed.

The hide had managed to stay wrapped around the box. With both hands holding the container, Joe pushed upwards. A snag ripped through his baseball jersey. He pressed harder into the branches. A souvenir on the chest of the jersey came unhinged. He felt the outside of the breast pocket where, somehow, the pin had managed to drop inside.

Joe tried his best to wedge the kit through the tree's prison bar branches. Turning the box so the narrow side faced up, he pushed until finding a gap. Joe pressed it through two wrist-thick branches and maneuvered the kit to lay fairly flat. On tiptoes, and with all his strength, Joe pushed until the encased stash broke enough twigs to be pressed against the trunk of the cedar. Wedged within the limbs, gravity wouldn't allow the wrapped box to fall to the ground. The stash seemed well hidden, but without the flashlight it was impossible to know in the dark of night how well he'd secured it within this weave of branches. His fingers told him the hide covering the First Aid kit was still intact.

None of this took more than a couple of minutes. He'd get back to the China White soon enough, and they wouldn't need to visit Gunnar after all. Even Joe knew these contraction things took time, not to say that it wasn't the time to get Mary to the closest hospital.

"Joe!" Mary screamed. "Don't be such an idiot. We really gotta go."

"I'm coming." He exited the densely limbed tree, hurried to the shrine, and scooped up the flashlight. Keeping to the outside of the ring of stones, he hustled to the Pathfinder.

Joe brushed off bits of cedar when he reached the car. "Our fortune is turning." He jumped into the driver's seat with enough adrenaline kicking in to maybe give Mr. Jones a monkey nap. He plunked the flashlight on the console beside him, reached out and, in one motion, kissed Mary's cheek while pulling the baseball souvenir from his jersey. He clasped the pin through the thin ginger braid closest to him.

Joe was pretty sure his girlfriend was ready to punch him in the shoulder for wasting time, but his mind stayed on the stash. He'd return soon enough for the kit and its white treasure delivered to him straight from the cosmos.

"What's wrong with you?" Mary demanded, her voice much more even than he expected.

Joe knew he needed to get clean. He needed to man up to his cravings. That crap was taking over. Who was he anymore? Think this through. What was he messing with? This crazy, big stash didn't belong to nobody. Should he just leave it be? More than a lifetime worth of smack sitting in that tree. Serious dough. Whether for the money or a junkie's perpetual paradise, he didn't have a clue about the box he'd opened. Maybe he needed to forget he ever found it, step back, keep on driving and embrace the family way. They'd eke by with regular old jobs and his old lady's offer of housing. "I'm sorry, Mary. I've just been stumbling."

She held both sides of her womb and glared at Joe sternly. "But what's wrong with you? You smell like the wood in a sauna."

When Joe pulled a twig from his hair, a few sandy blond strands stayed with the cedar. He dropped it between his seat and the driver's door, but didn't answer her.

CHAPTER TWO

(Friday, August 18th)

Joe's heart raced. He wasn't sure if the pounding was from jonesing, finding and moving the stash, or Mary's blind date with giving birth, but knowing what her overreaction would be, he wasn't about to mention the first aid kit. When he engaged the clutch, the Pathfinder spit sand and fishtailed.

He stopped and made sure the 4-wheel-drive was still engaged while Mary removed a small towel from between her thighs and reached behind the seats into her suitcase for another. He turned away when she started to dab up more moisture from beneath the ruffles of her skirt.

"The emergency room can't deny us help." She tilted the passenger seat back.

Suck it up, dude, Joe told himself. Maybe he really had found a stopgap solution to their money woes.

Joe took a breath and eased forward. This time the SUV spun on the sandy surface that was not quite a road and not quite a path. "Just a few miles to Moses Lake, baby. Can you hold on?"

"Contractions!" Mary clutched her womb.

Joe tried to watch both the road and Mary. She arched her back and grimaced while pressing into her seat with a pained expression he'd never seen from her before. He probably wasn't looking much better.

Joe sped up, but needed to stop fishtailing if Mary was going to make it to the hospital. There was no time for any of this, not the whole labor mess, not his own sweat kicking in, not for any of this crap. Mary wasn't supposed to drop the kid until the end of August. That's why he agreed to let her come north with him today—that and the fact she owned the ride to get him here. Her old Nissan had decent 4-wheel drive, that is if the tires held up through all his spinouts.

"Watch the bumps!" Mary slapped his elbow when the pain hit her again.

Joe pulled a towel from his duffel bag behind her seat. "Bite on this," he insisted. Mary winced just as the SUV sputtered and rolled to a stop with a pothole seep pond on one side and a few crude parking spots for fishermen on the other. "I thought you filled the tank the whole way up when we left."

"You were there when I did, Joseph. The gas gauge broke the day you drove like a manic Mountain Goat up that hiking trail."

He remembered hauling a dumb mattress to his summer hideout. Joe turned the key, but the ignition ground until it ignored him. "I can't believe this crap." He pounded the steering wheel.

"You can't believe this? What about me? Help me before it starts again." Mary pushed her wavy, black-dyed hair over her shoulder and rolled the towel until it was thick enough to bite and muffle her screams. He sat stunned, staring at Mary until she removed the towel, and hit him over the head with one end. "Do something! She's coming, Joe. I can't stop her!"

Mary's body tightened and forced her to start pushing. "I need to lie down."

They'd only come a couple hundred, sandy, slow yards, so Joe craved a run back to the cedar tree. He shut off the headlights instead and left on the inside dome lamp. He grabbed the flashlight again and hustled to the back to lift the rear hatch. Most of all, he ordered himself to make a nest for the hatchling, to get tougher on his bird of withdrawal, and don't freak out. Otherwise, Mary would lose her grip and really fly off on him.

Joe gathered up as many clothes and belongings as he could and threw them onto the driver's seat until the pile covered the steering wheel to the level of the dashboard. A few trips from back to front and he'd cleared enough space.

"I found the air mattress and pump." What a piss-poor consolation prize for needing to give birth in the middle of nowhere.

"Just hurry." Mary's voice was quieter, no doubt dreading the next round of pain. Joe did his best under moonlight to unfold the mattress on the empty road and hook up the plastic accordion foot pump.

Hooking up. It was so close by and free for the taking. His body had thinned from relapsing and camping, but Joe wasn't out of shape. His hard breathing was either nerves or the muffled gobbling his angry turkey was starting to make. His sweat began to pour.

In the heat of night, he was tempted to shed the Chunichi Dragons baseball jersey that he'd been given by his family's exchange student. He'd worked hard to convince Mary he was clean. It was just a light maintenance habit he told himself last May, and it was just that until he indulged a bit more often, with a bit more smack each time, and one day his maintenance demanded to be maintained so often that it owned his sorry, bony backside. He'd quit for real when the baby came. Even if he snagged that stash and sold it, he'd go clean. Joe promised himself, but his hands were starting to shake.

"You gotta hurry!" Mary leaned back hard against her seat.

Once Joe felt the mattress fill, he groped for the plug to keep air from escaping. He slipped the light mattress inside the rear of the SUV. The thing covered most of the space between wheel wells. Joe leaned down to blow air into the pillow at one end. The effort gave him fresh energy, not resolve exactly, but a touch of determination. Mary's lime-green fleece blanket brightened under the dome light. A trip to the cedar was all he needed, but this was no time to be slip sliding away. Joe draped the blanket like a sheet over the mattress so Mary's own sweaty skin wouldn't stick to the plastic. "Let's get you in back, Lady Quinn," he said and helped her to her feet.

"Smells like rotten eggs out here." Mary had one hand on her womb, the other held her nose closed.

Bulrushes and cattails filled the edges of the pothole pond beside the dirt road. Moonlight cut up the surface of the pond like bits of jagged glass. The same marsh vegetation grew here as it did a couple hundred miles downriver in their Oregon part of the Gorge.

"What's that?" Mary asked, pointing towards more carefully arranged stones separating the road from the pothole pond, probably to give fishermen a place to sit.

Joe shined his light and squinted towards where she pointed. Walking closer, he spotted a fat, bloated, scaly fish rotting atop the landing of stones. The thing had to weigh ten pounds. "Moses Lake carp. They taste as good as they smell."

Or, even more like the way he felt inside, he wanted to say. Joe placed a palm over his nose and mouth before going over to kick the dead garbage fish off the landing. It splashed into the pond. Joe needed to puke. Even though the carp gave him an excuse to upchuck, he took deep breaths to calm the urge.

Mary went to the rear of her dented SUV where she raised her arms and held on tight to the back edge of the open lift-gate. Joe hustled back to her when she doubled over from a wave of pain. "I don't want to do this here." Her eyes were as big as a freaked-out owl's. "I want to go home."

Joe stepped back when she ripped off the front buttons from her wide skirt and let it drop. "It's too HOT here!" He steered clear of her temper outburst when that heated word pulled more sweat through his pores. She stomped on the skirt and kicked it to the stone landing, where it fell directly on top of where the stinking carp had been.

Mary didn't have much patience for her sleeveless blouse either. When the first button wouldn't come undone, she yanked like she meant it and ripped off a whole row of buttons until they clanked against the Pathfinder and bounced into the sand. No way was Joe not going to do his duty here. He may be jonesing, but he wasn't ready for her to fling him away like some broken fastener.

Joe took one step forward, but sidestepped the garment she threw towards the closest reeds. The blouse all but stopped in midair and opened like a parachute before drifting down and landing like a canopy over the nearest tall cattails.

"I hate this place!" Mary's scream insulted the scablands. Her bra and panties landed on top of the pile of stuff on the driver's seat.

It all came in waves, the sweats, the urge to puke, his insides wanting out. Hate didn't begin to describe Joe's loathing for letting heroin bully him into his wonky state of submission, even though there were the lulls, too, like this one. He stepped towards her.

"Just keep away from me!"

Joe——young, brave fool that he knew he was——stepped in and kissed her cheek anyway. He ignored the inevitable elbow to his chest.

Mary reached up to hold the raised lift-gate again. From a good yard behind her, he rubbed his rib. Joe found himself admiring her well-rounded hourglass that had hidden a growing womb for the better part of her pregnancy. She cried softly, expecting any minute to be slammed by another inevitable contraction, the way that too soon the smack would mock his pride again. This was never going to be him, he'd remembered thinking. It was always someone else, some weaker user. This was just a maintenance thing this summer. Man, how the monkey would lean in his ear and ration out the little lies, until Joe aped what he believed he could handle. Man, how the monkey-mind came to own him.

The real Joe loved how Mary's breasts were bigger than ever and full like they were ready for what they'd been made to do (besides pleasin' him!). Moonlight bounced off the freckles on her back. Joe moved all her hair over one shoulder so it covered a breast and allowed him to trace her cool tattoo. His touch calmed her and took his mind off Joe, the addict. Naked, Mary seemed to be biding time. No way did she want to climb into the back of the stuffy Pathfinder on the hottest flippin' night of the year. But they were going to have a baby. It was really happening. Two kids having a kid, that part was the craziest thing of all.

Joe's fingers traced the image of She-Who-Watches, a Columbia Gorge petroglyph that covered her upper back. The dark brown design had been inked on Mary's ivory skin all speckled with freckles. She had the tattoo inked a few weeks before he got out of juvie. Said she'd used the five hundred dollars her mom, Bonnie, had left her on her 18th birthday. That would have been right before her mother split for Branson, Missouri to become a Country-Blues, or Bluegrass singing Ozark star, or some such thing. Mary said that the tattoo needles had been brutal. Joe guessed the pain of the inking had nothing on what she was about to feel.

Positioned just below her neck and covering both chicken wings of her upper back, the tattoo stared back at him, and letters dropped one at a time along her vertebrae:

T

S

A

G

A

G

L

A

L

A

L

The bottom letter stopped between her dimples of Venus, what Mary called the two indents where her waist widened into her hips. Joe traced the letters and then those two dimples. The design was cool, very cool to Joe's eyes, but She-Who-Watches was watching him.

"You have eyes on the back of your--back," Joe said and, for the moment, despite her mind-of-their-own contractions, and despite him becoming a soup of chaos inside, they laughed. *Tsagaglalal*'s ears, like a bear's, sat atop the tattooed head. His chieftess, Mary Quinn, was listening, too. He never figured why she hadn't caught onto his relapse.

"We can do this, Joseph."

He didn't know if by 'doing this,' she meant a life together or bringing this life into the world. Even though they were way too young, both of them accepted what a big deal this birth was. They could figure out the mom and dad thing, but not if he was always scrounging for his next fix. Other than that minor detail, he was sure they could raise a kid. "I'm no midwife or baby doctor," he added.

"But it's your turn to be *my* nurse," Mary smiled and told him. This was a lull for her, too. She reached behind her naked body. With one hand, she cupped him and, ever so lightly, squeezed. "Just like I helped you heal."

Joe enjoyed standing still together. Mary faced her birthing vault inside the Pathfinder. Joe sensed how afraid she was to budge, still dreading the hard labor part. As softly as he could, Joe lifted his fingers from her tattoo and, from behind, placed his hands on the small of her waist. His chin rested on her crown, a head shorter than his own. All summer, once she'd told him, they'd made love as often as they could. Not having to worry about getting knocked up was the oddest benefit of her being pregnant. "I hope she has your blue eyes," Mary whispered.

He kissed the nape of her neck. "I don't know. Those green eyes of yours are pretty fine," he countered, his cheek against hers. As lightly as he could, Joe set the palms of his hands on the top of her belly that was so hard and ready. Joe thought he felt it move. Mary dropped her hands from the raised lift gate. She tilted her head back to Joe's cheek before squeezing each of his wrists parked on her belly.

"I've been channeling the ancient chieftess," Mary told him and climbed inside the Pathfinder, getting as comfortable as she could on the air mattress, feet against the backs of the front bucket seats, and looking straight up at him.

"Why the channeling?" Joe asked, knowing that Mary wasn't kidding.

"So I can always watch over you and Grace."

Across the small seep lake, a night owl hooted and frogs took up a chorus. He watched Mary grimacing from inside the back of the Pathfinder. She lifted up her neck as far as she could and pushed. "Hold me forward," she demanded. Joe placed his hands on her shoulders to help her ease towards her knees. She roared in pain and reached back to grip him. Fingernails dug deep into his forearms. Joe resisted the urge to react. Under the dome light he could see where she'd drawn blood. Nothing hurt, but even if it had, he wouldn't have minded her wringing out her pain on him. When the contraction backed down, he helped lower her head onto the air pillow.

His bird of withdrawal returned, ready for action. Joe's pores dripped with sweat and he stood behind the Pathfinder growing more nervous about this whole birth-giving thing. All he wanted was a nice snort of China White, so close, but so far away.

"She'll be a world baby," Mary told him just before her next contraction hit. She wailed. Mary was so sure it would be a girl that she didn't get an ultrasound reading to tell them the gender. She lay face-up clutching the edges of the air mattress, her feet spread-eagle against the backs of the front bucket seats.

Mary was in for real laboring. Middle of nowhere, middle of the night and with a bone dry gas tank, she was primed to drop their kid. He ignored the urge to bend forward when his own stomach cramped. The white meat, dark meat, dressing, and giblets of his insides had turned rancid. How much longer could he hide this from Mary?

"Harder, Mary. Push harder," he kept insisting. His own cravings ate at any sympathy he should be having for her. Stopgap--just a tiny fix from this surprise stash to get him through. In the spare tire compartment beneath Mary's head, he'd stashed needle, spoon, cotton and syringe for whenever that elusive fix might come his way.

Having a kid could be the coolest thing ever if they made it a good thing, if he could get over this bad thing--for good. "Relax, baby," he said, but she wasn't in any mood to be soothed. She squirmed on her back. Joe listened to her deep breaths, the kind they'd been teaching her in Lamaze class.

"I need some water." Mary was moody for sure, but this was hardly one of her spells of depression. She closed her eyes and breathed even deeper.

Joe lifted his body up, bumped his head, and with his knuckles, pushed away some of the sweat covering his face and neck. He rummaged in the front for a water bottle that was no doubt buried deep in the pile of belongings he'd just heaped there. He returned empty-handed to his place behind her. "You really gotta push harder," he demanded, hoping to distract her.

"Stop going off on me!" She sat up, still naked. Joe helped hold her in place. Mary winced and moaned from her biggest contraction yet. When it eased off, she ground her molars and spoke real low. "I don't want that mean voice of yours being the first thing Grace hears."

Joe bit his tongue about the Grace name, even when she continued. "Promise me we'll call her Grace. Promise me, Joe. She'll be Grace Rochelle Gardner."

"No reason why not," he said. 'Gardner' was Joe's last name. 'Rochelle' would be after his mother and not Mary's own. That surprised him, but his mom and Mary were crazy close. Too bad he hadn't talked to his mom all summer after getting booted.

He and Mary had thrown out a slew of first names, even ones like Sandy or Shawn that could work for either sex. They hadn't settled on any and she'd never mentioned Grace as a possibility until, in the thick of this labor, he guessed that her signature song was coming on strong for her.

"'Grace' is a cool name, I guess," Joe said, "if it's a girl."

"It's going to be a girl. I told you that."

Why argue an impending truth? Joe positioned one foot sideways and farther back to really dig in through the sand and hold up her shoulders for what he hoped would be the home stretch of this birthing mess. He didn't want to think it could be hours of labor, not with his withdrawals starting in on him. Secretly, Joe wished for a son––for Joseph John Gardner, IV––even though he hadn't talked to his father, J.J., since he'd left his mom in May. And, to keep all the Josephs straight, he and Mary could call their son, 'Jo Jo.' At the time of the bust, J.J. had let him know how disgusted he was about the heroin, so maybe naming this baby 'Jo Jo' would repair those ugly things with his old man.

The frog chorus went quiet. When the hot breeze died down, their croaks were replaced by buzzing from the swarm of mosquitos blocking out most of the moonlight. The baby hadn't even dropped, but he'd need to get gas as soon as 'Jo Jo' or 'Grace' came––after he'd snorted just enough, that is.

These flying bloodsuckers from this scabland swamp started landing on his skin, his shirt, his pant legs. There was no mosquito repellent to spray over the skin he'd already scratched raw. Mary, three weeks early, yelled like her thick locks were hissing flares. This nonstop itching under a glaze of sweat wasn't much fun for him either.

The contractions came quicker. Try as he might, Joe clawed his arms more and more. "Gawddammed mosquitos!" At least the kamikaze insects gave Joe an excuse for scratching right in front of her.

"That'll only make their bites worse, baby," she told him, until another contraction seized her. Joe had never seen labor up close. The only thing he'd experienced that compared to her pain was his baseball injury, the one he blamed for everything bad since the accident. He didn't want to think about that at-bat again for the ten-thousandth time, especially not now.

Joe's sweating got worse with the swarm attacking in formation; it took all he had to keep his hands placed on Mary's shoulders and away from his skin. She screamed again. Sandwiched between the Pathfinder's interior vinyl and Mary's naked body, the plastic air mattress squeaked and annoyed Joe more than his girlfriend's labor cries. He couldn't believe that the mattress hadn't popped under the pressure of Mary's round, pregnant, antsy, pounding butt. She groaned again and begged for Joe to hold her tighter and push on her harder.

He kissed her sweaty temple. "What do I do next?" he asked quietly when more contractions came, one right after the next.

"Like I told you, Joe, hold my neck up. Also get rid of this stupid air mattress. I hate the thing." She was losing patience all around, so he quickly pulled the mattress from under her and slipped it on the sandy ground beneath the chassis of her Pathfinder. The palms of his hands had grown rough from two-and-a-half months of summer escape-camping, and were no doubt too rough on the soft skin of her shoulders. Her next scream came out so loud that the mosquitos stopped buzzing. Joe reacted by clenching her collarbone. He told himself to be more gentle.

"I've gotta follow the freeway to get us some gas," he said, hoping he could visit the cedar tree first. Just one good snort. Joe stepped to the side of the beat up Pathfinder and unhooked the bungee cord holding an empty plastic gallon gas can to the top of her car. It bounced off a round rock on the road before stopping in the sand at his feet.

"No! Don't leave me, Joe!"

"Of course I'm not leaving right now, Mary, but I want to let you know before the baby comes so you don't freak out then."

"I don't care about then. I just want to get this over with--like right now!"

He knew Mary could do better than staying hooked up with a high school drop-out like him. He lifted his face to breathe.

"That baby will be a saving grace for this hard world. I've been singing her song, Joe."

Mary sure wanted to believe that her new baby would be that special somehow. It was fine and well by him--even if he couldn't bring himself to believe it. He remembered her talking about this baby being a bodhisattva of the earth, and the daughter of humankind, or, however she put it. He'd be cool with a healthy, normal kid, not one who'd grow up greedy, full of himself, or unable to make smart choices, like getting sucked into a junk-hole like his.

Joe started itching crazy-like and put his wet hands on Mary's sweaty shoulders again. "Breathe harder; keep yourself calm, Mary," Joe told her, despite his stomach going to war. She ignored him and screamed again. Joe clenched his teeth. "What else do you want me to do?" he asked, again worrying if this would go on for hours.

When her next contraction hit, he used his forearms to prop up her shoulders. Mary pushed the sole of one foot so hard that the passenger seat popped loose and slammed forward against the glove box. The driver's seat was so full of clothes that it wouldn't budge forward no matter how hard her foot pushed.

Mary let out her wildest groan yet. The eyes of *Tsagaglalal* widened when Mary bent forward and cut loose with a long moan. Joe ignored his worst itching yet. She lay back and pressed her sandals against the ceiling of the car. Her primal yell filled the night, and she cracked the dome light with her sole. The inside of the Pathfinder went dark.

"She's here," Mary whispered. Her head collapsed back on the overinflated pillow.

The baby came out way faster than Joe expected. Mary slumped back, eyes closed. She begged faintly. "Let me see her." Her request jolted him into the moment.

Joe walked to the passenger side of the Pathfinder and, after pushing the front seat back to its normal position, he leaned in to fish out his flashlight hiding alongside the bucket seat. With no rear side doors, he tilted the front seat forward again. Nervous to find out the sex, Joe pointed a weak beam over the glistening form. The newborn lay partly on crumple up fleece and partly on the vinyl floor between Mary's legs. He set down the light and lifted the infant.

"'Grace' it is," he said in a soft, low voice, inspecting the baby that filled his palms. Right then, he knew he didn't mind in the least having a healthy girl to raise. Most surprising to Joe, the baby didn't cry. "Am I supposed to pick her up by the ankles, hold her upside down, and spank her?"

"No, Joe! But pleeeeze let me see her."

He agreed with not spanking the already breathing newborn. Why should they upset the kid during her first minute on planet earth? He placed the girl in the crook of his arm and lifted the weak flashlight just as Mary grimaced and her placenta fell.

Joe turned away and shined the light on Grace. "Definitely a girl, but..." He stopped cold. The infant was alert and stared back at Joe. This first impression of the baby stayed with him forever.

"Let me see her, Joe." Mary held her arms out, not quite ready to sit up. "I really need to see her."

Joe left the placenta between Mary's legs. With the umbilical cord attached, he lowered Grace into her new mother's outstretched arms. There was a small pool of blood beside the bright green blanket and surrounding the placenta, a couple feet from the back of the front seats. At least the darkness inside the Pathfinder hid the mess of Mary's birthing. The dim flashlight showed moisture, but not much color. Joe handed Mary the polar fleece. She snuggled the newborn approvingly in the crook of her arm and covered Grace with a corner of the blanket before singing the newborn her special song, the searing lullaby he'd never grown tired of hearing Mary perform:

Little Grace, sleep soft and long,
the oxen soon awaken.
On the trail they pull us strong,
when we are weak and shaken.

Both Joe and Mary, at age eleven, had played the role of pioneer kids for an Oregon Trail living history celebration. Joe still pictured Mary, only eleven, dressed in a bonnet, standing tall, hands folded across the apron of her small pioneer petticoat, singing soulfully into a lowered mic.

Joe leaned the passenger seat back and shined his flashlight beam on Grace for closer examination. He closed the door, but in the darkness edged towards the rear of the Pathfinder to stand behind Mary and Grace. His surge of mixed emotions was as bad as the withdrawals that were kicking in with full-force itching again. He clawed at his skin just to feel anything. Was it really betrayal just because in his gut it felt like betrayal?

He watched Mary kiss the baby's downy hair. "Isn't she perfect?" The new mom lifted her head just a bit, and smiled sweetly at Joe.

"I'm taking off," Joe answered. "I can't do this."

Joe picked up the empty gas can.

"Can't do what, Joe?"

"Yeah, she's..." he started to say, and ran his nails over an itching shoulder. "She's totally, fricking perfect."

He scratched as far onto his back as he could. "She's the perfect Tokyo baby."

Joe could see Mary twisting on her side and trying to focus through the dark to see his face. She took care not to squish the newborn cradled in her elbow. Joe started walking away from the Pathfinder.

"Wait, Joseph!" came her voice, filled with alarm.

He pivoted to face her.

"Don't leave me!" she cried.

Joe knew why she sounded so desperate. No way had Joe mistaken those black, Asian eyes of Grace's. Mary's plea thudded in his ears. There was no way she hadn't noticed the same thing.

"Wait on what?" he bellowed through the hot night air. "In what world are you thinking that I'm going to raise Kuma's kid?"

"It just happened, Joe." Her voice was too exhausted to protest. The next words came faintly through her sobbing. "You told me we were broken up, not to wait for you to get out of juvie."

He ripped off the Chunichi Dragon's jersey he was wearing; the buttons flew when he threw the thing as hard as he could towards the pond. Kuma's token of appreciation landed in the pond just beyond the stone landing. The winter before, while Joe was serving three months in detention, the family exchange student had been drafted by the Nippon Professional Baseball team. The jersey wasn't the only token Kuma left behind.

Joe opened the driver's door and pulled out the first tee-shirt he could find, one with a Full Sail Ale logo on the front. When he yanked on the pile, everything on the seat tilted, fell, and kept him from slamming the door shut. He could hear Mary screaming, "Don't leave me, Joe! Please don't leave!"

He grabbed the empty gas can and two plastic bottles of water that rolled free from the collapsed pile of clothing. "Have faith, Mary. There's your water," Joe told her when one bottle landed below the rear bumper of the Pathfinder. He turned and ran into the night with the other bottle and gas can. His running rage kept his insides from spewing out.

Joe stopped, set down the empty fuel container and ran his fingernails over every bit of skin he could reach. Then he trudged up more sandy excuse of a road. Was it all in his mind, or was he hearing her pain carry through the distance? Whether from his own memory or her tired lips, Mary's Oregon Trail voice drifted like a hot breeze:

Fording streams of hope and woe,
Wagons brimmed with treasures go.

Dust to dust, we're taken.

CHAPTER THREE

Joe concentrated on his footing and squeezed the handle of the empty gas can until his knuckles hurt. "Kuma!" came his bitter yell. With his other hand, he wiped more stinging sweat from his eyes. After sprinting a few dozen yards, Joe grabbed his knees again until he could catch his breath. From there he started walking fast instead of running. Angry memories raced through his head as fast as his chills came on.

"This Japanese kid will be a good influence for your son," he could hear his baseball coach telling his parents back when Joe was on the local American Legion team.

Next thing Joe knew, a flame throwing southpaw from Japan—this foreign kid with loads of promise—had moved into one of three upstairs bedrooms of their old, two-story Victorian. Kuma's English wasn't too bad since he'd been taking the language in Japan since he was eight or nine. He also had the same dream as every local player on the Columbia Gorge Hustlers. With a good showing on the elite squad, Kuma hoped to be drafted by a Major League team like the Dodgers, Yankees, or even the Seattle Mariners. Joe once had the same dream, too.

Instead, the talented Kuma accepted a big bonus from the Chunichi Dragons as the team's first round pick in Japan. Kuma returned to Japan after eight months in America. Tonight, while trying to trudge up the sandy road, Joe pictured Grace. But why did Kuma leave the way he did in the dead of winter? Was it homesickness, this good rookie offer, or the need to avoid his shame over Mary? Joe had his own shame at the time, still stuck in detention when Kuma decided to leave The Dalles.

The Japanese exchange student was a cool, tall handsome kid, too stiff and polite at first, but then fun to hang with, until--

--until last August when Kuma jinxed his life.

The Gorge Hustlers were scrimmaging. In came Kuma's fastball on Joe's hands. Swing and miss. Kuma was only seventeen then like Joe, but the radar gun hit the low 90s which was outstanding for a lefty this young. A rubbery smooth arm motion. Deceptive, too. He had a little hitch. With his leg up high in the wind-up, he would stop cold before coming towards home plate with the pitch. Japanese pitchers liked the surprise timing from that hesitation. Joe tried to concentrate harder so he could pick up the ball out of Kuma's grip. Fastball on the outer edge. Swing and miss again. Too slow with the bat.

Joe figured that Kuma wouldn't throw him three heaters in a row. He knew Kuma's out pitch. He even guessed right. His 12 o'clock curveball dropped slow and downward to six o'clock when the ball crossed through the strike zone. Such a hard-to-read bend to that pitch, but Joe waited and waited in what was really only a nanosecond of hesitation to his swing. Full concentration. Inside out with the bat. Hard, hard solid contact into the nether zone.

Just remembering the moment had Joe stopping on the sandy road, hands on knees again, this time reliving the impact in sync with his withdrawals. The scream inside him didn't fill the night, only every cell of tissue from his marrow to the outer reaches of his skin. He'd never shake the memory of that one Kuma curveball--or this night's curve. Was that pitch the worst feeling of his life, or was it not being the father to Mary's baby?

Kuma had backstabbed him. Joe reached down and hoisted his ball sack as he speed-walked, itched, sweated, raged, and kept going. After the surgery and a full year to heal, at least his testicle no longer tormented him. Tonight made him wonder if he'd always be firing blanks on the baby-making range. One thing was certain. For the last nine months, Mary's oven had belonged to Kuma.

And then there was that fat turkey wattle shaking his mind. Joe's inner ear turned up with gobbler ferocity. The mockery echoed through his guts and down his bowels. The gobbling didn't stop for over a minute, reminding him that this was all the time he would have needed to snort enough smack through the puncture hole. One good hit would have kept the demon fowl from slam-neutering him again.

That's the moment angry Joe threw up. He'd been so focused on getting away from Mary and Kuma's baby that he didn't sneak back over to the cedar. How could he backtrack, slip past Mary in the dark for just a snort? Simpler to get the gas, get back, get the hit of dope, then get Mary and Grace to the hospital, or even straight back to The Dalles if that's what Mary decided. He sure didn't need his cousin's heroin now.

Joe swished the vomit from his mouth. Strangely, there was less pain when he jogged than when he walked. Maybe it was the real sweat mixing in with the inner turkey sweats to keep the chills from knowing the source. Besides, running kept the mosquitoes from settling in. He scratched his drenched torso anywhere his arms could reach before hurrying his pace. Sheer agony. Like finding out Kuma had seduced his girl when he was sent down. Joe knew it could only have been Kuma. The round-faced, newborn looked too much like him––mainly those dark Asian eyes.

Maybe Mary had been badly hoping the kid was Joe's. There was no doubt she hadn't wanted either him or his mom to find out she was pregnant until the truth couldn't be hidden. Or maybe Mary would rather fly with Grace to Japan so they could raise their precious 'world baby' together.

To think he'd never questioned that Mary's baby wouldn't be his. What a fool he was. On Thanksgiving Day, she was still beyond pissed about his heroin bust. That evening, he'd promised to never touch smack ever again. Joe had meant it with all his heart. He was fully set on staying clean. That night she believed him. They'd made love nine months before the due date so, of course, he was the daddy. In their afterglow, Mary had really wanted to know where he'd scored his stuff. For the forty-ninth time, he wouldn't tell her. "Oh, hell, Mary, you know full well you can do better than this junkie punk."

"If you're gonna keep on keeping secrets from me, then I sure can do better," she'd countered, pulling on her clothes and storming out of his bedroom.

That was Thanksgiving Thursday. The next day--his Black Friday--they sent him away. While in detention, she didn't write or visit him once. She didn't get in touch at all.

Joe didn't tell the cops anything when they busted him. He wasn't a rat; he never snitched. His lawyer, the one his mom and dad hired for him, said he could have gotten him off if Joe had simply cooperated with the drug investigation. Mary, his parents, and his baseball coach were all pissed off when Joe held his tongue and got sent away. As for Kuma during all of this, he'd seemed mostly confused by Joe's legal problems.

After serving his time, the skipper hadn't wanted Junkie Joe anywhere near his American Legion Hustlers. The skipper liked the All-Star Joe and could sure use his power bat and hot corner glove at third base, but after detention he'd be a bad influence on the other boys. Joe might have gotten his diploma this summer, but losing out on baseball and then relapsing had killed his will.

Joe's feet glided faster across a hardening road surface that grew steeper near I-90. He was totally sweating now with his eyes fixed on the lights of town still off in the distance. How had it gone down? Had Mary come on to Kuma, or had Kuma put the moves on her? Had they been screwing every night until Kuma flew back home?

Where the sandy path ended at the freeway frontage road, Joe's stomach erupted. The pain bent him over, drove him to his knees. Face in his palms and elbows on the gravel, the memories came fast forwarding through his brain. He heard an enormous swarm buzzing overhead. Every single bloodsucking mosquito in North America flew towards his sweaty flesh.

Out of juvie, only Mary had shown up to believe in him. Too bad he didn't know she was pregnant until the beginning of summer. If Joe had known, then he wouldn't have relapsed in May. He caught his wind again, even though his gut felt like it had been sucker-punched.

Joe's hard swing had driven Kuma's curve off the underside of his bat, full contact into his testicle. His nut wasn't just bruised, and it wasn't just traumatized. No. Kuma's pitch punched through the ball sack. The hardball fully ruptured that testicle leaving Joe on home plate in a huddled mass of pain––deathwish-wretched, horrible pain.

They said he'd fainted, but Joe was certain he hadn't been so lucky. He remembered keeping his eyes closed after impact, and then during the ambulance ride. He'd left his lids shut during most of the deafening helicopter flight to Portland for emergency surgery. He'd never forget the contact pain, the whir of attention, or the lonely agony.

Joe stayed down on his knees when the puking began. The pain had him feeling helplessly sick. He heaved. Semis roared past on I-90 and his vomit landed on a poor, gnarly, low-lying sage. He upchucked bitter gut fluid.

When Joe was released from juvie and back in The Dalles, most of his old teammates and school friends shunned him. On that first night of freedom, though, right after he went upstairs to bed, a small pebble pinged off his bedroom window. No letters, no visits to the detention center, no relayed messages through his mom, but there stood Mary in the backyard staring up, but not sure how she should act. She didn't smile and she didn't step towards him, but her emerald eyes told all when she shrugged and forgave Joe on his first night home. During his time in juvie, Joe had desperately wanted to be back with Mary.

So why was he being such a hard case with the new baby? They could both lose their cool. Maybe he should figure out how to apologize, what to say. He hoped she wasn't freaking out––baby resting on her heart––thinking he'd split for good. By now, she knew him better than that. Didn't she?"

Plastic gas container still in hand, Joe forced himself to get up and press on towards Moses Lake. He wondered if he should defy the freeway's no hitchhiking sign and climb through the barbed wire and stick his thumb out along I-90.

No, Joe kept hoofing it––a combination of trudging and speed-walking towards the lights of Moses Lake. Joe could tell that Mary had been hoping the baby would be his. If so, then he wouldn't have melted down or ever known about Mary and Kuma. She never would have needed to tell him. Joe counted months on his fingers. Yep. Just under nine since he and Mary made love late on Thanksgiving Day.

He gritted his teeth. When he went to detention, Mary and Kuma sure didn't wait long to get it on. Get over it. Joe knew he was the one who broke it off with Mary. He deserved what he got.

The post-midnight stillness was broken only by freeway and the rustle of his clothes, but the flat straight road seemed to go on forever. At least he didn't have anything left inside to puke. Finally, the glaring Chevron sign illuminated an all-night mini-mart and he could see the edge-of-town onramp.

Under the florescent lighting, Joe fished out a fin and handed it to the cashier hidden behind a thick, glass window. "I'll take a bottled water along with however much gas this can can hold." The attendant set his fiver on top of his cash register.

Joe pushed the button for the lowest, cheapest octane. A bit of the gas splattered on his fingers. Couldn't anything go right? At least the chills had stopped. Was it just another lull, or was he over the worst?

The owner of the *taqueria* next door chased off the last of his Mexican customers. Joe thought about asking one of them for a ride to his turn-off, but their laughing faces turned cold and expressionless once a new pair of headlights appeared from the frontage road. A white Jeep with a silver-on-black Wanapum County Sheriff logo pulled in front of the mini-mart window. Joe went and collected his change.

"Run out of gas?" the friendly voice asked from behind.

He turned to see the sheriff deputy standing behind him and pointing to his full gallon container. Joe's heart raced. "Yes, sir. The gas gauge on my car is broken, so I was caught flat-footed tonight."

"Where's your car?"

Joe pointed away from the town lights of Moses Lake and toward the wildlife refuge.

"I'll call the desk sergeant and see if he'll let me take you. First I'll need to see some I.D." The wiry, tall officer, about thirty, acted low-key and smooth like it was just another quiet night on patrol. His uniform was crisp but his shoes and the tires on the sheriff SUV had the same sandy grit that Joe had just kicked-up for over an hour.

Joe had no intention of mentioning anything about Mary and Grace. Now that the baby was safely born, there was no pressing need to bring in the authorities. If Mary wanted to, she and the kid could go to urgent care back in The Dalles. A ride to the turn-off would be great though.

Before pulling his wallet out, Joe set down the plastic gas container while the cop bought a pop. Joe had been told that his juvie bust was wiped from his Oregon record on his eighteenth birthday, so he was pretty confident that nothing bad would show up. Somehow, miraculously, he'd managed never to get a moving violation, so there would be nothing there either. Besides, not showing the cop his license might trigger ugly suspicions.

When Joe's wallet opened, a small slip of paper fluttered to the ground. The deputy reached down to pick it up. "Gunnar Larsson," he read under the mini-mart marquee. "Local 509 number. Name sounds familiar."

Joe traded the address slip for his Oregon driver's license. "He's my cousin."

The light inside the SUV patrol Jeep reflected on the cop's name tag. Joe was able to read, *Deputy Zach Riggleman: Wanapum Co. Sheriff Dept.* There was something about the cop's easiness that made Joe uneasy.

"Too late to drop in on my cousin. Sleeping in the car made more sense."

"Why not wait until morning to get gas?" the sheriff deputy asked with the same down-to-earth tone.

"My rig's smack in the middle of the road, so I need to move it." Joe wondered why he'd chosen the word 'smack'? And why did his plans matter so flippin' much to the deputy?

"You couldn't call your cousin for an emergency like this?" the deputy asked in his gliding voice. Darkness hid the man's eyes, so Joe had no idea if they were casual or harsh.

"I can't exactly afford a Blackberry," said Joe. Or any other of the new flip phones, he thought. Why had he told the cop that Gunnar was his cousin? Why hadn't he stuffed the phone number and address deeper inside his wallet?

"The Dalles, Oregon. You're a long way from home." The cop examined his driver's license.

"A three-hour drive is all."

"And it takes just a bit more than a tank of gas," said the cop.

Joe started to repeat that the gas gauge was broken, but noticed the deputy's sly grin. "Yep. Just a tiny bit more." Joe smiled as best he could.

He asked how long Joe was planning to stay in Moses Lake.

"Don't know yet. Just up for a visit."

The cop got into the driver's seat and Joe tried to listen in, but the deputy closed the door of his vehicle and talked low, except for the light ringing of a cellphone, only a dull murmuring could be heard from inside the cop car.

After a few minutes, the deputy stepped from the sheriff Jeep and handed him his license. Joe felt better when the cop went to the rear of the SUV and opened the lift-gate. The cop made sure that Joe set the gas can inside a plastic trash bag before putting it in the back of the SUV. There was another full, sealed trash bag in the back. The cop gave him a Handy-Wipe to get rid of the smell on his fingers.

The deputy continued around the vehicle to open the front passenger door. Joe climbed in and tried to guess the function of all the electronic support inside the sheriff Jeep. The pain returning to his stomach made it hard to concentrate on anything except for trying not to puke again.

"You're sure sweating a ton."

"Ran most of the way."

Riggleman climbed in the driver's side and they headed along the lonely frontage road away from Moses Lake.

"Full Sail Ale," the cop said, gesturing toward Joe's t-shirt. "My uncle, Will Riggleman, is the brew master there. My cousin Billy, his son, is about your age."

Joe tapped at his chest, recalling how he'd angrily ditched his long sleeve Chunichi Dragon's jersey in favor of this tan tee-shirt. "Sorry, don't know anyone named Riggleman. Hood River's close, but not my town." Joe scratched himself, hoping the cop wouldn't see, but the cop seemed to notice. The deputy would glance from the road and back to Joe's nervous fingers and probably at the discolored flesh on his bare arms.

Joe's thoughts stayed with Mary and all the focus it took to hide his gut pain. In the distance, a pair of taillights disappeared over a slight rise in the frontage road and the cop surprised Joe by turning at the primitive road he needed.

"Thanks a lot for the ride," said Joe, slapping at a mosquito buzzing his ear.

The deputy stopped the Jeep. "You've been walking plenty tonight if you're staying down by the ponds."

Joe spoke as pleasantly as he could, but tried to open the locked door. "Seriously, I can walk from here."

"No worries," the deputy told him when he paused at the unmarked intersection. "I even have permission from the desk sergeant." He kicked into four-wheel-drive and edged onto the soft sand of the primitive road.

Joe couldn't bring himself to thank him, smile, or even nod. He thought he'd be walking back to Mary on his own, to breathe better and plan what exactly he'd say to her. Instead, he had to think of the right thing to tell this cop. There'd be no hiding the messy reality of what the cop would see.

And there would be no hurrying over to the cedar tree stash with this cop in tow. "My girlfriend just had a baby," Joe blurted.

The cop shot him a glance. "Then why are you out camping by yourself in this wasteland?"

"No. That's why I'm getting gas now." Joe pointed directly ahead of them. "My girlfriend is with me. We weren't expecting her to have her baby in the back of her SUV out in this dust-bit place."

The deputy wasted no time. He called dispatch, told them about the childbirth, then gave the directions. "Like I said in my last dispatch, I'm on my way there now with the father of the newborn."

"I'm not the father," Joe said once the cop put the mic back onto its bracket.

"Then what's going on here?" Riggleman asked while trying to concentrate on keeping traction in the loose sand. This time his voice came off as anything but congenial. "Why would you leave her there? If me and my wife could have kids, I'd be holding her hand every minute, before and after. Your stupid gasoline should have waited until morning."

Joe had no idea how to respond to Riggleman's outburst. What an about-face in tone.

"Mr. Gardner, I've been working this job long enough to see the same sweating and that same jittery stare you've got going. Some of us cops aren't blind. What else are you hiding? Is your girlfriend a druggie, too?"

Joe folded his arms and glared at the deputy. "You saying it's a crime to jog for gas so I can hurry and take care of my girlfriend and the baby? Of course, I'm sweating. I ran all the way to where you picked me up." If Riggleman only knew how hard Joe was working in his head to convince his turkey not to make him blow chunks again.

The cop took off his cap and tapped his temple to show Joe that he wasn't stupid. "That was quite a few minutes ago when you got to the mini-mart, and you're still sweating like a pig. Those forearms of yours are sporting obvious track marks, and you're antsy as hell."

When the words left the cop's mouth, dispatch came across the radio. "Officer, do you have a more specific location and any information on the status of the mother and newborn?"

The cop stopped again and answered the call. Joe tried to open the passenger door again. The deputy gave him a cold expression after telling the dispatcher he hadn't arrived yet to be in a position to respond any more accurately.

"Please let me out. And thanks for saddling us with a big ambulance bill we can't afford."

"There's a newborn and mother," he told Joe. "so this isn't about you anymore." The deputy turned on his flashers and swerved around stray stones. The deputy seemed to enjoy the opportunity to push the performance of his official SUV. Each fishtail had Joe clutching the elbow rest.

"I apologize, Mr. Gardner," the cop turned and said on a smoother stretch of road. Under the big moon, they could see the pond in the distance with the Pathfinder sitting on the gray road like a dark hole. Beside the SUV, the marsh glistened like polished black granite.

"Apologize for what?" Joe asked. He just wanted out of the cop rig so he could talk to Mary.

"It's just that my wife and I have been trying to have a baby for the last five years," the cop answered, his eyes on the sandy path. "I'm sensitive to the subject of newborns. She's Vietnamese, a culture where not being able to have babies is a stigma." He turned to Joe. "Let's get your girlfriend the care she needs. That's all."

"Let's," said Joe, his voice terse. There was nothing to say that he and Mary couldn't have a kid or two of their own someday. That's definitely what he would tell her rather than some blanket apology. He needed to stand, to breathe the night air, without this cop butting in.

But why didn't Mary warn him that the kid might not be his? She had to know it was a possibility. "A definite effing possibility," he muttered under his breath.

"Come back with that," said the cop.

"You and your wife should keep on trying for that kid." Joe said, twisting to glare harshly at the cop.

"I swear I heard you say the 'f'" word."

"That's what it'll take," said Joe, "but who am I to school you on the birds and the bees?"

Deputy Riggleman laughed, his easy manner restored. He pulled into the fisherman's parking spot closest to the Pathfinder and turned off the engine. With ambulances on the way, a cop pitching him crap, and a newborn getting most of the attention, Joe wondered if he'd even have a chance to talk things through with Mary, let alone sneak over to the cedar tree. Joe's saliva told him more vomit was coming.

Big wings swooped down to land in the back of the Pathfinder below Mary's lift gate. The descent happened fast. When the deputy turned on his spotlight outside his door, Joe saw what was definitely a Great Horned Owl lifting something into the air, something dangling below its talons.

"Let me out," Joe told the cop. No bird would have flown that close to Mary. Even through rolled-up windows, Joe could hear the night owl's wings pounding to escape their arrival. It hooted in anger and flew straight above them. "That's the bloody afterbirth," he told the deputy. One glance showed a cop looking more annoyed than grossed out by the big splotch of bright blood splattered across the white hood of the Sheriff Jeep.

The deputy got out and stepped around to open Joe's door.

"Mary?" Joe asked gently when he got out and followed Riggleman to the back of her SUV. The spotlight was to the side of the Pathfinder and didn't offer much of a beam inside Mary's vehicle.

It took the flashlight from the deputy's service belt for them to tell what was inside the back. The owl had already hinted that the vinyl flooring would be empty of the people and the placenta. Towards the front seat, Joe could see a blob of glistening blood where the placenta stained the vinyl flooring of the Pathfinder. Where was the baby? Where was Mary?

"Mary!" His voice boomed through the night.

Joe turned back towards the deputy to see a Glock trained at his face. Riggleman steadied his service pistol. "Mr. Gardner, place your hands on top of your head."

"Why?" Joe asked, but did as directed. Riggleman's aim added a churning horror in his guts where a Howler monkey and ugly gobbler were playing tug-of-war with his intestines.

From three yards away, the cop kept the gun trained on Joe's head and pressed the two-way microphone clipped to his shirt. "Clear the channel. This is Deputy Riggleman. We have a 10-33, repeat, an escalated 10-33. Please send back-up along with the emergency help. Over."

The deputy waved his gun nervously. "Very slowly, place your hands behind your back," he ordered. Joe did as the cop commanded and allowed him to cuff his wrists. "Now kneel, but keep your body tall," Riggleman added. Joe got down on one knee and then the other. The cop added a thick plastic Flexi-Tie to Joe's ankles and tightened it too much for Joe's liking. "I'm placing you under investigative arrest." Joe listened to the cop read him his Miranda Rights.

"Mary!" Joe stayed kneeling upright. "Where are you, Mary?" With no response, his words got lost in a landscape of darkness.

"That's my question to you, Mr. Gardner. Where's your girl-friend?" Riggleman hovered above Joe, flashlight and gun in his face, waiting for an answer that the Joe couldn't give. The cop shined his flashlight deeper inside the back of the Pathfinder. "I hope that's blood from her giving birth." He went to the pile of clothing and belongings that flowed down from driver's seat to ground like a mudslide. "Did you two have a fight?" the cop asked.

"It's not my kid," said Joe. His arms shivered and his legs shook. "I wasn't happy to find out, but we didn't fight in the way you're thinking. I've never laid a hand on Mary, ever."

"I'm thinking you better tell me what's going on here," Riggleman demanded. There was no mistaking that the cop could see the pathetic state of Joe's worsening condition.

Nausea or whatever, Joe knew enough from his first bust to clam up and ask for a lawyer if the cop pressed him, not that it would do any good out here in this scabland, kneeling all alone near this armed and antsy cop. "Mary!"

Riggleman ignored Joe's yell and, with his flashlight, scanned the ground surrounding her SUV. Nothing. The cop then moved the Jeep's spotlight towards the seep lake.

At the instant Joe saw Mary's sopped, pale, naked form, facedown and floating motionless, something like battery acid flowed through every vein he had. The horror outside mimicked his poisoned insides where a toxic brine seeped from his zip-tied ankles through calves and thighs, into his hips, and up his torso with an acid-reflex spew. Unable to help the cop, he saw himself as a big, wounded trash fish flopping and spinning in a big, slow circle around Mary's body. Joe would have slapped himself if he wasn't cuffed, if only to see if any of this nightmare was real. Only an outpouring of rage kept his throat from seizing shut.

"Over there!" Joe tried to stand, but forgot for an instant that he was hogtied. He tipped over and hit his hip instead. Joe lifted his chin from the ground. "Mary!" The only shape Joe could make out under the Jeep spotlight were her arms out wide like on a cross. "Save her!" Joe rose up again, but fell and winced after landing on the exact same spot of his same hip.

Riggleman stepped onto the landing and eased to the edge of the pond. He unbuckled his belt and set it on her skirt to keep his police gear dry. He also took off his sheriff's uniform, all but his boots and boxers, and draped the clothes over the landing stones.

Everything smelled sickening, like brimstone. Joe watched the cop step into a slot of open water between the willows and iris clusters. Mary's body floated just a few yards off shore. The deputy pushed his legs towards the body, shoving the bloated carp off to one side before he reached her. The pond was over three feet deep there.

Riggleman grabbed Mary by the heels and overlapped her legs until she rolled onto her back and her arms splayed wide again. He rotated the body so he could grab Mary under the armpits and pull her limp body to shore. The lean, tall cop was stronger than he appeared. After backing up, Riggleman pulled Mary's naked frame on top of the hard landing of stones. Mary's ankles dangled in the water along the shore. The naked, wet body lay lifeless even though Joe watched keenly for any sign of movement.

The cop glanced at his police belt still dry on her skirt, before pressing Mary's rib cage at the sternum. A surge of water from her lungs spewed through open lips. She didn't gag or open her eyes wide. The air pouring back into her lungs didn't pull the life back into her body. Riggleman turned Mary onto her stomach, straddled her hips and pushed down over and over. His repeat pressure had the vibe of desperation. The cop seemed to be doing his best; the pond water that had spouted from her mouth was only a trickle.

But the baby. "Where's the baby?" His stomach convulsed like winged monkeys shoveling a new melt of wicked witch goo deeper into his bowels. Despite his ankles being bound together and wrists cuffed behind his back, Joe wriggled closer to the boulders to help.

"Not another inch towards me," Riggleman looked up and ordered.

Joe froze and watched the kneeling cop reach towards the service pistol in his belt.

Joe fell back. "Mary!"

The deputy flipped Mary onto her back to resume mouth-to-mouth. After trying over-and-over with no response, he turned her on her stomach again and pushed on her back repeatedly, and in vain. Mary wasn't coming back. Riggleman took his tired palms off Mary's tattoo. His face, even in moonlight, seemed nearly as defeated as Joe felt inside.

"Did you see the baby?" Joe asked with a somber voice, his eyes closed and feeling waves of shock.

The cop got on his feet. This time, his voice boomed. "You knew right where this girl was, so why don't you tell me where the baby is!"

Joes upper arms ached from wrists bound too tightly behind his back. The Flexi-Ties on his ankles dug into his skin. Joe shook his head side-to-side; his eyes felt wild and helpless. Disbelief and denials looped through his head.

"Please just find the baby. Please, Officer!" Maybe the formality would jolt Riggleman away from the failure that had just hammered the man's face into grimness.

Joe sat up higher on his knees. Beyond Mary's still body, he couldn't see much of anything in the night except for dark marsh plants casting moon shadows over the pewter-hued surface of glassy water. On Mary's wet back, *Tsagaglalal* glinted and stared upwards, watching Joe's reaction when he wasn't sure if he'd heard something. The sound came like light mewing from a hungry kitten. "Did you hear that, officer?" Joe pointed with his jaw. "Over there. On the other side of all those cattails."

Riggleman slid over to the part of the landing where he'd left his gun and full belt. He picked up his flashlight and shined it in that general direction.

"No. Not there, cop! Through the tall reeds. I really did hear something." Joe had lost all faith in Riggleman.

The deputy glowered at Joe before guiding the beam in the direction that Joe had pointed to with his chin. Joe sat cuffed and several feet higher than the cop. "Like I said, the cry came from the other side of those cattails. It's gotta be her."

"What do you mean, 'It's gotta be her'?" the deputy asked. "Did you put the baby in this pond to float and die when you found out it wasn't yours?"

Joe tried to stand, but fell forward towards Mary's corpse. He was seriously fortunate not to crack his skull open when, by inches, his mouth and forehead found sand instead of stones. His bowels let loose. "Arrrrgh!" Joe kept yelling, but didn't explain to the cop his own private disgust.

"Why would I be here if I'd done something that wicked?" he asked instead. "What a douchebag!" Joe bellowed, not wanting to think of his own soiled pants. Even more than the cuffs, the fouled pants froze his body in place with him not wanting to move even an inch.

"Uncuff me!" he demanded, his chin half-buried along the edge of the landing. Joe was spitting out aggregate, and crapping cold turkey bile. "If you're too chicken, then let me save the baby myself."

Riggleman looked first at his belt and weapon, then up at Joe. Even tipped on his face, Joe watched the cop take a moment to realize that his new prisoner would be hard pressed to descend four feet of stones to reach the Glock, let alone have any way to fire off a round. Riggleman didn't know how lucky he was to smell the rotten carp instead of him. Joe shook uncontrollably. More involuntary emptying. The sweat kept oozing from every pore. Joe willed himself to avoid any movement that made matters worse.

Crap, puke, and itchy sweat, but he could hear the mewing continue from inside the bulrushes. Joe snarled and spewed from both ends. "Spineless bastard!" On the slant beside the sandy road, volumes of what wasn't soaked up by denim trickled down his thighs and calves to leak over the once hip Nikes. Joe felt too much withdrawal, too much worry, too much grief to care.

Riggleman stepped into the warm pothole water again. "Slip your slimy slim bones through those cattails," Joe tried to yell, but a new hoarseness stifled any volume. "Can't you do one thing right tonight?" was the best he could manage. He sounded like a raspy crow. "Those cries are coming from on the other side of the thick reeds. You gotta bulldoze your wimpy backside through the bulrushes."

Deputy Riggleman had actually paid attention to Joe. Every several feet, the cop cast his light back towards Joe, as if his prisoner could hop or roll or waddle away from the scene of the crime and, even if Joe could, would the sheriff deputy have the slightest of chances to climb out and catch him? "About twenty feet past where you are," Joe told him, his throat sore from all the acid reflux. "That's where she is, I'm telling you!"

Joe's eyes landed on Mary's unmoving body. What had happened? Why had he been so set on leaving Mary and Grace when he did? Joe managed to kneel tall again, hands behind him. Mosquitoes hovered and covered his skin, but Joe had no way to scratch himself, no way to escape the vulgar truth of his state. Tortured and rank, Joe watched the silhouette of the cop churning his feet and legs through the muck, pushing reeds to one side and the other, and plowing deeper into the bulrushes that were hiding Grace behind the wall of reeds. The mud seemed to try all the strength in Riggleman's wiry, long thighs as he willed his legs and feet through the mire.

More faint cries. Had to be. Had to be her, Joe thought. "You're almost there." The cop couldn't get through the marsh fast enough when trudging his mucky pathway. When the cop paused, Joe thought he heard plastic rubbing against the reeds. What if the mattress had popped, or sprung a slow air leak?

From I-90 in the distance, the sound waves of night sirens carried easily across smooth scabland. More sirens from Moses Lake drifted in from farther away. Waist deep, the cop pushed through even more reeds.

The infant cried.

"Thank, God!" Riggleman yelled. Under the full moon, Joe watched his shadowy body pull on the floating mattress until he was chest deep, but free of the reeds. The Jeep spotlight revealed hints of color from the cop's wet uniform when Deputy Riggleman lifted Grace to his face and inspected the newborn under the moonlight. His flashlight beam bounced from on top of the air mattress. Joe could barely make out the bright green fleece that swaddled the newborn.

Above the eerie cast of flashlight, the cop cradled the baby high against his chest and held a free hand high. The cop pointed past the full moon towards heaven. "Thank you, God!" he repeated, the words sounding less this time like a reaction of relief, and more a grateful prayer of thanksgiving.

"Thank God you did one thing right," Joe snarled at him, again realizing when the words came out that he was a complete zero himself and in bad need of a higher power pressure washing.

The drenched deputy grabbed the flashlight, but left the air mattress floating free in the pond. Guarding the newborn, he back-tracked step-by-mucky-step towards shore. Grace didn't so much as whimper. Joe watched Riggleman, his flashlight against the underside of the baby blanket, ease back along the shore and slowly closer to the landing where Mary lay dead.

Joe tested his zip-ties, not for escape, but for their twisted anchoring. He hated his putrid, self-defeating, addicted self. By resisting his binds, he tried every last bit of his strength to check his sorrow and see if any of this nightmare was possibly real. From his bound and stinging limbs, and from the foul stench, Joe knew there was never going to be any escaping the truth of this night. With Mary face down,

She-Who-Watches stared up from the landing stones to let him know his life would never be the same.

He wanted to ask what had just happened, but the chieftess couldn't talk and Mary couldn't talk. He didn't care what the cop had to say, and Grace could only cry.

After climbing free of the pothole and muck, Riggleman lay the baby and blanket on the rocks beside Mary's body. He cinched his service belt around his waist and stared at Joe who stayed upright on his knees, bowing his head, and shivering back-and-forth. The teen tried to rock away the night's cold horror. Worse than horrid withdrawals, puke, and diarrhea, Joe shuddered at the loneliness awaiting him.

CHAPTER FOUR

II.
of LIFE

~

"Not Mary. Please... not... her," she kept saying through tears and shaking her head. How could the girl give birth and suddenly drown?"

Rochelle teased up her burgundy hair that hid more and more gray roots. No time to mirror gaze through blurry eyes. After slipping on loose, crepe pants and a matching tan shirt to cover her lean body, she threw a change of clothes, toiletries and her cosmetics bag into a small suitcase. Putting on make-up could wait. No need to brew a thermos full of coffee. She had enough ugly adrenaline coursing through her veins. Rochelle winced and grabbed two bottles of water and a couple of Lunchables from the refrigerator, but felt her head pound when she couldn't find her comfortable blue Crocs, demos from a Nordstrom Rack. She always kept them—same place—by the front door. It was the one thing she wanted for this trip, besides learning that her son had been totally wrong on that phone call. Rochelle caught herself throwing one of those private, mini-tantrums, the kind where she swore at the high ceiling of her Victorian living room.

After a minute of core meltdown, she told herself that anger wouldn't help her grief. Immediately, she found the soft, plastic clogs stuffed far under the entryway bench. Rochelle walked across the living room to fold the wooden cover over the keys on her piano. She cried again. Maybe she'd never play the upright again, especially without Mary's sweet accompanying voice to help fill her big house with music.

Rochelle slid toes inside the Crocs, grabbed her oversized, brown-leather handbag, and closed the front door. She turned her key to lock the deadbolt. Once the van was rolling, Rochelle reminded herself not to speed. At the I-84 overpass, lights glistened off leaping aluminum salmon. Had her son really led Mary to her death? Rochelle merged onto the empty interstate. This couldn't be happening. No way.

Her eyes stared at the spot on the freeway shoulder where, last year, an Oregon State Patrolman had pulled Joe over and discovered far more Mexican black tar in his car than Joe could explain away for personal use only. She and the boy's father had no clue Joseph had been using, of all drugs, heroin. Who were his junkie connections? Joe would never say. He'd never brought druggie types around the house, mostly just Mary and his baseball teammates. Like most places in America, The Dalles, Oregon had plenty of pot and meth. Not much heroin here, she came to learn through Joe's ordeal. Keeping it that way was why the local cops wanted to clamp down hard on Joe by getting him to reveal his source.

Her son came back from his ninety days in detention harder and more withdrawn, especially when he wouldn't be graduating high school at the same time as Mary. Always a solid student, her 18-year-old had chosen to drop out for the spring. The most disappointing thing for Joe was not being allowed to rejoin his ball team.

Rochelle had watched her boy escape into who-knew-where. With him out of detention, she wondered if she'd reacted wisely after finding drug gear for shooting up heroin taped inside the tank of the upstairs toilet. Why wouldn't she boot him out of the house? Was she supposed to condone his stupid relapse?

Joe took a minimum wage job pumping gas. Rochelle would park her van down the street of the Shell Station and watch her boy's sandy hair and beard grow scragglier each week. If Joe had spotted her spying on him, he never let on, never asked to move back in with her. She knew that camping out in his secret hideaway would never continue through the harsh fall and winter in the Gorge.

With the new baby coming and the upstairs readied with a nursery, Rochelle had planned to wait. By freezing him out all summer with no intervention, who was really the stubborn one? Mary had been the one to soften Rochelle; she'd been the one to come up with a better plan.

To think that Mary drove Joe to Moses Lake so they'd be sure to have him home by Monday. Monday, when Rochelle and Mary had arranged the intervention. Do it before the baby came; get Joe cleaned up; get him on track for fatherhood; get him moved back home with his head on straight. All summer, Mary hadn't let Joe know that she knew he'd relapsed. Better that way, they figured, if she was going to be able to coax him back where he belonged.

Images, memories, and her worst realized nightmares triggered more convulsing tears. The crying jags forced Rochelle to the side of the road. She stopped just past the freeway off-ramp on the east end of town. At 3 a.m., there were no cars anywhere in sight, so why not sit and cry? After five minutes or maybe more, Rochelle regained her composure, at least partially, at least for the moment, and crossed the bridge into the state of Washington. An eerie glow of lights on The Dalles Dam penetrated the constant spray of water tumbling down the spillway and into the churn of current flowing below.

Churning. Her emotions wouldn't stop.

She crossed over the Columbia River on a faded bridge painted an odd shade of fuchsia. Vice President Richard Nixon had helped dedicate the big impediment in 1957, the year she was born, but the dam was most famous for having flooded Celilo Falls, a salmon netting mecca once called one of the eight natural wonders of the world.

Rochelle had no desire to turn on the radio in the van, but flipped on the light above her rearview mirror. At a quick glance, she could tell that her eyes would need more than a light touch of liner to help hide her swollen redness. Her sister and brother-in-law were not at home in Moses Lake, but off at some official potato growing convention in Idaho Falls, Idaho. Darla, upon being awakened to hear her sister's news, insisted she would drive back first thing in the morning, but there was no way she could get to Moses Lake until late afternoon. She gave Rochelle the address of Gunnar's new place. Her nephew had a spare key to his parent's home. "Make yourself comfortable until I get there," Darla had said, as if comfort of any kind would be possible.

Keep your eyeballs on the road, Rochelle told herself, trying not to pull over again. She hadn't even driven ten miles from her house when she turned onto Route 14, the Lewis & Clark Highway, and followed the Washington shore of the big river. Time to deal straight-up with her son, but what else was she about to discover?

She hit the gas pedal and spun out onto the empty highway before gaining speed––40...50...60...70...80 mph. Rochelle's mind raced and, again, she admonished herself to slow down in the van, the one filled with chamber literature, a fold-up table and chairs for indoor events. As the director, she was always on the go, always tenaciously selling the benefits of joining The Dalles Area Chamber of Commerce.

Mary. The baby. Her son. More tears. Her brain was about to detonate until Horsethief Lake appeared along with Mary. The girl's apparition glowed on the dark windshield.

Rochelle slowed and slowed until she could pull over on the shoulder above the small lake across the tracks from the Columbia. In the window––like a ship's figurehead––Mary faced away and upriver with hair billowing in the hot Gorge breeze. She was naked with that crazy tattoo inked into her ghostly white skin. Mary wasn't pregnant anymore, but appeared very alive. She couldn't really be dead. Maybe Joe had misspoken. Her son definitely sounded out of it. Maybe Rochelle had misheard.

Basalt outcroppings created a protective cove for the small lake and park. When she was a kid and out-of-towners came to visit, her family made this a regular attraction. She and Darla would run and lead the way to the petroglyphs. Hidden on low cliffs was She-Who-Watches, a prehistoric pictograph honoring a local chieftess from pre-pioneer times. Rochelle never understood why, but for some reason last winter, Mary, on her eighteenth birthday, had covered her upper back with a huge tattoo of the Native stone etching.

The van idled.

"Mary," she said softly to the tranquil image in the window. As soon as Rochelle spoke, Mary faced her. She pressed her palms together like a Buddhist monk; elbows squeezed her engorged breasts. Mary had to be alive. Where was the baby right now?

Palms still together, Mary bowed deeply while her gaze locked onto Rochelle's eyes. Dyed black hair trailed over her raised forearms.

"Please be alive," Rochelle begged through more crying. At this, the apparition faded and Mary Quinn was gone.

She eased back onto the empty highway and bawled, somehow managing to find a tissue to dab her eyes and keep the yellow dividing line in focus.

It wasn't until this ribbon of asphalt climbed steeply onto a bluff above the Columbia that Rochelle regained a semblance of composure. Next to the river, well below her van, one of those forever long trains rolled along the shore.

Beyond the train and under the full moon, river water shimmered where Celilo Falls once roared and tumbled. The Dalles reservoir lay still, an illusion that it could mask the history of this place. Next to the inundated falls, the locomotive howled like her own rolling nightpain. Had Mary's life really vanished so young?

Celilo had been a pre-European trading hub where the local fish Indians would hoop net, feast, and trade salmon to other Northwest Natives. Rochelle pictured what she'd seen growing up at her aunt Wilma's downtown photography shop. Her aunt had colorized her photos showing the grandness of these falls, the fishermen on rickety scaffolds, or of Tommy Thompson, the hundred-year-old chief who knew his people would never be the same. Humans from the Pacific coast and Columbia River plateau congregated here like nowhere else in the entire region. The dam had forever flooded and stolen the soul of their tribal way of life.

Rochelle—this white girl of The Dalles—felt for the first time in her life, the magnitude of that loss. She cried wounded tears not unlike those Tommy Thompson had so openly shed. In a blink, a prehistoric life-way had flooded into oblivion. Tonight, a precious loved one of hers also forever drowned.

Hot night, windows rolled down, and not caring if her teased hair blew wild, she could hear her son's voice return to her from their phone call a couple of hours earlier. They'd found Mary Quinn face down in the water. The home-sweet-home she'd planned with Mary, Joe, and baby was as likely as Celilo Falls yielding a great harvest of salmon again.

The train horn faded and Rochelle passed the amphitheater that was under construction at the new Maryhill Winery. Mary Quinn's mother, Bonnie, had performed at the Edgefield amphitheater on the Portland end of the Columbia Gorge, not to mention fronting blues-rock bands at every honky-tonk dive between there and here. Bonnie had taken off in May to start over in Branson, Missouri, but couldn't be bothered to give her daughter or anyone else in The Dalles an update. "It's time I followed my own dream," Bonnie Quinn had announced to her daughter before she uprooted and abandoned the high schooler. It wasn't as though Mary––a great kid––had gone out of her way to tether her mom to an 18-year-long prison sentence of doting motherhood. The hard partying Bonnie hardly bothered to honor any of her duties as a mother, but she was going to be a music star, just you watch. The woman didn't even know her own daughter was five-months pregnant when she took off, so who was going to tell her that her wonderful girl was dead?

Who else? thought Rochelle, tapping a forefinger on her forehead. It sucked to always be the responsible one.

Rochelle accelerated again.

Castle Nowhere appeared. Mary...Mary...Maryhill Museum––a cool and peculiar 1926 castle-museum with Auguste Rodin sculptures. The place had been built by Sam Hill, an eccentric pacifist. For Rochelle, everyplace was nowhere until she could get to Moses Lake, nearly three hours away. How much trouble was her son in this time? The person-of-interest stuff sounded foreboding.

Rochelle continued up the Columbia River and, a few miles past Maryhill Museum at Sam Hill's Stonehenge replica, she stopped to calm her mind. The monument was another part of the Quaker utopia he'd envisioned creating. Images of Mary and more confusion continued to clog Rochelle's head.

The pre-dawn, full moon had settled toward the west and cast wavering shadows over the dried up ground. Dozens of Stonehenge pillars, three times her own height, formed the outer circle. Shorter ones, inside the circle, framed a long altar stone.

She walked around the outside of the monument to catch her breath and recall last spring how--after Bonnie took off--she'd helped Mary with the girl's senior honors thesis. The teen had decided to focus on Sam Hill's Stonehenge.

"He created this as a tribute," Mary had told Rochelle the first time they visited the memorial for her project. Sam Hill constructed a replica of England's ancient Druid monument to honor the heroism and sacrifices of local soldiers who'd fought in 'the war to end all wars.' Mary's thesis argued that this Stonehenge had less to do with the Druids and served more as a lasting testament to peace.

She sat on the only smooth surface inside the Stonehenge ring. Enticing Joe into recovery was no more the permanent solution than WWI turned out to be 'the war to end all wars.' Her son would need to go deep inside his own soul to embrace the strength to conquer his war with addiction. She wove her way through the stone columns towards the van, hoping her fast steps would restore her equilibrium.

Starting the engine, Rochelle remembered in June when she watched her son peeking inside The Dalles High School gymnasium on the day that also should have been his own graduation ceremony. Scruffy from his camping exile, Joe stared only at Mary and didn't notice his mother or other classmates staring at him. Mary, as salutatorian, adapted the senior paper to her commencement speech.

"So I want to ask the same question of my fellow graduates that Sam Hill asked when he created his Stonehenge monument to honor the local military men of World War I," Mary had said. "Why do humans keep repeating the same folly? Why do we keep sacrificing soldiers to the God of War?" Mary Quinn urged her fellow classmates to learn from this fascinating bit of history in the Gorge and strive to lead lives of peace.

Peace? Putting the van in drive, she wondered if newly dead Mary was in a hellish turmoil, or had found the peace that surpasses all understanding. On this worst night of nights, any hint of calm steered clear of Rochelle.

Just east of Maryhill, she eased along the arid bluff above the John Day Dam. This was the third major dam upstream from the Pacific Ocean. Viewing the Gorge Aluminum plant above the dam, Rochelle wondered if the salmon that decorated the freeway overpass near her home had started out being molten smolts in this smelter.

The huge Gorge Aluminum plant had just started operating a single shift, but once operated around the clock. Her estranged husband, J.J.--the last foreman on the graveyard shift here--had caught wind of the closure the spring before and claimed it was the reason he applied for a foreman's opening at a big smelter north of Bellingham by the Canadian border.

Rochelle knew this was not the main reason. Their faltering marriage was why. J.J. knew full well she had no interest in moving away from The Dalles. Economic cycles in the global aluminum industry were one thing, but Rochelle had never expected her marriage to go bust--at least not so suddenly, at least not without serious counseling for their marital shortcomings, and at least not without some warning from her husband. With this night's news, everything in her life was going under.

During that all too brief call, Joe had said that the baby wasn't his, probably the kid of one of Mary's Native American friends. "Remember, Mom. I got sent to juvie. Mary and me were broke up. We weren't a couple when she got knocked up." So after readying her big, old house for Mary, the baby--and, hopefully, Joe--Rochelle learned on that call that the infant wasn't even her grandkid.

Her tears dried up like the landscape she drove through; she felt herself go cold again, the way she'd reacted in the spring when J.J. had left so abruptly and humiliated her throughout her hometown. And here she was, all alone once again to deal with their boy's crisis that was way bigger this time than even his deplorable heroin problem.

It was taking too long to get to Moses Lake. Above her, she saw tiny lights on the big-bladed wind turbines. Constant Gorge gusts blasted the top edges of ridges hovering above the big river. She needed to breathe. In her blur of driving, she turned up Rock Creek Canyon with its Native In-Lieu-Fishing site--nice boat ramps substituting as access to the shrunken salmon runs ruined by the dams. She stopped, as J.J. would say, to do some in-loo sacrificing in the Porta-Potty. Rochelle would ask him if the toilet seat had been stylishly anchored in Lucite. Their marriage wasn't without doses of lightness.

She continued 75 more miles past the Rock Creek tribal longhouse by climbing the steep and winding road over a washboard surface through Dot, a metropolis it was not, and onward to the Bluebird-Capital-of-the World at not-much-bigger Bickleton where she descended steeply into the Yakima Valley. She passed alongside orchards of apples--Fuji to Delicious--and rows of peach, pear, or apricot trees. Hops hung from tall trellises and she smelled the resins from freshly harvested fields of spearmint before ascending through hillside vineyards and out of the Yakima Valley to the top of another rattlesnake bitten ridge.

In the distance, from a great flood a bit older than the area's newly discovered, but ancient Kennewick Man, she could tell where the upper Columbia flowed invisible from her vantage in the van. The big river hid in an enormous ditch scoured through parched earth. Her boxy vehicle shuddered from a sudden wind gust. She stopped at an overlook.

Ahead, she saw a dust devil swirling in the first light of morning.

She'd never taken this shortcut, but last summer, on a road trip with Joe, Mary, Kuma, and Biff, they drove to this same barren plateau from a different direction. The excursion was in lieu of visiting the usual Northwest tourist sites like Crater Lake, the Sea Lion Caves, or Mount St. Helens. On a day off from summer baseball, Kuma had really wanted to come here. She remembered how politely her new exchange student had requested to see this specific place. Driving from The Dalles on that day trip with the kids, she'd gone a different route by staying along the big river the entire way and joining their tour in the Tri-Cities, a nuclear engineer's oasis.

This predawn morning, on her wretched drive to Moses Lake, Rochelle watched the little twister of gravel and dirt gain size and momentum and start to spin across the barren ground. The whirl of wind scoured shallow pockets of topsoil while picking up speed. It whipped faster-and-faster across the wasteland. The dust devil pulled at her attention like watching a soiled stage curtain beginning to open.

During his stay with them, Rochelle came to learn that Kuma's family had been against the military running Japan during World War II. Many of his Buddhist sect members, including his relatives, had been imprisoned. On the tour with the kids, her exchange student described how his grandfather had worked in Nagasaki and, after Fat Man exploded, radiation poisoning took several months to usher in his painful death. Kuma's father had been an infant and happened to be with his mother's family in Tokyo on that day of the blast.

From her van, Rochelle watched the veil of gritty haze lift. Dawn illuminated the B-Reactor, now an abandoned and isolated relic of the past. This was backstage in the biggest of all wars that followed the war to end all wars. The building served the Manhattan Project, human beings' first fully existential tragedy, a powerful production capable of extinguishing humankind.

"The bomb of all bombs is from devil," Kuma had said to his new friends.

Rochelle sat in her van on this morning knowing the day ahead of her would also feature a day of the devil's reaping. Examined from afar, the ordinary looking industrial remain of the second world war, had her hearing Mary say how the B-Reactor was no monument to peace, just another edifice to the God of War.

On the road trip with the teens, their tour guide had pulled in front of the towering, empty plant. 'The Bomb' served to shorten the war with Japan," the guide told them. Rochelle remembered how Kuma sat stoically, probably struggling to hide his disgust.

They toured the B-Reactor perimeter and were shown devastating WWII photos of Little Boy and Fat Man exploding in Japan. The tour guide told them about the protective concrete, and all the river water needed to cool the core of the reactor.

After the tour, their Japanese exchange student told the others, "I am from a family of *Kosen Rufu*. We wish that no more Fat Men or Little Boys will poison our planet."

"What's *Kosen Rufu?*" Biff McCoy had asked Kuma. Diminutive Biff was Mary's expressive, high-motoring best friend.

"Working for peace in the world must start with people finding peace inside," said Kuma. "This is *Kosen Rufu*."

"Who doesn't want world peace?" Joe asked, but before Kuma could answer, Mary sharply elbowed her boyfriend in the ribs. During the drive back to The Dalles, Rochelle remembered how their Japanese guest sat quiet and shut out the antics of the American teens.

On this morning, through her windshield, a big coyote climbed from a ditch and glared into Rochelle's puffy eyes. The sun was just above the horizon when she honked and the animal bolted into the bitterbrush.

Rochelle put the van in drive and accelerated. A few thickets of sage dotted the arroyos along the highway. Closer to the Columbia, the road flattened. The Manhattan Project building stood well off in the distance in its decayed façade of industrial innocence.

After crossing the big river, the last hour into Moses Lake swept by in a blur. Rochelle drove in a jangled, hypnotic rush. Her mind raced along with the van as the sun lifted with the morning. "It can't be true," she kept saying out loud.

Her high desert highway merged with Interstate-90 halfway between Seattle and Spokane. Huge metal cutouts of wild broncos dotted the dry ridge and reminded Rochelle of the aluminum salmon anchored in The Dalles. Wanapum Dam held the latest Columbia reservoir. How many of the spawn-and-die fish had made it up the big river to this, the sixth huge concrete barrier from the ocean? This was, also, the farthest upriver that Joe and Mary had made it together.

Welcoming Mary into her home had made sense for Rochelle, especially with the baby coming and with so much emptied from her own life. But that call. That horrible, horrible call. Joe had been beside himself. His voice had been so hoarse and upset that she could barely understand him.

Had he really said that Mary drowned to death? What of the baby? Where was she? Where was this newborn who Mary had chosen to called 'Grace'?

CHAPTER FIVE

"What had he done? What were the charges? Did you treat him here? And Mary's baby. Can I see the baby?" Rochelle asked.

"Mrs. Gardner, your son is 18-years-old," the gray haired night administrator at Samaritan Hospital said. "HIPAA regulations prevent us from disclosing this patient's medical information without his permission." The woman's voice remained calm, almost studied, so she wouldn't sound combative. "As for the rest, we've been instructed that there's a criminal investigation underway. We suggest you contact the sheriff's office. Your son's in police custody at the Wanapum County Jail in Smohalla, twenty miles north of here."

A graveyard shift security guard appeared through the wide swinging door, positioned himself several feet behind the hospital administrator, and tried to act like a sentry by listening in while pretending not to be.

"Is the baby here? Can I please see her?" Rochelle asked again when pointing to a small 'Maternity Ward' sign with an arrow directed down the corridor.

"You'll need to contact the Wanapum County Sheriff, Mrs. Gardner. I suggest you talk to one of the detectives there."

The guard moved ever so slightly closer to Rochelle. "Ask for Detective Roger Riggleman. He's the Sheriff Department's chief investigator." The security guard spoke like a wannabe cop, probably one of those guys who listened to police dispatches on the radio during his off hours. "I'm sure he'll be handling this case," he added after Rochelle wrote the name on a pad that she extracted from an inner pocket of her big purse.

Rochelle needed to talk with her boy. Maybe Gunnar had spoken to his cousin. She should stop at her nephew's place before driving another half-hour to the county seat. She double-checked the address her sister had her write down when they spoke last night.

"Where is Lake Vista Drive? Can one of you at least tell me that?"

"Not too far from here, Mrs. Gardner." The administrator said before giving the general directions.

Rochelle's brain was fogged up from stress and sleep loss. She tried her best to focus. Rochelle had visited her sister in Moses Lake enough times over the years to at least know the key town streets given to her by the administrator.

"I'm very sorry we can't be of more assistance." The woman's tone was similar to what she'd expect to hear in The Dalles. Nothing big city or too aloof. Both the lady and guard knew more than they could say and probably wanted to be of more help than allowed.

Walking towards her van, Rochelle could see the security guard standing a bit back from the Samaritan Hospital window and scoping out her movements. She got in the van, shut her eyes and worked to collect herself, unable to escape last night's memory of Mary's face–– her haunting, vibrant image in the windshield.

After plunking her big purse on the passenger floorboard, she started the engine. If she stayed gone long enough, then she figured, if she returned, then the guard and administrator would be replaced by the day shift. She turned the AC on high to counter what was sure to become a blazing high desert sun. Shutting her eyes again, she waited to drive until her wretched emotions allowed her to concentrate.

Rochelle did her best to remember the streets she should take and eased her way through light traffic to reach the section of Moses Lake where Gunnar lived. *Lake Vista Drive.* The name suggested much fancier homes than the twenty-five-year-old doublewide trailers sitting a half-mile back from the Moses Lake shore just beyond the city limits. Gunnar had moved into his manufactured home only a couple of months before, so she hadn't yet seen the place at the far edge of town. Each lot was over two acres in size and cars in all states of working order were strewn across the flat, arid landscape. Loud dogs on short chains greeted the early morning arrival of her van.

The numbers on the homes indicated that Gunnar's new place would be farther down the compressed gravel road. A mile into Lake Vista Estates, the road took a final turn away from shore. Rochelle made her turn, double-checked the address number scribbled beside her, and then looked up.

She hit the brakes. Gunnar's was the only doublewide on this ending stretch of road. A few Wanapum County Sheriff vehicles clogged the turnaround and his driveway. A van similar to hers had its side door slid open. The decals read: *Wanapum County Sheriff: Crime Investigation Unit.*

Her vehicle sat fifty yards from Gunnar's isolated lot. She pulled out small binoculars from her big handbag and investigated the investigators who were coming and going from both the manufactured home and the separate shop that Gunnar had built at the end of his driveway alongside a modest patch of backyard lawn. A couple detectives exited the shop and disappeared inside the doublewide.

Even upside down, Rochelle recognized Gunnar's Husky dirt bike on a repair stand next to the side of the shop. The thing was blanketed with gray grit. The front wheel had been removed and was leaning against the outbuilding. The rim was seriously bent and its knobby tire dislodged from the wheel. The motorcycle reminded her of how her nephew and son--who would borrow his uncle Nils's identical make of Husqvarna--explored the off-road trails in and around the Pothole ponds. Joe would tell her how tough it was to keep up with his hard-riding older cousin.

Lean, tall, handsome Gunnar stepped onto the porch, his blond ponytail as bushy and long as ever. His wrists were cuffed behind his back. Rochelle chose not to get out of her van. Two uniformed deputies escorted Gunnar to a Crown Vic squad car. Her 21-year-old nephew appeared to be calm, but he always did. Even when a sheriff deputy placed one hand on top of his head to lower him into the back seat of the police vehicle, her nephew maintained his unflappable disposition.

Rochelle opened the driver's door so she could go and talk to the two deputies guarding Gunnar, but before getting out, she watched a K-9 deputy with handlebar mustache exit the doublewide behind his dark Shepherd. Not bothering to remove his latex gloves, the officer wrote something on a clear evidence bag. Rochelle trained her binoculars on what he was carrying––hypodermic needles and syringes, the same red color that Rochelle discovered three months earlier taped inside the upstairs toilet tank of her own home.

Rochelle's binoculars dropped to the floor beside the brake pedal. The thud told her how braindead she'd been to have never realized. Gunnar, her only nephew, was always so hip and handsome, cocky for sure, but hardly the image of a druggie to anyone. He'd been hiding in her blindspot. In the glare of the sunny morning spotlight, her nephew was no longer in the shadows. Gunnar, the one Joe looked up to like the brother he never had, had been the one to hook her son on heroin. Her own nephew with regular access to Joe. Her skull pounded at the thought of Joe having had to rot in juvenile detention for not ratting out his own cousin.

Quietly, she shut her driver's door and backed away. Once she was far enough around the corner, Rochelle found a nondescript place to park by the nearest neighbor's home. There was no need to advertise her Oregon plates to these cops. She got out telling herself to stay cool, hardly an easy task after her realization. Rochelle reminded herself to channel her best curious-neighbor persona when her light Crocs crunched over the gravel and she slow-walked towards the crime scene. She told herself to act puzzled when approaching the officers, and eased behind the squad car that held her nephew.

"May we help you?" the nearest deputy asked politely, one of his thick arms resting on the window frame of the driver's door. A bare elbow on his other arm pressed against the strobe lights on the roof of the Crown Vic.

"Is this a drug bust?" Rochelle asked, glaring at her nephew. Once he recognized his aunt, Gunnar's cold-blue eyes widened and he turned away. She noticed a big strawberry that covered the outer half of his forearm, elbow, and up to his triceps. From the looks of that upside-down, wheel-wobbled dirt bike, she guessed he'd laid out hard and fast. Gunnar was no doubt letting the wound air out by going short-sleeved and not bandaging the big scrape.

The cop lowered his arms from the squad car, glanced inside towards Gunnar, and placed hands on hips to address Rochelle. "Do you know this man?"

"He's the new neighbor, officer." Rochelle wasn't quite lying. She allowed her voice to grow agitated. "And the young man seemed so respectable when he moved here. I just can't believe it." She stared into the back of the squad car again, but Gunnar still refused to look her way.

"What can't you believe, ma'am?"

"If this is a heroin bust, then he's the one who got the 18-year-old neighbor kid hooked on that horrible, horrible drug. I hope you lock him up." Rochelle glared at Gunnar and caught his eye before turning to walk away.

"At least I'm not a murdering thief like Joey." Gunnar's insult carried well beyond the open driver's door of the squad car.

"Pipe down, Larsson," the cop told him.

Joey. Gunnar and his parents were the only ones to call her son, 'Joey.' Rochelle was on the verge of openly asking Gunnar precisely where he was the night before. She wondered what the cops thought he'd done, or what they'd found here. After all, what did it take to earn a middle-of-the-night search warrant on the heels of her son's horrid news? And what in the hell did he mean by *'murdering thief'?* Her nephew was always a bit too sly about what he knew and didn't know.

She thought of how much energy she'd expended during her son's juvenile trial by checking out all those obvious suspects in The Dalles--leather-clad bikers in full colors, face-tattooed Mexican gangbangers, tooth-challenged tweakers--wondering why her son would never rat out the likes of those losers. But this here was a problem of the hearth. Joe had always revered his older and only cousin. So why was Gunnar backstabbing him?

Rochelle caught the officer's attention. "Please get this drug pusher off the street. We don't need his kind of scum polluting our neighborhood."

When she turned and walked back towards the van, she hoped her posture and steps didn't show how livid she was at Gunnar. Her nephew had ruined Joe, starting before her son's juvenile detention. It began the first time Joe shot up. Without the heroin, none of this chain of nightmares would have happened to her son. This morning, she had no doubt who'd been the one with Joe when he was introduced to the needle.

Rochelle walked around the corner and out of sight of Gunnar and all the sheriff activity. She had an uneasy feeling about the police raid she'd just witnessed. Something was horribly wrong for Joe. Had he somehow been in cahoots with Gunnar again? Rochelle climbed into her van and backtracked through Lake Vista Estates. There was only one person on the planet she needed to see more than her son.

Rochelle retraced the route she'd taken to Gunnar's. Back in the same parking lot, Rochelle knew she'd need a disguise and hoped that the night security guard and late shift administrator from this morning were off duty by now. Just to be safe, Rochelle reached behind her and pulled out a gardening hat she'd purchased for keeping the sun off, or in this case to obscure her face. The brim was neither too wide nor ostentatious.

Hidden deep inside her oversized purse, Rochelle found a packet of spring-loaded barrettes, the kind that resembled carnivorous dinosaur choppers biting air. She pinned up her unruly, burgundy locks, tried on the hat and, in the rear view mirror, tilted it fore and aft, port and starboard until she found a stylish angle that, for the most part, hid her face. Rochelle rummaged in her make-up bag, also hidden at the bottommost layer of the handbag. She applied more lipstick and rouge than usual and smiled into her mirror compact trying to project an emotion that was counter to everything she felt. The rouge didn't do a half-bad job of covering the remains of last night's crying jag.

From her small suitcase, she pulled out a neatly folded sundress with flower prints on the cotton material. She checked out the quiet parking lot to make sure no one was watching, Rochelle wriggled out of her pants and pulled on the dress covered with orange blossoming poppies. The irony had her, not laughing, but shaking her head from the imagined image of each poppy oozing with milky, white opium.

Several people climbed out of a different van. One of them held a

Mylar balloon with 'Congratulations for Baby Kayla' printed on the side. Rochelle jumped at the opportunity to walk beside them. No need to run into the same guard or administrator by reentering the hospital on her own. "Does your family have a newborn, too?" she asked with her most inviting smile, refined from years of running the Chamber.

"My sister," said one of them.

"Kayla's a great name." Rochelle pointed towards a large, helium-filled oblong. "Ours is Grace." When the group entered the main door, she stayed in the thick of their procession.

"We're back to see the Ford baby, Kayla," the lady told a different front desk person. The hallway door buzzed open and Rochelle continued inside with the crowd.

"Hey, again," Kayla's grandma said to the charge nurse in the maternity ward. The nurse smiled at the entourage, but immediately returned to her paperwork. Fortunately for Rochelle, Kayla's mama was in the room directly across from the nursery. When the Fords disappeared to check in with the new mom, Rochelle walked along the line of windows to view the nursery bassinets.

Rochelle adjusted her wide sunhat, and began scanning the name tags with date of birth, gender, and name: 8/14/00, Watkins girl, Heather; 8/17/00, Ramirez boy, Manuel; 8/15/00, Sanchez boy, Carlos; and 8/17/00, Ford girl, Kayla. Only the last bassinet had a label with no name for the child: 8/18/00, girl, CPS.

Rochelle inhaled before leaning in to see. Her son was absolutely correct about the baby he'd called Grace. High cheekbones, and dark, Native American eyes told Rochelle that the petite girl most definitely had a different father than pale-skinned, blue-eyed Joseph Gardner. Mesmerized by the brand new, stunningly delicate infant, there was also something subtler, maybe the bone structure of the face, showing her that this was Mary's child. In Rochelle's blurry state of mind, she was unsure how long she'd stared when she reared back, startled by a soft voice from behind. "Are you the grandmother?"

Rochelle turned to see a ginger-haired woman with long, wavy locks. "Pretty much," she said while reading a name-tag identifying the CPS caseworker as 'Amanda Skerry.' Rochelle stared through the plate glass again. "Isn't she gorgeous?"

"Adorable," said the caseworker. "I'm so very sorry to hear about your daughter."

Rochelle started to correct her, but placed a closed fist to her lips to hold back a torrent of tears.

"So, are you also from Oregon? That's what my preliminary information says about the mother."

Rochelle nodded and breathed deep, placing her palms on the window to maintain balance. The woman placed a hand on Rochelle's back to steady her, and also looked through the window at the baby. Rochelle pointed at the tag hanging off the bassinet on the other side of the window. "Right before she drowned, Mary named her baby 'Grace.' Can you?" Rochelle pointed and started to ask, but Amanda finished for her.

"Beautiful name. I'll have the floor nurse add 'Grace' to the tag."

Rochelle tried to focus through swollen eyes.

"The young man she was with last night claims the baby isn't his," said Amanda when she opened her notebook. "An initial blood test shows this. We're waiting on DNA tests to come back and corroborate those findings."

"That young man is my son." Rochelle decided to tell the CPS worker, knowing that her own connection to this case would surface soon enough. "Mary and Joe were sweethearts for their teen years. He told me he has no idea how Mary drowned. Do the police have any leads?"

Amanda eyed Rochelle. "I honestly can't help you with that. I'm not part of the homicide investigation, Mrs. Gardner."

Since she'd never given Amanda her last name, there was little doubt that the lady knew more about her son than she was letting on. "For the record, I can't imagine any universe anywhere where my boy would kill Mary Quinn." She expected the caseworker to react with shock or coldness, but Amanda remained calm.

"Do you have any idea who the baby's father is?" the caseworker asked.

"On the phone last night, my son claimed the father was Native American. Mary and Joe broke up for a while last year, and Mary had some Native classmates at her high school."

Amanda wrote this in her notebook.

"Without Mary, what's in store for Grace?" Rochelle asked. "Who'll care for her?"

Amanda closed her notebook and motioned for them to sit in the chairs by the nurse's station. Once they were both settled, Rochelle waited for the caseworker to speak. "This morning, Wanapum County Family Court will likely declare emergency jurisdiction over Grace."

Rochelle liked how Amanda already called the baby, 'Grace,' but the jurisdiction thing had her confused. "So why declare this in Wanapum County and not where Mary is from--in Oregon?" Rochelle asked.

"Grace presents an emergency situation with the mother deceased and no paternity established. I expect that CPS will be placing the baby into local, temporary foster care."

The realization hit Rochelle. As much as she treated Mary like her daughter, as nicely as she'd prepared a nursery for the newborn in The Dalles, this was another city, county, and state. Rochelle Gardner's eyes widened. She had no biological tie to Grace that would help her secure custody.

Amanda glanced down the hall toward the newborns. "Next step is to find the biological father. That process won't be expedited." Amanda spoke factually, without trace of emotion. "It's often grandparents or others with ties to the child who petition the court, but the parental rights of custody only belong to the biological father and mother. If the surviving parents cannot be found, a judge will award permanent guardianship. It's usually predicated on a thorough CPS review."

"What does a CPS review entail?" Rochelle asked, after forcing herself to stay composed.

"We visit the home, interview the prospective guardians, and conduct background checks. Afterwards, we advise the court."

"What about me being an out-of-state resident?" Rochelle asked.

Amanda hesitated. "I doubt that will work for temporary foster placement, but it won't disallow permanent non-parental custody, assuming the father is not located."

Rochelle handed Amanda a Chamber of Commerce business card.

"The Dalles," the caseworker noted. "A year ago over Memorial Day, my husband and I took our kids to a nice new museum there."

At this, Rochelle perked up. "Mary and my son worked there in the summers doing living history. Joe also helped care for the injured raptors. Mary Quinn sang with the End of the Trail Band. Incredible voice. *The Oregonian* called her singing 'spellbinding.'"

Amanda placed her hand to her mouth. "Did she have hair like mine?" the caseworker asked.

Rochelle nodded, but then laughed. "She used to--before dying it a deep Goth black a few months ago."

"I remember her," said Amanda. "Definitely spellbinding. A teenager, maybe seventeen. Petticoat and bonnet. Her singing gave me goosebumps."

"That was Mary Quinn alright. All the other musicians in the band were adults."

Amanda smiled. "During one solo, she walked around in her petticoat handing out braided sprigs of dried wildflowers for the young girls to pin in their hair. My little girl absolutely loved hers. Every weekend last summer, she insisted I put the same sprig in her hair until every last dried leaf and blossom dropped off."

"How cute is that?" said Rochelle, trying her best to sound upbeat.

Amanda stared at the newborn. "Come to think about it, I remembered her singing a song about a little girl named Grace out on the Oregon Trail."

Rochelle tried to smile. "That's the one Mary loved to solo."

"You know what my husband told me when she finished singing that day?"

Rochelle shook her head.

"He told me that, back when he and I first met in high school, I could have passed for that teen singer."

"I didn't want to say anything," said Rochelle, "but I was also thinking that you and Mary could pass for twins, that is if you two were the same age."

At this, the CPS caseworker teared up. "I can't sing much, but I definitely remember seeing and hearing Grace's mother."

CHAPTER SIX

III.
FORCE

I n his disgusting, grieving state, Joe remembered medics spraying his scratched skin with disinfectant and wiping him down with a rough sponge before allowing him inside their ambulance. Joe was also ordered to thoroughly shower at the hospital before being admitted into the emergency room.

"I need some morphine or Methadone to kick this crap," Joe all but pleaded to the emergency doc, who asked him how long he'd been addicted, and to what.

"Heroin," Joe said too desperately for his own liking, but at this point he didn't care. "I've been having major withdrawals all night.

He was told that, with his pending incarceration, neither Methadone or morphine were permitted. However, the hospital was just starting an FDA test trial for a pending drug called Suboxone. "The addicts being tested are put on an eight-day taper, no longer." The physician described how some participants would be given a placebo, while others would get the actual drug."

Figuring that his luck couldn't get any worse, Joe asked where he could sign up.

Joe needed something, anything, especially with the sweats starting up again. A Wanapum Sheriff deputy preparing Joe's release from the Emergency Room paid close attention when Joe signed the release form for the test program. The physician returned with the packets of Suboxone strips and had Joe take the first two. "Let it dissolve under your tongue," the doctor said and handed the remainder to the deputy. He instructed both the cop and Joe about the tapering––two strips to start, one-and-a-half to follow, and then one strip to a half-doses. "Again, no more than eight days total and the amounts are listed in the instructions."

The deputy told Joe that the infirmary nurse at the jail would give him the medicine. Why eight days in jail? he wanted to ask, but decided to hold his tongue.

"I failed to mention that your newborn girl is fine," the doctor said before leaving the room. This time, Joe didn't clarify about not being the father. Medics loaded him into another EMT ambulance when another bout of sweats ruined his showered skin.

Unlike the blaring sirens taking Grace and him to Samaritan hospital, they followed the speed limit for the half-hour from Moses Lake to Smohalla. A deputy sheriff trailed Joe's ambulance the entire way. His shaking continued worse than ever. Joe barely recalled being processed into the Wanapum County Jail. Stepping from the ambulance, he did remember one side of the place looking like a squat, metal coffee can. They bagged up his clothes and wallet. Except for his Nikes and own underwear that he'd crudely washed in the earlier shower, the jailers made him don loose jail coveralls that were the same tan color as the jail building.

The infirmary consisted of four beds and a stainless steel toilet. Sunlight streamed through vertical slits of thick windows too narrow for even Houdini to wriggle through. Joe lay in bed sweating and shaking until the Suboxone kicked in and his body started to calm–– finally. It definitely wasn't a placebo. Joe had lost his urge to puke and the itching mostly stopped, but in his half-sleep, he couldn't stop thinking about his life in shambles.

Joe, the only inmate in the room, waited in this stupor until a guard flung open the infirmary door. A another man stood behind him in the darkened hallway. "Come in, I guess," Joe muttered.

"Of course El Padre can come in," the stocky, short guard barked and left once the man entered.

The priest was close to the age of Joe's parents, mid-forties, but Hispanic and wearing a black robe with a large silver cross dangling on his chest. "You marked 'Roman Catholic' on the jail admitting form. I wanted to be sure and stop in for a couple minutes to introduce myself. You can call me Father José or El Padre, but for you gringos, 'hey priest' works, too."

Father José surprised Joe by sitting cross-legged on the floor against the wall beside the entry door.

"Are you a Yogi-Priest hybrid?" Joe asked, pointing to El Padre's lotus pose.

"This is how I practice Integral Yoga, a way to center myself into my Roman Catholic prayers."

Joe studied the large silver cross hanging from the priest's neck. "Cool cassock, Father, but just so you know, I haven't been to church in a year or so. My old lady made me go to catechism in grade school, but that's about it." El Padre was inspecting Joe's demeanor, listening keenly.

"I'm here as your jail chaplain, especially for the likes of good Catholics like you. I'm not here to discuss your case, but to offer spiritual support."

"Who's been spreading bad rumors that I'm a good Catholic?" Joe asked and tried to smile, but couldn't. He'd grown up Roman Catholic, but the variety that only went to mass on Easter and Christmas Day.

"Only good Catholics know what a cassock is," El Padre answered and laughed, but then turned serious. "From the radio news this morning, you've had a horrid night. If you feel moved, why not recite your devotional? I'm sure you remember your 'Hail Mary, full of grace.'"

"Then you don't know squat about my case, do you Father?"

The priest clasped his hands on his lap. "I don't know a whole lot. Teen girl found drowned in a pothole, her newborn rescued, and the admitting guard just told me that you're their person-of-interest."

"Mary and Grace, like in the Rosary prayer." Those are the names of my girlfriend and her baby."

"I see. Holy Mary, full of Grace," said El Padre. "I'm not so good with puns––even when I'm listening for them. The radio news wouldn't broadcast any names pending notification of kin, but I'm truly sorry for your loss, Joe."

"I'm beginning to think that Wanapum County is about to hang a noose around my neck."

"Higher truth will prevail, just not always in the way we expect."

Joe appreciated how the priest listened to him. Even the way he sat on the floor displayed a humble holiness.

Father José lifted his cross and made a soft suggestion. "Why don't you and I both listen to our 'Hail Mary' with fresh ears?" He pushed off the floor and adjusted his cassock. The priest crossed himself before closing his eyes to recite the devotional. Joe did his best to join in and only messed up a word or two:

Hail Mary full of grace. The Lord is with thee. Blessed art thou amongst women, and blessed is the fruit of thy womb––Jesus. Holy Mary, Mother of God, pray for us sinners, now and at the hour of our death. Amen.

"Amen," Joe added, and slid to one end of his narrow cot to press his back against the wall.

"I'm really pleased to meet you, Joseph. You're in my prayers now." The priest moved closer and extended his hand to shake. "My rounds are calling, so I need to be going," he said when they shook.

"So many sinners, so little time," said Joe.

"I'll definitely schedule more time with you next round."

CHAPTER SEVEN

"You got a visitor," the nurse-guard came back in and told him a few minutes after the priest left. Joe tried to focus and find his bearings when he was guided to the visitor's area. At least the cold turkey was locked in its pen. Joe couldn't wrap his brain around the night before, but froze at the sight of his mother standing on the opposite side of the window that separated inmates from visitors.

Except for on the phone the night before, they hadn't talked for three months, not since she kicked him out of their home. His chest forgot all of that; a surge of emotion rushed into his head, caused him to blush. His throat tightened and made him to want to hug her. Maybe it was the frightened boy stuck somewhere inside a hardened, 18-year-old frame. Joe forced himself to breathe and plopped down on the wobbly chair in front of the Plexiglas that divided them.

"Thanks for calling me," his mom said almost shyly. She looked more exhausted than ever. Joe no doubt came off plenty haggard, too. "Tell me again about Mary," she added.

"I would never hurt her," Joe said, clutching the well-worn chair arms. His voice went dry and he coughed.

"I just can't wrap my head around her——"

"She's effing dead, Mom!" Why did she start out grilling him on the gruesome details? His parents had raised him to never swear, and he never did, except for this time when he almost did. The whole raw mess made his temples throb.

Rochelle turned away. "I'll find you a local lawyer this morning," she told him and got up. "Maybe it's better if I go now."

The last thing Joe needed--after everything else--was to wound his mom again, the way he had by relapsing. That didn't mean he was in any mood to sugarcoat the ugly facts for his bitter drama queen of a mother. Ever since he was ten and she started working for the Chamber, his mom spent her workdays lime-lighting through town, but morphing into a sour lemon at home.

"Please stay, Mom." He spoke sweetly, knowing he needed to control his own outbursts. "I really do appreciate you coming. It's just--" His voice trailed off. After all, she'd just driven all night to see him. Besides, he might need an attorney, something he definitely couldn't afford on his own.

Rochelle lowered herself back into the visitor's chair. "I wasn't there for you this summer, Joseph."

He hadn't made any moves to patch things up, either. "They got me on this new drug being tested. *Suboxone*. I'm being given eight days to taper off the heroin." Joe's feet tapped nervously when discussing the subject. "It's already starting to work. I'll be taking smaller and smaller doses each day. Whatever happens, I'm done with smack. Totally done."

She didn't respond with encouragement or a lecture. The Suboxone may have been like horse without the euphoric ride, but for his mom, he could see that, this time, in the middle of grief, his drug problem wasn't registering. Her face stayed sullen. She stared at the jail wall behind him. "I know Mom. Mary's dead and you get more empty promises from *Mr. Relapse* here."

At this, she jolted back from whatever thoughts overwhelmed her. "Any time now, expect your favorite cousin to be joining you in the slammer." Her tone turned bitter. "That is, if he isn't here already."

"What's Gunnar got to do with last night?"

"Well Joe. I'd love to look my nephew in the eye and get a straight answer to that very question. The cops just raided his place. So, let me ask you straight up, son. Do you think he had anything to do with Mary's murder?"

Joe shook his head. "That was probably all due to the slip of paper I dropped in front of the deputy last night, the one with Gunnar Larsson's name and number scribbled on top." From the look on his mother's face, he could tell she had more to say on the subject.

"Or maybe you're covering up again for your cousin. I can't believe it took me until this very morning to figure out that you were protecting him last year." He watched her lips quaver and then freeze before she grabbed the fabric of her sundress sleeve and pressed a poppy flower image against the window for him to see: "He stole the son I used to know."

Joe told her it wasn't that simple. "His smack may have weaned me off Oxy last fall and got me hooked, but when I got out of juvie, Gunnar and me steered clear of each other. After Pops took off, it hurt me, too. I caved into my own cravings. Gunnar had nothing to do with my relapse."

He watched her collect her thoughts. "I know you, Joe... I know the boy with... so... much... promise." Joe fought to keep from turning away when she stared him in the eye. "I'll do what I can to be your ally, son." Then, she paused. He could barely make out her words. "Maybe I'm not as strong as you think I am, Joe. Maybe, just maybe... you're more on your own...than you've ever been." At this, he watched his mother lower her face into her palms.

He'd never seen his mom on the edge of defeat before. Not in this way. Then the bigger, most devastating thing hit him. "I think you loved Mary as much as I did," he whispered, his mouth close to the stainless-steel speak-hole cut into the Plexiglas. "You and me had some big-hearted love for that girl."

At this, she sat up. Tears seeped through her closed lids. "Mary was the daughter I never had."

Joe nodded, but Mary's absence kept hitting him harder than hard, and there was no hiding from the ugliest of facts.

"I saw the baby," his mom managed to say. "I went to the hospital first because I thought you might still be there. Very beautiful. But definitely not your child."

Joe turned away. "Mary never warned me that it was even a possibility. I didn't have a clue, until––"

"Until?"

"Until I first saw the baby and asked her if the father was one of her Native friends." Joe leaned into the window, almost nose-to-nose with his mother. He whispered through the speaker hole. "When Mary nodded, I got pissed and took off to get gasoline. Her Pathfinder was flat out of gas."

Joe wobbled on his chair and glanced around at the last place he expected to be spending the morning. "I have no idea what happened to Mary in the time after I left and before I came back." His fingers tightened around the ends of the stubby armrests. "As for this kid who's not mine, I'm not so sure I care who raises her."

Rochelle tapped the Plexiglas with the nail of her index finger. Her hard pings filled his side of the wall. "Listen here, Joseph." She gave him a stern glare to go with the harsh tone. "Mary Quinn will always be part of us. She's not the one who screwed up what the two of you had together. None of this is the baby's fault. There's no way Mary's child is going to be lost to the system, not so long as I'm alive."

They both leaned back. He refused to look her in the eye until she broke the silence. "For what it's worth son, whether you're called a person-of-interest or something worse, I do know that you would never hurt Mary."

Before he could thank her for promising to find him a lawyer, a guard came to tell them that the jail's visitation time was up. Joe kept picturing in his mind, not Mary, but Kuma. "I love you, Mom," Joe managed to tell her when the guard motioned for him to get up from the visitor room chair.

Why couldn't he stop picturing Kuma Kusumoto's athletic, Japanese face? Why was Joe so dead set on Kuma not being identified as the father of Mary's baby? Joe's jaw stiffened when the answer came. Simple. He never wanted anything to do with Kuma again.

He shuffled and slouched when the guard took his elbow to lead him back to the Shoe. "I love you, too, Joseph," he heard his mom say faintly through the speak-hole.

CHAPTER EIGHT

A fter he left the visiting area, a huge deputy corrections officer named Max ushered him in the opposite direction from the infirmary. The man unlocked the door into the E-Tank. The guard removed Joe's cuffs when they entered, and pointed to one of the lower bunks.

On this Friday morning, three men waited inside the admitting cell of the Wanapum County Jail. Across from Joe, a large, slow-witted man poured forth freeform poetry until he stopped and laughed robustly, probably impressed with himself as a colorful wordsmith. The other two inmates were badass bikers quietly talking at the far end of the big holding cell.

Joe was tilted back on his bed when a different guard ushered in a familiar face.

"Well, well, if it's not Joey Gardner. We've got a family reunion in the admitting tank." Gunnar sounded like the way artificial sweetener tastes when he stared down at him and spoke.

The crazy poet laughed and said something about rotten fish flying in formation through Walmart to buy their Air Jordan's.

Another set of guards entered to inform the two bikers that their cells were ready. The tough men allowed themselves to be cuffed and led from E-Tank.

When the guards left, Gunnar took a piss, washed his hands, and stared from the stainless steel basin through two thick, tall Plexiglas windows on either side of a door. When he tried the handle, it opened onto a wide, narrow patio with high, tan, cinderblock walls. The patio ceiling was covered with thick grating. He motioned for Joe to follow him into the outer enclosure.

Joe sat against the outer cell wall and noticed Gunnar standing a bit sideways with half of his body turned away. Once the door shut, his cousin stared up at the surveillance camera. Joe watched him smile for any hidden guard who might be tuned into the jail monitoring system. His tone was anything but happy when he looked back down on his cousin. "Not sure what they can hear, Joey, so talk really quiet."

Out of nowhere, a nearby church blasted the heavens with chimes. Joe looked up, dazed. "Mary sang this song last year for a local, all-denominational choir," he said just loud enough for his cousin to hear. Gunnar––over six-foot tall––loomed between Joe and the overhead grate where the music poured in:

Holy, holy, holy,
Lord, God Almighty,
Early in the morning,
Our song shall rise to thee.

This was the song she'd soloed. The church bells didn't come with words, but Mary's pure powering voice filled his head, and he turned away from his cousin when his throat tightened again from thinking about his girl.

"I want to throttle you, Joey, not sing hymns," he said over the looming chimes. "What in the hell were you thinking? Why'd you touch that kit?"

Joe tapped fingers on knees. "From your tone, I'm thinking everything inside that First Aid kit was stashed there by you, or intended for you."

"You think?" Gunnar shook his head like it was such a stupid thing to say. He didn't elaborate, except to say that when the "medicine' bundles inside the kit came out, then the "lettuce" went in to pay for it. "Problem was that the whole kit-and-caboodle was missing." Gunnar leaned down and scowled. "Except that you snagged it all."

"Finders keepers," said Joe.

Gunnar shook his head. "You jumped the wrong game, Joey."

Joe squinted. "And here I thought that old Bone Shrine was just a big pile of dead cows and coyotes."

"What with you being my cousin, the *Tramposo* gang will think I was in on your little prank."

"*Mess with me, and I mess you up?* Those guys?"

"How'd you know their motto?" Gunnar asked.

"The Bone Shrine. It's carved on the top of the altar. So were you the 'medicine' man or the 'lettuce' guy?"

Gunnar's ice blue eyes grew wide and discreetly motioned to the camera above them. "None of your business, Joey." Gunnar craned his neck to look at the roof grill. "For all I know, you're already as good as dead to them."

"I'm on some kind of hit list?"

Gunnar's steely blue eyes narrowed. "You are, unless you take the fall and say that you came up from Oregon to deliver the 'medicine'."

Joe turned away. "It's way worse than that."

"What could be worse?"

"Seems like you think this is only about the kit and all. I can tell you exactly where I hid it with everything inside, Gunnar."

"Too late for that. The sheriff's K-9 unit sniffed it out."

One thing struck Joe. His stupid fingerprints would be all over those plastic sealed bundles he touched. "After Mary went into labor, I abandoned the stash and never made it back to where I hid it."

"Labor? Are you saying that Mary had her kid last night? Sweet Jesus!" Gunnar gritted his teeth and shook his head even more.

"Last night in the car. The baby came early. Except she wasn't mine. I could tell the minute I saw her."

"Anything else I'm missing here?"

"You really don't know, do you?"

"Stop messing with my head, Joe."

"When I got back from getting gas––yeah, we ran out of frickin' fuel, too--Mary was face down in the pond. Some mutha drowned her and I aim to find out who."

"Mary Quinn is dead? Holy effin' Moses!"

Holy, Holy, Holy!
All the saints adore Thee,
Casting down their golden crowns
around the glassy sea.

"And I shouldn't have told the cop how I lost my cool after finding out the kid wasn't mine."

Cherubim and seraphim
falling down before thee,
which was, and is,
and evermore shall be.

On the hot patio, Gunnar's face turned red and beads of sweat dripped down his brow. "The cops didn't say a thing to me this morning about Mary being dead--too busy grilling me on the heroin they found."

Joe tapped the drainage grate with his heel again. "I think the cops are thinkin' that I killed Mary."

When Gunnar placed both hands on his hips and looked up again, Joe noticed the scrape on his far elbow. His cousin tried to turn away when Joe scooted over enough to catch a look at the entire arm. "What happened to you?"

"Didn't want you to see what a klutz I've become. There's a rough motocross spot behind my new place. I tried a small jump and totally laid out my dirt-bike yesterday."

That's some serious trail rash."

"It's nothing compared to your scrape. Taking out Mary is definitely the sort of hardline move those *Tramposos* would make." The church bells made it hard to think, but didn't lessen Gunnar's growing frustration. "I can't believe you two were out there last night."

"When me and Mary were in 9th grade. You were the one who showed us the Bone Shrine."

"But that was before I ever used it as a drop site. Face it, Joey, if Mary wouldn't say where the stash was, and then said she knew me, then, hell yes, she'd get snuffed."

Joe clenched his fist and slammed it against the door behind his ear. "Jesus, Gun, she didn't even see me move it; didn't have a clue about any smack. Mary's water broke right when I stumbled onto your China White."

The church chimes refused to quit.

Holy, Holy, Holy!
Though the darkness hides Thee,
Though the eye of sinful man,
thy glory may not see.

"You have any idea what kind of whirlwind you unleashed?" Gunnar asked.

Only thou art holy;
there is none beside thee,
perfect in power,
in love, and purity.

"No. I don't have the slightest idea," Joe said. "Mary Quinn is murdered because of me, and I'm clueless."

The chiming stopped, causing the cousins to stare heavenward with surprise. The late morning sun was high enough to beat down through the metal grating. The opening offered no cooling breeze on the dry, warming day. Joe thought he was finished sweating, but this was a more normal perspiration than cold turkey sweat.

Gunnar loomed over Joe and slowly opened and closed his eyes. Joe could tell from the silence that his cousin's mind was busy sizing up the situation and, from there, puzzling together bits of intelligence to figure out the best option for moving forward. Joe had seen the look many times before. Gunnar's mind usually stayed three or four steps ahead of everyone else's thinking. His cousin plopped down beside him and, without the blaring chimes to mask their words, he warned Joe again to keep his voice real low. Shoulder-to-shoulder, he leaned into Joe's ear. "So we have a drowning, a rescued baby, a major drug confiscation, and you're the person-of-interest for all of this. Anything else, Joey?"

"How horrible our luck has been," he muttered.

"Nothing to do with luck. That was a drop gone bad because you snagged the stash. So let's assume the cops want to saddle you with everything––murder, moving the smack, whatever. None of that solves our little problem with the *Tramposos*, does it?"

"Screw the *Tramposos*," Joe said in a whisper.

"Except, if you beat the rap and want to survive on the outside; or, if you take the hit and want to stay alive in prison, then things will need to be smoothed over with those *hombres*," his cousin repeated.

Joe furrowed his brow, puzzled. "Is that all I am in this life––everyone else's convenient fall guy?"

Gunnar pointed to the surveillance cameras and motioned again for Joe to keep his voice down. "You bring this crap on yourself, Joey." He paused. "I got a plan, though, the best I can come up with on the spot. If you go along with this, and I mean, once you commit, you've really got to stick with the approach and not change course. Can you promise me that?"

Joe didn't know what he would be promising, so didn't respond. He wanted to ask if he was going to be tailed for the rest of his life with *Mess Me Up* inked on the back of a shaved skull?

Gunnar whispered in his ear: "Get ice blood in your veins, unless you plan on joining Mary Quinn."

Joe lifted his hands in the air. "Just tell me your brilliant strategy, then." He got up and started pacing over and back on the small patio.

Gunnar motioned for his younger cousin to come closer. Joe squatted and Gunnar spoke quietly. "Mary was cool, but she also had some of the baddest mood swings I ever saw. So, if you're planning to survive this, then it has to look like she committed suicide."

"Suicide! Are you serious?"

"Dead serious."

Joe banged his temples with both palms. "Mary would never, especially with a new––"

"Pipe down, Joey!" Gunnar's voice boomed and then whispered, "If any *Tramposos* go down for either the confiscated caboodle or for

Mary's death, then our whole family is a pack of goners." He waited until he had Joe's full attention. "So you better get wise and stay wise."

The older cousin glanced up at the cameras and raised his voice so any eavesdroppers could hear: "Too bad your moody girl drowned herself when she thought you were dumping her again."

Gunnar grabbed the handle to the door and disappeared inside E-Tank. Joe's emotions went from numb to baffled, achy to angry when he followed his cousin inside and welcomed the cool rush of air conditioning.

Within E-Tank dorm, the happy, crazy man riffed about a ring of secret talkers plotting to land on Saturn with outlaw three-wheelers. Gunnar spoke with the old, loony dude he knew from somewhere in Moses Lake. "Are you still a Yankee's fan, Cecil?" Gunnar asked. "Who did you like better, Joe DiMaggio or Marilyn Monroe?"

Cecil laughed aloud and told Gunnar that Marilyn was the bigger hit.

Big Max and another guard entered E-Tank. "Cecil. Next time keep your pants on in the grocery store," Max warned him.

"Toodle-oo," said the man, laughing and tightening his belt under a huge belly. Joe watched Cecil waddle across the floor of the cell looking like the Penguin in those Batman movies.

"And, Gunnar Larsson," Max added. "Someone arranged your release, too."

When his cousin got off the bunk, he told Joey not to forget. "It's all about survival."

The guard ushered Gunnar from the big cell and Joe was left wondering what sort of hell he'd created for himself. An hour or so later, two more men were admitted. Each one had a tattoo the size of a thumb-tip over his cheek bone. The matching ink images featured the same howling coyote head. Neither new inmate glanced at Joe. Neither spoke a word until the guards left, locking the door behind them.

Each man sat on a lower bunk of the two beds directly across from him. The bigger, burlier inmate narrowed his eyes and asked Joe, "It true you kill your girl? Kill her once she has your kid?"

"Not true," said Joe.

"Yeah, nobody in jail never do nothin' them cops say they do, eh Pedro?" the same man asked his thin buddy.

"And nobody ever got shanked in here, Jorge," wiry, tall Pedro added.

You *Tramposos* are a pack of losers, Joe forced himself not to say.

"Look at them puffy eyes, Jorge. Lady-killer likes to cry."

"He's *Él Niño*," said Jorge, "'cuz of his warm teardrops."

"Baby-Daddy kills *la Madre*." The other one laughed coldly, goading Joe for a reaction.

He knew better than to get sucked in to their lowlife poking and prodding. No need to rile up these coldblooded killers. Joe sat stony, his eyes inspecting two surveillance cams and hoping this time that someone on the other end was listening in and watching.

Pedro, the thinner *Tramposo,* took off his coveralls and tossed his t-shirt over to Jorge. In only his boxers, Pedro washed his face and pits in the sink. Once done, he slipped his jail garb back on and took two steps closer to Joe's cot and stopped. Burly Jorge ripped off a few big sections of cotton from Pedro's t-shirt. He climbed up on one top bunk and then the second to tie the cloth around the two surveillance lenses. Joe tensed up, but did his best not to let it show.

"No one messes with the *Tramposos*." Jorge hopped down, tapping his cheek tattoo.

Joe sat on the edge, trying to watch both *hombres* without them noticing.

"*The Tramposos* ain't happy about last night," Skinny Pedro said staying between Joe and the E-Tank bathroom.

Joe grew uneasy sitting half-way between these two, but didn't see why he shouldn't stand up for himself. "Why did you hide your little kit right out in the open of the Bone Shrine? Anyone could have found it," Joe told the two fools.

"Your cousin told you when to be there, didn't he?" Jorge asked. He stared first at Joe, then beyond him to Pedro. "How else you know the exact time to steal the horse? Whatever you get paid from him ain't enough. Why? 'Cause you still gotta pay us way more."

Joe twisted his head and jolted back with surprise at the locked door leading into the admitting cell. The instant he could see the smaller *Tramposo* turn and look, Joe sprang from the edge of his bed and tackled the man. The lunge came faster and harder than even Joe expected--his adrenaline rush carried the thin man back with full force.

Joe's face was in Pedro's chest and his legs were driving like he'd exploded out of the batter's box towards first base, except the base of the toilet was where he heard the dull thud of the *Tramposo*'s skull crashing into stainless steel. Pedro's pathetic moan was not quite as sickening as the guy's body going limp beneath Joe's shoulder.

The quiet that followed was worse, but Joe only noticed during that instant when he rolled off the lean body. He had no time to check out the damage when stout Jorge rushed him, a right fist about to shatter his face.

Joe was still on his back when he threw a left punch that partially blocked the *Tramposo*'s fist; his knuckles only grazed the man's ear. Jorge's thick body slammed full force on top of Joe. Torso-to-torso, they pummeled each other on the cement floor and tried to land dirty blows. Joe kicked his knee into Jorge, but the man was too close for much impact. He punched Jorge's neck and tried to land a solid, short punch to the big *Tramposo*'s eye, but his fist glanced off the coyote tattoo, instead.

The two traded nasty body blows until Joe grabbed Jorge's thick hair to bend his neck sideways. Jorge's face contorted with pain, but the hair-hold exposed Joe to a hard shot in the ribs, part of a combo to the gut, too. Winded, Joe commanded himself to hold his breath and not show any sign of the impact. He punching back even harder. He may have landed a shot to the Jorge's jawbone, but the two were too close for him to tell. Clinched up like boxers, except for down on the cement floor, neither of them could land clean blows with fists or knees. The stalemate lasted until Jorge found a way to grip Joe's neck.

Joe never expected such a choke. Beefy, sandpaper-rough fingers crunched his Adam's apple and crushed his air passage. Joe gagged and tried to knee the man, tried to punch, but began to black out.

When Joe could breathe again--freed from the death grip--he regained his sight and consciousness and saw Jorge directly above him with his spine arched upright. Joe landed a solid Charlie-horse blow with a heel to his thigh. Jorge hardly responded to the kick. The man reacted instead like Frankenstein being jolted alive. The *Tramposo* stayed upright and stiff before toppling with a rigid thud to the cement floor. Directly behind Jorge, a guard clutched a Taser gun in both hands. Joe scooted away and watched Jorge writhe like he was suffering an epileptic seizure.

The formal uniform said: *Al Weaver, Chief Correction's Officer*. The boss guard stepped forward to zap Joe, but with back against the patio door, Joe held a mauled throat and vomited nothing but fluids over his own coveralls. Seated in puke again, Joe gagged, held his hands high and winced. When the boss guard stayed back, Joe was pretty sure that, if he hadn't barfed, then he'd have been Tasered, too.

"What are you idiots doing?" the thick-jawed jailer with a huge underbite asked, still holding the Taser gun like a wobbly pistol.

"We was attacked," said Jorge.

Joe wanted zero part of the fun so he kept his hands high, kept his eyes on the chief guard's big and wide black tennis shoes and tried his best to ignore both the horrible taste in his mouth and raw pain in his throat.

The boss jailer stared at the unconscious man, but skinny Pedro stayed down, nothing moving, his face still wedged where the floor met the base of the toilet. "Don't either of you even so much as flinch," the chief guard warned Jorge and Joe, his jaw making him seem downright angry all the time.

"I'm thinking assault charges, boss," said Big Max.

The chief didn't respond before glancing at Joe, his rear still on the cement floor, and hands clasped on top of his head. He asked Joe if being all over the front page wasn't enough excitement for one day.

"I haven't seen any newspapers, sir," said Joe, "but I was ambushed. Two against one. Self-defense."

"He is a liar!" Jorge countered from where they'd cuffed him. "He threw the first punch."

The jail boss glared at the larger *Tramposo* and pointed to the surveillance devices. "When? Right after you climbed up and blocked off our lenses?" He waved his Taser. Jorge turned away and decided to keep his mouth shut. The chief guard tapped the sole of Pedro's foot with his steel-toed boot. After the taps got harder, Pedro finally moaned, rubbed his skull, and rolled face up. His eyes were so glassy that Joe could tell the man had no clue where he was.

The boss guard turned to Big Max and pointed at burly Jorge. "Get the sweet one there into solitary. And when you come back to help me with our celebrity criminal here, bring him a fresh pair of coveralls." The boss jailer turned to the other two guards. "Take the loopy featherweight to the infirmary."

"What if he goes into a coma?" one of them asked his boss.

"Then get in touch with me directly. I'll be the one giving the orders on that skinny sack of bones."

Max cuffed Jorge and escorted him from the admitting cell. The jail boss waited for the two other guards to drag Pedro from E-Tank.

The chief corrections officer motioned for Joe to move away from the patio door. Joe shifted over a few feet but stayed seated, hands still on top of his head. The two were alone. The jail boss opened the door and checked outside before turning back. "You can lower your hands now, Gardner. I saw where you was having a long conversation with Gunnar Larsson," he said. "What were you two plotting?"

"We were just talking family stuff." The question being asked told Joe that the surveillance audio hadn't captured much, especially considering the nature of his and Gunnar's patio conversation. "This is all real tough, sir. We were all close to Mary." The raw words inflamed Joe's throat.

From the smirk on Officer Wheeler's face, Joe expected him to ask why he killed her then. Instead, the boss seemed startled when Big Max returned so fast with fresh jail coveralls. "I handed Jorge off to Sam. He'll take him to the Shoe," Max explained.

Joe slipped off his soiled jail garb and replaced them with the clean ones that Max brought back.

"Listen up, newbie," the jail boss leaned in and told Joe. "In my jail, when you got no clue, get used to the Shoe."

Joe zipped up his fresh jail garb and turned to the chief guard. "Actually Officer Weaver, after being jumped like that, I'd very much appreciate being kept in solitary for the time that I'm here in your jail." He said it in a tone where the chief jailer would have no doubt he was serious.

"We call our solitary hole, 'the Shoe'," Big Max explained.

The jail boss leaned in close and whispered. "And the Shoe's a good call for you, son. Just be sure you keep this little scuffle here under your hat. You understand?"

"I get it, sir." Joe rubbed his Adam's apple when he spoke.

"You're what we call real high-profile for little Wanapum County. Let's just say it won't help none to have you getting hurt again on my watch." The boss guard's mean jaw stuck out more than ever and he whispered something in Big Max's ear.

Joe couldn't figure why—with two against one—he'd only been jumped and not shanked. He guessed that their 'fall guy' would be more useful to them alive than dead.

"No more trouble like today and we'll keep you in the Shoe," the chief corrections officer said. "I'm assigning Big Max to be your personal protector. Do we have an understanding, inmate?"

Joe only knew he'd be safer that way, so he locked eyes with the rock-jawed boss guard, nodded clearly, and with his fingers, zipped his lips shut.

"He's all yours then," the head guard told Big Max who'd just cuffed Joe. Max held Joe's elbow and led him down the bending hallway of the can-shaped, county can.

CHAPTER NINE

IV.

WITH

Rochelle stepped outside of the jail into a blinding Friday morning sun and walked to the front of the Wanapum County Courthouse, a stately brick structure with grand steps and old by Pacific Northwest standards. How much trial time would be spent inside those walls?

There must be a decent defense attorney near this hub of local government. The offices should just be opening and Joe had to be ready, posthaste, for any arraignment. She expected to see the same alignment as in The Dalles, also a rural county seat. Most law firms wanted to set up shop as close to the halls of justice as possible. Rochelle started directly across the street from the courthouse when she spotted a plate glass window with black stenciled letters outlined in gold-leaf. 'Gates, Cobbler, and Gutierrez,' it read.

She opened the heavy, front door of the firm. Not a soul sat in the waiting room. "I'm sorry, but we don't accept walk-ins," the receptionist at the front desk told her. Smohalla, population 8,000, wasn't exactly a bustling New York, New York. "Here's a new client application form. Please return it so we can see if any of our attorneys have openings this week," she added.

Not so much as a simple meet-and-greet. Rochelle wasted no time walking out. Methodist Church chimes clanged out a familiar protestant hymn that was so loud she couldn't think straight. No need to divulge any information about her son's potential legal jeopardy or hint at the accounts receivable these horribly overworked lawyers might generate from Joe's quagmire. That's not to say she wasn't hoping for Joe to be released without any charges.

At the Law Office of Vilhelm & Associates, a half-a-block away, she met the same formal receptionist with a different face who'd been cloned to process all the little people with the exact same plastic protocol. Again, in their polished tomb of a waiting room, she was told there would be no walk-ins allowed and appointments were always mandatory. Like in that first place, she wasted no time leaving. Rochelle decided to walk her concentric strategy one block wider. At least the church bells had stopped.

Wedged in a slot between the Dog-Eared Bookery and Baldy Bob's Barber Shop, Rochelle stopped and read the wood burnt letters on the plaque hanging from inside the door window: *Angus MacIntosh, ESQ.* The only 'Esquires' Rochelle had ever heard of were attorneys, so she guessed this narrow, long, one-room office housed a law firm. There was no receptionist to run interference for a gaggle of all-important attorneys. Only a line of file cabinets and a fancy bicycle filled the back of the cave-like space.

When a man came out of the only door in back, Rochelle watched him unhook a five-gallon, nearly-square, plastic bucket from on top of the rack that was mounted behind the seat of his bike. He didn't notice Rochelle outside the entrance peering in, but pried open the bucket and took out a newspaper with a few file folders. Still oblivious to her, he walked towards his big oak desk by the front door and neatly pivoted to sit facing away. She turned the doorknob and pushed. Both of them lurched back at the sound of another loud bell, this one jingling from the top of the door frame.

"Sorry. I didn't mean to startle you," Rochelle said, as he spun around.

"No. No. Good morning to you. Do come in." The man shifted his bucket to the side of a cluttered desktop.

Odd, but at least organized, she thought. The side of the bucket sported a sticker with a cartoon man in a polka dot moo-moo. A ribbon bound his few strands of hair to the top of a pointy skull: *Zippy the Pinhead for President, 2000.* Below the eccentric character it read, "Am I Elected Yet?"

"I haven't seen one of those stickers since I was in college," Rochelle managed. "I guess old Zippy's running again."

The lawyer smiled with just one corner of his mouth and knelt down to unhook the Velcro strap that kept his cargo pants from tangling with the bike chain. His big, brown eyes twinkled, but wouldn't focus directly at her. "Ol' Zippy will keep Gore and Bush on their toes this fall," the man said. She'd be ecstatic if his legal acumen was anywhere near as bright as his pullover bike-riding shirt––neon-yellow with cyan stripes on skin-tight polyester.

The man gestured politely to a hardwood chair across from him. "What can I do for you this morning?" he asked pleasantly, before shifting several folders into a single stack at his elbow. Rochelle put her elbows on the only clear space and leaned in between the bucket and tower of folders. "I'm from out of state and really need to speak to a lawyer this morning," she said, but he still wouldn't look at her. The man peered into the plastic bucket instead. She couldn't pinpoint why, but he struck Rochelle as being more shy than shady.

While he was rummaging, Rochelle checked out the cubbyhole of an office that was maybe nine-feet-wide by twenty-feet-long. She could hear flushing behind the same door that Angus had first appeared through, so she realized this must be a shared 'powder room' with bookstore browsers. After opening a small, black Day-Timer to this week in August, the lawyer scanned his entries.

"I can squeeze in a few minutes for you right now, if that works for you," the man offered, extending his hand to shake. "I'm Angus MacIntosh." He spoke firmly, but kept staring at his scheduling book.

At least one attorney in this bustling metropolis would meet-and-greet with her on-the-spot.

"I'm Rochelle Gardner." She handed him one of her Chamber of Commerce business cards.

"Oregon," he said, after studying the card. The bright glare from outside made it hard for her to focus clearly, but no doubt allowed him to see every line of fatigue on her face after a night without sleep and these ugly discoveries still rustling beyond belief. The lawyer swiveled to lower his bucket beside the big, oak office chair. "What can I help you with this morning?" he asked, looking toward her shoulder, and then at his bike, but not at her face.

Rochelle told him what little she knew about the night before. "I wouldn't be here right now if I thought my son was remotely capable of murdering Mary Quinn."

The lawyer glanced at her card again. "I understand, Ms. Gardner. To get started, let me explain how I work. Until I speak with your son and learn what I can from our local authorities, I will hold off on making any firm commitment to represent him." Now that they were discussing business, the Zippy fan seemed less quirky to Rochelle.

"And remember, there may not be any charges filed against him," he added. "My initial meeting with him will be pro bono. After this we will meet again to discuss any further representation, including a retainer's fee."

"Do you have a ballpark figure, Mr. MacIntosh, assuming that your meeting with my son goes well?"

He tilted back in his swivel chair. "We'll most definitely have that conversation as soon as I have a rough idea what the county prosecutors have planned. Rest assured Mrs. Gardner. I'm a fair man."

Angus fished for another file on his desk and asked her to fill out a contingent client form. She finished quickly and he glanced at what she'd written. I'm in court this afternoon, but first thing Monday morning I'll set aside time to meet with Joseph." He didn't lift his eyes.

Rochelle read the masthead of the local newspaper at the attorney's elbow. The Columbia Basin *Herald*. She squinted to read the upside-down headline of the morning edition. "Would you mind if I peeked at your paper?"

"Take it, please," MacIntosh offered. "I read it before I came in. Nothing much specific yet about your case, other than Sheriff Colton Usk saying they have an unnamed person-of-interest in custody."

"That would be Joe, of course." Rochelle's voice was low, but she wondered why this was the first time he'd hinted at knowing anything about her son's situation. Then again, he'd allowed her to present directly what she knew, putting no emphasis on the press account.

Rochelle accepted his newspaper and turned it her way. The photo showed the crime scene and seep pond. Klieg lights obliterated any darkness. The headline read: *Pothole Drowning Being Investigated.* Rochelle read the smaller block within the article: *Newborn baby found alive on raft, according to Sheriff Usk.*

At this, Rochelle folded the *Herald* in two. Angus shook her hand, even though he looked at his own knuckles instead of at her. She thanked him for taking the time to meet with her so promptly. "Please do your best for my son," she added, mostly for herself. "I'm heading straight away to Bellingham. That's where Joe's father lives now. I've been putting off talking to him about our divorce settlement, so when we're face-to-face, I'll also bring him up to speed on this little matter."

Angus ignored her sarcasm, but held out his a business card to take. Rochelle wondered why she was always the one in charge of fixing everyone's mega-problems. "Do you have an extra?" she asked. "As far as I'm concerned, the bum can help foot our son's legal costs in the event there are any."

Stone-faced, Angus gave her a second card. She slipped both inside the billfold she fished from her large purse. He jotted a note in his Day-Timer, but kept his gaze away from her eyes. "Please pull over whenever you feel the slightest need. These are stressful times for you." Despite any earnest eye contact, at least he expressed concern for her safety.

With purse hanging from her shoulder and holding the folded paper in her hand, Rochelle exited the thin office to the same clanging bell above the door. She breathed in the hot summer of high noon in eastern Washington. Time to take a prod pole and find the hidden den of Joe's father, the man who'd dumped her. Time to pointedly rouse Mr. Avoidance from his hibernation.

CHAPTER TEN

(Saturday, August 19th)

After leaving the lawyer's office, Rochelle drove five freeway hours to Bellingham. The trip across the Cascades Range was a blur and she welcomed the cooler, maritime weather. Closer to the Canadian border, she pulled into the LummiLand Casino-Hotel near the aluminum plant where she knew her estranged husband currently worked.

Beyond exhausted, Rochelle booked a room. When she woke up from one of those badly overdue and wholly unconscious sleeps, the bedside clock read 10:30 p.m. Fully clothed, her Crocs still on her feet, she nearly threw out her neck by sitting up too fast. A barrage of pained thoughts and her plan for finding J.J. Gardner had her fully awake. She set the clock alarm for 4:30 a.m.

Her strategy was simple. She knew he'd been hired for graveyard, so at the end of his shift at the aluminum plant, she'd wait near the employee parking lot. When night turned to day, she'd watch for his pewter dark '66 Ford Bronco to emerge. If that didn't work then she'd try again on Monday and Tuesday mornings, too. On Wednesday, if needed, she'd hire a private eye in Bellingham to figure out where the bum lived. Once she found J.J., she'd insist on having their overdue talk––the one that now included Joe's ordeal.

While sleeping in the hotel bed, Rochelle's Blackberry recharged enough for her to see that Darla had left a dozen messages of concern, but the last person she wanted to talk to or see was her sister, not with the raw outrage she was harboring towards Gunnar. She listened to more recorded messages from her office manager that could wait until Monday morning.

Rochelle wondered if the restaurant downstairs might have something on the menu that would go down easy. She also pulled out five twenties on the outside chance that her luck might improve at the slot machines, but mostly just to kill time this evening. She was tempted to bring her ample purse, but stuffed room key, I.D., credit card, and gambling money in the back pocket of her snug, lady's Levis and took one more pass at readying her hair in the mirror. She saw fatigue, but the same figure she'd worked hard to maintain, so why not show it off tonight? A crepe-sage blouse hugged her thin waist and she replaced her Crocs with summer sandals that weren't as comfy, but far more stylish. Rochelle touched up her make-up to mask the crow's feet. Another pass with the eyeliner accented her blue eyes.

When Rochelle exited the elevator into the hotel lobby, she asked the young lady at the desk where she could find their nicest restaurant. The plush carpet soothed each step in the direction she'd been sent. She was tempted to sit at one of the slot machines, but eating first made more sense. A stiff drink with dinner sounded fine, too, but why wait?

At a bar along the edge of the casino, she ordered a Bacardi and Coke, and stirred the ice cubes. When she concentrated harder on the drink than where she was heading, Rochelle nearly missed the turn leading to the Salish Seafood Bistro. In the awkward pivot, she didn't see the floor sign and nearly tripped, tipping over the base and poster it framed. Somehow, she held her drink upright, not spilling a drop. Rochelle did her best to slurp the last of the booze hiding beneath the cubes and placed the glass to one side before kneeling down to set the free-standing frame upright. She hooked the arrow back under the sign so it again directed the casino patrons into the open cocktail lounge opposite the bistro. The classic hard rock she could hear playing from inside was familiarly solid.

Rochelle picked up her empty glass, but almost dropped it when she stood upright. She re-read the words five or six times before righting the floor sign and releasing her grip. She stepped back in shock to refocus her eyes and make sure she'd read correctly: "Tonight Only. The Coolest Blues-Rock Sensation." The voice and delivery nearly floored her. The words, *Bonnie Quinn & the Igloos*, stared back at Rochelle. Inside the lounge, a few drunk patrons rocked out to her classic Sixties delivery. Bonnie––like the short-lived Janis Joplin she resembled––had no clue about the downbeat soon to rock her bluesy, boozy world.

On a different day and circumstance, Rochelle would much rather be joining these revelers on the small dance floor. She slipped into the pulsating, dark lounge and leaned against the back wall with eyes closed, listening to a voice reminiscent of Mary's in fullness, but with more rawness and rasp. She absorbed the earthy sound of Bonnie's familiar, let-it-all-out delivery.

When the cocktail waitress lightly touched her shoulder, Rochelle opened her eyes with a start. "A double Bacardi and Coke," she said and the waitress wrote the order on her pad. "And pleeeeze don't go light on the rum," Rochelle added, placing her empty on the woman's tray.

As the waitress was turning to leave, Rochelle asked her if this band played in the lounge very often.

"Every week or two. When the bosses don't have established touring acts for our larger event center, they go after fresh, up-and-coming bands." The woman smiled like she needed to get back to work, and turned towards the bar.

From the back of the lounge, Rochelle examined Bonnie Quinn. She sure wasn't getting any younger and, despite all those hard lines, seemed too weathered from drinking and middle-age to be launching rock stardom. But why, sometime this summer, hadn't she tried to get in touch with Mary, especially if she'd returned to the Northwest?

On stage, Bonnie sounded soulful and in her element––not the least bit pathetic. She led the *Igloos* into giving the lounge patrons her nightlife best. From the abandoned way she belted out more rock standards, Bonnie was no doubt loosened up by a cocktail or three of her own. When she finished wailing about being tied to a whipping post, her set closed with a bang.

Bonnie stepped offstage, obscured by the half-filled room of patrons. At the nearest table to the low stage, Rochelle watched the woman push back her thick mane of hair and lean down to plant a long kiss on a man, probably her manager, and definitely the latest in a long line of brief dalliances. The man stood and held Bonnie by the shoulders to kiss her again.

Rochelle's knees buckled and she pushed back hoping for the wall to stop her fall. She hadn't noticed the cocktail waitress return and managed to upend the tray holding her latest double rum & coke. The cocktail waitress tried to catch glass and tray in midair, but fell into Rochelle instead, drenching the arm of Rochelle's crepe blouse in the process. Both women sat in a heap on the carpet.

"I can't believe it!" Blood rushed to Rochelle's face.

"I'm so sorry for startling you," the waitress offered.

"Not that!" said Rochelle. "That slut, Bonnie Quinn. And, in front of everyone."

"Tonight's singer? Why such language? That man comes to every one of his lady friend's shows."

"That man's my husband!" Mary's mother and Joe's father were still locked in a passionate kiss. The cocktail waitress picked up her tray and the spilled glass. "I'll bring you a double. No. I'll make that a triple on the house."

She couldn't believe how J.J. and Bonnie had bolted from The Dalles last spring without Rochelle catching on to the tryst. But, then again, the tavern tramp Bonnie Quinn was the last old lass she imagined her husband snagging as some prize catch. Feeling foolish, she pressed her back against the wall and shook her mind-boggled head side-to-side.

The cocktail waitress returned straight away with her replacement drink. Rochelle handed her a twenty.

"It's on the house, dear."

"Then use it for my next one and keep the change." Rochelle held the lady's wrist and sucked down the ice-cold triple in one, very long pull through a thin straw. She left the empty on the tray and let the cocktail waitress leave.

Rochelle did her best to concentrate. She lectured herself to baby the next drink. No way would she confront J.J. and Bonnie together, not in between sets, and not so publicly with news this morbid. There was no hurry for the confrontation, especially for a man who'd dropped out of his son's life for months, but it didn't mean Rochelle was capable of averting her eyes from the table where the two of them sat. She snorted when Bonnie decided to nestle on J.J.'s lap. The other men sharing the front row table had the look of aluminum smelter workers, no doubt J.J.'s new colleagues.

Bonnie's raspy gut laugh carried to the back of the lounge. Rochelle cringed knowing this woman had no clue that the best thing in her besotted, inebriated, soused, and blotto-faced life was gone, no longer alive. Rochelle clenched her jaw until the cocktail waitress returned with the double and again thanked her for the gracious tip. "My pleasure," said Rochelle just as Bonnie returned to the stage.

J.J. started walking towards the entrance. Rochelle gasped, but then realized how well this darkened room hid faces and features. J.J. rushed between clusters of tables with his familiar 'bladder call' expression. Rochelle dropped her chin down. In the dark lounge, he hadn't noticed her standing fifteen feet away. She waited for him to pass into the hall before turning slowly to follow him out the same entrance door. Cradling her fresh drink, she stayed well back and trailed Joe towards the nearest LummiLand loo site.

She found an inauspicious place to watch the men's room door behind a cluster of slots. Rochelle struggled to wrap her head around his betrayal. She pinched herself and chomped on an ice cube unable to figure how J.J. Gardner could dump her for such a honky-tonk floozy.

When Rochelle married J.J., she knew she'd have to be the one to give their kids any genes for good looks. The boxer-nosed man was well-built with a chiseled jaw, but even into his mid-twenties he still had pock scars from severe teen acne. No one knew what Mary's father looked like, thanks to Bonnie, the closing-time hottie. Both Mary and Joe were far easier on the eyes than either of those two.

J.J. stepped out of the restroom seeming much too pleased with himself and planning on another pint of microbrew if she knew his habits. He wasn't all that ugly, she decided, even though she was reviled by the sight of him. He possessed the presence of a real man's man, which was partly why he earned promotions to become plant foreman.

She stepped from behind the slots and hurried to cut off his path back to the lounge. Rochelle belted out her best, faux-happy greeting. "J.J.! Imagine that!"

He torqued his neck in her direction, and once his eyes registered her face, the man stumbled. Before falling, he caught himself with an elbow against the wall. She wasn't sure if it was shock, fear, or a Freudian slip of a slip when he nearly fell. Like a stick-up victim, he spun around to face her, hands up. J.J. acted like he was guilty of the crime. His narrow-set eyes opened wide and his jaw dropped. No words came from this rugged-and-silent sort. Hardly a shock. In all their years together, he'd never been able to communicate much of anything requiring sensitivity.

With a big smile still forced on her lips, Rochelle clutched one hand on his forearm while the other held her drink. "What a huge surprise seeing you and Bonnie here. And so public with your affections!" she broadcast loudly. A couple of elder casino patrons looked up from the nearest machines.

"Rochelle, what are you doing here?" J.J. managed to ask. He tried to keep his voice calm, but she could hear the quaver, see his brows furrow and watched those slate-blue eyes glowering at her.

"I was planning to find you tomorrow or Monday," said Rochelle, "but here you are, a real rock star groupie," she added, still intentionally loud, but concentrating hard so the Bacardi didn't have her sounding like she was stepping on a wah-wah pedal when speaking.

"Why did you drive all the way here?" he asked. "You could have called instead."

"Like you gave me your phone number, jerk," Rochelle all but barked. "I came here, J.J., because your son needs you."

"What? Money for recovery?" J.J. countered, snidely.

"You should wish it was that simple."

At this, a woman behind them erupted with a shriek. Her slot machine joined in with a cascade of blaring bells and buzzers.

"What do you mean, 'I should only wish'?" J.J. shouted over the jackpot jubilation. "What's wrong?" He motioned Rochelle away from the commotion to a quieter row of slots.

"Our son will be needing some serious legal assistance. I expect you'll help pay." Rochelle gurgled down the last of her tall drink until only ice cubes remained. "And tell your rock star girlfriend not to drink her earnings away. She has a daughter to bury." At this Rochelle turned to walk away, but Joe grabbed her hard by the elbow and forced her to face him. In the spin, Rochelle dropped her drink. The tall glass bounced off the carpet without breaking. Ice cubes slid in all directions on the floor. J.J. being physical shocked Rochelle, one thing the cheat had never done before. "And you owe me a fresh drink, asshole!" she screamed.

Two security guards appeared. "Is everything ok?" they asked.

"No! Mary Quinn is dead," she slurred, "and our son is going to be charged with drowning her. And to top it off, the baby is about to be lost to the system."

"What baby? Joe's been charged? Drowned where?" J.J. yelled back when Rochelle stormed off toward the hotel end of the casino. When she glanced back, she could see that the security guards were not going to allow J.J. to follow her.

When she passed the lobby desk, she saw it, pointed, and stopped cold. "I'll buy that t-shirt."

"Perfect!" said the young lady at the front desk. After giving her a twenty, the woman packaged up the pink *Bonnie Quinn & the Igloos* memento and started to give change. Rochelle told her to keep it.

"I'll be wearing this perfect t-shirt at my divorce hearing," she said, to which the cashier again repeated, 'perfect!' These days of perfection were overwhelming Rochelle.

The bellhop stepped over from the main hotel entrance and asked if she'd be needing assistance. Rochelle nodded and motioned him off to the side with her. Discreetly, she also handed him a twenty-dollar bill. "*Bonnie Quinn & The Igloos* are playing in the lounge," she whispered, to which the uniformed man nodded. "Bonnie Quinn's boyfriend will be seated at the closest table to stage. He's a thick, rugged guy with a haystack of sandy hair. Can I count on you to hand him this?"

The guard read Angus MacIntosh's business card and assured Rochelle it would be no problem if she could give him the man's name.

"J.J. Gardner," she told him. "Please tell J.J. that if he wants to know what's going on, he should contact his son's attorney, but definitely not me."

The bellhop nodded again, and left for the lounge. Rochelle waited for the elevator, decided she'd call down for a room service dinner, but wondered if she'd get any sleep tonight.

CHAPTER ELEVEN

(Sunday, August 20th)

The hot, calm day had turned to early evening by the time Rochelle made her ritual pit stop at tall Multnomah Falls, thirty miles up the Columbia Gorge from Portland. She'd driven from home, north to Moses Lake, over to Bellingham, and then today down through the metro Seattle and Tacoma. Driving back into Oregon, her horrid, counterclockwise road trip was nearly complete.

On a walking bridge, Rochelle breathed mist from the white ribbon of waterfall. For a moment, the natural beauty helped her forget her human anguish. The 'island' parking lot for Multnomah Falls was wedged between the east and westbound lanes of I-84. Rochelle clutched her fresh cup of coffee when walking from the lodge through a pedestrian tunnel under the eastbound lanes. The wide Columbia River shimmered silvery under a clear, late sky. She set the coffee on the roof of the van until she could unearth her keys from deep inside her purse. At the edge of westbound freeway closest to the wide river, a ruckus caught her attention. Several birds chased off a bald eagle with dive bombing and raspy cries.

In the evening light, she saw the focus of attention. Ravens ripped at the flesh of a roadkill doe on the farthest shoulder of freeway. The large black, cadaver-eating opportunists took turns feasting. What bothered Rochelle wasn't so much the harsh survival habits of these scavengers, or that humans provided the road carnage meal, or even the bloody deer, but what she noticed next to the interstate.

She wanted to race across, dodging fast moving vehicles, and whisk it to safety. Instead, she held to the outside driver's mirror to keep from dropping to both knees beside her van. A fawn––in shock––waited at the edge of traffic, its mother gone.

There was nothing for Rochelle to do but cry and wonder when this nightmare would end. When the fawn hopped over the guardrail and disappeared into the brush, Rochelle grabbed the steaming coffee and climbed back in her van to wedge her way upriver on the last leg to The Dalles. I-84 followed a wide trough along the big river where evergreen cliffs loomed a mile high along each side. She barely noticed the Bridge of the Gods or the town of Hood River as she drove, but adrenaline and caffeine kicked in when she neared home.

At dusk, from well above the Columbia, she recognized Memaloose Island. Except for the tall grave spire that shimmered white in the twilight, the isle sat barren in the river below. For centuries, local Natives enshrined the bones of their dead there. The tribes stopped the practice after a pioneer merchant from the end of the overland Oregon Trail in The Dalles contaminated the ancient grounds. The man had his body entombed inside this pointy burial monument that he commissioned to himself. With Rochelle's last glance at the isle of the dead, she wondered what local native had fathered Mary's son. She'd have to ask Biff McCoy––delicately. If anyone would know who Mary had slept with last winter, other than with Joe, it would be her best friend, Biff.

Rolling past Rowena, Rochelle felt antsy for her own bed. Hometown lights glimmered in the distance. There was no moonlight tonight, and rare for this blustery windsurfing paradise, no gusts buffeted her van. From the oak leaves in her headlights, she couldn't detect a hint of breeze where the big river ran through a tranquil Gorge.

When she rounded a last bend of interstate before The Dalles, the

Columbia Gorge Discovery Center was strangely illuminated off to her left. At first Rochelle thought she was seeing a thick swarm of fireflies surrounding the building, except the Pacific Northwest has no lightning bugs. When she slowed to fifty, the people came into focus with most of them waving neon glow-sticks to challenge the darkness.

The new museum was often reserved for weddings, but there were far too many people outside. Since she was director of the Chamber, if there had been a major event scheduled in town, then it would have been on her radar weeks, if not months ago during that bygone era when her life wasn't insane. It was hard to see much flying down I-84, so she decided to backtrack. The aluminum salmon sculptures shimmered on the exit. Rochelle turned west on the Historic Columbia River Highway built in 1914 by Mary's pacifist hero, Sam Hill.

Sundays were not typically big time event nights in this small city of 12,000, but a dozen or so cars guided her to the Discovery Center entrance where the gate would usually be locked by this time of night. Cars were parked along the paved entry road which Rochelle found unusual since there was normally ample event parking in the lot next to the museum. She took one of the last available spots before reaching the entrance gate. Before Rochelle got out, she put on an old hoodie of Joe's from The Dalles High with the school's Indian mascot on the back. She left her big handbag wedged next to the bucket seat and decided to keep it locked inside the van rather than lug the thing through the night.

"What's up?" she asked a teen getting out of the car in front of her.

"A vigil. Ain't you heard?"

Rochelle's heart sank. "Heard what?"

"It was in today's *Chronicle* and all over Q-104, even on the Portland TV news. Mary Quinn died. Drowned up in eastern Washington. Most of us didn't even know she was pregnant. Couldn't believe that the cops there arrested Joe Gardner."

"What a pity," Rochelle managed to say. The kid didn't recognize her, but she decided to pull the hood over her hair anyway. What could she possibly say to anyone about Joe? Not here, not with rumors flying, and definitely not when feeling so shaken herself.

"Yeah. Joe and Mary always seemed so tight," said the kid, "but then again no boy I knew ever messed with Gardner. That went double when his temper got triggered, so you never know."

Rochelle didn't react, unable to argue the couple's tightness or her son's outbursts. The high schooler excused himself and jogged ahead to catch up with some friends he'd spotted. Rochelle told herself that no one knew how to handle Joe's temper better than Mary, and that included the boy's own mother.

She walked in a slow, gloomy procession with other arriving locals and pulled her hood farther over her head. When she heard more high schoolers debating whether or not Joe could have done it, she walked with her face towards the ground, staring only at the heels of the people in front of her. The column of mourners edged into the dark, full parking lot.

For a city this small, she was shocked to see such a big crowd. So many had come, a couple thousand it seemed, but no one was in much of a hurry to get inside the museum. Even the scores of high schoolers were fully aware that rushing wouldn't restore feeling to their numb hearts, or breathe life back into their deceased friend. The glow-sticks were being freely offered and swooshes of light filled the parking lot. Outside the entrance to the museum, a couple dozen teenage girls clustered near the big doors and sang Mary Quinn's beloved solo:

On the rugged Oregon Trail,
We live beyond the ending.
Where littered bones are not our tale,
When springtime flowers are bending.

The girls leading the singing also honored Mary by wearing their hair jet-black, and most with lighter side braids visible in the dim lamps along the entry path.

After journey's wear and tear,
Grace fills the sunlit, frontier air.

Young laughter needs sweet tending.

Rochelle found a smooth rock beside the replica of an Oregon Trail wagon where, seated, she buried her face in the palms of her hands and kept hearing Joe's name in random conversations.

In the dark, she breathed in this night of rare stillness that seemed to honor Mary. Rochelle stood up from the rock and walked towards the bluff to the trail alongside the interpretive center. A split-rail cedar fence separated visitors from the edge of the cliff. From inside a raptor cage, the hooting startled her. Joe's favorite Great Horned Owl seemed to be asking the dark question. Who had drowned Mary Quinn?

She stayed close to the cedar fence. Across the big river, the Klickitat slopes on the Washington side would turn golden under the first rays of rising sun, but those same Gorge walls rose up as the blackest of backdrops under tonight's moonless sky.

Along the closed end of the museum, a large grid of picture windows framed the actual Columbia River. But that was only when standing inside and looking out of the museum's main hall. In the darkness peering in, Rochelle focused on a snaking, shimmering rendition of the Columbia River that centered the 140-foot-long main hall. Dull, dark brick flooring channeled glassy black granite that mapped the meandering river's flow. Behind her on this still night, Rochelle heard the actual river lightly lapping on the shore well below these cliffs.

Rochelle could see all the way through the length of the Discovery Center's grand hall with huge timbered posts framing basalt brick walls. Beyond the windowed entrance, glow-sticks were still being waved.

The museum entry doors opened wide to welcome a flood of mourners. Rochelle brushed away her wave of tears to see the museum director, Jill McCoy, standing beside a podium set up to allow for eulogies. Outside, peeping in, Rochelle didn't stay for the tributes, but long enough to watch Jill's daughter, Biff, tending a table in front of a screen that showed a loop of photos and a few familiar video clips of the End of the Trail Band. Rochelle stared at the visuals from a harsh angle.

Biff and Mary--Joe too--had worked at the museum part time

since it opened. Rochelle stayed transfixed on Joe's girlfriend growing up again. For reasons Rochelle could guess, she saw no images of her son. A fifteen-year-old Mary in her petticoat already possessed such a ladylike presence on stage. Standing on the outside, Rochelle couldn't hear the snippets of film where Mary mesmerized the crowd with her singing. There was no denying the thunder, though, when the standing room crowd inside burst into loud, polite applause for Mary and her searing voice.

Mourners walked towards the open area below the podium and deposited offerings into a large punchbowl. Rochelle watched the mound of bouquets and roses grow wider and higher beneath an easel that held Mary's greatly enlarged high school graduation photo taken only months before.

Everyone wanted to fix this, but no one could do a thing. The punchbowl next to Biff's sign began overflowing with bills. Her calligraphy read: *Contributions for Mary's Baby.* The teen emptied the money in a big paper grocery sack wedged between her ankles. A fresh line of mourners crept through the great hall and the big bowl filled again.

Rochelle planted her feet in darkness while the bawling and affection inside those walls burned forth like the wildfires that would scorch these grassy Gorge hillsides during dry summers. This vigil–– kindled by a burning grief––had ignited with spontaneous planning. The outburst of love flamed high for her precious life remembered, for one of their own, gone.

Rochelle had no consoling thoughts, not when she desperately needed the same. There was nothing she could explain, no clarity, nor salve to soothe the rawness of Mary's death.

Into the night, Rochelle made her way unseen to an empty home.

She left her Crocs in their place inside the front door and followed an urge to go into the dining room. In the small recessed niché, her statuette of the Virgin Mary and Christ Child was positioned in front of dusty Rosary beads that dangled from a hook. Carefully, Rochelle took the Rosary into her palm, and set the statuette on the formal table last used the Thanksgiving before, a feast that served less as an appreciation of blessings and more as a bleak send-off for Joe to serve his three-months of detention.

From a wall shelf on the opposite side of the room, she lifted a framed photo of Joe standing inside a large cage with the Great Horned Owl on his fist. Rochelle recalled taking this picture at the Discovery Center the summer before--before the baseball accident and before his addiction. Her son radiated with joy, so happy to be holding the big, trusting raptor. This was the son she wanted to remember. In the photo, Joe was all-boy, rugged, but with a sweet, caring streak, the same kid who watched ravens and raptors religiously when the large birds navigated the near constant gusts pushing along the cliffs of the Gorge.

Holding Joe's image like a finely painted egg shell, Rochelle centered the framed photo inside her niché. She stepped back to look. The sight of her son at his best convinced her not to move the photo until Joe was flying free again.

She turned and lifted the statuette from the dining room table realizing that she hadn't been to Mass since before Joe had gone to detention. Suffering one test after another, she questioned how God could be so cruel to keep heaping woe after woe upon her life. Rochelle had nowhere near the perseverance of Job.

Rochelle took barefoot steps up the narrow stairwell that led to the three bedrooms upstairs. One hand held the statuette and the other her Rosary beads. Rochelle ignored the handrail and, just to feel something when she continued up the steps, her toes tapped each closed riser hard enough to make her wince. The balls of her feet weighed down each oak tread of the staircase until they creaked the way they always had the thousands of times anyone went up or down. On the upstairs hallway with its own vintage slats of flooring, Rochelle eased past Joe's bedroom towards the one Mary had used since she moved in last spring. The slats in front of Mary's room were the only ones that didn't make a noise.

She turned on a nightstand lamp and set the statuette and Rosary on the room's antique dresser. She opened the top drawer. When she saw that Mary had left behind her flannel nightgown, Rochelle buried her face in the freshness of the fabric. She found a thick lock of Mary's natural reddish hair dangling from a brush in the back. Freed from the bristles, the wavy strands coiled in Rochelle's palm. She clenched the hair in her fist before setting it next to her Rosary.

She took off Joe's high school hoodie, stripped away her traveling clothes, and snaked her arms inside the nightgown. The sweetness brought the girl alive in her mind. In the same way that Rochelle started this nightmarish journey only to stop her van in grief by Horsethief Lake, she desperately craved a visit from Mary.

Gently, Rochelle ran her palms down the flannel fabric that hung loose to her calves. She embraced her own shoulders and remembered late last May when Mary wore the same nightgown. That evening, the girl had allowed for the truth of what wouldn't stay hidden any longer. When Rochelle had hugged Mary, there was no crying, no reprimand, just a loving acceptance.

Rochelle opened the door to the walk-in closet. She held only her Rosary beads. The bedroom lamp showed the closet altar in silhouette. When Kuma first arrived in America, she insisted that he make himself at home. When he asked in that ever-polite manner of his, she assured him it would be fine to place a small shrine inside his closet. Kuma's parents in Tokyo shipped him a modest crate filled with what he needed.

When Rochelle had expelled her son last spring and invited Mary to live with her, she'd wondered why the girl had chosen to stay in this bedroom, rather than Joe's. Then, faintly, she would hear Mary's chant. Usually, the words came late at night from this closet and the shrine Kuma left behind. Mary used the same rapid words that Kuma had taught her: *Nam myoho renge kyo.*

Rochelle set her Catholic Rosary on the closet altar next to the Buddhist *juzu* beads that Kuma gave to Mary.

"What do you chant for?" she had once asked Kuma.

The young man closed his eyes to think before answering. "To chant is like sun of wisdom. Sun of wisdom melts away frost of karma. I chant to take heavy karma and receive it light and warm."

Thinking back to those words, Rochelle wished her jailed son would find a way to transform his heavy karma. "Karma, as in 'what goes around comes around'?" she recalled asking Kuma.

"I do not know this go and come around, except for home run in baseball."

Rochelle remembered laughing loudly and patting Kuma's shoulder. She sometimes wondered if learning to receive karma lightly was akin to the Catholic forgiveness of sins.

While Kuma had lived in their home, she would hear him chanting every morning. He used a mandala like the Tibetan Buddhists did, and engaged in more ritual chanting than the Zen Buddhists. His practice held to a similar Zen emphasis on mindfulness and the honoring of life force. "To find Buddhahood within is like Holy Spirit inside Christians," he once told her. Late last winter, the young man departed for Japan after the Chunichi Dragons selected him in the first round of the Nippon Professional Baseball league draft. For some reason, he never arranged to ship the shrine and its contents back to Japan.

Rochelle went to the dresser beside the bed and lifted a thick candle and matchbox. She struck a wooden match, lit the wick, and with this illumination, she entered the dark, windowless, walk-in closet. Inside the carpeted closet was a silk floor pillow; no clothes hung from the rods. Rochelle stood before his Buddhist shrine and used the big candle to light four small ones on each corner of the altar along with igniting the sandalwood incense within a little burning box.

Kuma's dove-jointed *butsudan*, made of light Japanese cypress, sat closed. The small cabinet was centered towards the back of the altar. Most impressive for the sacred cabinet were the handles for opening the little doors. Two Sperm Whale teeth arched inwards and served as adjoining knobs. Scrimshaw etchings of lotuses decorated each tooth. The lily pads were painted green and, in the flickering candlelight, the magenta lotuses shimmered.

Rochelle did not open the *butsudan* doors, but kept the four candles lit. She went into the bedroom with her Rosary still swaying below her hand. She lifted the statuette and also carried it into the closet. Inside, she set Mary and her newborn Christ child on one side of the altar. Maybe this would call Mary back to her again.

Rochelle knelt on the silk pillow and faced the statuette. She crossed herself in the way she'd been taught as a girl and held the silver cross at the end of her dark Rosary up towards Mother Mary and her newborn. Rochelle recited the Apostle's Creed that ended with believing in the Holy Spirit, the holy catholic Church, the communion of saints, the forgiveness of sins, the resurrection of the body, and life everlasting. Amen.

She waited, but Mary didn't appear inside the windowless closet.

Rochelle went again to the bedroom dresser. Gently, she lifted a small, framed photograph of Mary performing in pioneer clothes. The girl started singing inside Rochelle's head. She placed the picture on the side of the altar opposite the statuette. Holding the first and largest Rosary bead, she bowed to the framed photo and recited the Lord's prayer. For some reason, she heard the words differently than ever before. The kingdom of heaven didn't come only after dying, but always surrounded us divinely. This evening, more than she ever had, Rochelle needed to taste heaven as though this were her daily bread. She needed to feel even the slightest bit of divinity; she needed help with all this evil she didn't understand, this evil that had stolen Mary's life and was stealing her son. She needed Mary's comfort.

Rochelle stayed transfixed on the statuette and photo, but the girl didn't appear. She bowed and pushed herself again to her feet. From the altar, she lifted a small Japanese saucer. In the candlelight she admired the glimmering of lotus blossoms painted along the rim of its ivory-colored surface. Rosary in one hand, the saucer resting in her other palm, Rochelle went out to the dresser top in the bedroom. She lifted Mary's lock into the center of the porcelain saucer and watched it spiral within the ring of lotus blossoms.

Returning to the closet shrine, she bowed and set the lock and saucer front-and-center on the altar. On this night of the vigil, the third day following the girl's death, Rochelle knelt before the whale-bone adorned shrine and ran her fingers over the grooves of scrimshaw on the whale teeth. In one easy motion, she pulled the bone handles outward and opened the small doors.

Inside, on rice paper print, the mandala, or *Gohonzon* as Kuma called it, welcomed her eyes. The characters were Sanskrit and ancient Japanese. Rochelle loved the way the figures at the top of the columns resembled arched peaks of little pagodas. The roofs seemed to protect all that was inscribed beneath. She did her best to recite the mantra and honor the mystic dharma of Buddha's lotus sutra: *Nam myoho renge kyo.* Mary wasn't dead, but eternal. Rochelle repeated the chant to honor her again: *Nam myoho renge kyo.* Mary still didn't appear.

No one she knew in The Dalles held any allegiance to eastern spiritual paths, not after that new age guru with his ninety-three powder-blue Rolls Royces tried to take over the entire county. On the day his followers poisoned a downtown restaurant salad bar with droplets of salmonella poisoning, Rochelle had chosen, at the last minute, not to take a prospective Chamber member there for lunch. Not that she'd ever be the pious Catholic that her sister was, but to openly practice Buddhism wouldn't serve her well as director of The Dalles Area Chamber of Commerce. In her private grief, though, she would accept any help for Joe and Grace, whether Catholic, Buddhist or from any spiritual force offering justice and healing.

More of her *nam myoho renge kyo* chants filled the closet shrine. Mary was present in the hearts of so many in The Dalles tonight. When Rochelle stopped chanting, she forced herself--with slow movement and high respect--to rise from the pillow and kneel tall. Leaning in, she bowed to the Mary and Christ child statuette, to the Buddhist mandala, to the ginger curl of Mary's hair, and lastly to the framed image of Mary winning over the crowd. Rochelle couldn't begin to fathom the beautiful young singer, the daughter she never birthed, gone much too young.

Lightly, Rochelle ran fingertips over the whalebone knobs and slowly closed the doors to the *butsudan*. She pulled her nightgown over her head and folded it neatly to place on the shelf beneath the altar. She vowed never to move the garment for as long as she lived in the old house. She kissed the cross of her Rosary and recited a "Hail Mary, Full of Grace." Rochelle lifted an etched stick from the altar and struck the bowl-shaped bell to honor the girl.

Rochelle blew out the candles and placed the lid of the burn box over embers of sandalwood. She gently eased the closet door shut, but when the ringing stopped, she had no desire to sleep in her large bed downstairs. She slipped naked limbs inside the sheets of the bed in the upstairs room and breathed deeply. On the pillow, in the liminal state between waking and sleeping, Rochelle breathed in more of Mary's sweetness.

Beneath the same thick comforter, this was the moment she came to realize the truth. Her son surely knew who the father was, but to own up, he still needed to release all the anger he held towards Kuma especially, but also towards Mary. In this very berth, nine months earlier and nowhere else, Mary's child was conceived.

Nestled within Kuma's and Mary's bed of conception, Rochelle accepted the truth in peace. Tonight it wasn't Mary, but the baby who appeared to her. She clutched the sheets fast to her face and curled into a fetal ball, drifting into a numinous, newborn dream of Grace.

CHAPTER TWELVE

V.

IN

～

Over the weekend, Joe's throat closed up from Jorge's stranglehold. He couldn't swallow without harsh pain, not to say that much of an appetite had returned. Except for his Adam's apple and the hard shot to the ribs that stabbed him when he breathed in too deeply, Joe still had his teeth and, unlike that skinny punk he got rid of before the real fight started, he hadn't suffered a broken skull; even his bones were intact.

The last of the day's sun streamed through the skinny excuse of a window above him. When Joe tried stretching upwards for the sill, a shot of pain zagged through his ribs again. He quickly lowered his arms. His chest pounded when he lay on the lumpy, thin bed. To get comfortable, he repositioned himself across the small area of cement floor. Flat on his back, he used only the folded, thin jail pillow to softened the back of his head.

At least the Suboxone still kept him from sweating or puking or worse. With the toilet at arms-length, and barely enough space to stand and turn, he could see why they called the solitary confinement cell, *The Shoe*. Joe had no desire to stand, so he stayed glued, spread eagle on the floor, and stared up. Passage of time was *Enemy #1* in this place, but how could he stop thinking about the haunting days, hours, minutes when he already had way too much time to think? All weekend, his brain had him reliving the grossest of nights.

When the calm and balmy evening dimmed into darkness, Joe opened his eyes. He did a double take. Mary appeared, her skin glowing. His breathing stopped and he sat up too quickly. His ribs convulsed and he gasped for air. Once he forced himself to calm down, her presence brought random smells into the cell along with haunting images and sounds from that night. He wished she could show him what she'd seen. Tonight there was something vibrating and more alive than alive in Mary. Three nights after the drowning, most who knew her back home had to have heard the news, had to be mourning her. So how much did Mary, so freshly gone, sense any of this love for her? So many people were big fans of his gifted girl.

When Joe closed his eyes, the Great Horned Owl flew through his cell, hooting. Bulrushes rustled. He opened his lids to see Mary facing away, standing behind cattails and beside the locked door of the shoe. Naked and wholesome, the sight of her reminded him of the lull before she climbed inside the Pathfinder and gave birth.

Joe stared at Mary's wavy, jet-black hair. She pulled her dyed locks around the side of her neck and down the front so the tattoo of *Tsagaglalal* glistened on her back. The chieftess stared at him, watching. Mary turned sideways, but she didn't speak. She was no longer pregnant, but her breasts were full of mother's milk. Mary was ready for a suckling baby, ready for Grace, wherever the infant might be. He couldn't read her expression, whether sad or content. Joe didn't know if he should stand and go to Mary, or whether he should allow his lover's spirit all the free rein it desired. He chose to lay as still as possible despite the concrete beneath his spine.

She knelt down beside him and touched his forehead with cool fingers. He sighed a thankful note that she hadn't come to haunt him. Mary cupped his ears to look closely into his face.

Ever so lightly, she knew to touch his ribs, but not hard enough to cause more pain. Somehow, miraculously, Mary pressed down with perfect pressure. The throbbing halted from that moment forward as though she wished to show him she was every bit as real as she was unreal. Joe felt no more waves of harsh discomfort. She applied her touch to his Adam's apple with the same soft but firm magic. The pain disappeared from his throat like a sip of water cures the desert thirst of a parched man. With emerald eyes, she enticed him to slide with her from the floor onto his narrow bed where they sat hip-to-hip. The luxurious mattress was covered with a soft, thick comforter stuffed full of Arctic goose down, as sublime as it was fanciful.

Joe closed his eyes to welcome her soft fingers across his brow and hairline. He placed his hand on her upper back and started to trace the outline of her tattoo when Mary whipped around and pushed him back so they were stretching out on the comforter together. In the same smooth motion, she melded into him. Joe gasped at the calmness surging within his chest, stomach, and through his pelvis and legs. Inside this tiny isolation cell, he breathed with complete ease realizing how smoothly his lover––the only girl he'd ever been with––was one with him.

They saw a gilded shaft of moonlight streaming through the sliver of window high above them. Mary stared through Joe's orbs––her nose, teeth, and ears were also positioned inside his body as though his frame and skull was an Eskimo parka with hood serving to hold her and to warm, not Mary's flesh, but her spirit. Joe was her cloak in this, the in between. Mary's fingers were one with his and softly touched Joe's temple, the bridge of his Roman nose, his small ears, brawny chest, hard stomach, and below. The fingertips were all hers. This was the Mary he knew so well. He melted with her gift of peace to him. Was she telling him not to worry? She didn't speak inside their oneness, but Joe filled with her white glow. Too soon, he knew she would need to let go for the other side, the place where dead people––good souls like her––departed to. In his tumble into solitary confinement, Mary's presence penetrated impenetrable walls.

CHAPTER THIRTEEN

(Monday, August 21st)

Joe had no idea how long he'd slept when Big Max clanked his flashlight-club against the door and opened the Shoe. "You got company, Gardner."

"Again?" he asked through a groggy mind and sore body that had no desire to wake up. When Joe sat, his cheeks were wet with tears. Fragments of the lucid dream returned. Mary had been weeping with him, yearning for her baby. Joe took his time to sit up on the hard cement, the hardest surface he'd ever crashed on. He'd never made it to the jail cot, to the divine comforter. Mary vanished with the opening of the cell door. She-Who-Watches was the last bit he saw of her as Max entered. Joe sat on the edge of the bed, pressed his ribs and rubbed his Adam's apple, feeling no pain whatsoever.

"It's your lawyer." Max stood at the door looking impatient.

"I don't have a lawyer."

"That's not what your attorney says." The huge guard opened the cell door wider. Joe slipped into his coveralls and extended his arms straight out. Short, squat Sam, another corrections officer, cuffed him.

The two guards escorted him to a stark meeting room with hard oak chairs and a plain, sturdy table. The room was a bit brighter than the jail cells, a bare-bones space designed for lawyer-con conferencing and maybe cop-con interrogations.

"Hello, Joe. My name is Angus MacIntosh." The compact, fit man extended his hand to shake, but then pulled it back and chuckled. "Sorry, I forgot you were cuffed."

At least the dude could laugh at himself. The salt-and-pepper haired lawyer with wide, brown eyes pulled out a hard chair and likewise gestured for his prospective client to take a seat in the chair across from him.

"When did I hire you?" Joe asked, checking out the Spartan room that was slightly more accommodating than talking to visitors through a speaker hole in Plexiglas. This man, about the same age as his parents, came dressed in summer khaki shorts and a bright bowling shirt, not Joe's image of most lawyers. He carried only a Manila envelope, thick with paperwork.

"A woman named Rochelle Gardner is thinking of hiring me. She claims to be your mother."

"That Rochelle lady hasn't been my mother, not this summer," said Joe, pointedly, "but yeah, she's my biological mom." His old lady had actually done good by following through with getting him an attorney. Looking across the table at this man, he realized that no mom could save him from his own grownup, screwed-up self. "You said she's 'thinking of hiring' you. So you're not officially my lawyer?"

"I never take on clients indirectly. We need to meet face-to-face and come to an understanding regarding my services and the expectations moving forward."

A face-to-face understanding? The sight of all that high-end China White bagged inside the First Aid box flashed through Joe's mind. "So are you saying you'll need to discuss with me the fees you'll expect from all the cash I've got buried away by my homeless camp?"

Angus shook his head. "Your mother is open to handling the retainer and fees, along with your father, perhaps." He took long pauses before formulating his sentences, not that what he said didn't sound professional, just overly crafted in his brain before he spoke.

"Mommy Rochelle and Daddy J.J. cooperating? Ha! That'll be tougher than winning my case, especially since I didn't do anything."

The attorney didn't react with a smile or frown or shrug when he pulled a typed list from his envelope. "Let's talk about your case, about what you might be facing."

"What I 'might' be facing? Some cop must know."

Angus pulled a notebook from the Manila envelope and set it beside his list of talking points. "You've been placed under 'Investigative Arrest' until your arraignment. At that hearing, any formal charges against you will be filed. I spoke briefly this morning with a contact of mine in the Wanapum County Prosecuting Attorney's office. There won't be any leeway to plea bargain."

Joe tried to get comfortable on the table with metal cuffs chafing his wrists that were already scratched raw. He leaned forward until his elbows dug into the hard wood surface. "Why would they charge me at all? Like I said. I didn't do it––any of it––so there's nothing to plea."

Angus placed his hands, palms down, on the stout, oft-visited table. "These aren't minor charges, Joe. For starters, they're looking at homicide along with felony intent to distribute heroin."

Joe shook his head side-to-side in rapid disbelief. "So they're going to say I drowned Mary and was in the middle of peddling a donkey-load of smack, the stuff I just happened to find a full minute before she went into labor? That's a heap of b.s.!"

He could see Angus studying him, not in a way to make him uncomfortable, but as though to tell him it was time to face up to the legal reality that might not be the real reality. "There's a preliminary match of your fingerprints to those on the heroin packets that the K-9 unit found. I couldn't learn much about the murder investigation except that, currently, there are no other persons-of-interest in this case. You seem to be the only one in their crosshairs."

Joe didn't need to argue his innocence to some lawyer he'd just met, but he couldn't keep from sounding miffed. "So you're saying I'm in their crosshairs, the truth be crucified."

Angus stayed even-keeled. "No. I'm telling you what you'll likely expect at your arraignment. Namely, don't be surprised to be facing serious felony charges."

Joe rolled his eyes. "That's just lovely!"

Angus glanced at his list of notes. "After the arraignment, we'll learn more about the prosecution's evidence. That's all part of the pre-trial, discovery process," the lawyer explained. "Namely, the prosecution isn't allowed to spring their findings on us by holding back evidence until the trial."

Joe plugged his nose. "Seems like Lady Justice is about to land in the same stink hole that Mary drowned in."

Angus ignored the theatrics and continued matter-of-fact. "They're also investigating the circumstances surrounding the newborn found on an air mattress in the marsh."

Joe sat up tall, his eyes staring fiercely at the locked door. "It may not have been my kid," Joe said, "but I helped rescue her baby. At least I assisted the best I could with my hands and ankles cuffed. That cop wouldn't let me help save Mary or Grace. I'm guessing he's the reason I'm being railroaded."

Angus face showed a sudden curiosity. "Why's that?"

"Just as soon as the deputy drove me back to my rig with my filled gas can, he treated me like I was guilty as hell. How does the nimrod explain that I pointed out to him where Mary was. I heard the baby crying before he did."

Angus wrote this down on his notepad. "We'll carefully scrutinize your arrest step-by-step throughout that entire night. Do you have a police record, Joe?"

The question surprised him. His mom hadn't bothered to tell the attorney about the big blight on the short history of his life. Joe nodded and described his bust, conviction, and the three months in juvie. "I relapsed this summer. And since they're doling out this test drug called Suboxone so I can taper off the smack, the Wanapum County cops and jailers also know all about my addiction."

Angus jotted down more notes. "To be frank, your recent history with heroin isn't helpful." The lawyer didn't lift his head from what he was writing. "That and the needle and syringe they found under the spare tire help link you to the cache of heroin they found."

Joe spoke firmly. "I'm gonna stay off smack for good. I promise." He knew full well that his addiction would never win him any sympathy points with the authorities, but he never guessed it would have them thinking he was a murderer.

Angus leaned forward. In a reassuring voice, he told Joe that there was no need to promise him anything. "For the record, Joe, my job is to make sure that you're allowed due process under the law."

"Will you let me pitch my side of the story to the jury," Joe asked, "I mean, if I decide to let my mom hire you for me?" If I decide to let my mom hire you. Joe realized how pathetic that sounded, even though his mom hiring this guy would be the nicest thing, the only thing, his mom had done for him since last spring. No time to be choosy.

"It's rarely wise for a defendant to testify in his or her own trial," Angus answered. "That's not to discourage you from sharing with me, in full confidence, any information you think will prove useful for your case. I'm hired to work as your advocate to make certain you receive a fair trial."

Joe could tell that the attorney was pitching his services, but not urgently. No doubt that Angus had seen plenty of his kind––a druggie dreg.

Joe stared at the man's Hawaiian shirt. "Do you wear a suit and tie, that is if we go to court?"

Angus laughed. "Definitely. I've got a tie-dye dress shirt to go with either my Peewee Herman bowtie, or Jerry Garcia necktie. Do you have a preference?"

Joe smiled. "How about a Wünderland tie?"

"I actually have one of those," Angus said, looking surprised at the request. "I grew up near Seattle. Believe it or not, Growling Elmer, the lead singer, went to the high school prom with my little sister. They had matching Glam-Rock hairdos back then."

"Growling Elmer. Really?" Joe asked, now the surprised one. "A couple of years ago, my cousin took me to Grungefest where we saw Wünderland play. It was close by in the Gorge Amphitheater. Killer pipes on that dude." When Angus grinned with a knowing nod, Joe told him what he probably already knew. "The band broke up due to Elmer, and all because his monster habit got to be too much. That was about the same time they released their CD, "Rabid Hole.""

Angus's jaw clenched. "Aren't we all in danger of falling down our own rabbit hole?"

Joe didn't answer. He'd just spent a year gurgling through Wünderland.

"Growling Elmer definitely sells what he's singing," said Angus.

Joe closed his eyes tight and nodded. "The way he delivers the hooks of his dark songs is like he just mainlined the soul of them." His eyes opened real wide. "Big time blissful smack sneaks up so nice and quiet, but then you can't tell the exact day when it owns you bad. In the days after that, though, there ain't no doubt about what's in charge."

Angus listened and seemed to nod. "Like my little sister's ugly truth."

"What truth is that?"

"She's buried six-feet beneath her rabid hole."

Joe stared grimly. He decided that any lawyer who knew about ugly addiction through uglier death could relate to his legal problems. "Do you have something for me to sign?" Joe asked.

Angus, his eyes looking upset, pulled out a contract. "Just to be sure, you are eighteen aren't you, Joe?"

"Eighteen-and-a-half," he answered, immediately wondering why he put it this way. It made him seem younger rather than older. Joe scanned the Representation Agreement the lawyer set in front of him until he found the line to sign. Awkwardly, one hand cuffed next to the other, he guided a pen to the spot. Joe definitely had a vibe that this lawyer would do all he could for him.

"I was upset when I saw that her baby wasn't mine." Joe set down the pen. "She freaked out when I split to fill our empty gas can."

"Did you fight?"

"I yelled at her. That's all." Joe tilted back in his chair and stared up at the ceiling. "With her bi-polar stuff, I'm pretty sure Mary drowned herself."

Angus seemed surprised. "Suicide?" he asked. "Really? A brand new mother?" He didn't wait for a response, but glanced at his watch and got up to shake Joe's hand. "We'll take this up again and discuss your case in full after Friday's arraignment. Right now I have another new client appointment scheduled."

CHAPTER FOURTEEN

(Friday, August 25th)

The arraignment was short, but not sweet. The big, white-haired judge had a voice that fell over his court like God echoing down from heaven to Moses in that really old movie on the ten commandments. "Due to the charges of homicide and major drug distribution, and because of the out-of-state defendant's prior legal history, the flight risk is high. Bail is set for $2 million dollars."

A short glance at his mother's wide eyes showed Joe all he needed to see. No way was he getting out to await trial. Joe took as deep a breath as he could. At least his parents were springing for an attorney. According to Angus, his dad agreed to foot the legal bill. His mess was costing his mom plenty in missed work, hotel bills, and the like. Joe knew that having a paid lawyer was definitely better than him getting a public defender from under some scabland boulder.

Felonies of class 'A,' 'B,' and 'C.' There was even a 'D' for Drug gear possession, a misdemeanor:

The State of Washington VS Joseph John Gardner, III
• *COUNT ONE: Second Degree Murder (Class A Felony).*
• *COUNT TWO: Intent to Distribute a Controlled Substance (heroin)*
(Class B Felony).
• *COUNT THREE: Child Abandonment (Class C Felony)*
• *COUNT FOUR: Possession of Drug Paraphernalia (Misdemeanor)*

In the Shoe that night, Joe pulled the blanket over his torso and stared. He spoke to the sliver of light along the edge of the tiny window in his isolation cell door and thought she might be in the hallway listening: "They say I'm your killer, Mary, but you know I was your lover through and through. My head may be sick, but you climbed back inside when I came home from detention. You know you did. So why?" His voice carried. "Why did you have to sleep with Kuma?"

"Stuff it, or I'll Buck-50 your tongue," came the pissed-off voice from a nearby cell.

Mary wasn't there. She'd disappeared again. Why did she have to vanish on him tonight? The legal charges were like vapers of poison oak anointing his skin. Maybe Mary had also vaporized. Joe scratched and couldn't stop.

Angus's best guess was three months being locked in the hole until his trial started. From the juvie stint, Joe knew all about ninety days. Too bad Mary couldn't have waited one single season of the last year for him to get out of detention.

In the darkness, Joe kicked at his sheets. Moonlight quavered through the slit of a window high on the wall just to tease him with shimmers of freedom. He couldn't bear imagining Mary screwing Kuma. Then it hit him. Mary was never much good at being a Goth chick. Even though growing up under Bonnie's boozy influence gave her plenty of reason to be angry at the world, Mary wasn't wired to be jaded. So why had she died her ginger locks so dark? It had to have been a sick tribute to Kuma and his thick, jet-black Japanese hair.

Maybe she deserved her fate--the Kuma karma. Seducing Kuma was no show of devotion. Why hadn't she waited for Joe?

No. She was right to run. He'd warned her, told her to find someone better. But why did she come back to Joe's twisted world when he got out of detention? So what if he wasn't her only one? He didn't deserve to be. He was definitely no better than Kuma Kusumoto.

The Suboxone tapering had just ended. Tonight, he'd surely score a fix if out on bail, that is if he wasn't stuck in this box with locks. He'd be lying if he said he didn't crave some milk blood as much as a newborn wanting her mama's teat. For Mary and Grace, that would never be.

Joe burned with a fresh wave of craving. He yearned for Mary, too. What if he never escaped a life behind bars? He tried to push his feelings away, but Mary was his best addiction. Maybe a fix would be second best. A whistling wind blasted against the prison wall, buffeting the jail like hate. Earlier in the day, hatred was all he heard when the charges were read in court. At least a fix would steel him to the loss of hope, to the forever loss of Mary. Or would Mary forever straddle life and death the way she sponged Joe's feet one minute and the next 60 seconds the vinegar of her words would sting his wounds. Still, it had been Mary and only Mary for him.

Joe stared without blinking, seeing nothing. He scratched his elbows and knees, cold-turkey-lite. "Why have you died, Mary? Why? Maybe I'm the one who's not alive, the addicted one, the stupid one who flirts with death. I'm the one who was treating heroin like an attraction bigger than the way you always attracted me. I took you for granted. I should be the one cut down by the reaper, but I'm still here rotting. I'm here, but craving a there, and once I'm there, I'll find hell. Life will be hell without you, Mary."

Joe spent the night electrocuted by loss, like he'd already been sent to fry in the chair. He tried and tried to wake up and discover the wickedness of his dream, but he was too wide awake. Joe's raging darkness kept Mary far away. Where that was, no one on this side could ever know.

Joe found his body in the morning contorted half under the jail cot and half-sprawled again on the concrete floor. His scratchy blanket was the mattress, forearms were pillows, and he had nothing over his body to warm the skin on his bones, but he wasn't the least bit cold.

"I love you too much, baby, maybe that's why it burns."

CHAPTER FIFTEEN

(Friday, October 13th)

"Look who's here," Joe heard Big Max say when he opened the cell room door and watched Father José walk in. "I gotta say Father, this Joe Gardner kid is doing his burpees and squats, sit-ups and weird stretches every time I come in."

El Padre smiled at the guard. "This kid's an Oregon All-Star. I asked my friend at the diocese in Portland to inquire. Sixteen-years-old in the state's American Legion tournament. Joe here won the championship game with a walk-off single."

Big Max seemed impressed, and before he left, he told the other two that his brother had just been hired as the facilities manager in the Tri-Cities. "The Dust Devils. Brand new affiliate of the Colorado Rockies. They'll play their very first game ever in the spring."

"Seriously?" Joe asked.

El Padre leaned in closer to Joe. "When you beat this rap, you should check it out."

"Maybe my brother can set up a meeting with the new skipper there. It's Single-A minor league for guys your age. Maybe you can get a tryout."

Before Joe could respond, Big Max closed the door and locked Father José inside the cell. The priest would stop by once a week or so. "Dreams and hopes are vitally important for you, Joe."

El Padre sat on the cement floor in his usual lotus position. It was nice the priest was taking such an interest in him. Sunlight through the narrow window reflected off the blackness of El Padre's hair and cassock. The room shimmered like a lake rippling dark and light in a dawn breeze. The priest had an everyman's peace about him. "I know you like to read, so I brought you one of my favorite novels," the Father said, reaching into his satchel.

"*The Exorcist?*"

El Padre chuckled. *One Flew Over the Cuckoo's Nest*. Read it like a Christ allegory."

"What's an allegory?"

"In this case, that's the key to understanding the hidden meaning behind rebellious Randle P. McMurphy and his struggles with Big Nurse. She's the authority figure in this story."

"So the hero's a Christ-figure dying for our sins?"

"I don't want to give away the story, but allegorically speaking, it's something along those lines." The priest smiled. "I thought you could relate––maybe not the part about going insane, but the incarceration. Besides, the author's from Oregon."

"Cool," said Joe and slipped the book under his pillow, "about the Oregon part, I mean."

When Joe wasn't thinking about Mary, which wasn't often, his mind went too often to Kuma. Joe knew his anger was emotional, probably all rooted in ego, but why did his feelings about Grace not being his own kid overrule his rational side? Mary hadn't cheated on him and he was pretty sure Kuma hadn't hit on Mary when Joe and she were together. Why was this eating at Joe? It was one thing that he couldn't wrap his mind around. Maybe the Black Robe could help him make sense of things.

"Talk to me about divinity, Padre."

"In what way?" Father José asked.

"I don't believe that Catholics own some monopoly on divinity any more than Protestants, Jews, Moslems, Hindus, or Buddhists."

"I'm a Jesuit Priest. Of all the Catholic orders, we're the most open to converging spiritual pathways."

Joe examined the backs of his own hands when he continued: "We had an exchange student at our house last year. Kuma was Japanese, my age. He chose the smallest bedroom upstairs because it had the biggest closet." Joe described the shrine. "Every day he knelt and chanted to the same image that was covered with Japanese scrawl. He called it his *Gohonzon,* or something like that."

"Like an idol?" the priest asked.

Joe shook his head. "I was thinking of our Catholic statues to the Virgin Mother and all those crucifixes of Christ when I asked him the same question. Kuma told me that his Buddhist practice honors the mystic law. Claimed he isn't worshipping anything that isn't already within himself and part of his inner quest for enlightenment."

Father José nodded. "It's the same for Catholics. Our statues help us focus our full attention on some aspect of prayer or worship."

Joe rocked and hesitated before continuing: "So doesn't the difference between Christianity and Buddhism come down to being saved from the outside-in compared to awakening from the inside-out? Christians worship the grace of God sent from heaven above, while Buddhists tap into the grace of being, the stuff of peace that we have inside of us from birth."

The two had a gift of sharing stuff like this without the heat of arguing, so Father José answered Joe calmly. "Without God's divine grace, we're unworthy sinners. Divine grace can be bestowed upon each of us only during this one blessed life, so I don't believe in Buddhist or Hindu notions of reincarnation."

Joe waited until El Padre finished. "But isn't Christ reincarnated from crucified flesh into God's divinity so we can all be saved?"

Father José laughed. "You argue like a Jesuit!"

Joe focused on the thin window again before telling the priest how Mary, before getting pregnant, had cradled a Madonna and Child figurine in her palms. "She was the only one I ever saw brave enough to touch Mom's statuette."

"Maybe the Lord was preparing Mary for this fate, blessing her with grace," the priest said.

"I heard what you did so gracefully there, Padre." Joe laughed. "Unless she was feeling real depressed, Mary had a talent for tapping into her own calmness, like it was divinity, like it was the silver lining of growing up with a drunk for a mom."

The priest nodded. "God's way of gracing her with the resolve she needed."

"That's not how Mary would view it through her new Buddhist faith."

Father José shrugged. "Our religions are fundamentally different, but also closely enough linked that hundreds of years ago, Buddha was venerated as a Catholic saint."

"Seriously?"

El Padre smiled. "Our Roman Catholic Church rejects nothing that is true and holy."

Joe scratched his head. "So maybe the holy spirit inside us is no different than the spirit of enlightenment in a Buddhist. In whatever way your heart taps into the divine, then whether it's in-out or out-in, no matter how you get there, grace will become you."

El Padre seemed to be deep in thought about this question. "So, from what you witnessed with Mary, you believe there is a Buddhist equivalent to being born again in Christ?"

"Eternal enlightenment, transcending karma and death––that's what Mary called it––those sound like a different way of saying what Christians say about salvation and everlasting life," said Joe.

El Padre reached for the cross at the end of his neck chain. "I'm not seeing how almighty God, our creator Father, fits in."

"Or how forgiveness works if we're all stuck––life after life after life––on some wheel of karma," said Joe. "I'm having a tough enough time as a Catholic with the whole forgiving thing." He paused.

"A tough enough time, how?" the priest asked.

"Kuma, our Japanese exchange student. He's the father of Grace. I can't forgive him for that, Father."

El Padre lurched back in surprised. "Was Mary cheating on you with this boy?"

Joe told the priest she hadn't been untrue. "I thought she would wait for me when I was going into juvie, but like a stupid idiot, I told her we needed to break up. I didn't expect Kuma to make a move on her."

Father José pressed his palms together and propped up his chin with the tips of his fingers to think over what Joe had confided. "Forgiveness is tricky," Father José offered. "If you can't forgive someone, it's as though you're wishing them ill will, but drinking that poison yourself. You forgive––first and foremost––for your own inner peace."

Joe tried his best to comprehend, but grimaced instead, realizing how much the notion challenged every impulse he had. "It's mind bending. You're saying how Christian mercy is grace from above, but forgiveness is a choice we make from within us to show mercy."

El Padre looked up at the thin window before answering. Like Christ on the cross, nothing in the realm of forgiveness is easy. Nor is loving thy neighbor as thyself."

"It's just that I thought he and me were better friends."

The priest got up to leave, but stopped. "Then, I suspect that you two really are friends." El Padre didn't elaborate, but left to continue on his rounds.

CHAPTER SIXTEEN

(Wednesday, October 18th)

That evening, following the coarse jail cell dinner of sausage gravy and hard biscuits, Joe tried to remember the chant he'd heard from Kuma's closet through thin walls each and every morning. Thinking he needed to be polite to their exchange student about something spiritual, Joe never complained to Kuma when the chanting woke him.

Tonight while relaxing flat on his back, he instead went with his own engrained devotional and hailed *Mary, full of grace, the Lord is with thee*. She startled Joe. Mary appeared instantly and sat on the edge of the jail cell cot pressed firmly against his hip. For fear of losing her just as quickly as she'd come, Joe continued:

Blessed art thou among women
and blessed is the fruit of thy womb
--Jesus.

Joe reached up to trace her tattoo. This time, as soon as he touched her back, Mary leaned down and pressed her ear against his. When he closed his eyes, she melded into him and they recited the words together. Joe was surprised when his non-Catholic girlfriend didn't miss a word:

Holy Mary, mother of God,
pray for us sinners now,
and at the hour of death.

After they repeated it in unison for a second, flawless, time, Joe stopped and she didn't speak another word. Instead, she transported them from his cell all the way back to their first kiss. The whole thing had started as a colossal public embarrassment.

During the grand opening and ribbon-cutting for the Gorge Discovery Center and Museum, Joe stood beside Mary. The senior senator from Oregon, Mark O. Hatfield, gave the keynote speech applauding the hard work and wonderful vision of this world-class museum that he was so pleased to have helped fund. Most surprising to Joe was seeing both of his parents standing together. His mom had insisted that his father shake off the cobwebs from his graveyard shift and attend. She'd also forced him to wear a blazer to go with his blue jeans. It was as dignified and formal as J.J. Gardner ever allowed himself to be.

The End of the Trail Band was set up to perform close to the speaker's podium on the brick walkway leading into the new museum. Mary's fifteen-year-old curves filled her pioneer petticoat and blouse, and a baby-blue bonnet covered the top of wavy, ginger hair that covered her shoulders and fell halfway down her back. Bonnie Quinn hadn't been kicked out of the End of the Trail Band yet, and waited by one of two microphones ready to accompany her daughter with the vocals.

Joe, also fifteen, already needed grown-up pioneer clothing to play the part of a wheelwright apprentice for the celebration. During the grand opening speeches on that clear May day in 1997, the U.S. Senator sounded dignified with his deep voice. Earnest eyes below the thick, white hair focused directly on Don Dufur, president of the museum's board of directors. He thanked Dufur for taking the time to cut a television commercial that proved pivotal in getting Hatfield reelected for his fifth term. At that moment, Joe made his big mistake.

He touched Mary's elbow and pointed at someone from their high school, a hot girl in their freshman class. "Do you think you could ask Angie if she likes me?"

The senator's words seemed to drown him out. "Without Don Dufur spotlighting my opponent's support of the Rashneeshee cult, then I wouldn't have been in the U.S. Senate to support this impressive new center. Not only did these evildoers poison Don, but they had designs on taking over your wonderful--"

Cymbals fell with an arrhythmic crash next to poor Joe. Hatfield's speech stopped cold and he stared from the podium when Mary's strong shove upended Joe into the End of the Trail Band's drum set.

Everyone in the opening day crowd stared when Joe sat up-- astonished. Mary stood with fists on hips and her freckled cheeks an angry shade of Bing Cherry red. He'd never seen her so mad. Mary stormed off through the large crowd.

Without him realizing, Joe's parents had edged directly behind him. His father laughed gruffly. J.J. bent down and whispered into his son's ear: "What a thing to ask a girl who really likes you."

Joe withered, but hustled through the crowd to catch up with Mary.

Senator Hatfield, unfazed, continued his amplified speech to the large gathering. "As I was saying, you have my deepest gratitude Don, and I want to commend you for your years of diligent work to create this truly wonderful museum."

Following the applause, Dufur nodded and waved with modest acknowledgement. Before continuing his speech, Hatfield looked over the heads of the large crowd. "And best of luck with your election, too, young man," Hatfield said through his mic.

The Senator of Oregon couldn't possibly be talking about him, could he? Joe spun around. Sure enough, every pair of eyes in the courtyard stared when Mark O. Hatfield waved at him. A stunned Joe waved back. Just as quickly, he turned away again. Mary Quinn was moving fast, disappearing through the gate that led out of the parking lot. Joe ignored everyone in the crowd, but ran towards her. She was already part way down the steep and long grassy slope to the river shore.

The trail was narrow and nearly vertical where he caught up with her. A big Oregon Ash had taken root in the only semi-level spot there. Mary stood with her back towards Joe, arms folded fiercely, and facing the big river. She seemed to be staring down at the railway cut right below them. Joe was winded with his hands on his knees, and he could tell by those crossed arms that touching her would be risky, unless he didn't care if he was somersaulted onto the tracks well below them.

"I didn't know," he told her, out of breath.

He sat down in the shade of the ash. Mary refused to turn his way.

"I really didn't know how you felt, Mary," Joe told her, once he caught his breath. "'Cuz if I'd known. Well, you know. Angie's got nothing on you."

She spun around, her freckled face nearly maroon from crying. "Just shut up, Joe Gardner." She took three quick steps towards him and he braced himself for another shove. Instead, she pushed him a bit more gently onto his back. He sighed in relief when she straddled him for their first kiss--at first hard, and then more tenderly. He rolled her on her side and framed her face in the palms of his hands to kiss the pioneer girl some more. What an idiot. He really hadn't known.

They could feel the rumbling even before the noise rolled down the track, not that they cared, except for when, directly below them, the whistle blew insanely loud. They fondled to the vibrations covering their skin. On the steep slope, they lay nearly above the locomotive. Mary bit his earlobe. Hard.

When the train trailed away downriver towards the Port of Portland, Bonnie Quinn's powerful blues voice carried to their Oregon Ash hideaway. Her vocals were raspy and strong, but not as smooth as Mary's. Next came robust applause for the End of the Trail Band.

Joe and Mary sat up when a second, long train approached in the opposite direction. Mary pointed to the turn. The locomotive seemed to be rolling too fast and blasted another warning into the air. Were all those cars really about to crumple like an accordion closing too fast? Mary took her hands off her ears and laughed when all the cars managed the bend and disappeared the wrong way up the old Oregon

Trail. Joe pulled the bow of her bonnet that was neatly tied under her chin and held to the free strings so he could pull her lips to his.

"Don't you ever do anything like that again, Joseph," she whispered after the train noise stopped and before they kissed again. When enough was enough, she pushed him away and got up. Mary took his hand and wrist before leaning back to let the gravity of the steep hillside do most of the work of helping her new boyfriend bend forward and onto his feet. When they climbed the walking trail to the Discovery Center parking lot, she didn't let go of his hand––not once. Joe was more than fine letting the world see that he and Mary were together.

She led Joe back to the museum where the grand opening day crowd had greatly thinned. They'd never been inside the newly inaugurated interpretive center and looked around in awe of the tall gallery hall. Joe followed her past a replica war canoe and huge timbered posts framing basalt brick walls.

Mostly emptied of visitors, the museum was preparing to close. The two still held hands and hurried to inspect replicas of antique wheat thrashers, pioneer trading posts, harness and saddlery shops, huge side-wheeler boats, salmon wheel traps, and Celilo Falls photos. "We'll go a whole lot slower next time," Joe remembered Mary telling him.

They breezed through the Ice Age and a display describing the colossal flood that scoured the Columbia River plateau and this gorge over 10,000 years ago. They glanced at the Native prehistory and descriptions of the wet-dry, up-and-down terrain with a wide variety of plants and animals. Mary––still in her bonnet and petticoat–– snapped one of Joe's pioneer suspender straps. He winced. "My boyfriend should buy me an ice cream," she demanded, the first time she'd called him that.

"Definitely." Joe guided her into the Basalt Rock Café. They selected ice cream bars and Joe paid.

"Please come join me," they heard an older man say. His deep, authoritative voice resonated through the empty café and startled them. Seated alone, U.S. Senator Mark O. Hatfield motioned for the two teens to sit with him.

"I'm delighted you two saw fit to come back. Isn't this a fine new museum?" Hatfield asked, and nibbled on a roast beef sandwich that he was washing down with ice tea.

"Definitely a cool place," said Mary, licking her Klondike Bar and in a much better mood than during the senator's keynote.

With a conspiratorial grin, Hatfield motioned the two of them closer. "I kissed my first girl beside a blackberry bramble."

Mary turned scarlet. The senator momentarily patted Mary's forearm and smiled. "I only share that with you two because, when I leaned in for that kiss, I was deathly afraid she was going to push me into the thorny vines."

Joe smiled, but blushed, too.

"I was hoping, when I saw you two come inside the café, that you'd sit with me," said the senator. "I need to apologize. I hope I didn't embarrass you two during my speech, at least not too much anyway."

"Joe deserved to get shoved," said Mary, meekly.

"But, I think we're okay now." Joe pressed his shoulder lightly into hers.

"I guess we'll see about that." Mary winked at Senator Hatfield.

"I'm told we all missed out on some fine singing from you, young lady."

Mary beamed and fished in her cloth pioneer purse for an unopened CD by the End of the Trail Band. "Sorry I took off like that," she said. "For interrupting your important speech, I owe you my recording."

"You should sign it for him, Mary," Joe said to her, and told Senator Hatfield to be sure to check out "Grace Amazed," her solo on the CD.

"I'd love that," said the senator, handing over his expensive fountain pen for Mary to borrow. "I promise to listen to your solo on my drive down the Gorge."

At this, Mary peeled off the plastic wrapping and opened the CD. In an open space on the disk itself, she wrote:

> *For Senator Hatfield*
> *A Gift of Oregon Music*
> *From Mary Quinn*
> *May 24, 1997*

"How old are you, Mary?" Hatfield asked, after she'd handed him the CD and his pen. He was inspecting the song titles on the paper insert.

"I'm fifteen, same as Joe."

Under the date and her signature, he printed in smaller letters on the last available space:

Age 15
Grand Opening
Columbia Gorge Discovery Center

"This way I'll be sure to remember our eventful day together," said Senator Hatfield before finishing his sandwich.

That night––back in jail––Mary and Joe were still fifteen, newly christened in their love, melded and sleeping as one, until the morning came and he woke up shivering. The one he adored was still dead. It should have been me, he thought.

CHAPTER SEVENTEEN

(Tuesday, October 31ˢᵗ)

"Nice 'do," said Joe. "Just like Mary's."

Joe had done a double-take when, through the visitor's window, he saw jet black hair and light side braids along with her same not thin, but nice, full figure, and realized it was not Mary standing there. Biff was three or four inches shorter with sharper cheekbones and nose, along with light-blue, not green eyes. "How's life on the outside, Biff?" he asked Mary's best girlfriend, and also his nemesis.

"I'm like a tumbling tumbleweed," she answered, which was pretty accurate for the nonstop Biffilator.

Actually, it was cool to see Biffy. He'd known her since third grade. "Welcome to my sweet new digs." Joe swept his hand towards the jail corridor behind them. Like with most visitors, he hadn't been given any advance warning. Joe sat down quickly with a big smile. "And thanks for doing Mary's vigil at the museum. Mom told me. Best thing you could have done for her." The two bantered and also knew how to deal straight-up with one another, but not so much that he was going to tell her how he was the one Mary appeared to on the evening of the vigil.

"Amazing night," said Biff. "I couldn't believe how many people Mary touched during her lifetime, but I've gotta say…" Biff looked away and fidgeted.

"'Gotta say what? You're never at a loss for words."

Biff turned back to address Joe through the Plexiglas. "How much she wanted to raise a family with you."

This time it was Joe who turned away. "Mary deserved better than me."

Biff leaned forward and waited for Joe's full attention. "Wasn't that for her to decide?" she asked. "When you haven't stumbled and fallen from getting in your own stupid way, you two made a pretty cool couple."

It unsettled Joe for her words to sound so wise. "Why are you finally visiting me after two-and-a-half months, only to kick me when I'm down?"

Biff reached into her daypack and pulled out an envelope with Japanese characters scrawled across part of the front. "Because it's time to get real, Joe. No more imaginary Native American lovers for Mary."

"How do you know whose baby it is?"

"Because Mary and me were best friends. She told me what happened. Besides, this is about Grace and not your wounded ego." When he didn't react, she continued. "Mary told me she felt pretty guilty about sleeping with Kuma."

Joe crossed his arms. "Pretty guilty?"

She tapped her envelope and whispered. "No matter what you think of him, Kuma's a stand-up guy. He's totally sick about the news. Even sent me a clump of his hair. I talked with that CPS caseworker, Amanda Skerry, before I drove up from The Dalles."

Joe wasn't impressed. "She came and talked to me, too, last week. My own mother didn't tell me squat about my dad, but without trying to, the CPS lady lets me know that it was Mary's friggin' mom that my father split with."

Biff squeezed one end of her rice paper envelope. "That part's whacko, but the fate of Gracie is a way bigger deal than J.J. Gardner and Bonnie Quinn staging some stupid midlife crisis together."

Joe couldn't argue that fact.

"I gave the Wanapum Family Court most of Kuma's hair, but held some back just in case his follicles get accidentally-on-purpose dumped in their loonie bin."

"What did you talk to the CPS lady about? She's the one who won't let my mom visit Grace."

Biff told him that she didn't go into any of that with the case-worker. "I guess Bonnie Quinn moved to Moses Lake a couple of weeks ago. She thinks it'll help her get custody of Grace. The case-worker asked my opinion about Mary's mom."

"What did you tell her?"

"The truth. I told her that your mother would be a far better parent for the baby."

Joe laughed. "Me, too. I said that––even as screwed up as Rochelle Gardner's son was––there was no comparison between Bonnie and my mother." Joe turned when it sounded like a food tray was dropped down the hall in the jail cafeteria. "I got along with Mary's mom," he faced forward and told Biff. "I kept her lawn mowed and mouse traps cleared, but it was always bluesy, boozy Bonnie––queen lizard of the cocktail lounge."

"And, yet again, she couldn't stick it out with a man for more than a few months, not even your laidback father." Joe knew what she said wasn't funny, but painfully true. It didn't surprise him when Biff laughed.

He chuckled, too. "I told the caseworker that Bonnie Quinn didn't even know her own 18-year-old kid was pregnant. If she couldn't finish raising her own daughter through high school, then why would CPS let her raise the granddaughter?"

Grace's custody issues were hardly Joe's foremost concern. If things didn't break right for him, he'd never know Mary's daughter until the girl was an adult.

Biff slipped out of her wool jacket and placed it on her lap. The first thing Joe noticed was the sprig of braided wildflowers pinned to the breast of her blouse. "I think Mary knew she was about to die," he said and pointed through the window at Biff's broach.

"Why do you say that?" Biff asked, almost taken aback, but peeking down at her dried flowers.

Joe fidgeted in his chair. "Because last spring, after I was first out of the juvie, Mary and me went on a little hike. Mostly, she bought flowers from a nursery to braid, but on that day she had me pick a cluster of them over by Horsethief Lake. You know that purple spring flower only grows in the Gorge, don't you?"

"The Poet's Shooting Star," said Biff. "*Dodecatheon poeticum*. Purple blossoms above a yellow collar, like feathers bound to a dark-tipped dart. The tip points towards the ground like a shooting star."

Of course Biff––daughter of the director of the natural history museum for the Gorge––would know this. "Mary had us take five nice blossoms. She braided up one for her mom, one for my old lady, one for her Pathfinder, and one for your Subaru. As for the last one, I don't know where it went."

"Is hers still hanging from her rearview mirror like mine is from my Loyale?"

Joe shrugged. "It was, but the Pathfinder's been impounded for as long as I've been locked up in this hole."

"She never told me how you guys preserved the delicate blossoms so well?" Biff tapped her own broach. "Her unpreserved sprigs usually don't hold up for long."

Joe described how his dad supported the Shooting Star stem with wire. "Everything was braided together with this blossom hanging below. Then Dad had Mary dip the whole thing in a small vat of resin he'd mixed." Joe sat back and realized that this was the last project he'd done with his father before he split with Bonnie Quinn.

"So you think Mary really saw herself dying this young?" Biff asked.

He focused his eyes through a small window behind her to a darkening Halloween afternoon sky. "Yes. I think she was resigned to her fate."

"What made you think that?"

Before answering, he thought about the way she chose him to be hers when they were fifteen. Time, especially not wasting it, mattered to Mary more than it did to most teens. "Little things she did and said," he finally told Biff. He described the hike when Mary spotted the Shooting Star cluster wedged in a cliff face beyond her reach. He told Biff how Mary insisted he shimmy up a basalt crevasse to snag the best blossoms. "When I climbed down and handed the tiny bouquet to her, she made me drive us home. That way she could keep them safe in her lap, almost like the little flowers were sacred."

"Once Mary sets her mind on something."

"When she held up one close to her nose, I remember asking her how long she thought the delicate flower was going to last," said Joe.

"What did she tell you?"

"'Forever,' was what she said. 'This blossom is me.'"

Biff's eyes watered, but Joe kept his own emotions in check by changing the subject. "Too bad Mary could never set you up with Kuma. Then he wouldn't have slept with Mary. Too bad we couldn't find a way to turn you into a mellow, almost obedient, sorta-Japanese wife."

Biff stiffened and her face grimaced, but it didn't take long for her usual shotgun blast of words to return. "Get serious, Joe. Mary was hoping and thinking that you were the father of her baby. She wanted you to move back with her and your mom to start your family, but nothing lined up that way. Nothing would have happened between Mary and Kuma if you hadn't broken it off with her."

Joe rolled his eyes. "That night before I started my juvie sentence, she kept pushing me to rat out my source."

"Trust me, I know how Mary could get. On the matchmaker front, I had to call her out for butting in." Biff surprised Joe by laughing. "Kuma became my friend, despite Mary."

When Joe didn't respond, Biff attempted to lighten the mood. "I'm actually dating someone from your old Hustler's team."

"Good for you, Biff. The shortstop, no doubt."

Biff hid her grin. "Maybe."

"Remember Derek, your almost first boyfriend in 6th grade? Remember when he leaned way down and tried to kiss you? Before he opened his eyes, you made a move that had him French kissing the sod."

"Everyone was taller than me in school, but I was never close to being the weakest."

"I think you shamed Derek's family into moving to Alaska."

Biff flexed a bicep.

Her brute honesty made him wonder if she was here to ask him the ultimate question about Mary. "I bet you think I killed her," he whispered through the speak-hole. He wanted to see her react. Why else had she stayed away from him for over two months?

"Knock it off! I never believed that," she said, glaring back at Joe. "But there is one other thing Mary shared with me that she didn't share with you."

"Are you trying to say that you two were closer than Mary and me were?"

"Hardly. It's just that Mary hated your cousin."

Joe tilted back again on the wobbly jail chair. "I knew Gunnar wasn't one of her favorite people, but she never said anything about hating him."

Biff stared straight at Joe and spoke low through the speaker hole. "When Gunnar first got you to shoot up after your surgery, he also tried to get Mary to try some smack, just him and her."

"Are you saying he was making moves on her?" Joe clenched his cuffed hands into fists and had to tell himself not to overreact.

"No. I don't think Mary ever gave Gunnar the chance. She was so royally pissed when he pulled out the needle and whatever other stupid gizmos you junkies use. When he opened the foil and held it out, Mary slapped the heroin up and out of his hand. The white powder flew up and covered his pasty face."

"What did Gunnar do then?"

"After she lit into him, Mary said he came unglued right back at her."

"What do you mean?"

"I'm saying that Gunnar went hard-nosed on her. He told her that she wouldn't have any big problems with him if she kept their little drug secret between him and her. Mary told me that when he tried to salvage a bit of the spilled smack, he kept scowling at her and calling her a stupid bitch. The whole thing gave her the willies."

"If I'd known any of that, then I would have never––" Joe started to say, but pointed instead to the camera and audio surveillance on the ceiling above him.

Biff leaned into the speaker hole and whispered. "That's why Mary kept asking you who gave you the smack. She got so mad because you failed her test to see if you would trust her." Biff checked to see if any guards were listening before whispering again. "I sure wouldn't rule out that slick scumbag taking out--"

"No way! Don't even go there, Biff." Joe was in no mood to even imagine his cousin as a cold-blooded murderer.

"Your mom is sure going the extra ten-thousand miles just to see your precious cousin. Did she tell you she's flying with your aunt on a weeklong trip to Sweden?"

Joe nodded. "Did you know someone torched Gunnar's workshop here in Moses Lake and he needs his parents to deal with the cleanup before selling the place?"

"Sure," said Biff. "Your mom and me were thinking it was someone tied to the Bone Shrine deal, maybe a gang who figured out that Gunnar's doublewide was abandoned and decided to set up a meth lab in the detached shop. Gosh, how sad it is for our amazing planet that your cousin's playpen exploded."

Joe ignored her sarcasm. "I'm not completely out of the loop. Did you know Aunt Darla happened to have an extra plane ticket since Uncle Nils couldn't go?"

"Yeah, but that's hardly enough reason for your mom to take off right before the trial." Biff got up and tapped the Plexiglas with her nail. "There's only one reason your mom is going. She wants to confront Gunnar, to find out exactly what he knows about that night at the Bone Shrine."

Joe shrugged. "Gunnar's only going to tell her what he wants her to hear. Nothing more."

"I guess we'll see," said Biff. "Too bad he's afraid to come back and testify on your behalf."

"Maybe he has a better plan."

"What's that?" she asked.

"Wait for the trial and you'll see."

Biff's eyes fired. She didn't like being left out-of-the-loop on anything. "Why do you always have Gunnar's back, Joe? He knows way more about what happened that night than he ever told you."

"He didn't off Mary. No way."

"You revere that creep way too much."

Joe started to remind Biff that Gunnar was his only cousin, but didn't. He touched his Adam's Apple instead, almost expecting to feel pain from that lowlife, *hombre's* chokehold.

"Mary drove you to Moses Lake that night because she wanted to make sure you were home by Monday for the intervention she and your mom had arranged." Biff looked away. "So, Joe, how bad were your heroin cravings?"

"The truth?"

"What else?"

"At my worst, I'm not sure which I loved more, Mary or that frickin' smack." He kept his voice low.

Biff spoke way too loud. "You loved heroin more than Mary? That's totally sick, Joe. I mean seriously stupid sick."

Joe wasn't in the mood. "Are there any other confessions you'd like to hear from my lips?"

Biff leaned next to the Plexiglas, her jaw set. "I already know what to think about Gunnar, the almighty drug lord."

Joe leaned his face into the speaker hole. "I own every fix I ever had, Biff. As for my cousin––hell, I don't know what to think about him."

Biff had no sympathy in her voice. "Then banish your cousin from inside your head. Exile him like he exiled himself, like how he's letting you take the fall for him––again."

Joe crossed his arms and glared at her, stone-faced.

"Mary would want you to stay clean and stop blaming Kuma," said Biff. "Stop waging war on peace."

CHAPTER EIGHTEEN

VI.
The WORLD

(Friday, November 3rd)

Sweden. Joe's trial was set to start mid-month. Turbulence over Greenland rattled the plane. Rochelle wasn't keen on leaving the country––not with Joe's case about to begin––but with the airplane ticket offer, she jumped on a free chance to confront Gunnar face-to-face in front of his own mother, to figure out what her nephew knew versus how much he was hiding.

Her sister was never fond of flying and fidgeted in the aisle seat of the long range SAS Airbus. She had rounder cheeks and fuller curves than Rochelle, but shared a similar youthful face with the same bright, blue eyes. At least Rochelle was thinner than Darla.

The two shared an eerily similar fashion sense. Without ever conferring, Rochelle marveled at how they'd wear the same brand of Lady Wranglers, and the same style of Meier & Frank blouses. In the same week at different hairdressers, both of them chose similar burgundy hair coloring to mask their creeping grayness.

After resting her eyes turned into an unexpected nap, Rochelle startled awake when the flight attendant rolled her cart down the aisle with a last call for drinks. Rochelle asked for coffee, no sugar or cream. This trip to confront Gunnar demanded a semi-alert aunt. Rochelle sipped, glad that Scandinavians liked a strong, black, wide-awake brew.

The overnight flight from Seattle made an early Friday morning landing in Stockholm. Their SAS puddle jumper flew them to the middle of Sweden. Darla's in-laws still worked a potato farm between Linköping, the market city of flax, and Vikingstad, the village of Vikings. After the long flight, Darla and Rochelle would have both preferred to chill out, but Gunnar had arranged to meet first thing. Darla rented a compact Volvo at the small airport.

When Gunnar was little, the Larsson family spent three full years at the family farm before Nils landed his position running the Columbia Basin Potato Growers Association. Nils and Gunnar spoke Swedish routinely which allowed her nephew to remain fluent. Her nephew's permanent move to the Scandinavian country would be more like exile on a luxury cruiser than the dungeon-shackling that Joe faced.

"He'll be meeting us here," her sister said and pointed up at a long and looming cathedral with patina green spires.

"In some massive church?" Rochelle couldn't hide her surprise.

"Linköping *Domkyrkan.* Gunnar insisted." Darla fluffed her hair in the visor mirror as she drove.

"Nils and I have traveled all through Sweden and are convinced that this *Domkyrka* is the most impressive Catholic remnant here. It's sleeker and more stylized than even the central cathedral in Uppsala. Darla zigzagged around the block past the high school Gunnar had attended for a year, a modern library, and a lush park blanketed with gold and red leaves. Oh, look!" She hit the brakes when a local Swede vacated his parking spot.

Rochelle hugged her big purse like a deployed airbag. Out on the sidewalk, the sisters shivered in the chill, autumn breeze below the towering place of worship. Rochelle breathed deep and focused skyward.

"That spire reaches 349 feet towards heaven, taller than a football field set on end," said Darla.

Rochelle wished she'd worn a sweater beneath her thin, REI parka. She wasn't looking forward to colliding with Gunnar, but expected a raw gleaning of truth.

Darla pointed to the cathedral's weather-protected awnings. "Check out the gargoyles." Grotesque statuettes were embedded along the *Domkyrka* walls. "Those trolls and griffins––or whatever they're called––were put there to ward off evil spirits."

Rochelle shielded her eyes from the glaring, mid-morning sun to better see. "Too bad Joe wasn't wearing a gargoyle pendant all last year," she said under her breath before leading the way towards the thick, wooden entry door. She stopped to read an English language plaque.

The cathedral, originally Roman Catholic, was started in 1230. Darla opened the main entry portal under a gray statue of Jesus who welcomed them from above the door. Arching over and behind Christ were his disciples, bishops, angels and Christian soldiers, all in bas-relief.

Inside, they found a grand place of worship––completely empty. Gunnar was nowhere to be seen. Rochelle followed Darla down the wide aisle, but midway her sister sat in a pew and kept checking around for her son. "He told me he'd be waiting for us here, and we're right on time," Darla whispered, her eyebrows furrowed.

Rochelle eased towards the church altar that was spread across the far, closed end of the cathedral. In contrast to high walls of gray, the morning sunlight illuminated hues of stained glass Christianity. Above the large altar, a huge crucifix hung down from the arches. Rochelle's tired mind imagined centuries of peasants and nobles filling the cathedral to pray below the same skin and bones of this thin, tortured Christ.

Her eyes locked onto dead Jesus. A children's song came to her. It was the one she would recite to young Joe with the finger bones connecting to the hand bones. Here, those palms were nailed to the cross. The arm bone connected to the shoulder bone and the shoulder bone connected to the collar bone, but what about that rib cage speared by some Roman soldier? The collar bone connected to the neck bone, and the neck connected to the jawbone. Rochelle stared up like she was Mother Mary seeing Christ's royal skull connected to eternity with a mocking crown of thorns.

The Lutheran shrine seemed surprisingly Roman Catholic. Maybe the two Christian denominations weren't all that different. Rochelle walked two-thirds of the way towards the back and set the oversized handbag on the bench between her and Darla.

"Where is he?" Rochelle whispered, but the reverent echo reminded her that Gunnar believed life adhered to the design of his own almighty, narcissistic making. For as far as they'd flown to meet him, was there any excuse to be stood-up by the boy? Her ever self-important nephew would no doubt waltz in eventually with some glib alibi.

"*Nam myoho renge kyo.*" The familiar Buddhist chant boomed deeply through the cavernous, Christian cathedral. Darla nudged Rochelle and they turned to see Gunnar perched tall in the Lutheran pulpit attached high on the long, left wall. The gilded gazebo offered an illusion of being suspended from heaven. Her nephew's fingers were laced through his Buddhist *juzu* beads. "*Nam myoho renge kyo.*" Rochelle shook her head. Under an awning of trumpet-blowing angels painted gold like the pulpit, her nephew chanted from the depths of his diaphragm. "*Nam myoho renge kyo*" poured out rapidly and echoed through the cathedral again and again.

"What do you think you're doing?" Darla yelled up at her son. Her question filled the gothic tall interior, although Rochelle was far more interested in what crime Gunnar had actually committed on the night of August 17th that compelled him to bolt to Sweden permanently, it seemed.

Gunnar dropped his hands and stepped down the narrow twist of stairs to the main level. He wore normal, American, everyday clothes––Levi jeans, a plaid Pendleton grunge shirt, and Converse tennis shoes. His tall, blond, angular features were classically Swede––definitely from his father, Nils.

After Gunnar edged along pews to meet them, Darla hugged her son. "Where is everybody?" she wanted to know. "No ministers, no parishioners?"

"*Nu fikar de på konditeriet,*" said Gunnar in perfect singsong Swedish. He turned towards his aunt, no doubt knowing she had no interest in hugging him. "On coffee break," he translated for her. "This place––the coolest Lutheran cathedral in the world––is amazingly empty most of the time," he said and made a grand sweep of his hand. "During the year I attended *Katedralskolan*, I'd come here to study." He motioned for them to sit. "It's quieter than the new library."

"What's with launching into a Buddhist chant in a Christian holy place?" Darla asked. "You're so full of disrespect lately."

"It's all in how one views it, Mom," he said, his own voice all but booming. "The Buddha of the North––that old Christian seer, Emanuel Swedenborg––is interred with kings and queens inside Sweden's main Lutheran cathedral. Millions of Nichiren Buddhists, just like Kuma, practice a Martin Luther brand of Buddhism. So I ask you in the name of protestants from all faiths, why not honor Buddha inside the walls of Linköping's grand Lutheran cathedral?"

Rochelle tried to connect the dots of Gunnar's contorted logic leading from Buddha to Swedenborg to Nichiren to Kuma to Luther so that we might all find our own inner, protesting paths to divinity, or something like that. This wasn't the weighty question she came half-way around the globe to ask him.

"I'm still Roman Catholic," Darla said instead. "So why would I care if your Buddhist chant is tolerated or not by these Lutheran Swedes, other than I can't believe you would be this rude inside someone else's house of worship?"

"When did you start chanting?" Rochelle asked her nephew, who never struck her as the spiritual sort, Christian or Buddhist.

"Your exchange student taught me to chant last winter after I first got clean. Ever since then, I've chanted every day."

"And, back home, as soon as you moved to Sweden, I took your little Buddhist shrine from the doublewide and placed it back outside your basement bedroom. But what's this about coming clean?" Darla asked, dumbfounded. "You weren't actually shooting up heroin, were you?"

Gunnar turned halfway away as though to say that there was much he chose not to share with his mom about his private life. "Aunt Ro, did Kuma ever tell you about *Sho-Hondo?*"

"I don't think so." His 'Aunt Ro' was growing impatient with how thoroughly her nephew controlled a conversation that had nothing to do with why she'd flown so far.

"Kuma's sect had the *Sho-Hondo* temple built in 1972 for $100 million. The sanctuary hosted their most sacred mandala--a *Gohonzon* created by the founder, Nichiren, in the 13th century."

"Now I remember," Rochelle said, recalling the photos Kuma received from his mom at the end of last year.

"Where was the temple built?" Darla asked.

"At the base of Mount Fuji," he told her. "Top Japanese architects stylized the building to resemble a crane taking flight. Thousands of Nichiren Buddhists chanted *nam myoho renge kyo* there. Italian marble channeled a chorus of voices through the sanctuary towards their most sacred *Gohonzon.*"

"Maybe your dad and I will visit it someday," Darla said.

"Impossible," Gunnar told her.

Rochelle knew this, too. It was why Kuma, at seeing the photos, had grown so upset at the images of the temple reduced to rubble at the foot of Fuji. She fidgeted when Gunnar continued his little history lecture. "Martin Luther was excommunicated by the Roman Catholic Pope for insisting that anyone, not just the priesthood, could pray to God. Same thing for these Buddhists. Their modern priesthood excommunicated all the lay followers of Nichiren for chanting to seek their own Buddhahood within themselves. Last winter, the Nichiren priests blew up that incredible temple."

Darla shook her head. "So a fine, new temple at the base of Mount Fuji was exploded to bits after only 27-years, but Linköping's Cathedral--originally Roman Catholic, mind you--is still standing magnificent and tall after 800 years."

"Kuma and his family back home were pretty upset," said Gunnar. "The loss of *Sho-Hondo* was the main reason Kuma went back to Japan when he did."

Rochelle hadn't considered this possibility. She'd always thought his early departure had to do with being drafted by the Chunichi Dragon team in the first round. As for the pregnancy scaring him back to Japan, if Mary didn't tell Joe until June, and always acted like she expected it to be Joe's kid, then why would she have told Kuma about being pregnant in February? If the kid had turned out to be Joe's, then why would she have ever told Kuma about any suspicions she'd had?

"Did Joe get Kuma involved with heroin, too?" Darla asked.

Gunnar didn't show much patience for his mother. "More like Kuma got hooked on Mary when Joe was sent to detention." He said it with a cocky, sideways glance at Rochelle. "Kuma did leave his shrine in Aunt Ro's house as a gift of sorts."

The large, marble baptismal font in front of the big Lutheran altar caught Rochelle's eye when she responded. "Mary stayed in Kuma's old bedroom last summer. She didn't know I knew, but I could hear her chanting to the miniature *Sho-Hondo* he left behind."

"I chanted there, too," said Gunnar. "So did Biff McCoy. *Shakubuku!* Kuma was slyly converting all of us."

"Is that like Christian proselytizing?" Darla asked. "Is that why you took the liberty of climbing into a Lutheran pulpit to bellow out a Buddhist chant? Frankly, son, you have to know that was rude."

"Drop it, Darla. You and me are the only ones to hear his immature prank." Rochelle cut loose on her naïve sister. The jet lag was trying her patience. "If your son hadn't invited Joe into his world of heroin, talked him into using smack instead of his prescribed painkillers, if Gunnar hadn't had his cousin deliver his contraband for him, then my son never would have gone to juvie, never would have touched that blasted Bone Shrine stash!" The accusations boomed.

Gunnar's smugness evaporated into a mean stare at his aunt. He pointed at the emaciate Christ on a huge cross. "It started before that, Aunt Ro. I never should have shown Joe and Mary the Bone Shrine."

"I can't believe you!" Rochelle got on her feet and stood over her nephew. "Your druggie drop site is no excuse. You showed Mary and Joe the Bone Shrine three years ago." Her voice carried up and through the high arches. "What you never should have shown Joseph was your glorious needle!"

Staring at Gunnar, Darla shook her head and started to cry.

"Get real, Darla! Not everything is about Gunnar Larsson. Your precious son poisoned Joe's life. It could be too late to save my son."

Gunnar focused straight up at the same pulpit he'd descended a few minutes earlier. "Did you fly all the way to Sweden just to unload on me? It's not my fault that Mary and Joe stumbled into the thick of a drop gone bad. It's not my fault Joey messed with that stash."

"That big heroin drop was intended for you, wasn't it?" Rochelle asked him, most annoyed at how Gunnar thought his vagueness and deflection would substitute for anything resembling a confession.

"The details of the transaction don't concern you. I'll just say that I'm clean, but I needed one last score, one last big deal to get out of the biz."

"And retire at age 21 while your cousin spends the next 21 years in prison? Knowing how you were involved or not involved could help lead to Mary's killer. Why won't you tell me what your active part was in all of this?"

"That's none of your business. The less you two know, the better. I was planning to move to Sweden before any of this went down."

Rochelle's face flushed red. The brat was simply covering his own backside. "And Joe pays the price for you skipping the country."

Gunnar glared at his aunt. "Don't think I can't get snuffed here. Not if someone wants me gone bad enough. It's a small world. Hell, Sweden isn't even Switzerland. Unlike in that little kingdom in the Alps, I can be extradited from Scandinavia if the U.S. authorities want to go through all the hoops and expense of dragging me from Viking Valhalla back to the seers of Smohalla."

"Just look me in the eye, Gunnar." Rochelle waited for what was only a quick glance. "Tell me you didn't drown Mary Quinn."

"Jeez!" he blurted. "The confessional booths were removed from this cathedral by the Lutheran's several centuries ago." Gunnar's jaw clenched and he looked up at the pulpit.

"Lower your voices." Darla's throaty voice sounded more like a growl.

Rochelle sat back down, but whispered harshly. "Mary's dead and Joe's whole future is on the line. That means I need to get very real with you, Gunnar."

"Not by throwing dart after dart at my face." Gunnar looked away from his aunt and waited until his mom had his attention. "I intend to do what I can to protect my family's lives, including my lovely Aunt

Ro here, and certainly Joey behind bars. Setting up a meth lab on my turf and inside my workshop behind the doublewide was a big time message. Those who exploded my shop won't back off if they take the fall for Mary or the drug bust at the Bone Shrine. That includes them not getting reimbursed for what the Sheriff confiscated."

Rochelle leaned closer to her nephew. "So did they pay for that heroin and you stiffed them after you couldn't deliver, or did they deliver you the heroin and the cops found it before you paid up?"

"Like I said, Aunt Ro. That doesn't concern you. The gang was left high and dry."

Darla tapped her son's shoulder. "But why not fly back and testify against these gangsters?"

Gunnar's eyes grew incredulous. He stared at his mom. "Didn't you hear a word? You, Papa, Aunt Ro, Joey--if he's in or out of prison--will all get hurt or offed if I finger any of them."

Darla's eyes widened. "So your father and I will need to watch over our shoulders constantly?" Her voice trembled.

Rochelle collected herself and spoke calmly. "Allow me, Gunnar. It's not like I haven't been puzzling this together nonstop for the last two months: Mary drowned; she didn't kill herself; Joseph didn't drown her; the cops confiscated that huge stash of heroin that was mysteriously left at the Bone Shrine; somehow--and you know, but won't say--the gang is out $250k; the Sheriff raided your place before dawn on the night Mary drowned; the investigators didn't find any drugs at the doublewide to hang on you; the gang wants reimbursed; they want my son to take the fall for the heroin bust, not to mention for Mary's drowning; you were released from jail and fled the country that same day; everyone of us in your family is endangered, and; you're now a devout Buddhist and living beyond reproach. So, unless you're the one who killed Mary, am I missing anything?"

At the question, Darla's eyes bulged. "Shut up, Rochelle, right this minute!"

Gunnar placed his large hand on his mother's shoulder. "It's okay, Mom. Other than lamely pinning a murder on me, I don't think Aunt Ro has missed much of anything here. The gang wants both a fall guy and repayment."

"Hold on. For just being in the wrong place at the wrong time,

Mary Quinn was drowned. Somehow, my dear nephew, you were an integral part of this big time drug deal. So please don't act as though you haven't the slightest clue who was at the Bone Shrine that night?"

Rochelle watched Gunnar start to talk, collect his thoughts, before finally speaking. "And that's the main reason a drop is used. It keeps the parties from having face-to-face interactions. The dope would be left in the First Aid Kit and, when it's retrieved, the cash is put in its place. Even from here in Sweden, I'd be starting a drug war if I simply named who might have killed Mary."

Rochelle tapped her elbow and pointed to his. "Aren't you already a road warrior for those very drugs? Has that wicked road rash of yours healed?"

Gunnar looked up at the pulpit and ignored her. "Like I said, I'm out of the biz. I know the kingpins back home and they know I know too many of their key players. When I'm over here, they know I'm out of the game. If I keep my mouth shut, that is." Gunnar's voice turned colder. "Enough ugly accusations, Aunt Ro. Joey's lawyer needs to convince the jury that Mary drowned herself. That's the only safe course we have short of him pleading guilty."

"Safe course? What about the truth?" Darla asked her son. "What happened to 'the truth and nothing but the truth, so help me God'?"

Rochelle cut in. "As in Joe *not* pleading guilty to a murder he didn't commit or a drug deal that wasn't his."

Gunnar sat angry and beleaguered when he reached into a zipped up pouch to pull out a manila envelope that he handed to his mother. "This will take care of the money the gang lost." He held a Wanapum County quit claim deed form, sales agreement for $1.00, and legal property description. He explained that he and his mom needed to go to the American Embassy in Stockholm to have it notarized. "I'll also pay to have the remains of my workshop removed. Once any trace of the meth lab is gone, you and Papa must sell the property. The proceeds will pay off the gang and get them out of our lives."

Darla held the packet uneasily and stared up at the tall arches. "Son, by asking us to negotiate with these drug thugs, aren't you inviting more trouble for me and your dad?"

Gunnar placed his hand on his mom's shoulder. "Let Papa negotiate. He knows how to be tough."

Rochelle turned to her sister. "I haven't figured out Gunnar's involvement, and he's hardly been forthcoming. That said, at the very least, he's no longer running away from a quarter million dollars of gang debt." Rochelle leaned back against the wooden pew. "Not sure how this helps Joe, though."

Gunnar leaned closer to her and spoke firmly. "If the jury has reasonable doubt because they believe Mary drowned herself, then Joey's acquitted of murder. And even if he gets a bum rap, he won't have a huge target on his back if behind bars. The money will be settled when my doublewide sells."

"What's the name of this gang that Joe's supposed to take a fall for?" Rochelle asked.

"Once again, you're better off not knowing any more than necessary."

Rochelle stood up abruptly. As much as the cathedral's empty gothic arches were intended to contain something holy, her insides were hollowed out. "I'm done here. I'll see you when you get back to Moses Lake, Darla. I'm flying back today."

"Seriously?" she asked.

"I never would have flown here with you knowing that the only fresh thing we'd get from Gunnar would be his misplaced chanting for Buddha."

Gunnar and Darla didn't need her help to work out the property transfer. She didn't need their help to meet with Joe's lawyer to push the suicide angle. If Angus wouldn't do it, some other attorney would. "After you get home Darla, don't mention one single word about who you think committed the murder that night. Mary drowned herself. Do you understand?"

Darla stared at Gunnar and didn't answer until he lightly nodded. "I really hate every last bit of this," she said, "but, yes, I understand."

Rochelle zipped up her REI parka, slipped the strap of her big purse over a shoulder, and walked beneath the towering gothic arches towards the exit portal. Only when she reached the tall door did she turn and face the pulpit, altar, and crucifix.

"You don't even understand how much you stole, do you Gunnar?" Rochelle's question ushered out full and strong. She didn't scream, although her words could be heard throughout the *Domkyrka*. Darla and Gunnar twisted around in their pew.

"I want Mary and Joseph back!"

She paused. "I want Grace!"

Her voice was resolute. "I want my old life again!"

Rochelle stepped into the brisk, sunny, autumn day and didn't allow herself to look back. Two black dressed ministers approached through the park as though walking across a sea of fallen leaves.

Rochelle turned the other way and, filled with painful thoughts, walked slowly towards the city market. She hailed a taxi to the airport. Joseph would be the one crucified––again.

She needed to see her son. Fairness was an abstraction, as abstract as flying halfway around the globe for a one-hour encounter. She secured no revealing truth from her nephew, only a perilous strategy.

CHAPTER NINETEEN

(Tuesday, November 14th)

Thirteen weeks had elapsed between that horrible night when Mary died and the beginning of the trial. Darla and Rochelle approached the front steps at the time they expected the wide entry doors to open.

Of the dozen-and-a-half media representatives, including two camera crews outside the courthouse, the only one Rochelle knew was Naomi Seufert from The Dalles *Chronicle,* a local reporter and solid contact of hers who covered Chamber news and events. Darla stepped forward and hugged the journalist. The two of them were from the same high school graduating class in The Dalles. Rochelle, two years younger, embraced her more lightly.

"I don't know how you keep so shapely and trim," Naomi told Rochelle.

"It's called the Trial Diet," she replied, "very stressful and never to be recommended."

Naomi told them that she'd be there, off and on, for Joe's case. Rochelle warned her that, with her swirl of emotions, she wouldn't be keen on offering up any quotes for publication. Naomi completely understood.

"Oh, my word! I can't believe she's here." Rochelle's face flushed when she saw Deputy Zach Riggleman approaching the courthouse steps with his petite, Asian wife pushing a baby stroller. "How about a scoop?" she whispered to Naomi.

"I'm all ears." Their reporter friend held pen and pad in hand.

"I stumbled onto the biggest conflict-of-interest," said Darla. "My hairdresser runs the place right by that woman's nail salon. In September, she and her husband were given foster care custody of a mixed race newborn. Apparently, she and her husband have been trying to have a kid for years."

"How is that a scoop?" Naomi asked, a bit confused.

Rochelle pointed discreetly and they watched the deputy lean inside the stroller and kiss the baby before giving his wife a peck on the cheek and double-stepping up the courthouse stairs. Beside the thick column at the top, he pivoted to see his wife still watching him. "Oh, honey, don't forget Jade's one-thirty appointment with the pediatrician."

Rochelle leaned in closer so no other media people could hear. "Oh my Lord! Can you believe they're calling Mary's baby, Jade?"

"Are you saying that they have Mary Quinn's baby in the stroller?" Naomi asked.

"Most definitely," said Darla. "The timing of the foster placement, the photos in the nail salon, and how they were given temporary custody of a half-Asian newborn from right here in the Columbia Basin."

"Not to mention that Linh Riggleman was never pregnant," said Rochelle. She could tell that Naomi's journalist brain was still processing the connections. "If Mary Quinn's baby was placed with the prosecution's key eyewitness in a trial concerning Mary's death, then I'm pretty sure that reasonable people would think it's a colossal conflict-of-interest." Rochelle rummaged inside her oversized purse until she found Amanda Skerry's card. "This woman is the CPS Caseworker for Mary Quinn's baby. Take the card. She can help verify whatever you find."

"Okay. I'm seeing the light," said Naomi, tapping her temple. "Let me do some gentle inquiring with the source. I'll catch up with you ladies a bit later." Darla and Rochelle thanked Naomi and watched her hurry to catch up with Mrs. Riggleman who was disappearing towards the parking lot around the far corner of the courthouse.

Inside––the second morning of the trial––Angus was already seated when the bailiff ushered Joe to the defense team's table. Rochelle took a moment to appreciate the professional appearance of her son with his cropped, sandy hair, and the dress clothes she'd brought him. Today he sported a blue blazer and khaki colored Dockers with a crisp button-up Oxford shirt and broken-in penny loafers, the dressy outfit he wore for things like baseball award ceremonies. There was no necktie since he never wore one, especially the kind he'd have to knot himself, a talent her son had never bothered to learn.

Angus had told her that this was a fast turnaround for launching a case of such magnitude and visibility. The Mary Quinn Murder Trial was Wanapum County's biggest case of the year. The courtroom was nearly full.

Rochelle noticed Joe trying not to stare at the twelve jurors when they filed in. A jury of one's peers. The notion still made Rochelle cringe. Her 18-year-old son wasn't from the area. Only one juror looked to be under thirty, six were women, five were Hispanic, eight were over sixty, and she noticed all of them sneaking peeks at her boy, the accused murderer and big-time, supposed drug distributor. What if Joe's jury consisted of high school seniors from The Dalles, or American Legion baseball players? Would the verdict of his actual peers turn out differently?

"Stop stressing," Darla whispered in her ear. "It won't help."

After Darla returned from Sweden, she never mentioned their cathedral clash and Rochelle did nothing to resist her sister's moral support when Darla offered to join her for the duration of the trial. The peaceful return from Sweden indicated to Rochelle that her sister was onboard with the suicide strategy even though they avoided the subject. Angus, without any shred of evidence pointing to any other viable suspects, decided to go along with his clients' wishes, especially when Rochelle and Joe, separately, insisted that Mary was suicidal and had drowned herself that night. During a visit at the jail, Joe and

Rochelle discussed with one another how it would hardly matter to Mary how she died, especially if it kept Joe and his family safe.

Gunnar kept his word and signed over his property to his parents. Nils and Darla wasted no time contracting a specialized contractor to dispose of their son's shop with its meth lab remains. The removal wouldn't come cheap due to Department of Health mandates. They asked their Realtor to plan on listing the doublewide at the turn of the year.

Superior Court Judge Thomas G. Kantadillo, a huge man with shock white hair and ruddy cheeks, seemed fair, but day one had only featured the prosecution questioning its key witness, with the defense cross-examination set for this morning. Kantadillo lowered his black-rimmed glasses. "Please be seated." His tone showed that he knew how to take control of his court when needed.

The modest courtroom featured blond hardwood throughout. The benches were like the hard pews in the Swedish cathedral. The presiding judge in his black robe reminded her of the bulky, Irish priest from her parish in The Dalles.

Angus MacIntosh wore nothing eccentric and looked dashing in his natty tweed suit with a blue dress shirt. Most surprising to her was the professional manner in which he'd been carrying himself in front of judge and jury. She even liked the way he whispered to her son. Rochelle couldn't hear a word, but she could see he was treating Joe like an adult, listening to what her smart, but not always wise, son had to say.

Late the week before, Rochelle monitored the jury selection. "Do you have family members with substance abuse disorders?" Angus would ask this same question to each potential juror, clearly wanting to acknowledge rather than avoid Joe's addiction to heroin. The issue needed to be framed in a way that wouldn't help the prosecution paint him as some depraved, drug dealing junkie capable of such a murder.

The chosen jurors, those with her son's adult life in their collective hands, seemed more self-conscious than overconfident. Rochelle could only hope that they would discharge their duty conscientiously. During the jury selection, Angus made the twelve selected jurors feel as though they had the honor, rather than the hassle, of deciding this important case.

Deputy Zachary Riggleman, arrow-tall and lean, sat in the witness box after being reminded of the oath he took the day before when the prosecution laid out its case. Pushing thirty, he was the closest the prosecution had to an eyewitness, not quite a rookie, not yet a veteran officer. Undoubtedly, he'd testified in court many times, and showed no nerves when he waited to be cross-examined.

Joe's lawyer lifted a pristine attaché case to the defense team's table that looked brand new. When Angus reached out to open it, Rochelle, seated a few rows back, worried. Not a single scuff. What if Joe's attorney couldn't remember the seldom tested combination? She smiled at the thought of Angus, in front of the new jury, pulling out a crowbar to pry open his expensive briefcase.

When the latches popped up, Angus pulled out a tidy folder full of typed notes and bullet points. Rochelle struggled to reconcile a quirky man, so proud of his *Zippy-the-Pinhead* bucket, to this formal attorney-at-law seated two rows away from her. Angus combed his salt-and-pepper hair with a stylish part along one side and greeted the deputy politely after glancing at the first bulleted question written on his legal pad.

"Deputy Riggleman, when you first saw Joe Gardner filling up a gallon gas can just after midnight in the first hour of August 18th, 2000, did you immediately offer him a ride?

"No sir. I first asked him where his car was. When I realized he had a few miles to backtrack, I told him I might be able to give him a ride, but I'd need to first see his identification. I secured permission over the radio from the desk sergeant before transporting him."

"So, in your assessment, this young man seemed to genuinely need a ride."

"Yes, sir."

"When Mr. Gardner pulled out his driver's license, did he drop a piece of paper on the ground."

"Yes, sir. I picked it up for him. It had a phone number and name on it."

"Did you tell the defendant that the name sounded familiar?" "That's correct. He said it was his Moses Lake cousin."

"Was the name, Gunnar Larsson?"

"Yes, sir. That was the name."

"Are you aware that on the night in question, your colleagues with the Wanapum County Sheriff raided Mr. Larsson's home prior to dawn and he was temporarily jailed the next morning?"

"I wasn't apprised of the raid until I came back on duty, late the next afternoon."

"Was Gunnar Larsson ever a person-of-interest in this case?"

"No, sir. In my initial report that night, I noted that the defendant said he was planning to meet his cousin. Due to the large stash of heroin covered with the defendant's prints, along with ongoing local suspicions of him interacting with known drug dealers, a search warrant was secured for Gunnar Larsson's home. I was informed that there was no evidence of any illegal drugs on Larsson's property to hold him in this case."

"Deputy, do you know of any crime lab able to test evidence and return the results to sheriff investigators within five hours?"

"That's not my area of expertise, sir."

Angus stood studying his notes when Rochelle noticed her sister turning red. Rochelle figured that the investigators showed up at his house about the time he'd been planning to head out to the Bone Shrine to either pick up the dope or collect the money owed. How else would a search warrant have been issued by a sitting judge that same night if the investigators didn't give a compelling reason to suggest that Gunnar was a key player in the China White transaction?

The possibility had entered her mind that Joe, busted the year before for heroin, might have been trying to deliver the China White to Gunnar from some big time, Portland connection. But, if so, why would he have needed a drop like the Bone Shrine? If he and his cousin had been on two opposite sides of the deal, they would have met in person. The cousins were tight. After what she learned about Joe taking the fall for Gunnar the year before, the two definitely trusted one another enough to deal face-to-face.

What a mess. With all the fingerprints on the plastic bundles of heroin, she didn't see how Joe could free himself from the distribution charge without Gunnar's sworn testimony. But as Gunnar pointedly showed, in order for that to happen her nephew would need to incriminate himself and also finger other key players in the biz. The consequences circling over and over in Rochelle's head kept leading her back to Mary's supposed suicide and Joe simply stumbling on the stash. Of the two, and the truth be damned, she believed the suicide would be an easier sell to this jury.

Angus continued. "When you drove Joe Gardner to the seep pond, did he tell you there was a girlfriend and newborn baby waiting for him back at the stranded car?"

"No sir, at least not at first. He was sweating and scratching suspiciously like the junkies I've arrested before, but he didn't bother to tell me about a newborn until I turned off the freeway frontage road towards the pothole pond."

"Didn't my client tell you he'd been running to get gasoline and that this was why he was sweating?"

"Yes, sir, but he was still sweating and scratching long after he stopped for the gas and we were driving back."

Angus jotted something on his sheet of notes. "Deputy Riggleman, yesterday you testified that you had been disappointed in Joe Gardner for going to get gasoline instead of staying with his girlfriend and the baby. Please tell the court what you did immediately upon learning that there was a newborn at the destination you were headed to."

"I called dispatch to send an EMT unit to the scene."

"You are calling it 'a scene,' but for clarification did you believe you were going to a crime scene?"

"No. Not at that point in time. I only knew there was a newborn and mother to be attended to on a remote road."

Angus stepped close to the witness and faced the jury box. He spoke softer. "So from your testimony you're saying that it was professionally appropriate for you to seek medical help for a new mother and child, but you were critical of Joe Gardner for doing the same when he went to get gas in order to take his girlfriend and baby to the hospital. How do you explain this discrepancy, Deputy Riggleman? Weren't the mother and baby the exact same people in the exact same circumstance needing help? Why did you deem this proper for you to do, yet improper for Joe Gardner?"

Rochelle leaned in and whispered in her sister's ear. "Because the hypocrite already had it out for Joe."

Riggleman squirmed, but after a deep breath spoke calmly. "Assuming a healthy birth, then I could not imagine if that were me, that I'd leave my wife and baby alone. I would have waited until morning."

"So, you don't view your words and actions as hypocritical here?" Darla elbowed Rochelle. "Great minds, you and Angus."

Deputy Riggleman glanced towards the county's criminal prosecutor and then back at Angus.

"Objection, your Honor," said Judith Rose, seemingly because of the deputy's prompt. The county's chief criminal prosecutor stood and faced Judge Kantadillo. "Deputy Riggleman may have told the defendant what he might have done, hypothetically, if his wife had given unexpected birth. However, this has no bearing on an officer-of-the-law calling for medical back up after the defendant had abandoned his girlfriend and her newborn."

To Rochelle's eyes, the lady lawyer wore too much make up and carried herself like a stiff. Even her words were labored.

"Where are you going with this, Counselor?" Judge Kantadillo asked Angus.

Rochelle watched as Angus stayed standing tall. Smoothly pacing his words, he told the judge that the prosecution's eyewitness had developed a prejudicial opinion towards his client even before they arrived at the site of this unfortunate drowning.

"Your Honor, this hypocrisy was step one of showing the deputy's premature bias toward my client." Angus, then turned towards Judith Rose. "And, for the record, even the prosecuting attorney is attempting to establish bias against my client by stating that, quote unquote, he 'abandoned' Mary Quinn and her baby. Your Honor, the opposite is true. Joe Gardner was running through the night with an empty gas can so he could return and help drive his girlfriend and the newborn to the hospital."

"The prosecution's objection is overruled," said the judge, "and I will ask the prosecution to be more careful in its characterization of the defendant. There has been no evidence presented of any 'abandonment.'"

"Yes. My apologies, your Honor," said Judith Rose.

Rochelle noticed the muscles on the prosecutor's cheeks tensing. The woman didn't appreciate the reprimand.

Angus half-sat and half-leaned on the railing in front of the prosecution and defense tables. His voice was calm. "Deputy Riggleman, when you arrived at the birthing scene to find afterbirth blood in the couple's vehicle, Mary Quinn and her baby were nowhere in sight. You immediately arrested and restrained Mr. Gardner, did you not?"

"Yes, sir."

"Had you witnessed any crime at that point of time?"

"No."

"But as soon as you pulled up, you pointed your gun in Mr. Gardner's face and cuffed his ankles and wrists. As you stated, it was not yet a crime scene. Why did you view this young man as such an immediate threat?"

"From all the blood in the car and his girlfriend and baby missing, I felt more secure by having the defendant cuffed."

"You just mentioned that 'all the blood in the car' was part of what impelled you to pull your service pistol and aim it at my client's face. Mr. Gardner had already told you to expect a childbirth. What made you suspect that blood in the back of the only logical place out there to give birth was anything other than from a woman having a baby?"

"Because the woman and her baby were not there. I was the only officer on the scene and needed to investigate immediately to find them."

"You say you wanted to investigate immediately. How many precious minutes did you spend forcibly restraining Mr. Gardner when Mary Quinn was face down in the water a few feet away?"

"Objection, your Honor," said Judith Rose. "From Deputy Riggleman's testimony, it is clear that the officer had no idea, at this point, where the woman's body was, and it is highly speculative for the defense to state that she was still alive and not already dead."

"Objection sustained." The judge didn't seem too bothered by Angus's potential embellishment of Mary's state at the moment of arrest.

"I'll rephrase my question, your Honor. Deputy Riggleman, how long did you spend restraining Mr. Gardner? More than five minutes? More than ten minutes?"

Riggleman paused before answering. "My adrenaline was pumping, so time slows down. I don't believe it was any more than five minutes, maybe only two or three. I wasn't timing myself."

Angus nodded slowly. "Have you read the coroner's report?" he asked.

"No, sir."

"Your Honor, I would like to submit as an exhibit for this trial the Wanapum County Coroner's report for Mary Quinn. It states that the time of death was indeterminate. Accordingly, there is no evidence to indicate that Mary Quinn was deceased at the time my client was being forcibly restrained."

"Objection, your Honor," said Judith Rose. "There is also no indication that Mary Quinn was not dead at the time the defendant left the mother and baby to go get gasoline."

"The defense's request to submit this portion of the coroner's report as 'Exhibit D' is allowed," said the judge, "and the court reporter shall duly note that the official estimation of the young woman's death is indeterminate relative to what the prosecution has established as the timeframe for the drowning in this case."

When Angus glanced towards the jury, Rochelle did as well. She noticed three jurors rock forward in anticipation of the next question. "Deputy Riggleman, can you tell the court once again why you chose to spend precious time next to this pond by restraining Mr. Gardner instead of having him unencumbered to help you find his missing girlfriend and her baby?"

Riggleman seemed unfazed. "At that moment in time, I had discovered blood in the back of the SUV. There had been a birth and possibly something worse, but mother and baby were missing. This alarmed me. Again, I was alone at the scene and needed to investigate immediately without the defendant interfering."

"Had Mr. Gardner in any way threatened you physically or verbally?"

"No. Sir."

"Was Mr. Gardner struggling or yelling?"

"He kept shouting 'Mary, Mary!' so I didn't want him getting in the way of my initial investigation."

"You say Mr. Gardner kept repeating, 'Mary, Mary!' I can't imagine anyone in this courtroom not understanding why my client would be calling out for Mary Quinn, his long-time girlfriend. Why would that in any way alarm you, Deputy? Did you rule out the chance that Mary

Quinn might answer her boyfriend from somewhere nearby in the dark?"

"I was alarmed that his girlfriend was not at the car. I'm trained to take reasonable precautions, so I made an investigative arrest of Mr. Gardner. I wasn't ruling anything in or out at that juncture."

"So, is it correct to say that you took precious time and used excessive force in a way that hindered Joe Gardner from helping you find Mary Quinn?"

"Objection, your Honor." Judith Rose jumped from her chair and furrowed her brow. "The defense is badgering the witness who has already explained the rationale for his actions. Deputy Riggleman has described, in full, the professional steps he took as an officer arriving at this scene.

"Sustained. The jury will please disregard the question and the court reporter will please strike it from the court transcript. Counselor, you've already established the deputy's less-than-gentle restraint of the defendant. Please refrain from repetitive questions."

"Yes, your Honor."

Rochelle was impressed with Angus's composure. He wasn't rattled when he pressed forward with his next question. "Deputy Riggleman, you testified earlier that Mr. Gardner told you to expect a mother and newborn when you arrived at the scene. Why do you now suggest you thought Mr. Gardner would 'interfere' in helping you find the missing mother and child he told you to expect?"

"It wasn't that he wasn't pretending to help. It was Mr. Gardner's nervousness. I worried he might do something unexpected. I've been trained to mitigate the uncertainties that might arise in situations of this sort. This is why I placed the defendant under investigative arrest and restrained him."

"Deputy Riggleman, your own police report states that Mr. Gardner was the one who first saw Mary Quinn in the pothole pond. You also stated that Mr. Gardner, not you, was the one who heard the infant crying in the cattails of that marsh. Did my client call out to you the moment he saw Mary Quinn's body face down in the pond?"

"Yes he did."

"Despite being cuffed, Mr. Gardner helped you find his girlfriend. As a professional police officer, how can you possibly suggest that Mr.

Gardner was simply, to use your word, 'pretending' to help you? To the extent that you allowed my client to assist you, he was overtly helping you save her, was he not?"

Riggleman, for the first time, showed nerves by hesitating to respond. Rochelle almost leaned over to point this out to Darla, but didn't want to miss the cop's response.

"He helped, but his frantic vibe and sweating suggested that he might be hiding something significant."

"Mr. Gardner has been charged, among other things, with placing a newborn baby on an air mattress and pushing her into the reeds of this pothole marsh. Deputy, did this young man in any way interfere with your efforts to find the newborn? Specifically, did he misdirect you when you trudged through the muddy pond?"

"No, sir."

"For the record, Mr. Gardner was fully restrained and would not have been able to dive in and help rescue either Mary Quinn or the baby, is that not accurate?"

"Yes. That would be accurate."

With this question, Rochelle turned to study the reaction of the jury. She expected one or two might nod ever-so-slightly when Angus mentioned Joe's helpfulness, cuffed as he was. None of them so much as blinked. It wasn't that they seemed bored. The jurors were simply a hard bunch to read. Their stony expressions didn't encourage or discourage Rochelle, but made her nervous. At least Angus seemed to be, gradually, turning up the heat on the witness.

"Deputy, at what point in this initial part of your investigation did you become suspicious of Mr. Gardner being the one to drown Mary Quinn?"

Rochelle liked the timing and forcefulness of the question, especially how Riggleman leaned back and paused before responding.

"Not during the actual rescue attempts. At that time, I was too focused on trying to save the woman and child." His voice broke up enough to make him take a long drink of water. "She's the victim based on the evidence. During the rescue attempt, I saw her as a motionless, young woman."

"So Deputy Riggleman, speaking of the evidence, did you, or anyone on the investigation team ever consider that Mary Quinn was not a murder victim, but drowned herself after placing her newborn on a raft to protect the baby from predators?"

"No. I have a hard time imagining any woman killing herself after she's been blessed with a baby, not with what...."

"Not with what, what? Please finish your sentence, sir."

"Nothing. It's personal."

"Did you not share with Mr. Gardner on the night in question that you and your wife have been unable to have children?"

Judith Rose got up from her prosecutor's table. "Objection, your Honor. The Deputy's personal circumstances on such a private matter are in no way relevant to this case."

The judge lowered his glasses and crossed his arms when he answered the prosecutor directly. "Overruled. Had the witness not shared this highly personal information while on the job and transporting the defendant, then I would agree with you, Prosecutor. Counsel may continue."

"Deputy Riggleman, you've stated more than once that Mr. Gardner's behavior made you suspicious. Was there anything about his helpfulness in finding the mother and baby that added to your suspicions?"

"Yes, sir. He found the mother and child too easily."

"But if he was pretending and already knew she was drowned, why wouldn't it make just as much sense for Joe Gardner to distract and delay rather than frantically help you find the mother and child?"

"Not if he wanted to appear helpful as part of his cover-up."

"But officer, are you trained to tell the difference between 'actual' helpfulness and what you are trying to call 'pretend' helpfulness?"

"Not trained for that specifically, sir, but as a patrol deputy, I am trained to recognize the likelihood that criminals are lying to me."

"So, are you suggesting that this teen was being less than forthright just because he wanted to help you locate his girlfriend and her newborn?"

"I was simply answering your question about my training, sir."

"Deputy Riggleman, in your police report you state that, before arriving at the scene, you were told by Mr. Gardner that he wasn't the father of his girlfriend's baby. Is this true?"

"Yes, sir. And that comment of his factored into my decision to restrain the defendant prior to investigating the scene."

Angus glanced at Joe and then at the jurors. "Deputy Riggleman, is there any way you can construe that Mr. Gardner was not helpful in finding the mother and child?"

"No, sir."

"So, the facts as you have presented them are that Joe Gardner directed you to the pond where you expected to find his girlfriend and her newborn both alive. Secondly, my client first noticed Mary Quinn's floating body in the most open part of the pond directly next to the road and you were unable to resuscitate her. Third," and Angus gestured toward the eyewitness. "Joe Gardner had told you on the drive to the pond that he was not the biological father of the baby, but he, and not you, first heard the crying. The defendant directed you towards another man's newborn on an air mattress farther out in the marsh. Fourth, you stated that the defendant acted 'frantic' during the attempted rescue. Is that an accurate summary of your testimony?"

"Yes, but--"

Angus cut him off. "Again, I ask you. Other than being in cuffs, frantic, and beside himself to help you rescue Mary and baby, is there anything Joe Gardner did to hinder you from rescuing them?"

Riggleman sat tall, flared his nostrils, and seemed to address Judith Rose when he answered. "Not that I can think of, but his *acting* skills were impressive."

Angus turned away from the deputy, leaned over the rail, and slapped his folder on the table near Joe who, completely startled, jerked back. The lawyer pivoted to face the judge. "Your Honor, the defense moves for a mistrial. This last comment, this brazen opinion by the prosecution's key witness, ascribes a personal motive to my client."

Angus paused only for a breath.

"This young man didn't abandon his girlfriend or the baby, and Mr. Gardner most assuredly wasn't *acting* when he did everything that he was allowed to do to save the two."

Rochelle could see her son's eyes widen. Joe couldn't have been expecting this onslaught of accusations by his attorney towards this cop who possibly--no probably--had it in for her son.

"My client, from the deputy's own report, first heard the infant's cries. This is what allowed him to pinpoint the location of the raft. His response is hardly the *act* of someone who already knew where the baby would be. Deputy Riggleman's premature bias towards Joe Gardner is appalling. The defense is not convinced that the officer's unwarranted delay by cuffing my client didn't cause Mary Quinn to drown."

The judge leaned forward. "Are you through, Counselor?"

"Please bear with me, your Honor. The prosecution's entire case rests on forcing all evidence into the assertion that Mr. Gardner was behaving like an actor at the time of the rescues. This wasn't a theater performance for my client. When he and the deputy arrived at the pothole, this young man simply wanted to save Mary and Grace Quinn, not play a sick game of dramatic cover-up as the opinionated Deputy Riggleman coldly suggests."

Rochelle couldn't read the reactions from jurors or judge.

"Your Honor. This sworn officer of the law has just slandered Joe Gardner and created an unsubstantiated bias in the mind of our honorable jury. This case has been irreparably prejudiced. Again, the defense moves for a mistrial."

Rochelle didn't know if the judge was going to pull both attorneys into his chambers, but Judge Kantadillo didn't hesitate with his response.

"Motion for mistrial is denied. The witness, as an officer sworn to uphold the law, shall be reminded to answer the questions before him without inserting his personal opinion as to what the defendant may or may not have been thinking, or what the officer believes the accused was intending at the time of this incident. Deputy Riggleman, you will not be warned again."

"Yes, your Honor. I understand," the officer said, pursing his lips.

"The defense may resume its cross-examination."

"No more questions, your Honor." Angus was still steaming when he turned and sat next to Joe.

CHAPTER TWENTY

(Thursday, November 16th)

The November grass in front of the courthouse, normally a dormant brown, looked worn and white. There was no snow, just frosty ground hardened from an arctic front blasting through the Columbia Basin. Darla insisted they stay off the icy concrete sidewalks. Rochelle took her advice, but nearly slipped on the frozen lawn. She managed to regain her balance and, after shuddering, hurried up the salted steps. A security guard waited just inside and quickly opened only one of the big matching courthouse doors before shutting it just as fast to keep the arctic blast from deep-freezing its way inside.

The mix of curious locals and media waited in the courtroom, but she and Darla found side-by-side seats behind the defense team's table and next to Mary's friend Biff, her mop of hair still dyed black. Darla wedged the winter coats and scarfs between her and Rochelle. When Joe peeked back, she blew her son a kiss. Biff's mother sat on the other side of the teen since she was being called to testify later in the day.

Rochelle introduced Darla to Biff and Jill McCoy, but her sister insisted they'd already met in The Dalles, more than once, in fact. "You're the museum director in The Dalles, aren't you?" Darla asked Jill, as though just to be certain.

She nodded with a smile.

"Mom loved both Mary and Joe when we all worked at the museum," Biff told them with a smile. "Did I tell you, Mrs. Gardner? The attorney we hired in The Dalles heard back from Wanapum Family Court. He was told that they won't be awarding permanent custody for Grace Rochelle Quinn prior to the turn of the year, unless, of course, the biological father is found. The only problem with the lawyer I hired is that I shouldn't have told him how much was donated. He tried to tell me he was giving me a special rate and then found a way to snag every last buck that was given to benefit Mary's baby."

The barrage of words had Rochelle wondering if she should nod to Biff or shake her head. "Mary naming the baby Grace Rochelle means the world to me," she told the teen and her mom, but talking with Biff sometimes rattled her brain. Rochelle's simple response made Biff tear up. The manic teen had mood swings like a chameleon changing colors in a tie-dye terrarium.

"I'm still waiting for word on the DNA test," Biff whispered while the press and curious locals finished filling the courtroom. "It's been over two weeks since they got my sample, but the custody attorney with Wanapum County won't say if there's a match, except directly to the matching person."

She reached into her day pack and pulled out a Manila folder. "I haven't had a chance to show you this." Biff spoke in a calmer tone. She held a document, the kind Rochelle had been reading too many of lately. "This is what all those donations from Mary's vigil paid for."

Rochelle scanned the document. Wasco County Family Court was asking its Wanapum County counterpart for justification of jurisdiction by citing the existing ties the baby had in the Oregon county. It described the outpouring of community support for the baby that was demonstrated by the memorial for the mother. Most importantly, the legal paper requested more time to locate the baby's biological father.

"That's great, Biff! Thanks, dear! We'll think of this as a temporary delay tactic, until paternity day comes."

"A lot of lawyer fees just to buy us time, but if it helps save Grace from getting swallowed by the foster care system."

Biff's mother, a character witness for Joe, stayed quiet, in stark contrast to her daughter. Biff shook her mass of Goth-thick hair and rubbed her upper arms to break the chill. "And just so you know, I'm chanting for Kuma to step up."

"I've come to the same conclusion. Kuma needs to gain custody," Rochelle said. "For Grace's sake, that is. Kuma's the best chance we have for that baby to stay in our lives." Rochelle hoped her morning coffee would kick in as a catalyst for another trying day.

Warm-blooded Darla, in only a long-sleeved blouse, leaned across Rochelle's lap and whispered to Biff. "And don't think my stubborn sister gave up easily on the idea of securing full custody for herself."

"Mary was definitely hoping it would be Joe's baby," said Biff, "and she talked about raising their child with good help from Grandma Ro here."

"But what if Kuma's not the father?" Darla whispered.

"I know you're Catholic, Mrs. Larsson," said Biff, "but there was no immaculate conception. Mary and I shared our secrets, and for this one, she forced me to make a vow of secrecy which I've kept. She told me the father was either Joe or Kuma. Let me tell you, it wasn't easy to keep my lips shut on that one––even for a girl of few words like me."

When Biff winked, Rochelle startled herself by chuckling.

Rochelle wore her bluest pair of Lady's Wrangler jeans with a snap-up Wrangler shirt for cowgirls, the outfit she saved for the Fort Dalles Rodeo every July. She was no cowgirl, but had on calf-high, suede boots. There would be no need for her Stetson hat inside the Wanapum County Courthouse, even though eastern Washington was horse and cattle country every bit as much as eastern Oregon. Rochelle had pinned her burgundy hair up high to accent her long neck.

Angus wore the darkest tweed blazer she'd seen on him. It comple-mented the attorney's fresh, dapper haircut. She caught the shy lawyer stealing a peek at her.

Joe's eyes couldn't hide their fatigue within a steely, unchanging stare. Rochelle could see how the jail time and trial were taking a toll on him. His stony expression was mirrored by blank-faced jurors, and today was no different when the bailiff ushered the twelve into the courthouse. They all seemed to sneak a peek at her son while seating themselves.

After Judge Kantadillo entered from his chambers, the bailiff instructed all to rise. After a hearty "Welcome to the North Pole," the judge asked those in his courtroom to please be seated.

Strands of Rochelle's hair set loose by the icy November wind were tickling the nape of her neck. She reached back and adjusted the barrette to batten her burgundy locks to the top of her head again. The first witness was called to testify. Knowing who it was, Rochelle forced herself not to turn around, but once the woman walked up and took her oath, she was surprised to see how nervous Bonnie Quinn seemed, something that never showed when she rocked out onstage.

"Mary was pretty wigged out when her mom abandoned her last spring," Biff leaned across Rochelle and whispered. "And to think it was with Joe's dad."

"Let's not talk about J.J.," said Rochelle, a bit too loudly.

"The gallery members are asked to remain quiet during the course of this trial." Judge Kantadillo sonorous voice filled the rural court-room. When Rochelle looked up, she could see him leveling a steady gaze at Biff, Darla, and most piercingly, at her.

Joe turned and glared. Rochelle could see Bonnie standing beside the witness stand, ready to take her oath. After the judge's warning, she smirked and left the expression in place. Rochelle felt a new wave of loathing welling up towards home-wrecker Bonnie.

With Mary's mother as a witness for the prosecution, Rochelle initially wondered if Bonnie thought Joe had murdered Mary. Yet, if that were the case, then by the end of August, Bonnie would have spilled her outrage to the press. Rochelle had never heard anything about Joe and Bonnie not getting along. She figured the prosecution was using Bonnie to fish for Joe's never seen murderous side.

Judith Rose, the criminal prosecuting attorney, spoke more softly to Bonnie than she had to Deputy Zach Riggleman, the Wanapum County Coroner, or the Deputy's father, Detective Roger Riggleman. Mary's mother, for some reason, was the prosecution's last witness. After asking Bonnie to establish, for the record, her relationship to

Mary Quinn and the defendant, the prosecutor asked how long Mary and Joe had been girlfriend and boyfriend.

She answered with her bluesy, smoker's rasp. "Since they were fifteen-years-old. The two of them met when we moved into the same neighborhood. Mary was in third grade, then." Bonnie's low, scratchy talking voice was hard to decipher, but she didn't suffer for volume when belting out the Blues.

Bonnie did her best to smile, but bloodshot eyes displayed the grogginess of someone with a hangover—a partier whose motor started purring at 9:30 at night, not 9:30 in the morning. To think that Mary never drank so much as a sip of beer or wine. The girl said it was because she never wanted to turn out like her alcoholic mother. But then, the sober girl dies in the crossfire of a different drug problem.

"Did you approve of the relationship?" asked the prosecutor who showed all the personal warmth of one whose idea of tight human engagement was a cool nod from far across a frozen courtyard, like the one outside.

"I approved until last fall when I found out Joe was arrested for having a half-key of heroin in his car."

The irrelevant sidetrack woke Rochelle up faster than the double espresso she'd swigged for breakfast.

"Did this juvenile prosecution occur in The Dalles, Oregon?" Judith Rose asked.

"Objection." Angus smoothed his John Lennon tie and buttoned his tweed blazer while standing up. "Relevance," your Honor. My client's fully adjudicated case as a minor has no bearing on this trial."

Judge Kantadillo stared over the tops of his glasses at Judith Rose. "Objection sustained. Please confine your questioning of this witness to her knowledge as relates to the charges in this case and the defendant's relationship to the deceased."

Judith Rose pursed her lips and rattled her notes, probably not realizing how defensive she seemed. "Yes, your Honor. Ms. Quinn, did your daughter break up with Joe Gardner when he was sent to juvenile detention a year ago?"

"Yes, but I didn't notice her dating anyone else during the three months Joe was sent away."

"Ms. Quinn, are you aware that your daughter's baby, your grandchild, does not belong to Joe Gardner?"

Bonnie sat up straighter and grew more alert with each question like she was stepping out of a dismal cave and still wincing in the bright morning sunshine. "Yes, but since the new baby is my granddaughter, I expect to be given custody."

At this Rochelle had the urge to slap the woman. How dare Bonnie use this trial to bring up––.

Angus immediately objected. "Relevance, Your Honor. Any custody questions regarding the infant, Grace Rochelle Quinn, do not pertain to this trial."

Darla elbowed Rochelle, and the two sisters looked wide-eyed at one another. Angus had used Mary's chosen name for the child and all but thrown 'Rochelle' in Bonnie Quinn's face.

Joe, who rarely turned around during the trial, glanced over his shoulder and winked at his mother. Rochelle loved the little gesture from him.

"Objection sustained," said the judge before turning to Bonnie. "The court asks the witness to confine her answers to the question being asked."

"I'm sorry, your Honor. It's just––"

"Ms. Quinn, did you ever see your daughter and Joe Gardner fighting?" Judith Rose asked, as though the interruption was intended to stop her witness from aggravating the judge with more off-track ramblings.

"Yes. Joe and Mary both had tempers that would flare now and then. And, I guess like most teen couples, the two would argue over the dumbest things sometimes, but I never thought he would hurt Mary in any way. It must have been the heroin."

Angus had barely sat down from his previous objection before he objected again. "Your Honor, the witness is speculating."

"Sustained," said Judge Kantadillo, his voice firmer and deeper. "And again, the court asks the witness to answer the question being asked. The court reporter will strike the witness's response, and the jurors are asked to disregard the opinion."

"Yes, your Honor," said Bonnie again, "It's just––"

"Ms. Quinn," the prosecutor interrupted, sounding more nervous than the last time. "Did your daughter mention to you that Joe had relapsed on heroin a few months ago?"

"No. I was out on tour last spring and summer and didn't have a chance to discuss anything with her."

The answer, revealing that this wannabe grandma hadn't communicated whatsoever with her own pregnant teen, seemed to catch Judith Rose by surprise. When the prosecuting attorney fumbled through her notes for a follow-up question, Rochelle nudged her sister in the elbow and got up to stretch. Bonnie seemed to stare past the lawyers and Joe, but definitely settled her eyes on Rochelle.

Rochelle had unsnapped her Lady Wrangler shirt and set it on the pile of outerwear. She kept her pose long enough to keep Bonnie's attention. The woman's jaw dropped when she read the pink t-shirt. *Bonnie Quinn & the Igloos* formed an arc of letters with black flourishes over the silver-sequined ice-hut beneath.

Bonnie may have reacted with a florid, Irish show of embarrassment, but Joe grabbed the wooden armrests on his chair and whipped his head around. Upon seeing his mom, he turned his palms up and glared, definitely wanting to know what in the hell his mother thought she was doing. Several jurors were also watching her, but with Joe's back towards them, they probably couldn't see her son's dim view of the interruption.

Darla tugged sharply on the *Igloos* t-shirt. "Try to be dignified," she whispered.

Rochelle, stunned at the unexpected reactions, stayed standing.

"Wow, you're really icing Ms. Quinn," said Biff, staring up from the other side of Rochelle.

"Quiet, Elizabeth!" Jill McCoy said sharply and placed a finger to her lips.

Biff winced, but did as told after the sound of her rarely used birth name.

Rochelle's eyes were frozen on the witness stand. Unfortunately, Judge Kantadillo lifted his gavel. In one quick, seemingly innocent motion, Rochelle remembered her legs and used them to melt into the bench with elbows crossed. For some reason, the Judge stopped himself from demanding 'order in his court,' or worse, kicking her out of the gallery.

Rochelle felt goose bumps on her arms and not from the arctic weather. In one fell swoop, she'd upset her son and aggravated the judge. What was she thinking? She'd let her disdain for Bonnie Quinn justify this stupid prank. In her embarrassment, Rochelle slipped into her cowgirl's shirt, snapped it all the way up, and then added her REI parka. Too bad the layering didn't hide her from every eye in the courtroom.

Time to kill the drama queen lurking inside, Rochelle told herself. Even Biff's mom wouldn't look at her. What had happened to her own sense of decorum? She zipped her parka to the collar. Reminder to self: This is Joe's trial. This is Joe's trial. This is Joe's trial. She almost leaned over to apologize to her sister, but couldn't bring herself to go that far.

A dour Judith Rose shuffled through her notes until she'd either found the question she needed, or didn't want to prolong the time Mary's mom would spend on the stand. She seemed to be eliminating much of what she'd planned to ask. "Ms. Quinn, are you aware that Mr. Gardner was suffering from heroin withdrawal on the night your daughter died?"

"Yes. I heard that."

"Objection, your Honor." Angus's tone was growing more irritated with every interruption of Bonnie Quinn, but nothing like the ire he had directed towards Deputy Riggleman. "Once again, this witness is being encouraged by the prosecution to give hearsay testimony without direct knowledge of the facts. The witness just testified that she hadn't spoken to her daughter in months."

"Sustained. The prosecution shall refrain from leading the witness to give hearsay testimony." The judge, once again asked the jury to disregard, and told the court reporter to strike the comment, even though this process had Rochelle wondering if there was some sort of intent behind the line of questioning by the prosecution.

"My apologies, your Honor." Judith Rose sounded as sincere as a soap opera star caught in the act of adultery. "The prosecution has no more questions from this witness."

"I hate how Joe's personal drug crap keeps getting highlighted," Darla whispered.

"I was thinking the same thing," said Rochelle. "Seems like every time the judge draws attention to comments like this by telling the jury to ignore them, then the jury members will remember what was said even more."

Darla leaned in. "But will it get in the way of the jurors determining what really happened on the night of Mary's death?"

"It's a sleazy legal tactic," said Biff.

The whole drowning and all had the teen put off entering college until next year sometime, but she really did have the quick mind and doggedness of a future lawyer, thought Rochelle, but motioned for both Darla and Biff to stay quiet when Angus stepped next to the witness stand.

"Good morning, Ms. Quinn. When was the last month that you saw your daughter?"

"Last April." Bonnie muttered her words in an even more gravelly voice, as though she disdained the thought of being cross-examined.

"So for the months of May, June, July and half of August you did not see or speak to your daughter. Is that correct?"

"I was on tour with my band then, so we didn't talk."

"Ms. Quinn, today you listed your address as a room at a Moses Lake motel. When you were subpoenaed by the prosecution to testify in this trial, your street address was in Ferndale, Washington. Is that the same address where Joe Gardner's father now resides?"

"Yes. J.J. Gardner let me use his address when I was out on tour." Her expression towards Angus further soured.

"Ms. Quinn, did you have a romantic relationship with the father of the defendant?"

"Objection, your Honor," said Judith Rose. "The romantic life of the prosecution's witness is not relevant to this case."

"Sustained."

"My apologies, your Honor." Angus didn't sound the least bit apologetic, but more like he was engaged in the prosecutor's same witness-leading game by hoping that Bonnie's less than sterling character would stick in the jury's collective mind more than Joe's juvie and addiction issues that were being so "accidentally" highlighted.

"Ms. Quinn, did you attend Mary Quinn's high school graduation when she spoke as her class salutatorian?"

Rochelle looked to Judith Rose and expected an objection, but the prosecutor glanced down at her watch like more objections by her would only delay getting Bonnie off the stand.

"No, sir. Like I said, I was on tour."

Bonnie's guardedness boiled up through terse responses.

"Did you ever speak by telephone to your daughter this summer?"

"No."

"Ms. Quinn, who gave you the horrible news that your daughter had drowned?"

"J.J. Gardner."

"For the record, J.J. Gardner is the defendant's father, is he not?"

"Yes."

"Where were you when you heard the horrible news about Mary Quinn's drowning?"

"I was finishing a show at the LummiLand Casino," she said, glaring at Angus.

"This casino is just outside Ferndale, Washington, north of Bellingham, is it not?"

"Yes." Bonnie squirmed visibly.

"Who told J.J. Gardner about your daughter's death?"

"Joe's mother, Rochelle Gardner, showed up for my gig and told J.J."

"For the record, Rochelle Gardner is still married to J.J. Gardner, is that not correct?"

"As far as I know." Bonnie spoke with a slight snarl. "J.J. and I split up a couple months ago."

"So you broke up with the husband of the defendant's mother, who is also your late daughter's boyfriend's father?"

Judith Rose slapped the table. "Objection, your Honor. We just established that the witness's romantic life is not relevant to this case."

"Overruled," the judge countered, immediately. "The witness has been warned more than once to answer the questions being asked. The witness has, once again, chosen to volunteer information beyond the question. For this reason, I am extending to the defense the latitude to pursue that line of questioning."

Rochelle, from deep in her lap, gave a thumbs up to Darla.

"Counselor––" the judge said to Angus.

"Yes, your Honor."

"You're treading on shaky ground here regarding the relevance of your questioning, but for the time being you may continue."

"Thank you, your Honor. With the court's permission, I would like to display the Wanapum County Coroner's autopsy report on the overhead screen."

Rochelle checked to see Judge Kantadillo's reaction. The imposing man seemed to be losing patience with everyone in this case––the lawyers, witnesses and, of course, with her, too.

"You've already submitted this as Exhibition F, Counselor, so permission is not denied," said the judge.

With a pointer, Angus had Bonnie Quinn look at one highlighted line. "Can you read here where it says that the coroner found no drugs in your daughter's body at the time of death?"

"Yes, I can read that. It's hardly a surprise since Mary didn't do drugs."

What surprised Rochelle was how this question caused Bonnie to become emotional, pulling out a tissue and dabbing the tears from her eyes. Finally, Mary's own flesh-and-blood mother showed a pulse. How many times over the years had Rochelle felt like she was more of a mother to Mary than Bonnie could ever hope to be? Maybe Bonnie losing her daughter had struck the last sober nerve inside the woman.

Angus didn't wait for Bonnie to collect herself before peppering her with more questions. "Ms. Quinn, was your daughter, when she was living with you, ever prescribed any medications for her depression?"

"Yes," Bonnie managed to say, although her rough voice was barely audible.

"Was that drug, lithium?"

"Yes. She started taking lithium when she was sixteen."

Rochelle pinched her thigh through thick Wrangler denim wondering why she focused so much attention on Bonnie? J.J. was half out the door when he'd run off with this woman. If it hadn't been Bonnie Quinn, her estranged husband would have escaped with some other bonnie lass.

"Ms. Quinn, do you ever recall a time when your daughter failed to take this prescription?" Angus kept his voice even-keeled.

"Yes. I had to remind my daughter at least once a week to take the drug. It helped her bipolar disorder."

"How did Mary behave when she wasn't taking her lithium?"

"She became unpredictable and moody."

Rochelle was also trying to tackle her own suffering, but those vexations had nothing to do with Bonnie Quinn. Even if she'd wanted to exorcise Bonnie from her life, such a thing would never be possible. The two of them were too entangled through Mary, Joe, and this baby. Roll with it; stop all the psychic battles with her; accept whatever might come, except that all of this was easier to envision than to embrace.

"Ms. Quinn, please think back to last spring before you left your high schooler to go out on tour with your band. Do you remember if Mary was taking her prescribed doses early this year?"

"Now that you mention it, I really doubt it. She wasn't exactly a honey to be around all last winter and spring."

"She was pregnant," Biff whispered. "Duh."

For Bonnie not to pick up on Mary's pregnancy with her first trimester of mood swings and morning sickness was surprising, too. Rochelle pinched her thigh again.

So what? Nothing would ever change how Bonnie was a piss-poor mother to Mary, but watching out for the girl had never been a contest between the two of them. Filling a maternal void for her son's girlfriend was more like serving as a safety net. Mary had fit into Rochelle's world easily, naturally, and always as a welcome addition to her home. She pictured the two of them in her living room, Rochelle at the old upright piano and accompanying Mary's magical singing.

"No way does this woman get custody of Grace," Darla leaned over and whispered.

"No way," Biff replied softly, but right away.

Glancing up at the judge, who again stared back at them, Rochelle didn't dare whisper her thoughts on this or any subject.

Angus continued his cross examining. "You testified that you never knew Mary was pregnant until after her baby was born. You stated that you left on tour in April, about halfway through Mary's pregnancy." Angus edged closer to Bonnie when he spoke. "According to the Wanapum County Coroner, Mary had no lithium in her system at the time she drowned. Ms. Quinn, were you ever directly aware of Mary taking her lithium at any time last December, January, February or March when you two still lived together?"

"No, sir." Bonnie folded her arms across the front of her sweater as though she thought it would ward off Angus's probing questions. "Mary turned eighteen last December. She was mature for her age. I was done babying her."

What a cut-and-run answer, Rochelle thought, but, then again, hadn't she done the same thing by booting Joseph out of the house when he relapsed this summer?

Angus paused before continuing. "Ms. Quinn, you just testified that your high school senior was very moody before you left to go on tour. Is that not correct?"

Bonnie unfolded her arms and fidgeted before responding. "Yes, she was moody and she was eighteen." Her voice boomed through the courtroom like she was driving home the Blues on a downbeat. "My Mary may have been bi-polar, but she was never even remotely suicidal, if that's what you're getting at here."

"No more questions, Ms. Quinn. Again, I'm sure I speak for everyone in the courtroom. We're all extremely sorry for the loss of your daughter."

Rochelle didn't take her eyes off Bonnie. Mary's mother turned red again when the judge dismissed her from the stand.

The harsh courtroom lighting hardly flattered her. Her face showed the years of heavy drinking. All of Bonnie's demons and crappy mothering stemmed from her alcoholism. The woman was unable to sustain any relationship, including her most important mother/daughter one. Imagine finding out—after a show and surely half-in-the-bag—that her only child was dead. Maybe this last gasp effort for a do-over at raising Grace was like putting a band aid on her core loneliness and inner desperation. When would Bonnie realize that floundering to raise another child was not the answer for her? Fronting another rock band wouldn't help her drinking woes, but at least she'd be showcasing her gift for the Blues, doing what she was actually pretty great at, and what she loved.

When Bonnie walked past Joe, Rochelle's eyes filled with tears. In that moment, she realized that somehow, miraculously, Bonnie Quinn had managed to raise Mary, a fine and special soul who also graced both Rochelle's and Joe's lives.

Somewhere deep inside, Rochelle felt a warming wave of peace, even though Arctic winds were flash-freezing everyone who was suffering this tragedy. For the first time, she realized that Bonnie's heart was just as frostbitten as any of theirs. On this bitingly cold day surrounded by the human bitterness of Joe's trial, Rochelle recalled Kuma's words. She could feel the sun of wisdom melting all the frost from her icy karmic brawl with Bonnie Quinn.

Judge Kantadillo slammed his gavel, startling both Rochelle and Darla. "Court is adjourned for lunch," he said. "We will resume our proceedings at 1:30 this afternoon."

Darla squeezed Rochelle's upper arm: "I can't believe how Bonnie offered up the suicide possibility without being asked. If only one juror buys this, then we'll have the 'reasonable doubt' we need for acquittal."

Rochelle started to answer, but little of this was rational. Much of Joe's mess was beyond her understanding, like she was groping along and just starting to feel truth taking form in a void of darkness. Her son's freedom still seemed strangely linked to Bonnie Quinn's daughter, and--startling to Rochelle--from her own sudden capacity to forgive.

CHAPTER TWENTY-ONE

VII.
WE

~

Joe, as usual, sat stony when Angus presented his first defense witnesses after court reconvened in the afternoon. The jurors would sneak peeks at him, so he didn't want to be digging in his ear, snarling, or holding a face-contorting goof-off with Biff while sweltering under a limelight that he wouldn't wish on his worst foe. His self-consciousness started with those twelve jurors who held the key to whether or not he'd be locked in a box for the best of his adult years. Problem was he couldn't read their shifty eyes. Day after day, the dirty dozen sat dwelling on him, a kid they didn't know from squat.

"Your Honor, the defense would like to call its first witness," said Angus.

Jill McCoy, director of the Columbia Gorge Discovery Center and Museum, took her oath and sat. Joe always thought Biff took after her mom, but Jill was a few inches taller with tamer hair, and she didn't sound like an auctioneer when she spoke. Angus asked about the

THE BONE SHRINE | 183

work Joe had done for the Oregon Trail celebration as a wheel-wright's apprentice.

"Joseph Gardner, at age eleven, participated convincingly as a youthful pioneer in our living history celebration," she said, "but four years later, he was even more impressive after the museum opened. He worked in our aviary with injured birds of prey. He'd clean the cages without complaint, and our chief handler relayed to me that the hawks, eagles, and owls always trusted the teen. It was gratifying to find a good, young handler the caliber of this young man."

Joe could tell when the raptors decided he was chill enough to hang with. He never wavered from treating the big birds right--the same way each and every time. Joe showed them he knew they were worthy of respect. In return, they were cool with him.

"So, overall, you were impressed with Joe Gardner?"

"The teen was hardworking and friendly, a very solid kid for us."

Joe almost blushed hearing the compliments, except it wasn't the sort of thing that would decide his case. It couldn't hurt, though.

"Ms. McCoy, you also worked extensively with Mary Quinn, did you not?"

"Yes. Regularly."

"Then, I don't need to ask you about her solid character, local popularity as a singer, or how bright she was, but there is a delicate matter I need to explore with you. Are you aware that Mary was diag-nosed with a mild to moderate bi-polar disorder?"

Jill McCoy glanced towards Biff before answering. "Yes. My daughter and Mary were close friends, so I knew her both at work and when she came over to our house."

"Did you ever notice her depression while she was working at the Discovery Center?"

"Yes, as a matter of fact I did. This was a particularly difficult year for Mary and it showed."

"What triggered your awareness of Mary's issue?"

The museum director, pressed her index fingers against her lips like a steeple when she thought through the question. "Well, there was an event we sponsored early in May where Mary couldn't bring herself to perform."

"Did you consider terminating Mary for failing to participate?"

"Heaven's no. Mary Quinn was a continuous draw for us at the museum, a Gorge celebrity. Besides, her clinical bi-polar depression was manageable. Mary has had a great deal of pressure on her this year, such as needing to cope with being abandoned by her mother, the woman who testified this morning."

Joe expected the prosecuting attorney to object to the word 'abandoned' just like when Angus objected to her use of the word when he'd left Mary and Grace at the SUV to get gas that night. This time, Judith Rose didn't so much as twitch in protest.

"For the record, in what month did Bonnie Quinn abandon her daughter, Mary, this year?"

"In late April or early May, several weeks before she and my daughter graduated from high school."

"Did you realize that Mary was midway through her pregnancy then?" Angus asked.

"No. I had no idea at the time. My daughter, Biff, never said a word. I didn't notice until mid-June when Mary definitely started to show."

"Thank you for your testimony, Ms. McCoy. I have no further questions."

When Judith Rose, the prosecutor, cross-examined her, she asked Jill if she knew about Joe's continuing heroin problem. Jill stated that she wasn't going to testify about rumors she might have heard, only about what she knew directly.

"Ms. McCoy, you just testified about being aware of Mary Quinn's bi-polar disorder. You have told this court that you were the boss of both Joe Gardner and Mary Quinn. You have said that Mary Quinn is a close friend of your own teenage daughter. Last winter, in late November, were you aware that Joe Gardner was remanded to a juvenile detention center in Oregon for a three-month sentence?"

"Yes."

"Yet, if you know about his conviction, how would you not know about Joe Gardner's heroin addiction?"

"Ma'am. I have never been an eye-witness to any drug issues with this young man, and certainly not when he worked at the museum. I am also not privy to whether or not he continues to have such a problem, which is the question you asked me."

"Did your daughter tell you−−"

Angus didn't allow her to finish the question. "Objection, your Honor. The prosecution is badgering this witness to give second-hand, hearsay testimony."

"Sustained. The prosecution was just told by this witness that she had no direct knowledge." The judge's tone was testy, even though his wording was polite. "Refrain from asking any more questions about what this witness's daughter might have told her. You've had ample opportunity to subpoena her grown daughter for direct testimony."

"Yes, your Honor." This time, Judith Rose didn't react to the slap on the wrist from the judge in the wounded way she usually did. "Ms. McCoy, you just testified that Mary Quinn went into a bout of depression when her mother left The Dalles last spring. A few months before that, when you knew that Joe Gardner was in juvenile detention, did Mary Quinn exhibit any signs of depression while at work or when she visited your house?"

Jill looked again towards Biff and back at Judith Rose. "During the winter and early spring, Mary would have only worked at special events. I don't recall any behavior being anywhere as severe as when Bonnie Quinn left her. Her mother forced this high schooler who was on the verge of graduating, to arrange for a place to live with someone else. We offered a bed in our home, but she ended up staying at Rochelle's Gardner's place instead. Rochelle is Joe Gardner's mother."

Joe loved how Biff's mom wasn't going to help the prosecuting attorney cut him down more than she already had. With this answer, Judith Rose thanked Jill McCoy for her testimony.

Next up for Joe's defense was Melinda Reiman. He remembered Gunnar's girlfriend from three years ago as a pretty, but older, high schooler. The young woman, now 21-years-old, moved gracefully into the witness stand. Sitting there, her black rimmed glasses seemed to add a dozen points to an already high IQ.

When asked by Angus, the University of Washington coed spoke about being invited to Gunnar's parent's home for Thanksgiving Dinner back when she was still at Moses Lake High. She described how Gunnar took Mary, Joe and her to see his cool, new discovery. "I was blown away to find this strange Bone Shrine so close to town, but still off the beaten trail."

"So there is no mistaking that Joe Gardner and Mary Quinn were fully aware of the Bone Shrine at least three years ago?" Angus asked.

"It's not something I can imagine anyone forgetting, especially those two."

"Why 'especially' not them?"

"Because while we were there, and then on the drive back to Gunnar's place, Joe and Mary kept saying how they wished they could make the altar of bones into a tall tower, a dozen feet high. Joe and Mary were overexcited fifteen-year-olds, girlfriend and boyfriend definitely, but it was like they were adventure buddies, too."

"Could you see the two of them thinking this would be a cool place to camp, even last summer?" Angus asked.

"Definitely," said Melinda. "On that Thanksgiving, Gunnar, or maybe it was Joe, suggested this very thing. I jumped in and suggested that next time we should haul in some firewood and kick off the campout with a big bonfire beside the pond."

"When you heard the tragic news of Mary Quinn's drowning, did it surprise you that it occurred in the small pond closest to the Bone Shrine?"

"Of course I was shocked and sad that she drowned, but the fact that Mary and Joe were camping there made total sense to me."

"Thank you for your testimony, Ms. Reiman." Angus sat next to Joe.

The prosecutor took a minute to jot down fresh notes, and Joe could hear Aunt Darla whispering from two rows behind him. "I remember that meal. There was nothing sinister about their Thanksgiving Day drive."

"Or revisiting it this summer," he heard Biff add.

Joe turned to see his mom smiling. Melinda's brief testimony seemed to give his mother, aunt, and friend a rush of optimism. He wished he felt the same.

Judith Rose stood and approached Melinda before asking about back when she was a high school senior. "Was the Bone Shrine a drug hangout?"

Melinda sat upright. Her big blue eyes turned fierce. "I've never been a doper, so I never paid any attention to the places where people took drugs. I do know that the Bone Shrine wasn't that kind of a hangout, though."

"Why do you say that?"

"Because hardly anyone knew about the place. Gunnar and I made a point of not telling anyone else about this spot that he happened to find when out exploring on his dirt bike."

Melinda had helped remove any stigma attached to the Bone Shrine. Joe also liked how she made him and Mary seem like a real couple, even though her words made his eyes sting with longing for his girl.

The part of his trial that still worried Joe the most was the drop. The whole bit where he accidently stumbled upon a heroin stash in an out of the way place like the Bone Shrine definitely wouldn't be an easy story for any jury to buy, even though it was true. His juvenile bust might be the clincher for these stony-faced jurors. At least Melinda painted a stronger likelihood of showing why what happened actually happened.

"Ms. Reiman, when was the last time you saw Gunnar Larsson?"

"I bumped into him at the hardware store in Moses Lake last spring."

"Do you know where Gunnar Larsson is now?"

"I'm not positive, but when I was contacted to testify someone said he was visiting family in Europe." Melinda looked squarely at the prosecutor. "Gunnar and I didn't hang out together after high school."

"Are you aware he's being investigated for distributing heroin?"

"Objection, your Honor," Angus said after bounding to his feet. "This man she is asking about is not on trial here, and was deemed *not* to be a person-of-interest in this case by the prosecutor's own investigative team."

"Objection sustained."

When Joe heard someone rustling behind him, he turned to see his aunt's face turn red. She started to cry. His mom wrapped her arm around her sister. This struck Joe as odd since he, not Gunnar, was the one being railroaded, creosoted, and torched into a public bonfire.

"Allow me to rephrase the question, your Honor. Ms. Reiman, are you aware of the defendant, Joe Gardner, and your ex-boyfriend,

Gunnar Larsson, using the Bone Shrine hideaway as a drop for any heroin deals."

Melinda glared back. "No," she said as bitterly as the short word can be uttered.

"The defense again objects!" Angus stepped forward with feet wide and faced the judge. "Your Honor, the prosecution persists on bringing back into their case this person whom was not of sufficient interest to them in late August. I will stress again that Wanapum County chose *not* to hold Gunnar Larsson, whom they arrested before dawn after Mary Quinn drowned."

Joe could see that Judge K. wasn't inclined to stop Angus from continuing, and his lawyer let it rip:

"This individual is now being implicated in heroin dealing via my client's case. Why was he released four hours after his arrest for lack of evidence? Most crime scene results could not arrive back from the lab at 10:00 a.m. in the morning following Mary Quinn's tragic drowning? Again, why did the county release Gunnar Larsson immediately and unconditionally?"

Angus paused, and took a sip of water.

"Your Honor, the legal consideration here is significant. What is the prosecution holding back as evidence that compels them to bring up my client's cousin yet again? I encourage the prosecution to extradite Gunnar Larsson. I have strong suspicions that the grounds for any successful extradition would vindicate my client of these drug charges. Simply put, Joe Gardner would not need an arm's-length drop site to conduct a clandestine drug transaction with the same cousin he openly told Deputy Zach Riggleman he was planning to meet in Moses Lake."

Judith Rose looked alarmed at Angus's comments when she hurried from near the witness stand to face the judge. She was several feet from Angus's shoulder in the same open area. "Your Honor," she shot back. "The defendant's cousin, Gunnar Larsson, fled the United States on the day immediately following the murder and drug bust at the Bone Shrine. The prosecution did not expect this, and was unable to serve him with a subpoena to testify—"

The judge, for the first time during testimony, hammered his gavel with such a severe blow that Joe could see most everyone in the gallery jolting upright. "This is the second time in one minute where I am sustaining the same objection from the defense regarding the expatriated cousin of the defendant."

During the trial, this imposing man had never turned red, but Joe thought the judge was about to have a coronary. Kantadillo wasn't done reaming the county's criminal attorney.

"Prosecutor Rose, did you bother to listen to the defense counselor's legal concern here? If the Prosecution knows of other parties involved in the crimes committed on the night in question and is seeking second-hand, corroborating testimony, then, you are out of order for this trial. You will not turn my court into a fishing expedition, do you understand?"

"Your Honor, the Larsson Family is the defendant's only known tie to the Moses Lake area."

Joe could hear Aunt Darla let out a short grunt behind him. The judge leaned forward, gavel still in hand, with a displeased scowl at the prosecutor.

"Ms. Rose, do not continue with this same line of questioning to a witness who has made it clear that she is not currently in the life of the defendant's cousin." The judge's face seemed incensed, but his voice totally in control. "Perhaps I haven't made myself clear. If the prosecution is withholding incriminating evidence pursuant to the charges before us, then you will need to convince me why your current case should be allowed to proceed on this particular charge."

"No, your Honor, I was simply expressing the challenges our prosecution has faced in securing Mr. Larsson as a witness."

"Ms. Rose, please do not compel me to sustain this same objection for a third time."

Judith Rose's face was now the color of her surname. "Yes," was all she could say before sipping water from her table. When she collected herself, she turned back and thanked Ms. Reiman for her testimony. "I have no more questions of this witness, your Honor."

CHAPTER TWENTY-TWO

(Friday, November 17th)

A ngus called his last witness forward to take an oath. Dr. Henry
Schloss, a well-known crime scene expert from Seattle, told the
court that his specialization was homicide case reconstruction. Angus
clicked on a remote to show the first of the prosecution's crime scene
slides already admitted in the trial as evidence.

Angus had told Joe that Schloss was the reason he hadn't
unleashed a vigorous cross-examination of the prosecution's chief
investigator. He was convinced that Schloss offered the best way to
counter Detective Roger Riggleman's testimony.

"Dr. Schloss, I'd like for you to focus on the illustration on the
screen. According to the prosecution's lead investigator who has
already testified, he concludes that this is the position Mary Quinn
was in when she gave birth in the back of her SUV. Sir, do you concur
with this assessment?"

The scientist pushed his black, horn-rimmed glasses up to the
bridge of a long, thin nose that made him appear even thinner than he
was. Despite the frigid weather outside, Schloss unfolded a perfect

square of white handkerchief from the breast pocket of the short-sleeved dress shirt he wore on this wintery day. Joe stared at the scientist who took plenty of time to wipe his lenses before answering in a nasally, but authoritative tone. "No, I do not concur."

"Can you please explain to the jury why, during the birthing, that Mary Quinn wasn't in this position?"

"Yes. A simple assessment of the floor of the vehicle shows blood concentrated 20-to-28 inches behind the front seats of the SUV. You can see this in the exhibit photo."

The man, a self-assured nerd, could pass for a 1960s control center scientist for a NASA space launch. "This concentration of afterbirth shows where the baby exited, directly below where the 5' 2" woman's birth canal would have been. From this and other corroborating evidence, I'm convinced that the new mother had her head 180° from what was proposed by the chief investigator in this case. In other words, I'm convinced that the young woman's head was to the rear of the SUV with her feet, knees and birth canal towards the front of the vehicle."

"Dr. Schloss, were there any traces of afterbirth found closer to the rear of the vehicle to show she could have given birth with her feet facing towards the back of the SUV?"

"No, sir. The afterbirth blood was concentrated in the location where I just testified it was. The birthing evidence would have been closer to the lift gate if what you ask was true."

Joe had told Angus exactly how the birth went down. Sometimes he didn't get why he shouldn't be allowed to testify and get the truth out faster and a whole lot cheaper than this expert.

"Why is blood placement enough to make this assessment?" Angus asked.

"The limited amount of space in the rear of a Pathfinder SUV does not allow for much variation of human positions," the scientist said. "This is especially the case while a woman is supine and giving birth. The process forces her to have her knees up."

Joe wanted to tell the jurors to stretch out in the back of that Pathfinder. He'd slept there many times on camp outs. He and Mary would spoon, him curled around her during part of the night. Then they'd flip so she could curl around him. The sleeping quarters were tight, but Joe hadn't minded when they'd nestle until dawn like fine silver cutlery.

"And, Dr. Schloss, did you find the bruises on Mary Quinn to be consistent with the alleged fight that the prosecution has reconstructed for this trial?"

"No. These bruises do not prove or even suggest that there was an altercation, and not remotely to the extent where the woman would have been forced into the pond."

Angus showed the prosecution's commissioned drawing of a man behind a standing woman and pushing her on the shoulders towards a small body of water. "Can you elaborate on this, Dr. Schloss?"

"I've spent many years replicating murders that included physical abuse or altercation. Unless there is evidence of a gun or knife being used as coercion, I've never seen or heard of an aggressor simply holding the victim by the top of the shoulders and pushing him or her from behind to their death."

Joe caught himself nodding.

"I should add that the prosecution's case argues for an aggressor physically drowning the victim. There is not enough bodily evidence showing how the victim was forced into the pond."

"So, if someone were to physically force another adult into this pond, then what would you expect to see?"

Schloss tightened his navy blue tie. "Any number of things. Bruising around the trunk of the body if the victim was lifted and carried. Injuries to the wrist or elbows, ankles or knees if the victim was dragged."

"Dr. Schloss, do you have any other plausible explanation for the presence of fresh bruises on the top of Mary Quinn's shoulders?"

"The bruises on this woman's shoulders were modest, far from severe," said the scientist. "In my opinion, they were too minor to indicate a forcible displacement of any sort."

Joe's memory was blurred, but the platoon of paramedics, sheriff deputies, and detectives arrived shortly after Deputy Riggleman rescued Grace. First, two ambulances came, and then another county cop followed right after. Joe was still cuffed when he watched a half-dozen vehicles fishtailing in a row down the small sandy road to the Pathfinder. They discovered right off that Mary was beyond reviving.

Joe didn't answer any questions for the cops when the paramedics sponged his fouled skin. After being so rudely cleaned, he was loaded into one ambulance, the baby in another. There were medics and cops everywhere.

Before the back of his ambulance was shut, the paramedics placed Mary on a gurney a few feet behind him. When they covered her naked body and face with a blanket, the sight was way too final for Joe. Flat on his back and looking straight up, his sockets flooded with tears. New sirens told him that more back-up officials were arriving on scene.

"Dr. Schloss, what else does your analysis tell you of the couples' bodies around the time of birthing?"

"There was only one set of scratch marks found on the defendant's body. Both were from fingernails gouging each of his forearms in roughly the same place." Dr. Schloss extended his own arm to show where. "If there had been a life-and-death struggle, then far more scratches would be expected on the defendant's body from the deceased woman's fingernails which, postmortem, were found to be quite sharp."

Schloss sipped his water before continuing. "In this case, during my forensic team's reenactment, we found that a woman having painful contractions could easily reach back and dig into the forearms of a person standing behind and gripping her shoulders. As you can see from the exhibited photo, our reenactment had a young man, the defendant's size, gripping the smaller woman's shoulders with both of his hands. This is the spot where the light bruising on the young woman was discovered."

"Would this have been possible had her feet been towards the rear of the SUV?"

"Not when assisting in childbirth. The distance and raised knees don't permit access to the shoulders. Conversely, his access to her over the backs of the front seats would have been unfeasible. The seats would have been too much of a physical impediment between him and the birthing mother."

Dr. Schloss took a sip of water.

"But, sir, during childbirth, why would the defendant not have been positioned to 'catch the baby'? How does standing behind the woman in labor allow for this?"

"I wondered the same thing. The eighteen year old boy was clearly not a trained midwife."

Several in the gallery laughed. Over the noise, Joe heard Biff say, "Joey Numbnuts can catch a baseball, but not a baby."

"Numbnuts?" his mother said even louder.

Joe felt blood rushing to his face.

"All in good fun. That's the nickname I gave him after his little baseball accident," Biff told Rochelle and Darla.

Joe could hear Aunt Darla chuckle. He twisted away from the jury to stare them down. The three of them, almost in unison, put hands to mouth and quieted themselves. At the same time, the judge tapped his gavel lightly to restore order.

Angus displayed the prosecution's photo of the landing at the edge of the pothole pond where Joe's Chunichi Dragon baseball jersey and Mary's blouse and skirt had been recovered and laid out.

"Dr. Schloss, as a former police investigator, and now in private practice, do you find it customary for evidence being used in proving guilt during a murder trial to be moved from where the investigators first discover it?"

"Absolutely not."

"Was this where these three primary garments were found when the Wanapum County Sheriff's department deputies and detectives arrived at the scene?"

"No, sir. From the reports made on the night of the drowning, the blouse was draped over cattails a few feet into the marsh, the baseball jersey was half-drenched in the pond and half on the landing stones. The first arriving deputy had set his belt on top of the dry skirt that was completely spread out on the landing. The officer took care to protect his weapons in this way before entering the pond to attempt his rescue."

"Dr. Schloss, were you allowed to have the skirt, blouse or jersey examined by an independent lab?"

"No, sir. The sheriff investigators indicated that the garments were contaminated and that further analysis would corrupt their evidence."

"For the record, Dr. Schloss, did you just say you were denied further analysis because you might *corrupt* the evidence that the Wanapum County investigators had already *contaminated?*"

The forensic expert's knuckles hid a bit of a smile. "Yes, sir. That would be a fair assessment."

"Objection, your Honor," Judith Rose got up and said. "The sheriff investigation team is not on trial here."

"Overruled," Judge Kantadillo responded immediately. "There will be no curtailing the defense team's prerogative to question the manner in which the prosecution has processed key evidence. Please proceed, Counsel."

"Dr. Schloss, if you'd been allowed to have an independent analysis conducted for this case, what specifically would you have asked the lab to analyze?" Angus seemed pleased by the judge's reprimand of his counterpart, but wasn't about to openly gloat.

"Two things have concerned me. I find it astounding that the investigators on this case did not analyze the skirt for evidence of afterbirth blood."

"Why is that, Dr. Schloss?" Angus pressed against the railing in front of Joe.

"Simple. If the prosecution had found even the slightest trace of Mary Quinn's birthing blood on her skirt, then they would have established how the garment was removed by the deceased following birth. The timing is key. Since the prosecution did not conduct such a basic test, then there is no way to show that the skirt may have been removed prior to her climbing in the back of this vehicle to give birth."

Yes, again! thought Joe.

Angus spoke as he stepped towards Dr. Schloss. "So on one of the hottest nights of the year in arid Moses Lake, you're suggesting that Mary Quinn stripped naked to give birth in the back of this SUV?"

Dr. Schloss shook his head and Angus stopped to listen. "Not exactly." He described how, in confined quarters such as the back of this vehicle, it was inconceivable that the deceased would not have blood on her skirt if she'd worn the garment while giving birth. The prosecution's argument hinged on a physical altercation between the defendant and deceased occurring *after* she gave birth. There was no forensic evidence to suggest that the dress wasn't removed prior to birth. "The prosecution found that, while the skirt did have the deputies weapon belt place on top of it, the garment was never in the pond." Schloss looked at the judge. "In other words, this garment was *not* too contaminated to be tested for afterbirth blood."

Joe glanced at the jury, hoping they'd get the logic here. Schloss had spelled it out like his favorite middle school science teacher. In no way did the evidence confirm that there had been a fight. Why? Because there had been no friggin' fight that night!

"Sir, what was the second thing that you wished had been better analyzed?"

Dr. Schloss sat up straighter. "Speaking as a forensics professional, I'm highly troubled that the investigators for the prosecution did not make any effort whatsoever to establish if there was evidence showing that the defendant was ever in the seep pond where Mary Quinn drowned. For example, when I asked to see the analysis of the defendant's tennis shoes from the night in question, I was startled to learn that the boy's Nikes had been worn by him ever since he was incarcerated for this trial."

Angus stepped in closer. "What was so startling about this?"

"Simple. According to the prosecution, the young man had climbed in the pond where, allegedly, he held the victim's head under the water. I simply can't imagine there wouldn't be far more than a trace of pond scum and muck on his shoes, skin, clothes or hair if he had, in fact, entered the seep marsh and drowned the young woman."

Angus leaned into the railing in front of the witness stand. "So, to be clear, the prosecution has not tried to prove for its case that the defendant was present in the pond to murder Mary Quinn?"

"Exactly. I'm saying that this is forensics at its most basic, especially with such a serious allegation of homicide. I did, however, request and was allowed the opportunity to examine the defendant's stored clothing from when he was arrested."

"What did this independent analysis show?" Angus asked.

"There was no trace of pond muck found on any of the defendant's clothing worn when the deputy picked him up that night. The shoes he was allowed to keep wearing while in jail were too contaminated after two months to provide valid test results."

Angus stepped closer. "So, you found no evidence of pond muck on Joseph Gardner's clothing. Were these clothes the same ones that the defendant was wearing at 07:40 p.m. on August 17th in the gas station surveillance video from when he and his girlfriend filled up with gas just before leaving The Dalles, Oregon to drive to Moses Lake?"

Schloss nodded slowly. "Yes, the defendant had on the same faded and ripped jeans, Nike tennis shoes, and Japanese baseball jersey. Again, I was quite surprised that the defendant's shoes and underwear, or his skin, hair, and nails hadn't been tested for pond muck."

Angus continued. "Dr. Schloss, are you aware that the Wanapum County Sheriff K-9 unit was used extensively at the crime scene early in the morning after the drowning?"

"Yes."

"Other than the three mentioned garments, did they find any clothes from the victim or the defendant?"

"From reading the report, the K-9 dogs were allowed to sniff the skirt, blouse and jersey where they were laid out on the landing. The dogs found matching scents on unworn clothes piled on and next to the driver's seat of the Pathfinder SUV. More notably, the dogs discovered the heroin confiscated as evidence for this trial."

Angus turned towards the jurors and then back towards Dr. Schloss. "So trained K-9 units could not find any muddy shoes or jeans belonging to the defendant at the scene of the drowning, yet a couple hundred yards away, wrapped inside a coyote hide, and well within the thick branches of a pungent cedar tree, they located a stash of heroin?"

"Yes. That's what the investigation team formally indicated."

"Dr. Schloss, had the defendant, theoretically, climbed into this mucky pond, and then walked five miles with an empty gas can, would there still have been residue from the pond scum on his shoes or jeans?"

The forensic expert nodded. "I fully expect that to be the case. The evidence would likely be wedged in the treads of the soles or adhering to the laces. Also, it would be embedded in the worn denim jeans he was wearing at the time of his arrest."

"Or, if the defendant had stripped naked before climbing in the pothole marsh, would pond scum and traces of muck have been found on his skin?"

"Yes. If he had entered that muddy seep lake with no clothes or anything on his feet, then, yes, traces of pond residue would have been present under his toenails or on his skin. Marsh muck possesses quite an adhesive quality."

"But, in your review of the prosecution's discovery process, they made no attempt to establish evidence on my client's body, clothes, or shoes to indicate he was ever in the pond, did you?"

"No, Sir. There appears to be no such analysis sought by the investigators in this case, so no such evidence was ever found."

"Your Honor, the defense has no more questions of Dr. Schloss."

Judith Rose waited for Angus to sit before she approached the scientist.

"Welcome, sir," said Judith Rose. "To fairly summarize your testimony, is it not true that your reconstruction of the homicide scene is predicated on second guessing what you think the prosecution should have analyzed?"

"Objection!" Angus had only just sat down before he got up again. His words came out both testy and rapid fire. "Your Honor, Dr. Schloss is a nationally renowned scientist. His forensic assessment of the crime scene investigation wasn't 'second guessing.' Rather, he noted the disturbing failure by the investigators to follow well-established protocol. Additionally, the investigators in this case denied the defense the opportunity to analyze critical evidence."

"On what grounds does the counselor wish to object?" Judge Kantadillo interjected.

Joe could see the jurors leaning forward, totally into the exchange. Angus hesitated like he was debating how to answer the judge's question.

"Discovery," Joe heard a woman whisper from behind him. She seldom uttered just a single word, so it took him a second to realize Joe was hearing Biff's voice.

He was even more surprised to hear Angus riff on Biff's hint. "Your Honor. What has surfaced today is a critical issue of *discovery*. The prosecution took unprofessional liberties to move key evidence of the clothing found at the scene, but then denied the defense the chance for *discovery* on the same evidence that they compromised. Without testing for blood, we are denied the *discovery* to know if there was even a skirt to be torn off Mary Quinn after she gave birth and before she drowned. Most troubling, the defense was denied the opportunity to *discover* the truth of whether or not the defendant was in that pond."

Angus turned towards the jurors and back toward Kantadillo. "Your Honor, this omission prevents the jury from knowing if the accused was ever in the pond and next to Mary Quinn when she drowned to death."

The judge responded evenly. "Counsel, the Court questions why you didn't bring up your concern over these specific discovery issues at the outset of the trial."

"Your Honor," Angus said uneasily, "Dr. Schloss made his request to examine the skirt just prior to the trial, but it was only last week when the prosecution formally denied us the opportunity to test this skirt for the deceased's blood."

Judge Kantadillo turned to the prosecutor. "The closing arguments for this trial are scheduled for Monday morning. Accordingly, I am asking the prosecution to secure a formal document from the Wanapum County Sheriff's Department detailing why Dr. Schloss's request on behalf of the defense was denied. Specifically, I want to know why he was not allowed to orchestrate an independent blood analysis of the skirt worn by the now-deceased woman on the night in question?"

"Yes, your Honor," said Judith Rose, "except we're headed into the weekend, so I don't know what I'll be able to obtain from the sheriff's office."

"Ms. Rose, the prosecution has unilaterally denied a significant discovery request prior to the beginning of this trial. This was done without notifying me. If the prosecution wishes to avoid a mistrial, then I suggest you get your investigative team to explain its actions by the time this trial reconvenes on Monday morning."

"I'll do my best, your Honor." For once she didn't turn red. If anything, she seemed overconfident.

"Please continue," the judge said.

"Your Honor, the prosecution has only one set of questions

remaining in its cross-examination of the witness." She waited for Kantadillo to nod.

"Dr. Schloss, you've questioned rather harshly how the prosecution examined and reconstructed this crime scene. In your testimony, you stated that you're aware of victims in other cases being coerced to obey aggressors who are wielding knives or guns. Is that not accurate, sir?"

"Yes, ma'am, but to be clear, the investigators for your case never suggested that such weapons were utilized in this drowning."

"Agreed, sir. However, you're not suggesting that a knife or a gun are the only way victims can be coerced, are you?"

Schloss shifted uneasily. "I'm not sure I understand how your question pertains to this case."

"A fairly obvious example from the night in question would be the threat of harm to the newborn baby would it not, Dr. Schloss?"

"Objection, your Honor. The prosecution is asking a hypothetical question of the witness when, once again, her investigators did nothing to prove that the defendant was ever in the pond with Mary Quinn and her baby."

"Objection overruled." Kantadillo adjusted the arms of his black robe and leaned back in his tall chair. "Counselor, two of the felony charges are directly relevant to the question being asked. Also, it is an established fact that the infant was in the pond. The prosecution will please pose a direct question to the witness that pertains to the night in question."

Judith Rose stood taller and more confident than Joe had yet to see her in the trial. "Dr. Schloss, in your assessment of the drowning of Mary Quinn, did you consider that the murderer threatened to drown the infant unless Mary Quinn did exactly as ordered, starting by making her climb into the pond?"

Joe couldn't believe his ears. It was exactly what he imagined the *Tramposos* doing to Mary. Jeez, this woman was painting him in the ugliest way.

Dr. Schloss sat adamant and tall when he answered. "No. As we pointed out, there was no reason to believe that the defendant was ever in the pond. Likewise, there is no evidence of a physical altercation between Mary Quinn and Joe Gardner. There was no evidence provided by your team, to suggest that any such hypothetical scenario in the pond warranted consideration."

Judith Rose edged in closer. "Except, sir, the attorney for the defense asked if you had any other plausible explanation for the bruises on top of Mary Quinn's shoulders, did he not?"

"Yes, and I said that the process of childbirth――"

She didn't allow him to finish. "Sir, was it hypothetical that the deceased died from asphyxiation by drowning in this pond?"

"No."

"Dr. Schloss, knowing this, can you tell the court why you did *not* consider that the shoulder bruises originated when Mary Quinn――from behind――was forced underwater until she drowned to death?"

The scientist's air of self-confidence evaporated while he thought about what to say. Joe's stomach dropped at the same time. "Yes, ma'am. Once again, my sequential, step-by-step analysis of the crime scene events as presented by your prosecution team showed no evidence of any violent physical altercation between the deceased and the defendant. "And, yet again, if the accused was never in the pond, why would I analyze something that could not have happened?"

"So, Dr. Schloss, since you did not actually prove that the defendant was *not* in the pond, allow me to simplify my question."

"Objection, your Honor," Angus said with emphasis. "The prosecutor is accusing the witness of *not* doing the prosecution's job for them."

The gavel came down firmly. "Motion is overruled. "The prosecution may continue."

Judith Rose, as though pausing for effect, allowed Angus to be seated before continuing. "Dr. Schloss, did you ever consider that the defendant caused the bruises on the deceased young woman's shoulders by grabbing her from behind and holding her under the surface of the pond until she drowned?"

Dr. Schloss was growing annoyed at the hypothetical questions."Again, the defendant was never shown to ever be in the――"

"Yes or no, sir." Judith Rose's interruption was grating and loud.

"No. For the reasons already given, I didn't consider it," said Schloss before she interrupted him again.

"Thank you for your testimony. Your Honor, the prosecution has no other questions of this witness."

Joe appreciated how Dr. Schloss attempted a grand response. What troubled him was how he, and not the team of sheriff investigators, had been the one to open the door for Judith Rose's questions on the shoulder bruises.

After the forensics expert left the witness stand, the judge adjourned for the afternoon. Joe was cuffed and taken back to the Shoe.

His whole trial had just taken a weird twist. Joe sat on his hard bed fearing how the jurors would picture him. Did they envision him in the pond directly behind Mary Quinn pushing her shoulders under the surface until she went lifeless. Did he then, in their minds, turn to the air mattress and, with Mary floating dead, push Grace towards the marshy reeds?

CHAPTER TWENTY-THREE

~

(Sunday, November 19th)

The icy, twenty-mile drive to Moses Lake from her Smohalla hotel required too much attention to withstand a crying jag. The sun seemed like a cold overhead streetlamp and subzero ice hid as grey patches on slightly darker shadows of asphalt. Each gust from the arctic blast ripping through the Columbia Basin threatened to tip Rochelle's clunky van onto its side.

When Rochelle turned on her sister's street, she could see where Moses had commanded whitecaps to cover his lake.

She slung the big leather handbag over her shoulder and reached in back of the van for the wine that was perfectly cooled from the drive. The bone-chilling wind made her shudder from the nape of her neck to the base of her spine. From van to house, she set each sole firmly on the frosty concrete to keep from slipping.

"This weather's even cold by Swedish standards," her brother-in-law told her when he opened the door to let her in. He shut it just as quickly.

Nils had a Scandinavian aversion for showing too much affection, but with everything unfolding, he embraced his sister-in-law. Despite his thinning blondness and thickening torso, Nils was a nicely aging version of Gunnar.

He placed her wine in an ice bucket already on the table. Rochelle put her handbag on the sectional couch beside her and noticed how it took up a whole seat cushion. She really did need to downsize.

Nils hung her REI parka and button-up sweater in the closet by the top of the stairs leading down to the daylight basement where Gunnar used to sleep. Her nephew had been allowed too much privacy while he was a teen living here. How else would he have launched a drug operation big enough to buy his own home outright, and manage to do all his dirty deeds right under the nose of his parents? Then again, upstairs in her Victorian, Joe had also gotten away with far too much.

She stepped from the living room to the dining room window which showcased the Moses Lake shoreline. Near their dock under a Quonset hut she could see a pair of jet skis, the ski boat, Nils's prized Saab Sonett sports car, and two Husqvarna dirt bikes. One of the Husky motorcycles was turned upside-down with the front tire removed.

"Isn't that Gunnar's broken motorcycle?" Rochelle asked. "I never heard how he crashed the thing."

Nils crossed his arms. "He wiped it out the day before he left. We brought the thing back here with everything else he left behind."

"Did he say where he crashed it?"

"Behind his new place," Darla said from the kitchen. "Said he wasn't familiar enough with the trails there. We took him to urgent care before driving to the airport in Seattle."

Nil's crossed his arms and clenched his jaw telling Rochelle to drop the subject and definitely not ask if the crash had happened during daylight or not. With the jury deliberation looming, she wasn't worried about stepping on anyone's delicate toes, but what good would it do to ruin a nice Sunday meal?

The Quonset hut opened towards both the house and lake, but mostly protected the watercraft and vehicles underneath. The main Moses Lake reservoir linked through an aquifer to the pothole ponds.

Today, the freezing mid-November wind forced the willows along shore to drop the last leaves of fall.

She made her way into the warm kitchen where Darla was baking, boiling mixed veggies, and sautéing asparagus. Rochelle leaned in and pressed an ear against her sister's before unfolding the Sunday *Chronicle* on the island counter. "Check this out. Naomi wrote quite the probing piece."

Bias in Mary Quinn Murder Trial? The font for the headline was huge and above-the-fold.

Darla turned down a burner and took a quick peek. "Front page, just like I predicted."

"How do we get the jurors to see it?" Rochelle mused. "I'm thinking that Angus can hold it up during his closing argument tomorrow. But would that be enough to help?"

"Too bad there's a question mark on that headline," Darla said. "A bold statement proclaiming 'bias' would be better," she added. "And, you're right, it may not help much since Grace's custody has nothing to do with what happened on that night."

"Nope. We lose Mary and now I feel like I'll never get to hold her baby."

Darla pinballed her way around the kitchen. "Did the article mention anything about Kuma sending hair samples to be tested?" She pulled a tray of golden-brown buns from the oven.

"Not really, except to say that there were still open leads on the question of paternity."

A burning pot on the stove interrupted them. "Oh crud, I've really got to stay focused here." Darla dumped the vegetables into the the garbage disposer, turned on the grinder and filled the blackened kettle bottom with faucet water that hissed back at her. The burnt smell filled the kitchen. Darla turned all her exhaust fans on max.

"Put me to work," Rochelle insisted when her sister replaced the veggies with fresh, deli-sliced pineapple that she mixed into a bowl of cottage cheese. Rochelle decided against making a quip about the kitchen smelling like an exploded meth lab.

Darla pointed and Rochelle took two side dishes to set on the dining room table near the unopened wine. Framed prints by Swedish artists Anders Zorn and Carl Larsson––bright summer shorefront scenes––covered the dining room walls beside the window framing their actual lake.

Nils rose from his recliner to see if he could help. "I don't understand why the only one on trial is your son. The losers who did this run free, but no one finds any clue."

"My question exactly, except all of that is too late now. Closing statements are set for tomorrow morning." Rochelle stepped back into the kitchen. Her brother-in-law's English was quite good, except for minor things like 'lose' sounding like 'loose' or 'loser' sounding like 'looser.' "Darla said she made you your favorite dish," Rochelle told him when returning to the dining room table to set the hot casserole dish on a trivet in the middle of the table.

"*Janssons Frestelse* is my second favorite dish," said Nils when seating himself at the head of the table. He looked up and smiled when his wife came in with her hot buns. "Darla is my number one dish!"

"Your hubby called you 'a dish'!" said Rochelle. "His English gets better all the time."

"His eyesight, too!" Darla laughed and sat next to him in a chair that kept her only a few steps from the kitchen. "The casserole has scalloped potatoes with onions, heavy cream, and something secret that Nils made me swear not to divulge."

Nils's face lit up. "We use only the best for our *Frestelse*." He took the serving spoon and tapped the edge of the Corning Ware baking dish so it rang out like a dull bell. "When I interviewed to be the director of the potato growers, Darla helped me prepare this dish for the executive board. She used my mother's recipe." Nils spooned decent portions onto both women's plates before serving up even more for himself.

Darla smiled proudly. "He landed the position, so I'm pretty sure the 'Jansson's Temptation' charmed them into hiring him."

"Yes. Like how I once tempted your great cook of a sister into dating me." Nils winked at Rochelle while lightly squeezing Darla's forearm.

Her sister blushed, placed her hand over his, and motioned for Rochelle to sit at the end of the table opposite Nils. When the three were seated, Darla lowered her head in prayer. Rochelle hadn't recited the Catholic blessing for supper since the last time she ate at her sister's and brother-in-law's. She decided to join in:

Bless us, O Lord, and these, Thy gifts,
which we are about to receive from Thy bounty.
Through Christ, our Lord.
Amen.

Rochelle could tell that Nils hadn't so much as closed his eyes, but she knew he wasn't about to censor his wife for saying grace. They both watched Darla cross herself.

"I hear that our Gunnar added some Japanese spice to that big, old Linköping *Domkyrka*," said Nils while lifting and uncorking the bottle Rochelle brought from the Maryhill Winery.

Rochelle chuckled. "My nephew claimed he wanted to properly greet his mom and me. '*Nam myoho renge kyo*,' sounded rather Goth beneath those looming arches."

"That's my son. The state church won't excommunicate him, though. Last I heard, there were only forty-seven Lutherans attending church in Sweden and, as of this year, it's not even going to be the Swedish state church." He turned to Rochelle. "Speaking of nephews, how do you think Joey's trial goes?"

"All of that can wait until after we eat, Nils," Darla scolded.

"I don't mind," said Rochelle. "Joe is dressed so handsome and sits tall and proud, and I think his lawyer, our lawyer, has been doing quite well. He established that the deputy was biased against Joseph even before he first got to the pond with my son." Rochelle blew on her first forkful of *Janssons Frestelse* to cool it a bit. "It's just too bad there's not a shred of evidence against anyone but Joe."

Nils watched her concentrating on what she slipped onto her tongue to savor. "So what is your guess on the secret ingredient?" he asked her.

Rochelle continued to take her time savoring the flavors on her palate. "The ingredients that Darla mentioned are easy to taste," she said, "but beyond those, I'm stumped." There was a full-flavored paradox to the Swedish casserole. Something definitely lurked beneath all the surface flavors.

"Tell me about the jury. What do their faces do when the lawyers argue?" Nils asked.

"Really tough to read those twelve," said Darla.

"Be sure and read the Sunday paper, the one from The Dalles that I left for you guys," Rochelle told her brother-in-law. "The reporter goes beyond Deputy Riggleman and his wife being allowed to foster Mary's baby. She questions why the lead investigator for the prosecution is also the father of the prosecution's key witness."

Darla wiped her lips with a napkin. "All we know is that the deputy son called his detective father, before the chief investigator could even visit the crime scene."

Nils finished a stalk of sautéed asparagus before sipping the Pinot Gris.

Rochelle also took a drink of the white wine. "The prosecution wants the jury to believe that only a conniving murderer with an elaborate cover-up could have found Mary's body as fast as Joe did."

Nils closed his eyes with pleasure when enjoying his *Frestelse*. "Joey would not harm Mary. Those two show much love to each other. But, if her face is in water and she is not dead, is not finding her very fast a good thing?"

"Apparently being helpful doesn't matter in Wanapum County." Rochelle took another bite of the Swedish casserole. This time when she couldn't pinpoint the secret flavor, her eyes bulged. What the hell was she tasting anyway?

"Can I ask the hard question?" Nils asked, and sampled more Pinot Gris. He spoke in a hushed tone. "Darla tells me about your cathedral visit with Gunnar. I hate how my own son turns his world upside down. I don't know, but I think and wonder if Joey was working with his cousin."

Rochelle swallowed a bit too fast when responding. "Are you thinking that the cousins were in cahoots, like they were last year when Joseph was busted?" she asked, trying to keep her tone even-keeled. Her stomach growled when she sipped and then stared through her nearly empty glass of wine at her brother-in-law and sister.

"Is there a reason not to think this?" Nils asked, dishing himself a second helping of *Frestelse*.

"No. I mean, I don't know." Rochelle didn't get why Nils was so casual about Gunnar's drug issues, the ones that his wife had only learned about in that Swedish cathedral two weeks before. She brought up the idea that there would be no reason for Joe to use the Bone Shrine to deliver directly to Gunnar, since the cousins would trust one another to meet directly. "Also, if Joe was Gunnar's mule and hauling the dope up from Oregon, why didn't he snort a line or two to keep his cold turkey at bay? Of course Joe stumbled upon the stash after he got to the Bone Shrine that night. It's the only thing that makes any sense." Rochelle took a bite of cottage cheese and fresh pineapple.

"It is very bad that Joey has fingerprints on each bundle of heroin," said Nils. "Too easy to tie him to the drug deal."

"Most definitely." Rochelle wanted to add that it also hid the players who were actually involved in this deal. Instead, she focused on the motive that was plaguing her son's case. "The fact that Joe wasn't the baby's father and actually told the cop he got upset--that hardly helps my son's case, either."

When Rochelle sucked down the wine in her glass, Darla leaned over and refilled it before topping off her husband's Pinot. "When we visited Gunnar, he told me way more than I ever dreamed to hear about his drug problems, but he said straight up that Joey was not involved with that Bone Shrine drop, except for hiding the stash when he should have left it alone."

Nils slapped the table like he was arguing the point. "I hate how Gunnar makes us clean up his messes."

Rochelle never remembered seeing such a visible show of anger from her controlled, Swedish brother-in-law. She sipped more wine while watching his face. At least Nils and Darla were no longer in denial about their precious son, even though it was Joe's life on the line.

She took her fork and stabbed what was left of her Jansson's Temptation. The eating utensil stayed straight up. "Joe is like the hidden ingredient of this foreign glop. My son pops up from out of nowhere and blends in just a little too well with every piece of this crime." She found herself raising her voice. "Once you tell me what this concoction is hiding, then I'm sure my taste buds will ignore or forget the other ingredients, even though they make up the bulk of the casserole."

After her *frestelse* frustration, she watched Nils and Darla stealing glances at one another. Rochelle pushed her half-empty plate away.

Nils pointed at the bit of casserole that Rochelle had left uneaten. "Anchovies," he finally offered. "They are like Joey. He is the red herring in his own case. Once my nephew was noticed by those doing the crimes, they feature him in the mix."

Anchovies. Of course. Reaching out for one last small bite, she could taste how Nils was right. She noticed nothing but the tiny, briny, strong bits of salt-cured fish so obviously hidden within this dish. Like no one else but Joe was involved, this devious trial had been stirred and baked to frame only her son's temptation.

"I hate to say it, but I'm so afraid that Joe will be the only one devoured," Rochelle said before pausing and glaring at the other two. "Your nephew may have stumbled into the mix by accident, but who created this concoction?"

CHAPTER TWENTY-FOUR

≈

(Monday, November 20th)

"Wear these, unless you're ready for some frozen gonads," Big Max, told Joe. "The courthouse furnace blew last night." He tossed fresh, tan coveralls across the cell.

Joe snagged them out of midair. The coveralls threatened the image he'd cultivated throughout his trial. Today he'd be looking more like a longtime prisoner standing before the parole board than a straitlaced young man seeking justice.

When Max and Sam escorted him under the awning to the old courthouse, the freeze still brought no snow, only lacy ice crystals battling crunched salt pellets on the sidewalk. He'd convinced Max to let him wear his blue blazer over the coveralls, a tight fit. The salt kept Joe and his guards from slipping, but the dry bitter cold was harsh, maybe lower than zero degrees Fahrenheit. The east side of the Cascade Range got plenty cold in late November, but rarely like this where his nose hair turned brittle. A facility maintenance crew and rental company rep adjusted the idle of a roaring, portable generator tucked behind the courthouse.

"Ain't that the junkie who drowned his girl?" Joe could hear the Rental guy ask the county worker closest to him. If he wasn't cuffed, Joe would have used both hands to flip them off and been ready to back up his double-barreled, middle-fingered blast. Big Max, with a simple glare, got the gawkers to turn away.

The diesel smoked and Joe thought he could hear church chimes over the din, but any melody was wiped clear by a surge from the Caterpillar. A couple workers trailed Joe inside and set up electric plug-in heaters along the perimeter of the courtroom. Despite the weather, the same media members and fewer diehard onlookers were bundled in thick winter outdoor wear. Joe took his seat next to Angus who poured over the notes he'd prepared for the closing. The lawyer paid no attention to what his client wore.

Joe turned around slowly and blew his mom and aunt a quick kiss. During the wait, he found himself watching fog spew from his lips in the frigid courtroom. He even tried forming his tongue to blow a misty ring. After nearly an hour, Kantadillo entered from his chambers at the same time the bailiff ushered the jury to its box. The judge apologized for the delay saying he'd been carefully studying the detailed affidavit from the Wanapum County Sheriff. The collar of a high-necked lobsterman's sweater showed beneath the judge's robe.

"As for this discovery issue," he said, staring down and over his glasses at Judith Rose and Angus MacIntosh, "rest assured, I'm troubled that the crime scene was not better secured immediately following the events of the night in question." His voice boomed through the frigid room and the fingers inside his black driving gloves squeezed the margin of a document he waved from the bench. He stared at the cluster of Sheriff personnel in the gallery. "It is not within my purview to comment on the investigative processual concerns raised by the defense, nor the role of the defense to dictate how the prosecution's investigation is conducted. The defense was allowed to test, independently, the clothing their client was wearing when arrested on the night in question. This helps me take at face value the level of contamination ascribed by the investigation team to these three garments and the need to prevent further deterioration. The court reporter will please enter this affidavit as Exhibit Q."

The bailiff took the judge's copy and gave it to the court reporter.

Angus, in his latest Scotsman's tweed, wasted no time standing. "Good morning, your Honor. The defense requests a delay, at least until this afternoon, so we can review, not the investigative process, but the prosecution's unilateral rationale for denying my client the opportunity to discover direct and potentially critical evidence related to the charges against him."

The judge did not seem the least bit agitated by Angus's request, but immediately denied it. "This is my ruling, counselor. Again, the timing of your belated discovery request asking for further analysis also contributed to my decision." His voice was calm. "You waited until last Friday to lodge your discovery concern over further testing of the skirt. There is no indication related to the condition of these garments that the prosecution investigation team discovered evidence that was not shared with you."

The dead end had Joe's stomach rumbling even before the closing statements began. He wondered why they hadn't hired Dr. Schloss earlier, like right after his arraignment, but then again he wasn't paying the bill.

At the judge's request, Judith Rose began her closing argument. Her PowerPoint presentation loomed on the large courtroom screen. The prosecutor's make-up was caked on thicker than usual, with blacker eyeliner and rosier lipstick like a corpse on display at a funeral. Unfortunately, she knew how to be persuasive when she spoke and, lately, the jury reacted with too many little nods, no matter what she said.

The prosecutor focused first on Deputy Zachary Riggleman's heroism in trying to save Mary. "If the officer hadn't been forced to wade into the pond, try to revive a drowned woman, and enter the pond again to save a newborn left floating in the reeds, then he would have been able to cordon off the scene prior to the arrival of ambulances and supporting law enforcement."

Joe remembered how he'd still been cuffed when the 'Keystone' clumsy cops and medics arrived to trample all over the crime scene with its critical evidence. The deputy had been sitting in his boxers on the stone landing with his face in hands, uniform in his lap, and sniffling over Mary's skirt. Him wimping out was the real reason the deputy cop didn't cordon off the crime scene.

Judith Rose took a pointer and touched a photo of Joe's Chunichi Dragon's jersey with all the buttons ripped off. "Members of the jury, if you have any doubt about Joe Gardner's motive, then this is your best evidence." She handed a document to the bailiff. "I know it's late in the trial, your Honor, but on Friday afternoon the county confirmed the paternity of Mary Quinn's baby. The child's father is an 18-year-old Japanese national and former exchange student to the Gardner family in The Dalles, Oregon. His name is Kuma Kusumoto."

After the judge agreed and Angus surprised Joe by not objecting, the paternity document was admitted into the record. The prosecutor continued by stating how the defendant was irate to learn that newborn wasn't his. "In the heated argument that led to Mary Quinn's drowning, Joe Gardner's jersey was torn from his body during the same fight where he ripped off her blouse and skirt."

She went on to show a photo of Mary's clothes where the investigators had moved them to the landing stones beside the pond. "Joe Gardner's emotional state was far from one of celebrating the birth of a baby. He was taking his anger out on Mary Quinn. For example, the forensic scientist on Friday went to great lengths to argue that there was not a physical struggle with the victim on the night in question." She showed the coroner's photo of her head, where a braid of Mary's ginger hair was missing. "That was simply not the case. As you can see, Mary Quinn's hair was violently ripped out at the roots."

The prosecutor failed to mention that the tiny side-braid was hardly thick enough to drag Mary into the pond.

"Again, the baby wasn't his, Joe Gardner admitted to losing his temper, and there were torn clothes at the homicide scene. We can only speculate, but only Joe Gardner knows if he threatened the infant's life to coerce Mary Quinn into the pond to drown her."

Of course she'd bring up such total B.S. She also ignored Dr. Schloss's concerns over the sloppy evidence collection and spotty lab testing.

"Joe Gardner has had a serious problem with heroin," the prosecutor continued. "Less than a year ago, at the age of seventeen, he was sent to juvenile detention in Oregon state for possessing a major quantity of the drug." She displayed a photo that Joe hadn't seen before. He did a double take when he saw six China White heroin pouches lined up in a row beside the First Aid kit.

"The defense asks you to believe that, at midnight, Mr. Gardner, a convicted distributor of heroin, just happened to stumble upon a quarter-of-a-million-dollar stash of heroin out in the middle of the Potholes Wildlife Refuge. Deputy Riggleman testified that Joe Gardner was sweating and scratching and agitated when he gave the young man a ride to fill his gas can. The prosecution contends that Joe's anger went beyond learning that his girlfriend's baby wasn't his. The defendant was also irate that Mary Quinn's childbirth interfered with his major drug transaction."

This was the part of Joe's defense that freaked him out the most. The lady couldn't be more wrong, but why had he been stupid enough to move the stash and put his prints all over so much smack that wasn't his? Now that he was clean again, he could see how stupid his cravings had made him. All the smack in the world didn't make him a killer though.

When Judith Rose pushed a clump of ironed hair away from the dolled-up face and went to the table to look at her notes, Joe leaned over to Angus. "Why do all the photos of the stash only show six quarter-kilo bundles? There were eight plastic sealed packets."

Angus turned full on towards Joe. "Are you certain?"

"I'm positive. I remember multiplying 0.25 kilos times eight bundles and realizing that I was staring at two full kilos. I remember because I knew this would be worth a quarter-mil on the street."

The prosecutor removed her stylish Afghan shawl and draped it over the back of a free chair by her table before continuing.

Angus whispered to Joe. "I'll definitely look into any discrepancies on the quantity of bundles."

Judith Rose remained poised with her spine straight. "Jury members, it is certainly true that Mary Quinn's Nissan Pathfinder ran out of gas before she was forced to give birth in the back of the SUV. The prosecution is also convinced that the defendant did not plan to murder Mary Quinn."

The prosecuting attorney came off as being kind enough to slow down her train. That way the jurors wouldn't think she was running over him at full speed.

"No. The defendant drowned her when he reacted with rage to his night gone sideways, with a surprise childbirth, a baby that wasn't his, and a major heroin deal that was interrupted."

She showed a photo of the newborn wrapped in a polar fleece blanket and being held by a paramedic. "The felony charges against Joe Gardner are straightforward." She pointed to the list of the three that were written out by hand in bold, block lettering on a large flip-board she'd placed near the jurors. "Ladies and Gentlemen, you will be deliberating on the second degree murder charge against Joe Gardner for drowning Mary Quinn. There is also the charge levied against the defendant for the intent to distribute nearly three-and-a-third pounds of heroin. Finally, the prosecution has levied the felony charge of child endangerment for placing a newborn baby at risk of also drowning."

She placed her pointer to the third charge. "Joe Gardner did not drown an innocent newborn, but he desperately needed to escape the scene of Mary Quinn's drowning. Deputy Riggleman helped the defendant return to his vehicle with gasoline. In doing so, he disrupted Joseph Gardner's planned escape after the murder." Judith Rose showed a photo of the stranded Pathfinder. "The defendant's intended getaway explains why he was so intent on not wanting the deputy to drive him to the scene at the pothole pond."

Joe recalled being cuffed, the feeling of thick, plastic ties on his ankles cutting into his skin, and the metal handcuffs wrenching his wrists behind his back.

"So what was the obvious reason why the defendant refused the deputy's help?" Her tone to the jurors was high-and-mighty. "Joe Gardner had no intention of taking the infant with him when he escaped the scene, so he had placed the baby on the mattress and into the pond for what he believed would be safe keeping from wildlife, such as coyotes. However, there was nothing safe about what he did. It's quite fortunate that the air mattress didn't sink. Once he put a bit of gas in the Pathfinder, Joe Gardner had every intention of escaping the scene alone."

Joe couldn't forget the sight of Riggleman's Glock aimed between his eyes. In the center of the frigid courtroom, he tried to wiggle the cold from his toes while the prosecutor pointed to the next item on her flip chart. Allow me to revisit the charge against Mr. Gardner of murder in the second degree."

Judith Rose stepped a yard or two closer to the jury box. "You heard testimony last week that Joe Gardner was a bright high school student and a paid living history actor," she said. "So when Deputy Riggleman insisted on taking the defendant from the I-90 frontage road to the Pathfinder, the quick thinking young man came up with a plan to act surprised when Mary Quinn and her baby weren't inside the rear of the SUV. He knew that the mother and child would be quickly found once anyone showed up at the scene, so, in order for the defendant to seem innocent, he decided to help Deputy Riggleman find them as quickly as possible."

Judith Rose kept her eyes fixed on the jurors. "As you heard the sheriff deputy testify, Joe Gardner gave a nearly convincing acting performance when the two of them arrived at the homicide scene."

The prosecutor walked close to the jurors and turned back to the next photo of Joe's syringe, hypodermic needle, and surgical tubing that were spread out beside the Pathfinder's spare tire. "The most minor of the charges against the defendant might be the most telling. Yes, the defense has conceded this lesser misdemeanor, but what you see on the screen are the tools of a heroin addict. The prosecution has in no way argued that Joe Gardner isn't a bright kid who has demonstrated true promise as a student, an actor, and baseball player."

Talk about an almost convincing acting job.

"This needle and that syringe represent the tragedy that is Joseph John Gardner." Her beady, dolled-up eyes were directed at Joe. He wanted to tell her to quit gawking at him like he was one more prop of her contaminated evidence. "This young man found himself sinking, at the age of seventeen and eighteen, into the illness of hardcore drug addiction. Again, possessing drug paraphernalia is a misdemeanor. However, less than a year ago as a juvenile in Oregon, the defendant faced the consequences of his actual heroin dealing. And here we are again. Only this time, Joe Gardner's major drug drop contributed to a night of horror where he also drowned his longtime girlfriend and endangered her newborn baby."

Joe tried to stare the truth into Judith Rose's tiny black heart, but she pivoted away from him and glanced up at the judge before resuming her focus on the jurors.

"Sadly, this young man has not shown himself able to behave as an individual who learns from his mistakes. Joe Gardner has been unable to overcome his addiction to heroin."

This was where Joe felt his hands squeezing the iron bars of a prison cell for as many years as his young brain could imagine. But who was this murderous, baby-harming, drug kingpin she described? Not him.

She clasped her hands at her waist and seemed to nod towards the jurors before continuing over the whir of heaters lining the court-room walls. "Ladies and Gentlemen, Joseph John Gardner is a serious danger to society and must be convicted on all the charges presented to you in this trial. I wish to thank you for your time and the serious deliberation of your verdict."

To the spinning whir of heaters, Joe rubbed his upper arms to combat a chill that might have been from the weather that had invaded the courtroom, or more likely from this court of ice cold injustice. There wasn't a murmur in the gallery. The prosecuting attorney's logical lies made too much sense to comfort him.

He shook his head. When Judith Rose eyed him from a few feet away as she sat, he didn't know how to react. Mainly, he didn't sense the slightest bit of hate from the woman. Her steely neutrality didn't unsettle him when he realized that the woman held nothing personal against him. That hardly meant she was on his side though. Every-thing was just another day at the office for her. He sat confused. Did the prosecutor even believe what she was trying to sell to the jury?

Almost more troubling was Angus. His own lawyer didn't look his way, nod, or show any emotion when it was his turn. Maybe he was still annoyed at being rebuffed on his request to have the skirt tested.

Angus came off stone cold. "Ladies and gentlemen of the jury, what you've just listened to is soap opera fiction. Allow me to cut through the prosecution's nonsense." Angus moved a yard or two in front of the jury box and spread his feet wide. Even from behind, Joe could tell he was making eye contact with each juror to his right and then slowly to the left, until he had the full attention of all twelve. "The prosecution is putting on a magic act for you. They are desperate to cover up a sloppy investigation that contaminated and left out key evidence, all of which would prove my client's innocence."

He paused strategically. "The only thing clear on that night was that Joe Gardner did indeed return to the scene with the cop to find his longtime girlfriend missing and tragically drowned. This horror was very real. It was by no means theater."

Joe leaned forward on his elbows. He hadn't paid hardly any attention to Aunt Darla or his mom behind him, not on this critical morning. He needed to stay focused on the details of these closing arguments.

Angus raised his voice just a bit, and made sure to emphasize every key word: "Members of the jury, the prosecution offers you nothing but utter speculation of what happened on that most unfortunate of nights. With this, they ask you to lock up this teenager for decades. The prosecution presents no direct evidence that Joe Gardner drowned Mary Quinn." He added that if Joe didn't drown her, then he wasn't the one who was in that pond to endanger Grace, either. "As for drowning Mary Quinn, where is the residue of muck to show that Joe Gardner was ever in that pond? Where was any sign of that mud on my client's body? Independent laboratory results confirm that there was no pond residue found on the defendant's clothes. Where is any proof, whatsoever, that it was on Joe Gardner's skin, hair, or nails? There is none, plain and simple."

Angus stood taller and reminded the jury that, despite the prosecution having every opportunity to prove that the defendant had been in the pond, "finding no muck on Joe Gardner's clothes or body would have forced the prosecution to search wider for Mary Quinn's cause of death. As it stands, this is a botched investigation. The entire homicide case hinges on the unfounded claim that my client drowned the deceased while standing beside her in three feet of water. The 'reasonable doubt' in this case is crystal clear since the defendant was never shown by the prosecution to be where the drowning occurred."

"Slide number one." Angus picked up the remote and displayed an image of the swaddled newborn being held by a paramedic at the scene of her mother's drowning. The attorney proceeded with a new force in his voice that Joe hadn't heard from him before. "The prosecution contends that Joe Gardner was simply *acting* when he helped recover both Mary and the baby from the pond," Angus began. "We have shown over the course of this trial that Joe Gardner has no history of violence toward the girlfriend he'd been with throughout high school. These teen sweethearts had a loving relationship at the ages of fifteen, sixteen, seventeen, and eighteen. No one, including Mary Quinn's own mother, has come forth to say there was ever any hint of abuse between the two. Now you're being asked to believe, beyond a reasonable doubt, that Joe Gardner committed the worst violence possible towards the girl he very much loved."

Joe felt his cheeks flush at hearing his love for Mary being announced for the world to hear. He could see steam rising through Angus's tweed blazer. His lawyer's engine was humming full-out like the diesel generator chugging outside the courtroom.

"No. The prosecution has not done its job to prove that Mary Quinn's boyfriend murdered her. Despite Deputy Zach Riggleman's unprofessional rush to judgment, the officer *actually* described for you how Joe Gardner was beside himself with *actual* fear and *actual* grief that night. In *actuality*, this was far from an *acting* job."

Angus stepped toward the witness stand and, with one hand on the railing, spoke softly to the nearest juror, but loud enough for all twelve to hear. "So no, Joe Gardner was not *acting*, but he was forced to face a very real and loaded police pistol pointed at his face and helped the deputy find his missing girlfriend and the baby anyway."

His lawyer continued forcefully: "To believe the prosecution's argument, you're required to convince yourself that Joe Gardner was putting on a show for this deputy's benefit." Angus hesitated, and then his voice boomed. "From the outset, Deputy Zachary Riggleman, the son of the Sheriff's chief investigator on this case, has had an over-sized impact on shaping the focus of this case."

Joe's coveralls fit too tightly under the suit jacket, and the denim itched on his forearms, but at least his lawyer seemed to be alive and completely on his game. Even the courtroom had gone from bitter cold to cool.

"Slide number two," said Angus. "Yesterday we heard from the leading forensic scientist in the state of Washington." The same photo from Friday's testimony showed the jersey, blouse and skirt laid out on the landing stones beside the pond. The lawyer summarized Dr.

Schloss's findings of a compromised crime scene and the failure to test either the skirt for afterbirth stains or Joe for pond scum."

"Slide number three." Angus had designed a chart. "This entire case started with a premature assumption of guilt by a low ranking deputy sheriff. This bias took hold throughout Wanapum County and has funneled from the chief investigator of this case down to you, the jurors." Angus paused. "A top-down investigation is to be expected, but the county's premature bias against my client from a low ranking deputy, son of the chief detective, corrupted this investigation from start to finish, from bottom to top."

Joe expected Angus's voice to boom, but he spoke calmly instead. "The contamination of the crime scene, the serious shortcuts and lack of customary lab analysis in the investigation, all contributed to the prosecution's false assumption of guilt. For example, why would Wanapum County not wish to know whether the young man they are accusing of murder was ever in that pond? I'll answer that. If Joe Gardner had no pond residue on his clothes or body, then he didn't drown Mary Quinn. From all appearances, the Wanapum Sheriff investigators didn't wish to muddy up their neat-and-clean murder investigation. With this convenient 18-year-old scapegoat, why bother finding the real murderer of Mary Quinn, or the real heroin distributors?"

Joe scanned the faces of the cold-faced jurors when Angus continued. He saw nothing from them.

"Last week, the prosecuting attorney litigating this case expressed frustration that Joe Gardner's cousin had left the country and, as a consequence, she couldn't subpoena him. Members of the jury, as the defense attorney in this case, you may be surprised to know that I also prefer that Gunnar Larsson had testified in this trial."

Joe glanced over his shoulder. Sure enough, Aunt Darla's face had turned red again. Angus wasn't fingering Gunnar, not overtly. His lawyer pressed the larger issue, though.

"Slide number four." Half the screen showed the Bone Shrine, the other half the closed First Aid kit. "Ladies and Gentlemen of the jury. The Bone Shrine drug deal has been reported as the largest heroin bust in Wanapum County history. My client, and no one else, has been charged with felony intent to *distribute* this heroin."

Angus went over and pointed to the screen. "Did Joe Gardner come from Oregon with the intent to distribute all this heroin to himself?" He paused before walking closer to the jury box. "That's absurd. However, there can be no felony 'distribution' if there is no transaction between parties. Where are the other parties involved?"

Joe watched Angus pausing to breathe. "As the jury has learned, Mr. Gardner is an 18-year-old kid. In May, he was kicked out of his family house for relapsing. He worked part-time and for minimum wage pumping gasoline in his home town. He has also been living homeless in the woods all summer. He talked his pregnant girlfriend into giving him a ride to Moses Lake. They didn't arrive until late at night and went to a familiar, out-of-the-way spot where they could car camp that night to save money."

Angus shook his head. "I'm sorry, but does this literally homeless teenager sound like the key party in a quarter-million dollar heroin deal?"

Joe's lawyer pointed again to the photograph and outlined why it made no sense for someone in withdrawals to have had possession of so much heroin all the way from Oregon. "No. Joe Gardner stumbled upon that Bone Shrine stash and was almost immediately interrupted. My client was hiding his relapse from his girlfriend, and then, inconveniently for him, Mary Quinn went into labor. He left the newly found stash to help her give birth."

Angus walked over and hovered over Joe. "There is one huge question for the jury. Until we know who was involved with the Bone Shrine heroin deal––the actual buyers and the actual sellers––then of course there is reasonable doubt that my client committed this crime? It's simply not logical that Joe Gardner had any extended time of possessing the China White heroin without taking enough to keep his withdrawals at bay that night. So where are the principles in this deal, the *actual* distributors, meaning the *actual* sellers and *actual* buyers?"

"Slide number five." Angus put up an exhibit from the prosecution showing Mary legs pointed to the rear of the SUV. Again, he hammered how the prosecution's investigative team, out to prove that there had been a physical fight between Joe and Mary, even got this wrong. "Joe Gardner may not have been much of a midwife, but even facing the wrong way, he was doing all he could to help his girlfriend give birth."

Joe thought he saw two of the women jurors glance at one another and nod, ever so slightly.

"Slide number six." Angus showed the prosecution's photo of Joe's needle, syringe and surgical tubing next to the spare tire. "Ladies and gentlemen, the defense is not contesting this misdemeanor charge against my client for possession of drug paraphernalia. In fact, you will recall the outset of the trial when we entered a *nolo contendere* plea. Joe Gardner has had an addiction problem stemming from a gruesome baseball injury to his testicle. This young, star athlete was overprescribed synthetic opioids for too long a period of time."

Joe was sick of how often his family jewels became the topic of conversation. The ball busting accident and painkillers played a role in getting hooked, but not with his relapse.

"As Joe Gardner's attorney, we are owning up to the one charge that has any validity. We are likewise fighting vigorously to refute this convenient yarn of fiction that the prosecution is spinning for you."

Joe nodded slightly, just enough so it could be noticed to anyone watching him.

Angus continued. "As we heard in testimony yesterday morning, Mary Quinn was prescribed lithium for her bi-polar disorder and depression."

Joe focused on the wood grains on top of the defense team's table. This was the moment when he realized more than ever, the weakness of their suicide angle. It didn't allow Angus a strong close if, after ripping the prosecution for not finding anyone else in the heroin deal, his lawyer didn't insist that the dangerous murderer of Mary was tied to the heroin transaction and still running wild and free.

Instead, Joe watched Angus shift gears to Mary. "Members of the jury, in the hour when Joe Gardner was getting gasoline, there is a distinct likelihood that Mary drowned herself in a postpartum state of depression."

Or maybe she'd accidentally slipped while rinsing off her newborn baby on the air mattress, Joe thought, realizing how pinning the drowning of the brand new mother Mary on Mary herself must have sounded flat to the jury. Joe's stomach started to ache.

Angus stayed close to the jurors and, again, tried looking each one in the eyes. "We still don't know what happened to Mary Quinn in the hour-and-a-half when Joe Gardner went to fill up his empty gas can and returned with Deputy Riggleman."

Joe's attorney paused before continuing. "On the hottest night of August, Mary Quinn removed her clothes prior to climbing in the back of her SUV to give birth. Joe Gardner never entered the pond. The two never had a physical altercation following the birth of Mary's baby. Joe and Mary loved one another deeply. My client, the defendant in this trial, did not murder his longtime girlfriend."

Angus turned and pointed to his client. "Members of the jury, Joe Gardner is by no means a perfect teen, yet no compelling evidence has been presented to you that this young man is the person he's being charged to be."

For some reason, the courtroom shifted from cool to overly warm within minutes. The portable heaters and gallery full of bodies had kicked the iciness from the room. Joe shed his suit jacket. He hated that the last image the jury would have of him before their deliberation would be in prison coveralls. The alternative was to be seen with sweat rolling down his face.

Angus's voice boomed again. "Members of the jury, I am asking you to consider the importance of *reasonable doubt* here. The prosecution's case utterly fails to prove Joe Gardner's guilt beyond a reasonable doubt for either murdering the girl he very much loved, or being a drug kingpin in such a major heroin transaction. We stand before this jury asking for justice. Sending this 18-year-old to prison for felonies he did not commit would be the height of injustice." Angus paused to catch the eyes of each and every juror. "I sincerely wish to thank you in advance for your fair deliberation as a jury."

Judge Kantadillo gave jury instructions. He warned them, as he had when the trial started, to steer clear of media coverage of the trial, and to not discuss any conversations in the jury room with those on the outside, including family members. Joe couldn't believe how quickly the case shifted from testimonies, evidence, and legal arguments to his fate resting with those twelve faces he still couldn't decipher.

CHAPTER TWENTY-FIVE

VIII.
INHABIT

(Tuesday, November 21st)

L ike a molten lake spitting out objections, Joe's brain erupted all
through the night. Liquid fire popped, spurted, and steamed
with details from the trial. Joe forced himself to remain still, but
wondering and worrying stole any rest.

Time plagued him. He suffered this torture with the hours,
minutes, and seconds drip, drip, dripping like stinging, wet salt on an
open wound. If he imagined the seconds, then time slowed into a kind
of madness. He tried ignoring the minutes, but then the passage
would drag on like the months he'd already endured in this hole.
Sleep often steered clear of him in the Shoe, but last night was the
worst. Like some kind of surreal thump to the head, he learned late
the day before that today would be verdict day.

After Max opened the jail door, Joe could see the huge man

holding his trial clothes. Behind him, squat Sam held his breakfast tray.

"Why do you think the jury's back so soon?" Joe asked. "All night I asked myself whether or not that's a good sign or not."

Max shrugged. "I gotta good feeling about this."

"Why's that? It means the jury didn't spend time arguing and discussing." Joe tried a bite of grub, but his knot of a stomach rejected the thought of anything staying down. If convicted, Joe would be locked up for longer than he'd been alive.

After taking Joe's full tray, Max brought up the baseball tryout possibility. "My bro said he mentioned you to the new skipper, including the part about you being an Oregon All-Star. The manager didn't see why they wouldn't give you a chance to show them your stuff––that is, if you can come in with your nose clean and keep your head on straight."

Joe pushed his uneaten food away and slipped into his dress clothes. He pulled on his same old Nike tennis shoes, and then held out his wrists like he did before every trip into the courtroom. "Having no cuffs on my wrists should help me, if I decide to become a Dust Devil."

"I'll bet you've been cuffed plenty of times by screaming grounders down the line," said Max.

Sam and Max escorted Joe under the long awning. Joe had decided against coveralls after Max told him the weather was predicted to be twenty-five degrees warmer than the day before.

Overcast clouds trapped warmer air at ground level and Joe didn't feel any breeze. It was quiet, too, mostly since the 'holy, holy' church bells weren't ringing. When Max and Sam led him into the court-house and handed him off to the bailiff, Joe scanned the late morning gallery to see the largest number of reporters yet.

He did a double take when he saw Biff's new 'do with bleach blonde coils. She sat next to his aunt and mom, and with the glam styling, she looked cuter than he'd ever remembered. They all sat closer to the back row than usual. Father José was there, too, the first day he'd attended Joe's trial, so maybe his presence would bring in the divine intervention Joe needed. El Padre had on his usual cassock and sat beside his aunt. Darla was in her element chitchatting with him. Father José wore the expression of a priest who'd been cornered many times before by good Catholic ladies.

Angus seemed uptight, as unsure as Joe about what lay in store from this jury.

The "all rise" order came from the bailiff. Everyone in the courtroom waited for the Honorable Thomas G. Kantadillo to enter and be seated. Judge Kantadillo hadn't cut his hair since Joe's arraignment three months earlier and his white locks had begun to resemble a powdered wig from the 18th Century. He asked those present to be seated.

The judge asked the bailiff to usher the jury into the courtroom. Days and weeks and months of Joe agonizing about all the years at stake, and then—–boom! The verdict would slam down like a gavel. Joe fiddled with the buttons on his suit jacket.

"The defendant, Joseph John Gardner, III, will please rise." Joe felt especially eerie when hearing his full name spoken by the imposing judge. His legs wobbled when he rose. This was it. The foreman of the jury was also asked to stand and the bailiff delivered the written verdict to the judge.

Joe took a quick peek back at the packed courtroom. His mom sat rigid, like a bundle of uptightness ready to burst. After winking at her, she forced a smile.

He turned his focus towards the jury foreman, a man hardly different looking than any number of ranchers around The Dalles. The judge went down the list:

1). *"On the charge of Murder in the Second Degree, a class A felony, how does the jury find?"*

"Guilty, your Honor."

2). *"On the charge of Intent to Distribute a Controlled Substance, a class B felony, how does the jury find?"*

"Guilty, your Honor."

3). *"On the charge of Child Abandonment, a class C felony, how does the jury find?*

"Guilty, your Honor."

Joe wasn't sure he'd heard correctly until Judge Kantadillo spelled it out: "The Superior Court of Wanapum County in the State of Washington, by this jury verdict, hereby finds Joseph John Gardner, III, guilty on all counts. This includes a prior plea of *nolo contendere* on the possession of drug paraphernalia, a misdemeanor."

Joe heard the judge's words and then the actual gavel falling just as fast and loud as he expected. His mind detached from the courtroom. He drifted unweighted, like a rush of heroin, but without any euphoria. Every word being said in the murmuring courtroom echoed through the veins of vents, one spaced-out sound after another falling on Joe's head.

Kantadillo called for order and thanked the jury members for their service. He said something about, with the long weekend, his sentencing was being scheduled in eight days for Wednesday, November 29th at 9:30 am. Joe refused to turn around even though, faintly, he could hear his mother's sobs from a few feet behind him.

This wasn't truth. This wasn't justice. What in his life wasn't a colossal lie? Judith Rose stood with her back towards Joe before waltzing from the courtroom. The judge, without any show of emotion, retired to his chambers. Angus told Joe that he'd like to go back to the jail and confer. Why not? Joe had decades of slammer time ahead. The bailiff cuffed him. Joe didn't lift his eyes from the floor when escorted towards the two waiting jail guards at the exit.

"There's always a phalanx of reporters when I leave out the front of the court," said Angus. "Another reason to leave with you via the back door."

Joe had no clue what a phalanx was, and he wasn't in any mood to care. When the bailiff handed him off, Max and Sam took charge. The blast of brisk air wasn't biting, but the two jailers and Angus closed their jackets tight to the throat. Joe––still cuffed––welcomed how the wind chill dried his sweaty neck and face.

"Why so many unmarked troopers parked in front of the jail?" Angus asked Max. "And why the ambulances?"

"Some sort of internal investigation. Everything's incredibly tight-lipped," Max said and stopped with Sam and Joe when Angus spun around a few steps ahead. They stood under the awning and halfway between the courthouse and jail.

"Is it related to Joe's case?"

"Not sure," said Max, "but when you was all in court just now, we noticed a kid oversleeping in his E-Tank cot. When the admitting guard shook him, he was stiff, deader than dead."

Squat Sam chimed in. "Looks like he snorted too much of some white smack we don't usually see around here. The medics tried reviving him. We're still waiting on the coroner to haul his sad ass to the morgue."

"White heroin?" Angus asked.

Sam nodded. "Most of the junkies east of the mountains are hooked on 'Dark', the Mexican black tar."

Max turned to Joe and gripped his mitt of a hand over his favorite jailbird's shoulder. "I forgot to tell you this morning. Last evening we put your old buddy, Pedro, in his own Shoe. Violation of parole."

"Why is some jail mate your 'old buddy'?" Angus asked. "I thought the only ones you knew around here were your Moses Lake relatives."

"Two *Tramposos* jumped me on the first day in the slammer," Joe told him, no longer caring what his lawyer did or didn't know.

Max nodded a bit too enthusiastically. "Two against one, baby. Joe here took out the skinny dude by ramrodding his skull into a stainless steel sink. Then he held his own against the bigger hombre."

Angus's eyes widened and turned to Joe. "So why am I first hearing that you had a jail brawl with two gang members?"

Joe shrugged. "It was before you were hired. Strictly a jailhouse survival move.

"But who did they find dead this morning?" Angus asked.

"Some white kid. Had that smack stuffed up his you-know-what," said Max. "He and a couple other new jailbirds snorted it out on the icy, E-Tank porch last night. The boy overdid it."

Stocky Sam spoke up. "Someone said he'd been the underage mule for that Gunnar guy who split for Switzerland."

Joe figured that, a year earlier, this dead kid might have been him. Same smack, same job, and he remembered just three months ago talking with Gunnar on the same patio, except that the sun beating down last summer had been brutal.

He turned to Angus. "We gotta find out if this white heroin matches that China White they pinned on me."

"That's not all I need to find out," Angus said in a huff and turned towards Max. "I've got to check on something before I confer with my client here. Could you please take him to the attorney-inmate room? I'll see you there in five minutes, give or take."

Sam accompanied Angus to the jail administration office while Max led Joe to the sparse meeting room. Max could tell he'd probably said too much already to the lawyer, so he simply locked Joe inside.

Seated on a hard wooden chair, thoughts ping-ponged through Joe's head. He imagined this kid about his age sitting in the slammer and snorting lines of China White. If the lab showed a match, then Joe might have an out––at least an out for the heroin charge.

A knock came at the door. Max let Angus into the room before locking the two inside. The lawyer didn't bother to sit. "What the hell, Joe? Why am I only now hearing about your jailhouse brawl, an all-out slugfest with *Tramposo* gang members, no less?" Angus was pissed, a side of his lawyer that Joe hadn't seen leveled his way before. "As if you don't know, those fine gentlemen run one of the biggest drug rackets east of the Cascades."

Joe wasn't sure what to tell Angus except to repeat what he'd already told him. "First day in the slammer and those two *Tramposos* jumped me." He tapped his cuffs on the table. "What should I have done? Like I said, there's a thing called jailhouse survival. I promised the boss jailer that I'd keep my mouth shut about the brawl. Makin' that bargain to keep my mouth shut and stay in the Shoe is what kept me alive."

Angus's face was crimson, but he stared squarely at Joe. "I'll do what I can to make sure we get those heroin samples compared. You're just lucky there wasn't a 4th degree felony assault charge filed against you for that fight, especially with a serious head injury involved."

Joe scratched his ear with a cuffed hand wondering why a 4th degree anything wedged between a misdemeanor and his 3rd and 2nd degree felony convictions would matter in the least. "Those punks tried to kill me. Then, poof, I never saw them inside the jail again. And that wasn't because I wasn't checkin' over my shoulder every time I exercised, or took a shower."

Angus wore a tired expression and placed his hands on his hips.

He continued to stand on the other side of the table from Joe and spoke low. "I just checked the jail roster from three months ago. They only have a record of three new inmates being admitted on August 18th, the day of your arrest. Other than our harmless, local nutcase Cecil, the log only lists you and your cousin, Gunnar Larsson."

"Seriously? I watched the two *Tramposos* being admitted into E-Tank that day. They might as well be saying that those two guys weren't even here."

Angus's jaw tightened. "That's exactly what I'm telling you. Wanapum County Jail shows no record of them in here. Officially, they were never arrested."

"Those two homeboys were here alright. After that thick dude's chokehold, I couldn't swallow for a couple of days." He wasn't about to say how in Mary's first visit to his cell, her touch had cured both his ribs and Adam's apple.

"Was there anyone else in E-Tank when these two joined you?"

"First thing when I got in there, the guards transferred a couple of bikers to their assigned cells. From their mussed up cots, you could see they'd slept the night in the admitting cell. Later, crazy Cecil and my cousin were sent on their merry way. After that it was only me in E-Tank for an hour or so until they locked those two *Tramposos* inside with me."

Angus paced. "There's a reason I wanted to confer with you after the guilty verdict. Dr. Schloss has been doing some follow-up with his colleagues at the Washington State Patrol crime lab. To be honest, I was very disappointed that the jury didn't deliberate for a couple days longer. Schloss wasn't privy to the specifics, but a former co-worker of his assured him that an internal review of the county's investigation has uncovered issues that are far more serious than what we were able to find in time for the trial. It's likely the reason the Troopers are swarming the place today."

Joe figured that the verdict had him as good as hanging from a noose. He didn't know what to make of his lawyer's news. "I want to say 'good,' but sure don't want to get my expectations up––not in Wanapum County."

"The *Tramposos* were one hell of a missed opportunity to sow reasonable doubt that you weren't the killer," the lawyer said, sounding almost bitter. "This suicide nonsense that you and your mom started pushing from the outset with me––let's just say it made my job near impossible."

Joe stared at Angus coldly. "I didn't notice any other leads pointing to Mary's real killer. Besides, you got paid. I'm the one still facing prison."

"I'm still pressing forward, Joe, but you held back this ambush to your own detriment. I would have made sure you were transferred from Wanapum County Jail. Knowing about those gang members sure would have helped me argue your case."

At this point, Joe had no interest in playing a game of 'what if?' "Gunnar pushed the suicide angle when he had us go out on the E-Tank patio on the day I was arrested," he said. "He was thinking that getting my jury to buy Mary's suicide would be the best way to get me acquitted, to protect our family from ugly paybacks. He even bought tickets for my mom and his mom to visit him in Europe a few weeks ago. Gunnar wanted to make totally sure that those two were also onboard with his plan."

His attorney's face turned red again. "To Switzerland?"

"Sweden, actually."

"That's a pretty major effort on Gunnar's part. And here again, why in the hell am I learning about this after the trial?"

"Ask my mom." Angus's ruffled feathers didn't concern Joe. Not now.

"Do you know how much speculating I did about your cousin's involvement in your case?"

"That Gunnar was the murderer?" Joe asked. "He was pretty shocked when I told him about her drowning."

Angus stared coldly at Joe. "When they raided Gunnar's home before dawn and arrested him, you seriously believe that no cop asked him if he knew you or Mary Quinn, or where he'd been the night before, or if he'd ever been to the Bone Shrine?"

"How would I know what he was asked?"

"Except you're telling me that––wham! bam!––Gunnar Larsson came up with the Mary's suicide angle the instant you informed him of Mary's death. That's some pretty fast thinking for your twenty-year-old cousin."

"Gunnar's twenty-one actually, and pretty smart," said Joe.

Angus stopped at the end of the small room and turned towards Joe. "And clever enough to always have his cousin take the jail rap for him. For right now, after those guilty verdicts, we need to focus on one thing."

"What's that?"

"We need fresh after-discovery evidence that will free you. It can't be anything we could have brought up in the trial. New proof would be things like finding the real killer, or even the actual druggies in that deal who, more than likely, also drowned your girlfriend." The lawyer ran his fingers through his salt-and-pepper hair and gathered his briefcase to leave. "The best shot is to somehow earn a mistrial."

Joe's spent brain worked through many scenarios on how Gunnar might have been involved that night. He considered that Uncle Nils––always gone on business trips––was the actual Larsson drug lord out brokering big deals all around the country. From working with Gunnar the year before, Joe knew his cousin's heroin trafficking never centered on deals with two-bit junkies. Joe had been Gunnar's mule to a major Portland connection at the time he was busted.

"I haven't given up on your case, Joe, but the bar to clear is high now, a good bit higher."

"What do you mean?"

"We need something more definitive than simply sowing 'reasonable doubt'."

Joe's head spun. He pictured those Husqvarna dirt bikes in the Quonset hut beside Moses Lake. His cousin knew every back trail through the scablands. Even at night, Gunnar could have slipped in and out on the pothole trails when Joe went for gas. From what Biff had told him, maybe his cousin had actually lowered the boom on Mary when she wouldn't tell him where the First Aid kit was.

Of course, the same could be said for the *Tramposos* during that ugly little window of time when he was off getting gasoline. Hell, Joe didn't even know if Gunnar had been the buyer or the seller. So, if Joe was wrong about Uncle Nils––and he seriously hoped he was off-base––maybe his cousin headed up the *Tramposos'* Gringo Brigade.

Angus seemed to read Joe's confusion and frustration. "To be blunt, I'm not being paid to find Mary Quinn's murderer," his attorney reminded Joe when he rapped on the inner door for the guard to let him out. "If legally possible, my job is to see that Joe Gardner walks free."

CHAPTER TWENTY-SIX

(Wednesday, November 22ⁿᵈ)

Biff assured Rochelle that she wouldn't mind slipping into the back of the van so that Kuma could ride in front once they picked him up. He'd arranged to fly into Moses Lake only a few days after the lab reports confirmed that he was Grace's father. J-Globe had an intermittent charter between Tokyo and Moses Lake where the Japanese Airline trained its big team of pilots and support staff. Find a day when they were coming in or going out with their Boeing jets and the savings were good.

She took a right turn at the Wanapum County International Airport sign. "Pretty big runways here," she told the teen, "and did I tell you how much better I like you as a blonde?"

"Decided to bleach it back a bit closer to my normal color, but I like me better this way, too. I mean I never thought of myself as much of a Goth chick. Wow, you're right. This is one big airport for such a small town."

"An old Air Force base. Host for the supersonic transports. Test site for Boeing's 747." Neither of them wanted to bring up the verdict, but both planned to stay for the sentencing and, of course, to see if Kuma could use any help with the baby.

A 747 Jumbo Jet sat closed up tight next to a huge hangar with a J-Globe logo painted on the side. Rochelle eased into an empty parking spot in front of the Port of Wanapum offices and next to a Ford pick-up with a Port logo on the door. "Darla said there's a one-man US Customs Office, mostly to monitor manufacturers in the Port's duty-free trade zone, but also for foreign trainees and those charter passengers like Kuma."

"Can't wait to see him." Biff pointed towards the J-Globe main office next to the Port's and hopped out before Rochelle could set the parking brake. "I'll double check on the arrival time, make sure he's on the passenger list, and meet you inside the terminal."

Rochelle reached into the open area of the van where she'd left her handbag. She dropped driving gloves and her Blackberry cellphone inside the big purse, then slipped it on her shoulder before hustling through the main entrance.

Once inside the terminal, she surveyed the long hangar-sized room until her eyes adjusted. On one side of the modest terminal were two long rows of vinyl chairs filled with uniformed J-Globe employees. All the fresh-faced Japanese professionals seemed newly trained and under thirty. Their baggage was piled neatly, like a miniature Mt. Fuji. They all waited politely for their departing flight.

Along the wall opposite the waiting chairs between the rest rooms and sole baggage carousel, Rochelle noticed a U.S. Customs sign on the front of the taller stand-up desk that adjoined the longer inspection table.

The lone U.S. Customs Agent looked downright bored while tapping the two passports and airline tickets. Rochelle expected that he was speaking to another J-Globe employee, and even when the woman turned part way around, it puzzled her that a trainee would have a baby stroller with her. The buggy was crammed full of diaper bags and blankets and other small luggage cases. It looked just like the same bright red one she'd seen in front of the courthouse when Naomi chased her story down for the *Chronicle*.

That was definitely the same woman pushing the baby at the

Wanapum County Courthouse. She was sure. Rochelle's eyes widened and she edged closer to listen in.

Two large suitcases on a passenger-sized, hand truck for bags were balanced on top of a fold-up crib. Her baby stroller brimmed with blankets, a satchel, and diaper changing bag. Rochelle could hear babbling from somewhere inside the removable bassinet that sat on the waist-high inspection table. From the newspaper article, Rochelle seemed to remember that Mrs. Riggleman's name was 'Linh.' The U.S. Customs Agent opened two passports and the plane ticket. He spoke quietly so only Mrs. Riggleman could hear.

The woman pulled her fists from a solid white, winter down jacket and edged her tiny body close to the gray-haired customs officer. "Why you need letter for Jade?" Her voice was loud enough for waiting onlookers to turn and stare.

Baby Jade. The name left absolutely no doubt.

"A letter from your spouse is required for you to take your child out of the country, ma'am." The gray-haired man stayed erect, but responded in a measured, open tone. He had a U.S. Customs patch stitched to his chest, but Rochelle didn't see a service pistol. She remembered the Iranian university students in the U.S. in the late 1970s. Several returned home after the Islamic Revolution with children that the American parent would never see again. It justified the need for written permission from the other spouse.

"We come back on New Year," Linh told the custom's official. She had a looming presence for someone so petite. "Baby Jade will meet her Vietnam grandmama and grandpapa."

Rochelle was about to step in and inform the Customs Officer, but decided she'd call the CPS Caseworker instead, the one whom she'd talked to a couple of times since she handed Rochelle her business card in the maternity ward. Amanda would set things straight here, and with official clout.

"We still need both parents to provide formal approval for the baby to leave the United States and enter Japan." This time the customs agent sounded more firm.

"But we not stay in Tokyo. We take first airplane to Hanoi."

"Ma'am, since the baby is an American citizen as your passport shows, then this concerns the United States." The agent's tone turned impatient, even harsh. "Such permission letters prevent international custody issues."

Custody. Maybe it was time to ask this kidnapper if she'd like to be in the custody of the Department of Corrections for a few decades.

"Maybe your husband should take a bit of time to provide you his letter before your flight leaves. Your plane is a bit late and not expected to board for at least an hour." The official's tone was even testier.

Mrs. Riggleman turned and leaned over the whimpering baby. It could have been the customs issue, but Linh winced as though she smelled a rank diaper.

The deputy's wife seemed to regain her calm. She wore a look that seemed to say she'd arrived at a solution of some sort. She addressed the customs agent sweetly. "I try. Can you talk on flip phone to Mr. Riggleman? I very sure he give permission."

"I'm sorry, ma'am," the official said in a resolute voice. "We need your husband's permission in writing to serve as a formal document in our records, that is unless he accompanies you and your child out of the country. Doesn't your husband live with you at your Moses Lake address here?"

She grabbed the two passports and plane ticket. "Please watch my things. I change baby diaper," she said. Before he could answer, she left her luggage hand truck and belongings leaning against the U.S. Customs desk.

Rochelle walked towards the big windows facing the tarmac and fished in her purse for the Blackberry. "C'mon, pick up the phone!"

On the fourth ring, the voice she needed spoke. "This is Amanda Skerry. May I help you?"

"Thank heavens!" Once the CPS caseworker figured out who she was, Rochelle's rapid fire words spelled out the situation. "Linh Riggleman is here at your big international airport with Mary Quinn's baby! She's been going through customs with Grace. She has the audacity to call the baby, 'Jade.' She's about to fly away to Vietnam via Japan!"

"Are you sure?" Amanda asked in a comparatively calm whisper. "Her husband just arrived at my Moses Lake office for our custody transfer meeting. He's outside my door waiting for his wife to show up with the baby. Deputy Riggleman already seems pretty annoyed about being stood-up, so I'm not thinking he has a clue about his wife's travel plans."

"And I'm here at the airport to pick up Kuma, the real father."

"Mr. Kusumoto may not have Grace in his own custody until the paperwork gets ironed out next week."

"He might not ever have Grace if she becomes Hanoi Jade. I really need you to I.D. the baby and fake passport for the Customs Agent."

"I'm going to speak with Mr. Riggleman right now about postponing our scheduled meeting. No need to alarm him at this point about what you're telling me. I'll try to head over to the airport now with my State Patrol contact. I'll get there just as soon as I can."

Rochelle dropped the cellphone in her big purse and hurried to where Linh Riggleman had disappeared inside the restroom. She could hear Grace whimpering inside.

A privacy-wall inside the bathroom entrance forced Rochelle to turn and face four unoccupied wash basins below a long wall mirror. On the other side of the partial barrier, she could hear the baby growing upset. Rochelle stepped inside and turned. She glanced across the restroom with its three stalls before focusing on Mrs. Riggleman who faced away and was lowering the changing table on the far corner wall. Linh found a fresh Pamper in the diaper bag hanging off the stroller before she lifted the crying infant. The baby bawled even louder when Linh placed her on her back and loosened the blanket. Rochelle could see the baby kicking her feet. Grace sounded as though she wanted free.

Rochelle rolled her eyes when the Blackberry rang from inside her purse. Linh turned and seemed to give Rochelle a hostile glare, or maybe the look was due to the baby shrieking. Rochelle hoped it wasn't obvious when every muscle in her body tensed. No need to check her phone until later. Rochelle muted the ring without checking for who called, and moved towards the wall mirror where she set down her hefty, leather handbag at her feet and turned on a faucet.

How long would it take for Amanda to show up? Once the first blast of sink water automatically shut off, she reached inside the purse and found an oversized makeup compact. The mirror inside gave her the angle she needed to keep an eye on Linh and baby while pretending to powder her cheeks. The small, round mirror also showcased Rochelle's sleep-deprived eyes. The powder she dabbed actually did mask her chronic stress.

Rochelle glanced over when she heard the trash lid open and saw the dirty diaper disappear with the clank of the cover. When Linh lifted Grace, the downy, auburn-haired baby calmed down, but wasted no time whimpering again once she was tightly wrapped in her blanket. When tucked into the bassinet, the baby's sudden scream had the impact of airplane tires screeching on a landing strip.

Linh's cellphone rang. She forced a pacifier into the infant's mouth. "Where are you?" she all but shouted into the phone over the muffled baby. Linh stared towards Rochelle, who was still faced away and observing through the mirror.

"I need permission letter to take baby Jade from U.S.A." The infant cried again. Linh reached in the stroller, grabbed the pacifier and stuffed it back inside the three-month-old's mouth.

As far as Rochelle was concerned, this Riggleman woman wasn't taking Grace anywhere. She slapped the mirror shut and threw the compact into her handbag. The brittle plastic collided with her hard Blackberry.

Mrs. Riggleman kept on arguing with Mr. Riggleman that the permission was a simple oversight. "It take you one little minute to write letter for customs man." Linh made it sound more like an order than a request. From the sounds of this call, Deputy Zach had been the one putting on an *act* with Amanda this morning. He was no doubt conning the caseworker into thinking that he and his wife as foster parents were planning to hand over Grace.

"Hurry!" Mrs. Riggleman's voice stayed angry. "I tell you this much. I have the cash money." She slapped her flip phone shut.

The cash money?

Grace spit out the pacifier once more and bawled again. This time Linh didn't bother to placate the upset baby. She pushed her stroller towards the exit.

The unfathomable death, her son's addiction, her husband's bonnie affair, and now a scream-filled kidnapping all stirred deep inside before swirling into rage. Her indignant mind twisted like an

Olympic hammer throw with its heavy lead ball spinning on a rope sling. She grunted like a brawny athlete squeezing the handle. Rochelle let out a primal grunt. At the privacy wall, Linh never saw her huge handbag coming, never knew what hit her.

The monster purse burst at the seams. The tiny woman flew back across the restroom floor and crashed against the changing table that she'd hadn't bothered to close.

Rochelle let loose with a primal yell from someplace inside that she never knew existed. Her cathartic roar drowned out the crying baby. Soft shrapnel poured over the restroom: makeup compact, Blackberry, keychain, loose coins, business cards, tampons, small binoculars, pebbles of Tic-Tacs, full key ring, six shades of lipstick, Moon Pie, soft brushes, eyeliner, driving gloves, wine opener, and other nonessentials.

Her Rosary string also broke free sending oval prayer beads rolling around the floor. The string of Mary's *juzu* beads, the ones Rochelle carried in the purse as a special reminder ever since the night of the vigil, bounced off the top of the baby changing table before dropping intact into the farthest corner of the floor. On the opposite side of the end wall, her ripped handbag landed in the far stall. A woman inside let out a surprise grunt. Linh Riggleman started to get up.

Rochelle rushed for the stroller. She heard her Blackberry crunching beneath one winter boot heel and the compact cracking under the other sole. The infant wailed. Rochelle grabbed the handle of the stroller, kicked her binoculars aside, and pivoted the baby around the privacy wall before pushing her way quickly around the privacy barrier and through the exit door. No way was this woman going to steal Grace. No way. A few steps into the terminal lobby, Biff's voice echoed from behind, from inside the restroom, "Mrs. Gardner! Watch out!"

Rochelle spun around. She held her hands out to stop Linh Riggleman's lunge. All she could see was a chunk of broken mirror thrusting down like a knife. She didn't feel the cut across her palm. Only Mrs. Riggleman's winter jacket told her how bad it was. Red splotches of Rochelle's blood were splattering across the white nylon of Linh's down coat.

"She kidnap my baby!" Mrs. Riggleman screamed.

More blood covered the small lady's face. Rochelle stood paralyzed until Linh lunged at her again. Rochelle fell back and knocked the stroller towards the middle of the terminal. The sharp point of broken mirror from the compact stabbed down towards her eye. She almost lifted her good palm in time.

Full Nelson. Before the mirror shard could gouge her into one-eyed blindness, Biff tackled the petite woman from behind. The gleaming chunk veered off course. Rochelle heard it shatter into more pieces. The strong, short teenager's arms wedged under Linh's armpits and her fingers laced together on the back of the woman's neck. The full weight of Biff kept Mrs. Riggleman's face pressed into the cold tile of the terminal floor.

"How can the baby you're kidnapping be kidnapped?" Biff demanded to know. Her raw voice with angry words blasted into Linh's ear.

Seated on the cool linoleum tile, Rochelle couldn't believe a chunk of mirror could cause the lightning bolt of a cut running across the meaty part of her palm. She pressed down to stanch the steady flow of blood. Between her legs, Rochelle could see herself in a remaining chunk of mirror. The bloody face, wreck of hair, and eyes of confusion barely hinted at the broken, ugly pain coursing inside her. She rocked to and fro and clutched her hand harder.

"That's not Jade Riggleman," she heard a voice say. "That's a fake passport. This baby is Grace Rochelle Kusumoto." The CPS Caseworker had pushed the baby stroller to the U.S. Customs desk. Rochelle watched Amanda lift Grace up and lay her on the inspection table before unwrapping the blanket. She probably needed to make sure the infant was unharmed.

Rochelle could hear the baby chortling. Her sliced hand throbbed, but she spoke to Biff who was still restraining Mrs. Riggleman. "Maybe someday I'll have an opportunity to actually hold that precious baby."

Biff looked up from her Full Nelson. "I'd say the odds are shifting in your favor. After they stitch up your hand, that is. You're a bloody mess, Mrs. Gardner."

The teen gave way to the Washington State Patrolwoman who had arrived with Amanda. The Trooper cuffed Linh Riggleman's wrists behind her back, ankles bound together. With a cheek pressed against the floor, Linh sneered at Rochelle.

Biff went to the customs inspection table and reached into the diaper bag hanging off the stroller. She unwrapped a Pamper while hurrying back to Rochelle. "You should press this against your hand."

"Yes, you're losing a good bit of blood," said the lady trooper to Rochelle. "I'm calling an ambulance for you."

The next pang hit Rochelle's stomach instead of her palm. She could have been killed or easily blinded.

Airport security placed a "Temporarily Closed" sign in the threshold of the ladies' room. A biting arctic draft poured into the building through the entrance by the automobile loading zone. Rochelle shivered despite wearing her REI parka and underlying sweater.

Through the window she spotted an unmarked cop car––the kind that fooled no one. Rochelle immediately recognized the face of the man hurrying into the terminal. He'd testified at Joe's trial. It was Riggleman alright.

With the assault, her cut hand, news of the impending verdict, and saving Grace, it took a minute for Rochelle to register the latest twist. Riggleman walked straight towards them and looked down at Linh.

"What the hell happened to you?" he asked, not masking his irritation, probably caused mostly by Linh's pushy phone call.

Mrs. Riggleman––wrists still cuffed behind her––contorted her body high like a coiled cobra and glared at him. Rochelle noticed how bruised and swollen one of Linh's eyes was, evidence that the big handbag had hit its mark. In addition to the splotches of blood, Mrs. Riggleman's white jacket had picked up streaks of grime from the well-traveled tile in front of the restrooms. Her voice hissed at Riggleman like a pissed-off alley cat. "Money is in crib," she said to him, pointing with only her chin towards the U.S. Customs inspection table.

He glanced quickly and turned back to Linh whose head dropped back down to the tile. "No way. That cash is all yours, honey. And I've worked with that CPS woman," he added when staring at Amanda. "With precious Jade in the arms of Child Protective Services, I'm guessing you won't need my bogus Riggleman letter either. Good botch job, Linh."

Rochelle watched Chief Detective Roger Riggleman spin around to walk away. Except for his gray, flat-top haircut and the added generation of age, the tall, lean man resembled his son. Or more accurately Zach, the deputy sheriff, resembled his father. Rochelle's mind wasn't working clearly; she had trouble piecing the puzzle together. Her pinkie and empty ring finger had lost all feeling, and the portion of Pamper pressed against the meat of her palm had soaked through with blood.

Something changed inside where her deep pain festered. Maybe it was intuition. Maybe it was faint hope. Maybe it was Riggleman freezing in place when two more Troopers hurried inside the terminal. Behind them, Rochelle could see two Washington State Patrol SUV's in the loading zone blocking the detective's unmarked sheriff vehicle from leaving.

Mr. Riggleman pivoted again and took three quick steps towards the opposite exit that led onto the tarmac. "Hands in the air, Detective!" Her arms were fully extended and the patrolwoman's service pistol aimed at the back of the sheriff detective while she stood over Linh. "You know the routine, officer. Hands where I can see them. No sudden moves."

But the sudden move came, not from Roger Riggleman, but at the trooper's feet. Linh rolled as hard as she could into the patrolwoman's legs. The startled trooper hopped into the air to keep from tripping. While off-balance and falling, her Glock fired off a round. Everyone in the terminal froze. Everyone except for her two colleagues, one uniformed and the other plain-clothed. The two patrolmen rushed forward to tackle Roger Riggleman.

Chaos had hit Rochelle's world since August and, in this moment, she'd found the eye of the storm. She sat still, afraid to shift even slightly for fear of chasing away the strange calm settling inside her. Rear end anchored to the ground and a tornado ripping through the terminal, there was nothing to do but to stay still and continue pressing her cut.

When being tackled, Detective Riggleman grunted in surprise when his chin bounced off the floor tile. Rochelle wasn't sure if the detective was reaching for his own service pistol when one trooper torqued his arm back and the other kicked Riggleman's pistol so it slid well beyond his reach. The Patrolwomen leaned down and picked up Detective Riggleman's weapon. The two other Troopers cuffed the man's wrists with such force that his next grunt echoed through the open terminal.

"I honestly don't know why she phoned me," Roger said, no doubt sounding more stressed than he intended. "My daughter-in-law is a little tough to understand sometimes, so I thought I'd better come to the airport and check things out in person."

The words hit Rochelle with a sudden crispness that had her sitting up higher, pressing her wound harder and speaking forcefully to the men who had tackled Roger Riggleman. "Corrupt cop!" The power of her words eradicated any newfound inner calm. "I heard her on the cell phone in the restroom. He was going to pretend he was Mrs. Riggleman's husband. This slime-bucket, Roger Riggleman, was going to write a permission slip for his daughter-in-law to kidnap Mary Quinn's baby."

The plain-clothed Trooper in his fifties reminded her of a cross between Detective Columbo from TV and a cerebral professor with mussed-up hair. The man looked strangely surprised, not at what she said, but seemingly because she knew so much.

"First things first," he told Rochelle when the other burlier patrolman helped him pull Roger Riggleman to his feet. They read the chief detective his Miranda Rights before he was escorted to one of the state patrol vehicles by the entry.

When the patrolwoman's gun discharged, Rochelle had turned towards Grace. Amanda was crouching with the baby next to the customs agent with only his tall desk to protect them from flying bullets.

The lady trooper had forced Linh to roll with her face down and kneeled on her upper spine.

The uniformed J-Globe trainees had been milling in the waiting area watching the commotion, but the moment the shot rang out, every one of them jumped up and hid behind the seats or swarmed for the tarmac. When they opened the exit door, Rochelle had felt another gust of freezing air and could hear the descending, vibrating roar of a heavy jet landing on the long runway outside. A spider web radiated from where the trooper's fresh bullet penetrated the window directly above the exit onto the tarmac.

Rochelle shifted to watch the burlier Trooper drive away with Detective Riggleman. The plain-clothed patrolman hurried back inside, ran his fingers through disheveled hair, and seemed preoccupied with processing all the crazy events.

Rochelle overheard the patrolwoman tell Biff that Riggleman wouldn't be going to Wanapum County Jail, but to a holding cell at the nearby State Penitentiary at Coyote Ridge. The U.S. Customs Agent came over to Linh and, with the plain-clothed trooper there, asked her to explain why she had so much undeclared cash hidden within the collapsible rods of her fold-up crib.

"I talk to lawyer," said Linh from the floor.

"So, it looks like we have currency smuggling to go with the attempted kidnapping charge," said the plain-clothed patrolman. He suggested to the customs agent that, in a few minutes, the two of them should jointly count the cash for proper verification. Mr. Customs Man didn't disagree. The Trooper acted like he was the one in charge.

Rochelle twisted her head to see Amanda still cradling the infant behind the customs desk. The U.S. Customs Agent returned to his post.

"Sir," Rochelle looked straight up and said three times until she got the Trooper's attention. "I would shake your hand, but don't want to get you bloody. My name is Rochelle Gardner. I'm the mother of Joseph Gardner. He's the victim of Roger Riggleman's corrupt murder investigation."

The state patrolman nodded politely while reaching into his pocket for a business card. "I'm Duke Condran, Captain of Special Operations within the State Patrol's Investigative Services Bureau." He slipped his card into the side pocket of Rochelle's parka and handed a second one to Biff.

"We just call him The Duke," the patrolwoman said as she carefully removed the clip from Detective Riggleman's firearm.

The captain winced slightly at the mention of his nickname. "As of today, the Washington State Patrol has assumed formal responsibility for the investigation of Mary Quinn's murder and the aborted heroin transaction at the so-called Bone Shrine."

"A bit late to the party, aren't you?" Rochelle couldn't help asking. "I mean with the jury verdict already in?"

"Trust me, Mrs. Gardner. The Washington State Patrol doesn't open a special operation like this one without an exceedingly strong reason."

"*The. Duke Condran,*" Biff said reading the business card. "Is your given name really *The Duke?*"

Both Troopers laughed. "Sort of," said Condran. "'*The.*' is short for *Thelonious.*"

"'Thelonious Duke Condran.' Your parents must have been some serious jazz freaks," said Rochelle.

"Except I was a colossal a disappointment to them. After my first embarrassing recital in second grade, my piano teacher pronounced me officially tone deaf."

Rochelle smiled. "I'll bet your parents are proud of you now. I'm not tone deaf, but I can't exactly say that six long years of piano lessons launched my career running the local Chamber of Commerce." They both chuckled.

"This is not the place or time, but I'd very much welcome a call from either of you ladies if you have fresh insights on the case. The sooner, the better."

Rochelle tried to smile. "I hope that man you're carting away, the chief investigator on my son's case, didn't destroy every clue for you." She looked through the terminal entry door when she heard the siren and watched the arriving ambulance pulling into the loading zone.

Captain Condran stared down at Linh Riggleman glaring at them from the floor. "The Wanapum County Sheriff's chief detective is off the case and in deep trouble, Mrs. Gardner. We've already started going over the investigation evidence and, in the next days, we'll be scouring the area for fresh clues. The judge in the trial has asked for a preliminary internal investigation report from the State Patrol by no later than next Tuesday. I've been assigned that task."

"That's the day before Joe's sentencing," said Biff.

"That's why my team will be working this weekend and overtime to comply with Judge Kantadillo's request."

Rochelle had some serious trust issues of late with the whole legal process and wasn't feeling waves of either light or heavy optimism from The Duke's belated assurance. A medic rushed into the terminal and offered to help Rochelle to a waiting room chair. "I might faint if I stand," she told him so he positioned himself on the floor beside her cut hand. Seated, the paramedic opened a first aid bag the size of Rochelle's former purse and said he needed to very lightly bind the wound for the trip to the hospital emergency room. Gently, the medic removed the bloody Pamper. When he saw the extent of the cut, he chose to leave it alone except for disinfecting the most jagged and open part of the wound.

Rochelle winced from the stinging and looked straight up to see herself encircled by Biff, Captain Condran, and the patrolwoman. Linh Riggleman, still flat on the floor, turned her face the other way and bellowed. "My husband come. He put you all in jail!"

The Duke issued a directive to the patrolwoman still standing over Linh. "I'd like you to transport this one up to the woman's jail in Wenatchee. And, together with your overtime slip, be sure to file an event report before you sign out tonight." He pointed towards the bullet hole through the far window. "I'll call for some backup to help me secure the crime scene here."

She handed an evidence bag to Condran with Roger Riggleman's gun inside. "Don't worry, sir, the clip is out and the chamber cleared."

"I'm pleased to hear that, Annie Oakley," Condran said.

"Who's Annie Oakley?" Biff asked.

"A sharpshooter from Buffalo Bill's Wild West Show," said The Duke with a wink to the teen before motioning for the patrolwoman to help him usher Mrs. Riggleman to the other waiting patrol car.

"Do you have any pain killers?" Rochelle asked the paramedic.

The EMT patted his first aid case. "I do have something to help," he said and started rummaging deep inside.

From the corner of her eye, she saw Amanda approach from the customs desk and did a double-take. For a blurry moment, Rochelle was sure it was Mary walking towards her. She only looked away when she felt the other medic lowering himself on the opposite side of her. Rochelle would definitely need help from both men to stand up. It took her a second when, cross-legged, the other man pressed into Rochelle's hip and knee. Shoulder-to-shoulder, he set a bundle on his lap so she could see.

"Look at my daughter, Grandma Ro! She is perfect. So perfect."

Rochelle's eyes widened when she could hear it wasn't the medic. She turned to see Kuma pressed against her good arm. The presence of the young man sent a wave of relief through her chest. "Oh yes!" she said when the reality hit. "Grace is perfect." Her hand stung from antiseptic and the wound throbbed, but she needed this great surprise. More than anything.

Rochelle wrapped her good arm around Kuma's muscle-hardened back, tilted her cheek against his shoulder, and felt a surge of calmness. Both stared amazed––their first great look at the gurgling, grinning baby.

CHAPTER TWENTY-SEVEN

(Thanksgiving, November 23rd)

That afternoon, Joe buried his face in a pathetic jail pillow. If he had a spoonful of milk blood to mainstream, he'd shoot up and maybe croak instead of suffering his stolen life. Monkeys pushed his face into an eternity of cold cinderblock.

The harsh dream came on with security lights above the courthouse entrance and cast dim beams over the base of wide steps. The Bone Shrine sat on concrete instead of sand. Four coyote skulls were placed at each direction—north, west, south, and east—along the outer edge of a ten-foot wide circle of smooth river stones. The noses pointed towards the same owl crucifix on top of an altar built up with crisscrossing femurs.

Joe's legs and upper body were strapped to a Greek-style column at the top of the courthouse steps. His arms were bound against his torso and only his head remained free enough for moving side-to-side or up-and-down. He wondered when the authorities would come and force him to face the pillar where they would whip him until all his blood leaked dry and flowed red down the steps to bring life back into the bones of the shrine so the coyotes and cattle could run free.

But not yet. Media photographers sprinted past his bound body with flashes that blinded him. The press disappeared from his bound up newsworthiness almost as soon as they'd arrived and once they decided his worth was no longer worthy news.

Joe watched his cousin kick the cow skull with his feet and toss the owl skeleton into the night. Gunnar squatted there in the middle of the shrine and held a lit candle. He squeezed the handle of a spoon so he wouldn't spill the contents that were gurgling above the flame. His syringe sucked up the smack and Joe watched the last promise of pleasure disappear from the spoon. After mainlining, his cousin tilted his head back with eyes of bliss. The rush lifted him above the altar. Gunnar levitated with the same anchored smile that Joe knew so well and craved. On indescribable waves of bliss, his cousin floated into the moonless night sky above the courthouse. Joe tried to twist away, but couldn't, not when knotted and tied up for the crime of being the craver anointed to take the fall.

Gunnar hovered above, waving his empty spoon and needle. "China White!" he told the courtyard softly like he was seducing any fool who would listen. A screeching Great Horned Owl, talons fully extended, swooped down to rip out Gunnar's eyeballs. Before the enraged night owl could tear them from the sockets, his cousin twisted away and fell. He dropped fast and hard through the altar's foundation with a thunderous crash. He crushed every skull, femur and fibula inside the circle. Gunnar's own bones and each Bone Shrine bone splintered, granulated and disintegrated into a pile of heroin, enough to fill a junkie's sandbox for a lifetime.

Joe tried to free himself from the pillar. He needed just a bit, just a snort, but was powerless to move, unable to free himself from the coarse rope that was binding his freedom. Below him, inside the ring of stones, a midnight dust devil began to turn and lift and spin in a blur of whiteness. Joe's jaw dropped. He stopped resisting his bondage when the heroin twisted higher, nearly close enough for him to inhale. Joe watched the column of smack swirl on a jagged path across the courtyard lawn. The dirt whipped away and all that remained of the Bone Shrine at the base of the courthouse steps were smooth river stones in a perfect ring.

The night owl perched on the gargoyle above Joe. The two of them watched the whirling heroin disappear in the dark. "Gone forever!" Joe screamed towards his disappearing dope cravings. But had his meddling monkey really stopped clinging to him?

In a waking grog, he slipped out of the rope, stretched his arms, and sat up to the sound of Max, the jail guard, telling him he had a visitor.

"I don't want to see anybody, not even my mother," Joe managed to say.

"Father José said to tell you that you aren't allowed to refuse his visit."

"Then why isn't he standing in the corridor behind you like he always does?"

"Because he's in the visitor's area."

Joe pushed himself up and, already dressed, slipped into his worn Nikes. "Tell him this better effing be good."

"You tell him. I don't swear in front of no priests."

Joe allowed himself to be cuffed. Father José waited on the other side of the Plexiglas barrier––tall, black haired, and dignified, as usual.

"I keep wondering how someone repents for something they never did," said Joe, unable to vanquish the verdict.

"Only repent for the sinful things you know you did," said the priest, not sitting, and sounding too pleasant for the circumstance.

"I only crave one thing right now."

"I hope it's not heroin."

"No. Well, sometimes yes, but heroin's like falling for a whore. Every time she gets you off, you realize you're paying for love." Joe didn't know why he was talking so coarsely to the priest. He wasn't the one about to hand down his sentence.

"Craving what then?" El Padre asked. Joe sat on the same wobbly chair, but the priest stayed standing on his side of the Plexiglas.

"I want to escape into the place of freedom where Mary is still alive and with me."

"Is she what you miss the most, Joe, being locked up like this?"

"Yes, that, and seeing birds navigating the winds."

El Padre told him that his mom, with her stitched up hand and still on pain medication, would try to come the next day to visit. "Anyway, when she called me to come see you, she told me to be sure and wish you a happy Thanksgiving. The priest went on to describe what he knew about the arrests of Roger and Linh Riggleman.

"Will any of that free me? Is that the kind of after-discovery evidence that my lawyer needs?"

El Padre, whether subconsciously or with intent, touched the silver cross at his chest. "That's not my department, but I will pray for the Lord to look after you, Joe."

It was the sort of response he'd come to expect from the priest. "I'm just about finished with *Cuckoo's Nest*."

"So what do you think?"

"I'm more into the crazy Indian character, Chief Broom, than Randle P. McMurphy, the alpha male in the ward."

"Why is that, Joe?"

"Choosing to be locked away in the Shoe all this time is kind of like how the Chief pretended to be deaf and dumb in the ward of his mental hospital."

"Except you're not crazy." El Padre listened calmly, the way he usually did.

"Maybe, but maybe life's just one big test for our sanity. The Chief only went a batty because his Native culture was killed off when the big dam came in. I've lost Mary and my freedom, so I get it. I totally get why the Chief thought he was nuts. I'm not convinced about him being insane, though. Chief Broom is paranoid and withdrawn for sure, but in his odd, reliable way, he tells the whole story with clear eyes."

"That he does."

Joe tilted forward on the wobbly chair. "You know he's from the Gorge and around The Dalles, just like I am."

"Why do you think I gave you my copy to read?"

"All my ugly stuff has been pushing me closer to insanity, it really has, but does that make me crazy or just wildly confused like Chief Broom?"

"You're far from mentally ill, Joseph. I see much strength in you.

We'll talk more about the novel next time." Father José had a warm-eyed expression. "I had a dream last week."

"Tell me about it," said Joe, more than ready to change the subject away from his own mental health.

"I performed a wedding."

"Who were you marrying?"

The priest crossed himself. "You and Mary Quinn. Even though it was high noon in my dream, a Great Horned Owl appeared overhead from out of nowhere. It hooted and circled before landing to watch us from the top of a nearby, bushy cedar tree. We stood on bare basalt in the searing heat and you made your sacred vows to one another."

"You know I'll never get to marry Mary."

Joe paused. "But, in a way, she and I have always been together."

El Padre pressed his palms together as in prayer. "Yes, I see that, too. That was the first dream I ever had where I married anyone. Mary will be your guardian wherever you are." His eyes locked on Joe's. "On that rock, under that sun, and in the realm of the Holy Spirit, we consecrated your marriage."

He wondered if this was El Padres' gift to him, a way of sanctifying Mary's and his connection so he'd be able to endure his prison sentence.

"When Mary appears in your cell, she finds a way to let you know what she wants." Father José motioned with his head for someone leaning against the same wall to edge closer to him.

Joe jerked back when he saw. On the other side of the Plexiglas––tall and noble––Kuma Kusumoto bowed.

Seeing the bow, Joe realized there was no blaming him for anything at the core of this mess, not the Bone Shrine, Mary's drowning, nor his own addiction. There was nothing left inside Joe for this unexpected surprise. After the verdict he'd suffered, Joe had no more rage inside, at least not today. He stared at Kuma standing there so dignified. Joe couldn't tell if their Japanese exchange student looked more like a disciple of calm for Buddha, or Zeus about to take the hill and hurl lightning bolts for strikes.

He felt defeated, but appreciated how Kuma traveled halfway around the globe to man up. "I never had a chance to tell you, but congratulations on the whole baseball thing, Kuma. You seem like a Dragon-breathing kind of guy."

"Thank you, Joe," he said, and paused. "I am so, so sad to learn." Kuma stood tall. "I made a large mistake with you and Mary. For this, I take much blame. I have much shame."

Joe couldn't find any words. His chair wobbled. He grabbed the flimsy armrests and gripped them until his knuckles turned white. Joe pulled his breath deep into his chest so he wouldn't overreact. At least he wasn't hearing alibis from Kuma for why the whole thing went down with Mary.

After a bit, Joe nodded. He'd never seen tears roll from Kuma's eyes. What Joe saw made him also emotional, but not quite tearful, and the opposite of anger. He figured his resentment towards his prison sentence would surface again and again when spending decades behind bars, but he realized again––his own false steps were none of Kuma's doing.

He glanced at El Padre and then back. "Mary's been trying to get a message through my thick skull." He tapped his head. "I know I must make peace with you, Kuma, but please answer me one thing."

"Yes, Joe. Anything."

"That tattoo she had on her back. You paid for the She-Who-Watches bear, didn't you?"

Kuma looked into Joe's face, surprised at the question. After a pause, he nodded slowly. "How do you know this?"

"Your name means 'Bear'. You gave everyone gifts before you went back to Tokyo. That included giving me a jersey for your new team. Of course you'd give the coolest gift to Mary. As fair warning, the chieftess is watching you and me right now."

Kuma circled his eyes with both hands like in the tattoo. "Last night, I was a guest with Biff at Aunt Darla's house." He pulled a photo from the inside pocket of his blazer and pressed it against the Plexiglas to show Joe. Wearing her petticoat, Mary was in front of an Oregon Trail wagon, shoulder-to-shoulder with his cousin. "I bring this picture to show you. It surprised me to see Mary pinned on Gunnar's bedroom wall. She told me she hated your cousin."

How did Kuma also know this about those two being at such odds when he had no clue? "Then tear the thing into little pieces," said Joe. "No wait. Don't do that. You never know."

Joe saw something more mature and confident in Kuma. Maybe it was the recent professional success. He didn't look any older, except for the way he carried himself.

After hearing Angus earlier, Joe didn't know what to think or suspect about Gunnar, or whether he should ever talk to his only cousin again.

"Gunnar set up a *Gohonzon* in his basement," said Kuma. "Last night, I opened his *butsudan* shrine. I chanted with Biff to help find Mary's killer and to free Joe Gardner."

"Why didn't you stay in The Dalles until last June for the Major League Baseball draft? I thought your dream was to play in the Majors."

"My parents were upset. They asked me to return when angry priests tore down our great Buddhist temple. Also, after I got drafted in first round by the Chunichi Dragons, I know I will not go close to so high in Major League draft. Before I flew home, Gunnar told me I was chasing the Dragon."

Joe shook his head. "That was a sick joke from my cousin. Gunnar and me didn't smoke no Dragon-smack, but we were the ones chasing that big time heroin high. I wouldn't be behind bars and waiting for sentencing if not for his stuff."

Kuma tucked the tails of his dress shirt deeper into his suit pants. "One night after your baseball surgery, I watched you through the crack of your bedroom door. Gunnar had the drug and the needle and a spoon over a little flame. He helped you shoot hot heroin into your blood vein. No one saw me watch you. Not Gunnar, not you. I never told any person, but I was sad. I don't know why you were doing this with your cousin."

Joe rocked his chair intentionally, maybe to find a soothing rhythm. "Hell, I don't know why I let myself get sucked into the dope vortex, but I'm clean now," said Joe, not daring to admit to Kuma or El Padre how often those cravings still monkeyed, limb by limb, through his addict's brain.

"I spoke with Mrs. Amanda," said Kuma. He went on to tell Joe that the caseworker was keeping Grace at her own home with her own children where she'd be safest this weekend. "Next week I will have custody of Grace. Then I will take my baby to Japan." He added that the girl would return to Oregon for the summer. "Grandma Ro will help raise my little girl in the summer when I play so many games with the Chunichi Dragons. My parents will help me when my girl is in Japan."

Joe found himself hoping that their best laid plans at sharing the child worked out for them. "A world baby," he said. "That's what Mary said Grace was. Those were last good words she said on planet earth."

For a moment, both teens stood in awkward silence. Then Kuma spoke softly. "Yes. Grace will be a girl of the big world."

"Yeah, but let's get real, Kuma." Joe couldn't help sounding bleak when the words poured out: "I should be married to Mary right now. Mary and me should be raising yours and her daughter right now. We should be talking about having another kid, maybe not right now, but down the dusty road a bit." Joe stared at his handcuffs. "But Mary is dead and here we sit. Just so you know, with Father José helping me get my heart in a better place, I'm only jealous of one thing with you, Kuma."

"What is this?

"I've been doing push-ups and squats on the floor of my jail cell, just in case that jury was going to set me free. You know I've always dreamed of playing serious hardball like you. Before the verdict, I was starting to hope I'd play for the new Dust Devils team this summer in the Tri-Cities, near the place where we visited that made the first atomic bomb."

"I remember seeing the B-Reactor. I still work for world peace," said Kuma, "for *Kosen Rufu*."

"A new minor league team is starting up there. Single-A level, for my age."

"You hit and play third base better than the rookies on my Dragon team."

"I guess I wasted my talent, then. I'll be going to prison instead for *not* killing Mary, for *not* abandoning Grace, for touching––but *not* tasting––that Bone Shrine temptation." Joe knew he shouldn't have been so blunt. "Just honor her."

Kuma stared at him, confused.

"What do you mean by that, Joe?" Father José asked.

"Grace," was all Joe could say before staring at his feet and swallowing his emotions.

Father José broke the awkwardness by turning to Kuma to explain. "Because of Mary appearing to Joe in his jail cell, he knows in his heart that you're the key for raising Grace into a fine young lady."

Kuma laughed in a way that startled both the priest and Joe. "Biff told me what Mary wanted. Biff wrote and wrote and wrote me. She said I was the father of Grace because the baby wasn't Joe's. She told me the sad, sad news of Mary. She told me of the murder and the drug trial. She told me what Mary wanted. I sent my hair to her to learn the truth. Late into last night, I talked with Biff again."

Kuma smiled. "She talked and talked and talked until I was too sleepy and closed my eyes. When they opened, Biff still talked and talked." He edged closer to the Plexiglas window. "Biff was Mary's best friend, so I listened and listened."

Joe surprised himself by smiling, too. "So, you're saying that you got royally Biffed last night."

"Yes, but yesterday at the J-Globe airport, I sat next to Grandma Ro. There is where I held the truth," Kuma looked squarely at Joe and rocked an invisible infant in his arms. "America to Japan, Japan to America––the farther shore will call for Grace always."

Joe felt a rush of peace. "Even if I'm in prison for all the time Grace is growing up, I won't be hating you, Kuma."

Kuma closed his eyes. "I don't stop, Joe. I keep on chanting for you to be free. Try to find life force inside you. Please send me your strongest prayer, too."

"Why would you need my stinking prayer?" Joe asked, and noticed El Padre wince at his question.

Kuma placed his hands in the pockets of his slacks. "Because I am just a boy who is paid many yen to throw a baseball. I am scared to raise a baby. I am scared, but I do wish to be a good father for my girl with no mother."

Joe knew how impossible it had been to forgive Kuma, but somehow he had. And what 18-year-old boy wouldn't be afraid of raising a kid by himself? Joe had been petrified of the same thing, even with Mary leading the way. "I can pray for you, Kuma, but one day I'll thump you good if you don't do right by Gracie."

The Japanese teen bowed low and held the position like a prayer. When Kuma stood, the voice was low and eyes sincere. "Thank you for being my friend again."

CHAPTER TWENTY-EIGHT

(Sunday, November 26th)

"One hundred days," said Kuma when Biff eased her Loyale to a stop at the stout gate closing off the Potholes Wildlife Refuge to vehicles. Fortunately, Darla had warned them about the new barrier. Kuma and Biff jumped out and, when the girl opened the trunk, he pulled out the Larsson's garden cart, the kind with bicycle wheels on the sides. The crisp day hinted at a touch of warmth to come.

Only official vehicles were allowed in or out of the sandy road to the Bone Shrine. From the rear seat, Rochelle, with her good hand, pushed a box towards the door for Kuma. He placed it inside the cart before pulling past the gate and ahead of them. "One hundred days is the exact number of days," Kuma said, somberly, when they trudged along the primitive, sandy road. "Not one day more or less." Walking behind him, his same silver Chunichi Dragon jersey shimmered under the bright morning sun.

Rochelle shifted her new leather purse higher on her shoulder and tried to ignore the throbbing hand still protected by her sling. Not quite as large as the last one, she'd found the handbag at a Black Friday sale, but wished the strap had as much padding as her old one. Near the bottom of the primitive grade, the eerie, wintertime pond came glistening into view.

She hadn't written anything for Mary's humble Buddhist service, her brain distraught from the verdict and too addled from the Percocet prescribed by the hospital doctor for the pain of her well-stitched palm.

On the drive over, Kuma said he wished that his mother was here to help with the ceremony. His mama's lifetime of practicing Buddhism would have helped Kuma and Biff know precisely how to conduct the ritual. With the prospect of sharing the upbringing of Grace, Rochelle wondered when she might have the honor of meeting Kiyomi Kusumoto in person. Maybe she and Kuma's dad could fly Grace to Oregon next spring and visit for a bit.

Biff discussed with Kuma what the layout for their memorial send-off should be. Rochelle surveyed the landscape around the seep lake––Mary's pond. Farther down the path, she spotted a silver SUV with taillights and lift-gate barely visible in the sagebrush at the edge of the road. Rochelle squinted and stepped to the opposite side of the road for a better look.

"There's a car right by the Bone Shrine," she told the teens.

The three of them watched intently when they heard doors shut, engine start, and saw the vehicle backing out. The Ford Explorer edged towards them and rolled to a stop. The tinted driver's window slowly lowered.

"It's The Duke!" said Biff, "Officer Thelonious himself."

"How fortuitous to be seeing you three out here," said Condran.

The captain and another man got out. Condran introduced them to his forensic's man from the State Patrol's crime lab. "I was lucky to commandeer Dr. Pember away from the west side, even if Sunday was the only day he could get over the pass to Moses Lake. He actually trained under Dr. Schloss, the defense witness."

"Sherman Pember," the slight man of thirty-something said before shaking hands with each of them.

"Did the Bone Shrine reveal anything new this morning?" Rochelle asked.

Pember nodded with a smile and gestured for Captain Condran to answer.

"In light of the old metal First Aid kit that contained the heroin bundles, Dr. Pember suggested that we use a metal detector to fully scan the Bone Shrine and the shore around the pond."

"Why didn't Roger Riggleman do any metal detecting?" Rochelle asked.

Condran shrugged. "As you know from the trial, there were a number of problematic oversights with this crime scene investigation."

"But we need something fresh to save Joe," Biff said, sounding impatient.

The professorial detective nodded just hard enough for his mop of wild hair to shake. "We came up with something very interesting. A sample dusting showed that those bones, especially on the underside and out of the weather, are covered with fingerprints."

He opened the lift gate and motioned for everyone to see. The Duke gave them all the expected warning not to touch anything. Inside were two trays, the kind resembling the ones that post offices use for sorting mail.

When the scientist lifted the covering of one, it held a Swiss Army Knife with the pointed awl-like blade opened. Imprinted on the red plastic side was "J.J.G. III."

"That knife is definitely Joe's," said Rochelle. "His father, J.J.G. II, gave it to him for his 12th birthday."

"And it has some sort of powder still caked in the thumbnail indention used for opening the blade," said Condran. "Whether it's bone dust or heroin, we'll know soon enough, but it was buried in the bone shards beneath the covered altar where your son reportedly found the First Aid Kit."

Rochelle nodded vigorously. "Joe has said that he stopped just when he was starting to take a snort of smack. When Mary's water broke, she yelled for him to come and help her. Joe said he never made it back to the stash that night, or ever actually."

"From what we've also gleaned, he most logically dropped the knife just after using it in the manner you suggest," Condran added.

"If heroin residue is found, it will corroborate this sequence of events."

"I never dreamed that heroin could be our ally," said Rochelle.

The Duke nodded. "And just consider how worthless this would be as evidence if it hadn't been largely protected from the elements for the last few months."

Dr. Pember lifted the cover from a second, much wider tray. An owl skeleton was spread out flat on its back. "We carefully removed this from the top of the altar. We'll be taking this promising evidence back to the State Patrol's forensics lab."

"Why would the owl have any metal in it?" Biff asked.

"A souvenir pin," said The Duke and motioned for Kuma to step closer and look inside the upside-down cranium. "Since you're wearing the same kind of emblem on your jacket, I was wondering. Do you have any idea whatsoever where the pin wedged inside the bird skull might have come from?"

Kuma leaned over for a closer look at the upside down raptor skull. His eyes widened with excitement. "That is the pin from the jersey I gave to Joe Gardner. It is the only Chunichi Dragon pin I had in America before I returned home to Tokyo. My new team sent me the pin in The Dalles when I was the Dragon's round one draft pick."

Then Biff leaned in for a better look. "And the hair. I know that braid. I know that color. That totally belongs to Mary."

Rochelle shifted the purse strap higher on her shoulder before placing the good hand to her mouth. "At the end of the trial, during her closing statement, the prosecutor showed how one of Mary's two ginger-colored braids was yanked from her skull. Hardly thick enough to drag her into the pond with, but this was the braid Joe pinned the Chunichi Dragon souvenir through just before she gave birth."

"Weird timing for him to give her something from you before Grace was born," said Biff to Kuma before quickly turning away.

"Definitely," said Rochelle, "but he would never describe himself doing such a thing during the trial, not if he'd been the one to then stuff the Dragon pin and hair inside that owl skull. More likely, some sicko stuffed it in the bird head after drowning Mary Quinn."

"Like a murderer's trophy token," said Dr. Pember.

"Or to honor the Bone Shrine," said Biff.

"Or both," said Captain Condran rubbing his chin. "Of course, we'll first test the bird skeleton to determine that no prints belong to the defendant. After this fact is established, then we'll look for the positive match. As for the pin, from what you said, there may be prints of Joe Gardner on the souvenir from him pinning it through Mary Quinn's braid. Perhaps we'll find fresher prints covering your son's."

"The braid, though," said Biff. "See how the thicker end was sliced off cleanly. The way we saw how it was yanked from her head in the Coroner's photo, it should have skin attached. If Joe was the one who cut the end of the hair, won't there be traces of Mary's DNA on one of his Swiss Army knife blades?"

"Who's side are you on?" Rochelle turned and asked her harshly.

"She has a good point," said Pember. "This can help eliminate Joe Gardner as the one who stuffed the braid into the owl cranium, that is if his knife has no evidence of hair on it."

Rochelle couldn't figure why Captain Condran was sympathetic to Joe's legal fate. Then again, he knew far more than he could tell them. Still, she had no intention of getting her hopes up.

"Did your son have any other cutting implements?" Pember asked.

"No. Joe used that little knife all the time," said Biff. "He always kept it razor sharp, and every single chance he could use it, he did."

Rochelle nodded in agreement. "Look how the braid is coiled around the pin and completely fills the bird skull. I'll bet the part of the braid holding Mary's ripped scalp couldn't be crammed inside, so that's why the thick end was cut clean off and tossed away."

"Consider the sequencing here," said The Duke. "Joe dropped his knife under the Bone Shrine altar when Mary yelled that her water had broken. This was pre-childbirth and just before he has indicated that he pinned the souvenir into her braid. We know that the birthing went exceptionally quick and there was no indication of Joe and Mary having an altercation prior to the baby arriving."

"Of course not," said Biff. "Joe was expecting the baby to be his."

Rochelle noticed Kuma look down at his feet.

"It makes far more sense that Joe lost his knife well before the braid and pin were stuffed into the skull," The Duke said while scratching his chin. "Any trace of heroin on the blade will help confirm this assumption."

Pember nodded. "In this chronology, if it had been the defendant with the severed braid and pin, then it would not have been the pointed blade, but his cutting one left open when he dropped and lost the knife beneath the altar."

Biff chimed in. "And it's not like there was tons of time that night for Joe to do everything he was accused of doing. Think about it. It's a couple hundred miles upriver from The Dalles to Moses Lake. The gas station video where Joe worked had them leaving at 7:45 p.m. The Pathfinder of Mary's wasn't a speed burner, so that's three hours plus to get to the Bone Shrine. That would have been 11:00 p.m. at the earliest. Then after the child birth and murdering his forever girl-friend, now you gotta add this whole step of Joe going back down to the Bone Shrine, *not* snagging any heroin to stop his cravings, and taking the time to stuff a braid and souvenir pin in a delicate owl skull. And that doesn't take into account the five miles of running, walking, puking and sweating for at least an hour if that cold-turkeying fool was going to get to the Chevron mini-mart by 1:30 a.m."

Rochelle always marveled at how fast Biffy's motoring mind could work. "I just wish we knew exactly when the baby came."

"Or how long it took Joe to hide his stupid First Aid kit?"

Dr. Pember was scribbling numbers. "Fifteen minutes to find the Bone Shrine stash and hide it after arriving. An hour to run out of gas by the pond and for Mary to have her baby. In medical terms, anything that fast is called a precipitous childbirth. Whenever Joe left, it was roughly another hour for him to get to the mini-mart."

Captain Condran nodded. "Two hours and thirty minutes from 11:00 to 1:30 a.m. would leave only a half-hour for the murder, bundling up the baby on the raft, cutting off her braid, going a quarter of a mile back to the Bone Shrine, and hiding the braid and pin inside the owl."

"So it's even more obvious now that my son didn't murder Mary."

"Yep," said Biff. "But is this the sort of after-discovered stuff to warrant an appeal of the jury verdict?"

"That's up to the appellate court," said The Duke.

Rochelle shifted uneasily on her feet. "It makes far more sense for other killers on vehicles of some sort, to take advantage of an hour plus to do all those things to Mary and her braid."

Biff looked at Dr. Pember. "I'm thinking that you and The Duke need to find an actual match for the killer's prints for us to be granted an appeal."

Condran placed his hands on his hips. "Thank you both for your solid thoughts on the timeline. The State Patrol is bringing an open mind to our role in this reinvestigation." He added that he wasn't at liberty to share all they'd found out in the last week, but anything definitive would be in Judge Kantadillo's preliminary report. "Mr. Kusumoto. When do you leave for Japan with your daughter?" The Duke asked.

"In five to seven days. First, Mrs. Amanda must give me Grace to keep. Then I must arrange for J-Globe to fly my daughter and me to Tokyo."

"I'm taking Kuma to the Japanese Consulate and U.S. Passport Office in Seattle on Tuesday so he can square away the paperwork he still needs for Gracie," said Biff.

The Duke turned to Kuma. "Would it be possible to set up an appointment for tomorrow morning with you so I can get your formal statement?"

Kuma looked confused and turned to Biff.

"It's all good," she told him. "For his investigation, he needs for you to tell him that you only had one Chunichi Dragon souvenir pin in America with you. Things like that."

"Yes. If you promise me it will free Joe, then we can meet tomorrow in the morning," said Kuma, turning to The Duke.

Captain Condran smiled. "Your comments surely won't hurt his cause," he said and gestured towards the box at the edge of the stone landing. "Lovely morning for your memorial," he said. "We'll leave you fine folks in peace."

"On behalf of my son, I can't thank you enough for continuing to unearth the truth," said Rochelle, extending her good hand to shake Condran's and Pember's. The Duke, likewise, thanked the three of them for their ongoing help.

When the Ford Explorer eased up the soft road, they didn't speak, but stood in the winter morning sun watching until The Duke and his Trooper scientist disappeared from sight.

The late morning November sun made Rochelle forget how numbingly cold it had been only days before. "Where in the universe of impossible happenstances did the appearance of those two investigators come from?" Rochelle finally asked.

"From Mary," said Kuma.

"Yes. Don't forget the power of our chanting, Mrs. Gardner," said Biff. "I'll bet that pin and hair are going to save Joe. And, Kuma, see how your gift to Joseph came back to him!" everything comes back around exactly the way it's supposed to."

Kuma unloaded a small bell, bell-stick, incense burning box, and incense on a level area of the landing stones.

The Arctic weather had cleared the pond of the dense green algae that Rochelle remembered from early September, the lone time she could bring herself to come here after the drowning.

"I sure hope Mary will approve of our memorial service." Biff's tone of voice was subdued, without its usual manic delivery.

"She'll love your loving gesture," Rochelle told her.

Kuma pulled two small pillows from the cart and placed them a yard apart at the edge of the clear winter pond.

Rochelle remembered when her devout grandfather had died. Their Catholic church held a 100-day memorial prayer service, too. The time-honored remembrance for Mary couldn't be on the 99th or 101st day, but only on this Sunday, the 100th since Mary had drowned in this pond.

Father José had invited Darla and Rochelle to a rare Mass he was presiding over at the nearby parish. Her sister had decided she was going to be a good Catholic this morning and attend, but promised her sister that she'd definitely go to any proper burial they had for Mary, once the girl's body was no longer being held as evidence.

Rochelle decided that she'd give her own eulogy at that service, but wasn't about to miss Kuma's and Biff's impromptu ceremony. "It was nice that my sister let you use her garden cart and what you needed from Gunnar's own little Buddhist shrine," said Rochelle.

She remembered Darla telling her that it was the least her son could do to honor Mary Quinn. Rochelle didn't dare ask what Darla had meant. She wondered how many times her sister suspected that Gunnar had drowned Mary in this very pond. She shuddered and clutched the elbow of her healing limb while thinking that her self-exiled nephew might well own the fingerprints on that owl skeleton and the pin inside.

One of the little pillows was shaped like a lotus blossom and made with red and purple silk fabric. Kuma placed it on top of a lone, level river rock. Gingerly, he set a black brass bell––the size of cupped palms––on top.

Biff placed the other pillow, flat and square, on several smooth stones that, together, created a fairly level surface. Also of silk, but a solid ivory color and one-foot wide and long, the fabric featured embroidered cranes in flight, wings spread wide.

The first thing Kuma placed on this square pillow top was a small burner box for incense. It also featured cranes in the shape of two gold medallions inlayed into the side of the shiny black box. The two large birds faced one another on either side with wings extended into perfect circles. The wingtips touched above their heads like ballerinas in *releve* pose. Rochelle wondered if the medallions were of solid gold. Even though Gunnar had claimed to be clean when he started his Buddhist practice last winter, her nephew was no doubt flush with plenty of drug money to splurge on such gold and silk treasures. Maybe her nephew had seen the error of his ways and, in addition to finding a spiritual path, he really was doing his best to protect his family.

Biff leaned a pewter frame against the gilded incense burner at the center of the pillow. Inside the frame was a photo of Mary in her petticoat without a bonnet. Kuma had shown her the picture that was taken the summer before last. Plumes of ginger locks framed Mary's beautiful, Irish-freckled face. For its use in today's memorial, Gunnar had been cropped cleanly out of the image.

Kuma motioned for Biff to kneel beside him and face the pond. He rang the bell with his etched stick. The rich tone reverberated through the morning stillness. Kuma poured sandalwood shavings into the black burner box. He and Biff––still kneeling––began the memorial by chanting *nam myoho renge kyo* three times slowly and then quite fast for several minutes.

The little seep lake was a foot or two lower than it had been last summer and lined now with stalks of reeds browned from the dormancy of early winter. When their chanting subsided, Kuma and Biff turned away from the pond to face Rochelle. "I told Biff that I did not wish to spend this morning for Mary at the Shrine of Bones." Kuma looked down and began reading from a stack of index cards that Biff had helped him write. "In Japan, our Bon-é is not a shrine, but a day when we remember the dead. One hundred days after death is a special time, a time for us to let go of Mary on this side, and for her to find peace on the other."

Biff made sure Kuma had finished before beginning her tribute. She took care to speak slowly and steadily. "This sonnet is inspired by *The Lotus Sutra*. Mary Quinn and I have been best friends since we were eight-years-old." Biff had to stop and take a big breath before beginning. "Even then, I knew she was very special."

She's the Dragon Girl who's always bringing
Instant dharma from the Lotus Sutra.
Perceive the sound and hear Mary singing
Her voice a pearl, the jewel she gives Buddha.

This is the day we shall usher our friend
to the pure land of true peace and delight.
Adorned seat upon the lotus, she ascends――
Bodhisattvas will bless her sound, her light.

Rochelle stared glassy-eyed at the small photo of Mary.

Singing forth a swirl of sandalwood haze
She vanquished the armies of birth and death.
Mystic flower, she'll forever amaze.
Peaceful waters like faith, lift her sweet breath.

Her sound the gift our hearts, boundless, will trace,
Unto her blossoming petals of grace.

The emotions seemed to come from somewhere beyond Rochelle.

Thoughts of Mary--gone from this world far too young--had Rochelle openly crying. Biff looked up and saw her. She cried, too, struggling to continue. "You both know that I loved Mary like a sister," was all Biff could say, but Rochelle knew for these two only children, their sisterhood was real.

Kuma leaned over the gold crane medallions and lit shavings of incense the color of Mary's natural hair. A deep, woody smoke, soft and floral, filled the Sunday morning air.

Rochelle's head began to spin, probably from the third Percocet she'd taken to make sure her hand didn't hurt like crazy during Mary's memorial. She'd been hurting enough. A loopy, languid calm flowed through her system masking the pain of her stitched hand.

The burning sandalwood left a thin layer of smoke hovering six feet above the pond like a duvet. Kuma lifted another card and kept reading: "My Nichiren teacher once instructed me that Buddhism begins with the inner self. We are taught to hold faith like water, not faith like fire."

On this clear winter morning, she enjoyed the smell of incense and felt her own delusion of opioid-tainted euphoria, a tiny taste of the kind that had engulfed her son inside his flaming addiction.

Kuma stood, turned first towards Rochelle and then to Biff before continuing. "Mary drowned in this pond. She is like a hungry ghost today. In death, she has been hanging upside-down with a mother's worry for Grace."

Kuma had remained outwardly patient during this long weekend before he could take formal custody of Grace. His inward worries sounded through his words. "Mary Quinn is still upside-down for Joe Gardner. The Bone Shrine brought too much fire into the lives of Joe and Mary. We are here to honor Mary in the same water where she left us."

He took the bell stick again. The sonorous toll rang over the pond. Rochelle did her best to join in with the same ancient words of devotion to the mystic dharma of the Lotus Sutra. Across the winter pond on the hundredth day since Mary had drowned, they chanted *nam myoho renge kyo*.

Biff knelt next to the pillow that held burning incense and Mary's framed photo. "Lotus seeds," she whispered when the vibrations calmed. She set three small bulbs of the pond plant in front of Mary's pewter picture frame.

At the edge of the road, Rochelle took her good hand and rummaged through the replacement purse. Zipped safely inside a pocket deep within, she pulled out Mary's sandalwood *juzu* necklace and handed it to Biff.

Mary's best friend draped the prayer beads over a top corner of the pewter picture frame. Cradling the square, thin pillow on top of her palms, she was careful not to upend anything. Biff placed the funerary raft into the pond and nudged the memorial free from shore. In silence, they all watched Mary's framed image drifting towards an open pool in the middle of the pond.

Rochelle found herself wishing that Mary's mother could have been here, both for the touching memorial and so Bonnie could meet her granddaughter. Biff heard that Bonnie had skipped the state following her DUI on the night of her court testimony. Apparently, she was going to take up a standing offer from some bar owner in Memphis, Tennessee. Bonnie Quinn would be performing on Beale Street at a blues-rock bar called Silky O'Sullivan's. Rochelle wished Mary's talented mother all the best in this difficult world.

Mary's tiny memorial raft drifted towards the same reeds that had hidden the newborn from the landing. Rochelle knew within that moment how Grace would grow up into a stunning woman. Kuma had such a handsome face and winning smile, while Mary was quite the natural beauty. Both held themselves with such a strong presence, too. Grace, from the start, had too much going for her. Wisps of burning sandalwood curled into still, cool air.

A dry autumn and the Arctic blast's killing cold had turned the still water crystalline clear. A minute or two elapsed after the raft floated to the most open part of the marsh. Water soaked the pillow. The beaming sun of the late winter morning sat perfectly in the sky for Rochelle to see Mary's raft beginning to list into the glassy water.

The weight of the pewter frame and incense box started sinking the pillow. Pond water gurgled. The burning incense came alive with a loud sizzle. After a few more moments, Mary's framed photo sank into silence. The glint of gold medallions shimmered like angler lures until the depths swallowed her raft darkly. Only the *juzu* and incense ashes, both of sandalwood, remained floating on the surface.

Mary had once explained to Rochelle how mud beneath the water was like suffering in life. The girl who had chosen Rochelle's care and love had said that a lotus required mud to grow and find wisdom-- and water, like faith, to blossom.

CHAPTER TWENTY-NINE

Wednesday, November 29th

S*entencing day.* Rochelle scanned the courtroom. Same defense team table. Same cast of characters, except there were no jurors. On Friday morning, Angus had filed a post-verdict motion with the court to deny the jury decision.

As soon as the judge sat, Judith Rose stood. "Your Honor, the prosecution objects on the grounds that we have found no precedent in Washington State for such a motion."

Angus jumped up and was granted the opportunity to approach the bench along with Judith Rose. He submitted a list of numerous cases, most all in other states, where his motion had been allowed on the same grounds.

The judge looked at the prosecuting attorney. "The defense has made a valid motion for me to rule on, Ms. Rose. Considering the magnitude of the after-discovery evidence, it would be a miscarriage of justice for me *not* to examine these new findings prior to exercising my authority in the sentencing of the defendant."

Judith Rose sat down at the prosecution's table in a bit of a huff when Judge Kantadillo ordered the State Patrol's investigative report to be formally admitted.

Biff and Kuma had entered the courtroom and joined Rochelle just as the judge came in from his chambers, so she didn't have an opportunity to discuss any new trial developments with the teens. The two arrived at the Longhouse Inn of Smohalla from Seattle late the night before after Kuma's appointments to secure Grace's needed documents.

Biff was wedged between Rochelle and Kuma when he leaned across her. "Mrs. Amanda said that the State will give Grace to me tomorrow. I will fly J-Globe with my baby to Tokyo on the next day."

Rochelle smiled for the first time that morning. "No matter what happens here, I'd love to spend tomorrow with Grace and you."

Biff elbowed him. "Me, too."

Kuma smiled and nodded to both.

While the court reporter was entering the report, Biff whispered at how shocked she was not to see Darla at the sentencing hearing. Rochelle shrugged at the sarcasm. She hadn't gotten over the shouting match with her sister.

On Monday afternoon, their nasty exchange played out in front of the two teens. On the heels of a State Patrol raid of her sister's and brother-in-law's home, they stood on the patio once the Troopers finished ransacking Gunnar's old bedroom, confiscated his desktop computer, personal effects, and the gritty, broken dirt bike from where it had been wedged upside down in a motorcycle repair stand under the Quonset hut beside the lake.

Darla's outburst resulted in Rochelle and the two teens leaving as soon as they could pack. Rochelle arranged for the hotel rooms. The family argument had centered around Darla's same double standard. Maybe Rochelle should have kept her mouth shut, but she was sick of Joe being nothing but junk and Gunnar always so golden. Rochelle may have been irate when they left, but ever-polite Kuma had turned back to thank his hostess so very much for her hospitality.

Judge Kantadillo asked Wanapum County Sheriff Sergeant Jack Pack to be sworn in. The head of the County K-9 unit approached the witness stand.

Rochelle noticed Biff beside her doing nothing to hide the crossed fingers on her lap. She watched Kuma also crossing his fingers. He probably thought this was the custom when attending an American trial. Rochelle found herself smiling a bit at the sight of them looking like such kids.

Pack twisted the ends of his handlebar mustache before taking his oath. The cop acknowledged that, yes, he had read the preliminary internal investigation report and did not disagree with any of its findings. He told the judge that, on the night in question, the Dutch Shepherd assigned to him had discovered the First Aid kit hidden in branches of the cedar tree near the Bone Shrine.

"My dog, Escher, is fully trained to locate several kinds of drugs, including heroin."

The canine cop testified that when he arrived at the cedar tree, he put on latex gloves and carefully opened the metal kit to see what it contained.

"Did you examine the contents thoroughly?"

"Yes, your Honor, I found eight labeled bundles, each stating: *China White, 0.25 kilos.* I shut the kit and called over our chief investigator, Roger Riggleman. He needed to see, right away, what my dog had discovered."

"Did you stay with Chief Investigator Riggleman to help him log the First Aid kit and its contents?"

"No sir. The chief already had his camera on a strap around his neck. He directed me to walk around the seep pond so I could investigate that area to see if we could locate any more drugs there, or additional torn clothing."

"So, are you saying that Detective Roger Riggleman was left alone with the newly found stash of heroin?"

The man's big mustache seemed to jiggle nervously, like he was ill-at-ease to say anything negative about the man who had been his boss up until a week earlier. "Yes, your Honor, he was alone there for at least five minutes. At that point, there were no law officers present near the Bone Shrine." He spoke his words haltingly. "The other sheriff deputies were over by the pond and in the vicinity of the defendant, the victim, and the vehicle."

Judith Rose stood up and spoke as though she'd heard enough. "Objection, your Honor. In all due respect, you reprimanded me for

not subpoenaing Biff McCoy, the young woman sitting in the gallery."
Biff sat up surprised, but didn't uncross her fingers. "Yet here, sir, you
are questioning a witness that, likewise, could have been subpoenaed
by the defense counsel during the trial."

The prosecutor had what seemed like a valid point. Why hadn't
Angus subpoenaed the K-9 cop when he could have and should have?
Then again, Roger Riggleman was still his boss then. At that time,
Sergeant Pack would have likely testified nothing more than an
inability to recall the incident.

"On what grounds are you objecting?" the judge asked Judith Rose.

"Sir. The allowance of this post-verdict testimony violates the
integrity of due process. The jury findings are being questioned and
on trial this morning."

The judge spoke firmly. "Objection overruled. After-discovery
evidence is part of the due process, Ms. Rose. Sergeant Pack's testimony is directly related to the new findings from the investigative
report that you've had the opportunity to read."

The prosecutor wouldn't back down. "Except, your Honor,
Sergeant Pack is currently testifying about the night of the drug bust
and drowning. Again, nothing he is describing was off-limits for the
defense to bring up during the jury trial."

"Again, the motion is denied," the judge told her as though unsur-
prised by her doggedness. "The State Patrol's involvement with the K-
9 sergeant revealed how the chain of discovery was violated that
night. For the record, your chief investigator also had ample opportunity to disclose any chain-of-custody incidents. He also had the
authority to direct the K-9 sergeant to remain with him to protect the
evidentiary integrity of your felony drug distribution charge." The
judge spoke quieter, as if only for Judith Rose's benefit. "And come to
find out that, after the verdict, two of the eight bundles of heroin had
been unaccounted for, that is, until one of those was discovered when
your chief investigator's home was raided on the day after our jury
verdict."

The judge turned to the witness and spoke more loudly again, but
still with a measured tone. "So Sergeant, are you stating that there
were many officers at the crime scene, but none, including you, were

directed by the chief investigator to assist him in verifying the quantity of heroin that was found by your dog?"

After what the judge had said to the prosecuting attorney, the K-9 sheriff seemed calmer and responded in a tone that came off as easy to believe. "That's correct, sir. Detective Riggleman was definitely in charge and acted in that way. He orchestrated all aspects of the crime scene activities."

Judge K. nodded slowly. "This preliminary report from the State Patrol also indicates that your same Dutch Shepherd assisted their investigation within the Wanapum Sheriff headquarters. Is this correct, Sergeant Pack?"

The head of the K-9 unit agreed, and described how the State Patrol had requested his help the prior week, on Monday, November 20th. In the room where Wanapum Sheriff Department officials check out police work items such as riot gear or cameras, his dog had discovered a trace amount of heroin inside one of the police camera bags.

"Was this the same camera bag checked out to Detective Roger Riggleman on the night in question?" Judge Kantadillo asked and tapped one of the stickers highlighting a page in the report.

"Yes, your Honor. Traces of heroin were detected inside the large, zipped side pocket of the same camera bag assigned to Detective Riggleman on August 18th at 2:45 am. Our Sheriff records show that the bag has only been checked out to the chief investigator in the months since. Frankly, sir, it is not uncommon for the bosses to drive the same vehicles or to have sole use of favored items. Chief Detective Riggleman asserted such a privilege over this investigation scene camera."

The judge nodded and turned the page of the report. "And was this discovery the basis for a search warrant at Roger Riggleman's Moses Lake home on the morning following the jury verdict, Wednesday, November 22nd, 2000?"

"Yes, sir. On the basis of my dog's findings, a search warrant was issued by Judge Beverly Quincy for that day. During the raid, hidden behind the wall of a basement closet, my shepherd also found a well-hidden, unopened bundle of China White. It was found to be a match to the vacuum-sealed bundles of heroin confiscated near the Bone Shrine."

Judith Rose stood and objected in the most calm-and-collected manner that Rochelle had yet to see from her. "Your Honor, in due respect, the prosecution objects. The jury was convinced, beyond reasonable doubt, of the defendant's guilt on the felony charge of attempting to distribute heroin."

Again, the judge was unruffled. "Prosecutor, the after-discovery evidence that has been procured by the State Patrol is hardly limited to the drug transaction. This is clear from State Patrol's submitted report you were given. We're focused this morning on a motion by the defense that is rooted on the question of whether new evidence clearly demonstrates a systematic obstruction of justice during the investigation of this case."

The judge thanked the officer for his testimony. When Judith Rose sat, she had the look of one whose sure victory was surely in jeopardy.

Rochelle recalled the conversation with Joe about his Swiss Army knife and how her son said he'd punctured one of the sealed, plastic heroin bundles when craving to snort just enough powder to stave off his cold turkey. Instead of finding his nostrils when Mary yelled for his help, the white powder must have seeped out of that hole later and lined the camera case pocket for the Shepherd to smell over three months later. To think that Riggleman had snagged the only punctured pouch out of those eight China White bundles in the First Aid kit. If not, the State Patrol wouldn't have had justification to obtain the Riggleman search warrant.

"That dog deserves a medal," said Biff. Hers and Kuma's fingers were still crossed. Rochelle crossed her legs and bounced her foot. She was much too bound up with anticipation to respond to Biff.

The next witness took his oath on the bailiff's Bible. State Patrol Captain Duke Condran told the judge that their forensic's lab had not yet established a positive match for the fingerprints found on the owl skull.

The Duke adjusted his glasses and ran fingers through his unruly hair. "Your Honor, no one remotely associated with the drug deal or drowning––except for Joe Gardner––had fingerprints on file with the local sheriff department. The report I compiled at your request also includes new findings from what we seized last Wednesday when raiding Chief Detective Riggleman's home. We also determined that the white heroin that caused the overdose of the young man in the jail admitting cell matched the China White confiscated at the Bone Shrine." Condran paused to sip from his water bottle. "The lab is still processing evidence from a related raid conducted Monday, November 27th. I expect there will be more search warrants before we're done. Our lab analysis work has been fast-tracked, but isn't completed yet, sir."

The judge thanked the trooper for his exceedingly prompt response dictated by the circumstances. "Captain Condran, you say you don't have a positive match, but do the fingerprints found on the bird skeleton at the Bone Shrine on Sunday match those of the defendant?"

"This was the initial test conducted on the owl findings and our State lab scientists are certain that none of the prints found on the owl skeleton match those of Joseph Gardner. There are partial finger-prints of his on the souvenir pin that belonged to him, but they are overlapped with additional partials that, in fact, match the whole prints on the owl skull. Again, the ones on the owl bones do not match Joe Gardner's fingerprints." The Duke rubbed his chin.

Rochelle hoped the prints belonged to a *Tramposo,* if only to clear both Joe and Gunnar. Judge Kantadillo looked up from the report. "Captain, can you tell me how you are certain this new evidence from the Bone Shrine is related to the drowning of Mary Quinn?"

"Yes, your Honor. The hair belongs to the drowned teenage girl," Condran added. "There is nothing presented in this case to indicate a physical altercation prior to her giving birth. The braid was missing from her scalp at the time Deputy Zach Riggleman arrived on the scene. This new evidence also makes it even less likely that the defen-dant would have had the time to complete all the things he's been charged with committing."

The judge shifted uneasily in his chair behind the massive desk. "Captain, for clarification, your report provides an event chronology from the night in question." The judge gave a rundown of the report time estimates of the known, undisputed events where from 11:00 p.m. the defendant explored the Bone Shrine, found and hid the First

Aid kit, drove the car to the pond, ran out of gas, helped with a highly precipitous childbirth, ran/walked to get gas; and returned to the scene at 2:00 a.m. "For the record and briefly, Captain Condran, could you walk us through the estimated chain of events in your report that immediately following the birth of the girl, including those related to your new after-discovery evidence from Sunday?"

"Yes, your Honor." The Duke spoke rapidly. "Following the birth of the baby, the defendant is accused of having had a physical altercation with the new mother. He then disrobed, carried the infant into the pond, coerced Mary Quinn into this same water that contained a rancid, bloated carp. He physically drowned her, yanked her braid and its souvenir pin from her scalp, abandoned the newborn on the air mattress, put his clothes back on, walked a quarter-mile away from the freeway to the Bone Shrine, carefully removed the owl skeleton from its altar, severed the end of the braid, inserted it and the pin inside the owl skull, replaced the delicate skeleton on top of the altar, returned to the car, gathered up the empty gas can and water bottle, and headed off to the closest open gas station. Your honor, not only is that exceedingly fast work, but the half-hour we've allowed as the maximum time he would have had available is exceedingly generous."

"Generous, in what way?" the judge asked.

"Considering it was the teen girl's first baby, a one hour childbirth is atypically fast. Also, the defendant was going through heroin withdrawals with vomiting and nausea when walking and running during the five miles to the Chevron mini-mart."

Captain Condran stopped and took a sip of water when the judge thumbed through the report.

Judith Rose slowly stood. "I'm not getting much respect with regards to my objections on this morning's testimony, your Honor. However, I just listened to this witness, with the jury no longer present. He is taking it upon himself to make a closing statement complete with a detailed chronology of what might have occurred on the night in question."

The judge set down the report and leaned back. "Ms. Rose, far more disturbing than the captain's timeline that refers to your own closing arguments and cross-examinations, I keep wondering why the Bone Shrine evidence unearthed three days ago was not found during the initial search of the crime scene. Increasingly, we are finding that such irregularities are not isolated incidents in this case."

Judge Kantadillo turned to the court reporter: "Note that the lab reports for the owl remains with the pin and hair are after-discovery evidence severed from Mary Quinn on the night she drowned, but not discovered by law enforcement until Sunday, November 26th, 2000––post-verdict."

Judge Kantadillo turned the page of his report. "Captain, with this being the post-verdict sentencing hearing related to after-discovery evidence and the related obstruction-of-justice concerns, what has the State Patrol been able to determine thus far?"

Condran immediately outlined his core findings from the past week. "Sir, the white heroin found in the Columbia Basin since the Bone Shrine confiscation, comes from the same core batch of what was confiscated on the night of Mary Quinn's drowning. Namely, the K-9 discoveries from Roger Riggleman's basement, the Sheriff department camera bag residue, and the drug in the overdose death at the Wanapum Jail last week all match the heroin from the First Aid kit."

"Captain Condran, in taking over the investigation of this case, is it your professional assessment that Sheriff Detective Roger Riggleman directly compromised the integrity of the evidence used to convict the defendant of these crimes?"

Rochelle expected The Duke to hesitate for at least a bit when being put on the spot, but he responded directly. "On the basis of the after-discovery evidence linked to Roger Riggleman, it disheartens me to say that this case was overtly compromised by Wanapum County's lead investigator. Beyond the recent heroin evidence directly linked to him, we also believe the chief investigator coerced the defendant's silence by orchestrating an assault on him after the placement of two undocumented assailants inside the jail on the morning of Joe Gardner's arrest."

Condran went on to say that Roger Riggleman was also directly linked to his daughter-in-law's attempted currency smuggling–– $70,000 in cash. "This, and the attempted kidnapping of Mary Quinn's infant daughter are also being further investigated." The Duke paused and looked directly at Rochelle, Biff and Kuma before continuing. "Your Honor, my investigation team has more work to do, but the State Patrol is convinced that Roger Riggleman has been an active and key player in the underground heroin trade of the Columbia Basin. It is the estimation of the Washington State Patrol that Sheriff Detective Riggleman took many measures to obstruct justice in this case and falsely pin his own drug activities solely on the defendant, Joseph Gardner."

"Thank you for your prompt, efficient work and for your sworn testimony today, Captain Condran."

The Duke left the witness stand. Angus sat erect and Judith Rose fidgeted, her eyes bulging with frustration.

Like on verdict day, Joseph John Gardner, III, was again asked to rise. The judge's words hit Rochelle's mind like fog: for the misdemeanor drug paraphernalia charge with its *nolo contendere* plea, Kantadillo stipulated a 90-day sentence with credit for time served while awaiting this trial. He added that the defendant would be required to attend a monitored drug rehabilitation program for the next two years.

The judge's voice then boomed. "There is much yet to be determined to solve the felonies committed in this case, but the after-discovery evidence is overwhelming. The defendant did not receive a fair trial from Wanapum County. Joseph John Gardner alone was singled out for prosecution for both the murder and heroin transaction. The court records will note that I have been informed that the arraignment of Roger Riggleman later today in a different venue of Washington state will include, among other crimes, felony charges for obstruction-of-justice during his official investigation of this case."

"Excuse me, your Honor," Judith Rose stood and shouted when the judge lifted his gavel. "Point of due process. That trial is not underway, nor has guilt been established. Accordingly, I make a motion for a retrial of this case."

"Objection, your Honor," Angus said standing a few feet from the prosecuting attorney. The judge was having none of it. Rochelle's ears rang from the slam of his gavel. When he ordered the lawyers to sit, they shrank into their separate chairs, almost sheepishly.

"I wish to thank both attorneys for their hard work in this difficult trial. Any consideration for retrial is out of order.

Judge Kantadillo scanned his courtroom to garner full attention.

"The defense motion presently before the court for *Arrest of Judgment* is hereby sustained." The looming judge, with no further explanation, lifted and slammed his gavel again.

The decision came fast. This strange legal term where the *judgment* of the jury had been *arrested* by the judge, took a moment for Rochelle to register. She watched Kantadillo retire to his chamber without turning back around. Only when Angus smiled and turned to shake Joe's hand did the implication sink into Rochelle's overwhelmed brain. Biff elbowed her good arm and grinned broadly. The girl turned to Kuma, held up her hands, and uncrossed her fingers.

"*Arrest of Judgment,*" she told him over the courtroom chatter like the term was commonplace. "Joe walks free!"

Kuma then smiled, too, and pumped his fist towards the courtroom ceiling. "Joe is a free man!" he yelled louder and with more enthusiasm than she'd ever heard from the teen. Rochelle held her own fist hard against her nose to keep the tears from gushing.

When Kuma yelled, Joe spun around and two-handed with cuffed wrists, held his arms up as high as he could. "I'm free, Mom. Hey you guys, I'm free!"

Judith Rose, the prosecuting attorney, didn't chase down the judge. She ignored Angus and Joe, gathered up her briefcase, and held her head professionally high while following the side aisle to the main courtroom door.

Angus slapped Joe on the shoulder, removed his Wünderland tie––a sepia-colored one with a three-legged dog on front––and looped it over Joe's head. He left the Wünderland noose hanging loosely and beamed at his mom. She ran up and hugged him, taking care to protect her left hand still hidden in the sling. One-armed, Rochelle took her sweet time before letting go of her boy.

Once she did, Biff stepped up and grabbed the noose around Joe's neck. She pulled him down and whispered in his ear. Rochelle overheard, just barely. "See, my friend, Mary was watching over your bony backside!"

Joe pecked her on the cheek and smiled.

Rochelle turned to see Duke Condran still seated, deep in thought, in the gallery. She waved her hand until she had his attention. "Thank you for your detailed report, Captain," she said, startling him.

He promptly stood with his worn leather briefcase and came over. "I'm pleased this worked out for you and your son," he said to Rochelle before turning to Angus. "And that was an innovative bit of lawyering from you, Mr. MacIntosh."

"Thank you, sir. And I was pleasantly surprised when the judge asked for your testimony."

Biff beamed up at The Duke. "My parents insist I start college in January. Looks like I need to inform them that it won't be at Columbia Gorge College in The Dalles."

"Where then?" he asked.

"Moses Lake. I was accepted in the criminal justice program at Big Bend College. I'm wondering if you might need a work-study intern," she added, pointing to herself.

Captain Condran rubbed his chin. "What do you see yourself doing thirty years from now, Biff?"

Biff pointed to the bench. "I'm going to preside over trials like Judge Kantadillo."

"Judge Biffadillo," said Joe and openly laughed.

"That's a long, long way away," Biff added, ignoring her friend. "Right now, if all your attention goes to cleaning out a corrupt sheriff department and taking down who knows how many drug lords, I'd hate to see Mary's murderer escape."

"I agree," said Condran looking first at Mary, then at Joe and Rochelle. "Trust me on that one."

"And this one can do anything she sets her mind to do," said Rochelle, putting her hand on the girl's shoulder. "Like finding the one who killed her best friend."

Captain Condran looked down at Biff. "The timeline you spelled out at the pond on Sunday really helped with my report for the judge. Thank you for that. After the holidays when you've started your program, give me a call."

"I still have your card from the day of the botched kidnapping," said Biff.

He shook each of their hands firmly, wished them all luck, and excused himself.

El Padre had been sitting in the back corner of the gallery for the sentencing, but was standing next to them now. "I'm so pleased for you, Joseph."

Joe's face turned somber when he looked at the priest. "And, for Mary, it's time for me to check out the Gorge and breathe into my head again, the good life we shared."

"And like Chief Broom, you get to have a fresh start," the priest told him. Joe, Biff and Father José walked with the bailiff to where Big Max and Squat Sam waited by the door.

Rochelle was left standing with Angus. She'd scarcely forgotten how tense it had been with him. Even without looking her in the eye, he'd laid into her over the suicide-defense. She stepped in front of him with her good arm extended. "You did your job, good sir," she said when he shook her hand, but didn't looked up from his briefcase. "Thank you for not dumping our case when you could have, or maybe should have. You freed him somehow. That's amazing, Angus."

The lawyer seem centered, like the first time she'd met him in his primitive office. "I doubt that Wanapum County has ever witnessed anything this corrupt before," he said quietly. "A motion for an *Arrest of Judgment* is exceedingly rare, but I thought it might work in this case, as fouled as the proceedings were on so many fronts." Angus kept his eyes on Joe and the others.

"And you made it work for us. Somehow, you sold the judge."

Angus laughed and leaned in so only she could hear. "Hardly. Judge Kantadillo is the only one to convince Judge Kantadillo on matters concerning his courtroom."

"I just hope the State Patrol investigators find Mary's killer."

Angus nodded and gathered up the report and his notes and snapped them shut inside his briefcase. "Nothing but potholes and perfidy. I doubt I'll ever have a case this confounding ever again." Angus excused himself, barely catching her eye.

Rochelle watched the shy man exit through a gauntlet of reporters waiting outside the main courtroom doors. She turned, scanned the empty jury box, judge's bench and witness stand before noticing Joe's jail guard standing next to the bailiff. "See, I told you that you'd go free," she heard the guard, Big Max, tell Joe when he unlocked the cuffs.

"And, just like me, you never had any doubt, did you Max?" Joe said, rubbing both wrists.

Rochelle listened in from a few yards away.

"I'm thinking it's time for me to call my brother again and get you that try-out," said Max loudly to Joe. "You can ride the Dust Devils to fame, so long as you steer clear of that dirty, smackdown tornado that's been chasing you.

"Then you'd better come down and watch me on opening day," said Joe, winking at Kuma and Father José.

"Only if you comp me box seats," said Max.

"Deal, but you may need to share my VIP section with Biff, El Padre, and my mom."

"A day at the ballpark sure beats hanging out with you jailbirds."

'Hey, I'm out of your cage now, big guy." Joe spread his uncuffed hands wide like wings. "This bird has flown."

CHAPTER THIRTY

December 1ˢᵗ, 2000

Joe walked free but uneasy into a sun about to set. Frigid gusts blew against his cheeks while he moved along a bluff of the riverfront trail. He didn't stop at the Oregon Ash, leafless in early winter, the place of their first kiss. The Discovery Center appeared in view. Catching his breath, he stared at the pioneer wagon near the front of the museum entrance. He hadn't come to hear the clear voice of Mary, but stopped to listen anyway. When his mind was right, here she sang, always.

This evening her hair--no longer dyed--reflected crimson-gold, the color of the sinking sun. Mesmerized, he soared with her last solo for the End of the Trail Band. Mary closed her eyes to find her signature song:

Once along the river shore,
between the marshy stubble.
Grace amazed, was peeking o'er,
the bank to see her double.

On this brisk evening, she was not with child; Gorge winds swallowed her words.

Mirrored in between the reeds,
in a flow that soon recedes,

a faceless girl is troubled.

Mary walked the crowd and smiled extra specially to Joe before handing him a protected sprig of braided wildflowers, one of the ones they'd dipped, one with a 'Poet's Shooting Star' dangling beneath.

Mary's song ended and the band vanished in the dusk. Joe pulled off his warm-up jacket and laid it out on the wooden driver's bench of the pioneer wagon. He enfolded Mary's delicately braided gift inside his quilted coat.

A gruff voice called him over. Joe stepped beside the anvil and fire to help the wheelwright the same way he had when he was eleven-years-old for the 150th year celebration of pioneers coming west on this trail. Joe helped position a length of the iron so the wheelwright could pound it into a belt-like strap. Joe was given the honor of pouring cool water over the nearly molten metal. He clutched his pail and poured the fluid evenly. The orange-red iron shrank and sealed tight to a wheel made ready to roll--tough and smoother--towards a new pioneering life.

A train raced below the bluff with wheels clanking. When the whistle died down and the long line of freight cars disappeared upriver, a loud hooting remained. Joe heard what he'd come for. Next to the trail between museum and bluff, Joe found the night owl standing atop his large cage, the door flinging open and shut in the bursts of wind. The Great Horned Owl stretched wings that would never fly and called out a never-dying urge to live fully.

The big raptor had hooted in chorus with trains ever since the first day Joe saw him caged here. Maybe the owl wanted to be a hobo, if only he could get the locomotive to stop. Tonight, at dusk, when the sound of the freight train trailed away, his friend kept beckoning anyone who would listen from his perch atop the small aviary.

Once the owl recognized Joe, he stopped and blinked, wide-eyed.

"That's right," Joe said. "Somehow, they freed my sorry behind." The bird nodded with indifference, not needing an explanation for Joe's arrival. "When I got home, I saw where Mom honored you and me with a framed photo. Can you believe she put the memory of the two of us inside her sacred niché?" Joe stayed a few feet away and didn't shout. His friend couldn't fly, but still had keen ears. "In the photo, I'm holding you on my fist." The owl calmed into soft chirps when they talked. "El Padre even had a dream of marrying me and Mary. You flew into his vision and became our witness."

The two of them scanned the lingering view of the big river beyond the bluffs. Strong gusts had turned the water into a layer of frosted white tips. Joe reminded the raptor of the night last week when his sharp talons pierced the craving eyes of the addict swirling inside of him. "I'm only two days free and not that strong," he confessed. Part of him wanted to watch those owl wings lift away from the box, like the way the raptor did in his dreams, but this wise nightbird understood more about the fate of captivity than Joe would ever need to endure.

"Remember the midnight when Grace was born?" Joe stepped closer and asked. "Full moon warm and so still, not anything like this icy blow." Joe pointed over the split-rail cedar fencing into the blustery onrush of early winter.

"You saw it all that night, didn't you?" Joe fixed his eyes downriver, but kept talking low and true. "I knew something had turned bad. I could tell the moment you swooped down hard and angry and veered away with the afterbirth."

The sun showed its last rays beyond the fold of hills in a gorge that turned from brown to green as the big river cut a path from the scablands through an evergreen range of mountains on its way to the ocean. Above them, Joe was sure he heard a different owl hooting. His friend grew animated and hopped from one side of his cage-top to the other, answering back in a special hoot:

Hooo, hooo! Hoo, hoooo, hooooo!

The other owl landed on the edge of the museum roof and, while looking down towards the aviary, continued a duet. Joe eased away from the cage and back in the direction he'd come, all the while trying to keep the two birds in view. Daylight dimmed and the two birds kept up their bluesy call and response. In the last glimpse of what the sun still had to offer, the bird on the roof flew down to land beside the bird who couldn't fly, but was still plenty spry.

Joe, smiling freely, remembered the Oregon Trail wagon to pick up Mary's braided sprig and his jacket. In a lull when the wind stopped overhead, Joe heard pounding wings of the Great Horned female.

Joe's heart beat wildly when a pebble hit his bedroom window like the peck of a beak. He sat up and pinched the bridge of his nose. "Have I been dreaming?" he asked aloud. The sound of very real footsteps on the stairwell up to his bedroom squeaked the way they always did, a wonderful sound.

Joe had been clutching his mother's statuette throughout his lucid dream. Try as he might, Joe couldn't remember where in his house he'd picked up the little sculpture of Mary cradling her baby. He set it on his nightstand and turned the braided sprig upside-down so the resin-hardened Shooting Star rested safely against the Christ child in Mary's arms. But, in his dream, wasn't he just given this same preserved wildflower?

He nearly knocked over both statuette and sprig when, shyly, his own beautiful Mary slipped into his bedroom. It was really her. "I want to drown in you, Mary," he begged, wide awake. "I really need to drown in you!"

Drowning with her or not, Joe took what Mary freely gave. His heart pain and fears dissolved within her soothing presence. Wind gusts rattled the window when her face landed cheek-to-cheek with his. He made room for her to sit, glowingly naked, beside him. Her hands lightly enclosed his on her lap. Joe could hear her breathing, but he wasn't sure.

Mary touched Joe's shoulder to tell him it was time to breathe deeper, time to recline on the shrine of his mattress that had never been quite wide enough for the two young lovers. His eyes blinked dryly, free of tears. He filled with Mary's fresh peace. His arms and hands belonged to her. Once again, she touched his temples much more softly than he'd ever touched his own face. Her tenderness waged war on his grief and won.

Joe gazed towards their shared recollections. Chimes of "Holy,

Holy, Holy" poured in from far, far away. Mary's will and Joe's voice powered the hymn until a mystic joyfulness rained down. He'd never sung with power or nearly as well. That part was all Mary.

Joe opened his lids, or rather, Mary opened her eyes with him. Mary's face was his face; Mary's nose was his nose; Mary's breath was his breath. He heard no noise; he had no taste; there was nothing to see and nothing to smell. All he possessed in his new world was Mary to sense it all for him.

Fully within, she pulsated with inner light, and life beyond life. She caressed his crown, his middle eye, his nose and lips, his chin. Onto his heart chakra, she pressed down softly with both hands to aid the opening Joe had latched so tightly within.

Her touch pulled energy through an ancient conduit he couldn't fathom, but could only allow. His solar plexus calmed when her palms hovered above. Delicately, she continued below to find him ready.

He was hers. On the shrine of eternity, far beyond their first breaths of life and the reaper's bone, Mary and Joe floated into essence. His lover's fingers were of silk and rhyme until all senses made sense and the pleasure wasn't desire, but perpetual joy. She was his and he was hers and the tenderness rose higher until Mary, full of grace, and Joe, full of Mary, burst like a fountain.

Thoroughly calmed and amazed, he watched Mary stand and kiss the statuette. She fixed the wildflower sprig into her crimson-gold hair. Maybe his and Mary's lives were meant to unfold in precisely this way.

Joe watched her rise from his ragged altar of a bed and turn to float face down. Illumination filled the dark room as though the universe were theirs alone. She glowed white--divine--until gone through his window into a night of stars.

He stood at the window and kept his eyes on the black and clear winter sky. Maybe her work on this side was complete and she'd ascended for good, but Joe doubted such finality. Nothing could steal her.

In freedom, he'd stopped dwelling on vengeance from that night, an impulse that would only keep triggering the worst in him. His own bad choices had brought on the horror. Today, he needed to hold, not his anger, but love, their love.

Mary's braided treasure to him was an ever oneness. Only a handful of sprigs possessing the rare Gorge blossom had been dipped. One went to her mother, another to his mom. One was for her best friend, another dangled inside the Pathfinder. She gifted the last Shooting Star to him and he gifted it back to her, always to be theirs––*Dodecatheon poeticum*––brightly in its season.

Joe never forgot how Mary lifted away.

∽

THE END

ATTRIBUTIONS

• "Grace Amazed" lyrics by the author ©2021. Inspiration from the traditional Swedish lullaby: "Vaggvisa för min son, Carl," by Carl Michael Bellman (Stockholm, circa 1787).

• "Holy Holy, Holy! Lord God Almighty" lyrics, Reginald Heber, 1826. The music, 1861, by John Bacchus Dyke.

ALSO BY SCOTT MACFARLANE

THE HIPPIE NARRATIVE:

A Literary Perspective on the Counterculture (2007)

"An important work of American Letters."

— GURNEY NORMAN, AUTHOR OF *DIVINE RIGHT'S TRIP,* A NOVEL SERIALIZED IN THE LAST WHOLE EARTH CATALOG (1971)/ POET LAUREATE OF KENTUCKY, 2009-10.

"Scott MacFarlane contextualizes the augmenting popularity of Vonnegut during the first wave of counterculture."

— HAROLD BLOOM, RENOWNED LITERARY CRITIC, FOR CHAPTER REPRINTED IN *BLOOM'S MODERN CRITICAL INTERPRETATIONS: SLAUGHTERHOUSE-FIVE* (2009)

ABOUT THE AUTHOR

Born and raised in the Pacific Northwest, the author lives in the Skagit River Valley of western Washington with his wonderfully supportive wife, Brenda, who is also an artist.

Key creative writing mentors have included the outstanding novelists Steve Heller, Ron Carlson, and Tom Legendre.

Throughout the writing of this novel, the story benefited greatly from Cate Perry, an exceptional critique partner.

Threads of inspiration for this novel:

• Served as founding executive director for the Columbia Gorge Discovery Center in The Dalles, OR.

• A transit operator for 9+ years, (and increasingly disturbed in recent years by the growing ridership of addicts and homeless).

• Studied one year at *Katedralskolan* in Linköping, Sweden as a Rotary International Exchange Student.

• Worked one summer at age 19 on the potato line at Basin Produce near Moses Lake, WA.

NEXT UP

Coming next from NichéEco Imprints:

WHO? The Bone Shrine Sequel
   (Book Two of the Shrine Series)

Newsletter, Blog, and Updates:
   www.nicheeco.com

REVIEWS & READER COMMENTS

A heart-pounding, page-turning story...

MacFarlane transports the reader to a world steeped in mystery and intrigue as eighteen-year-old Joe struggles to prove himself innocent of his teen sweetheart's murder. When Joe was released from juvie, all of his friends shunned him except for the lovely Mary who stood like a rock with him. But now Mary is dead, and Joe is behind bars, waiting for the trial for Mary's murder. What lies in store for Joe who has done nothing but destroy his life until now? MacFarlane's writing is fluid, drawing the reader further and further into Joe's world. Equal parts intriguing and suspenseful, the plot unfolds gradually, with constant tension at the back, merging real-life trivialities with supernatural elements. MacFarlane vividly brings his characters to life while conveying the underlying themes of love, teenage drama, fear, trauma, grief, family, and the real transformation of the human heart with utter conviction and thoughtfulness. A clever, smart, and utterly engrossing novel that fans of sophisticated crime fiction won't want to miss.

--The Prairies Book Review

"A great novel…"
  --*Mark Condran, Musician*

"What a fabulous and beautiful story that is both intimate and universal--a peek into the raw struggles of teen pregnancy, addiction, injustice, and forgiveness. The author's love for these characters and the places they go is impressive and inspiring."
  --*Dr. Carolyn Wortham, Public Health Specialist*

"Redemption of a naive teen tragically scapegoated by modern horrors. Set in real northwestern open lands, the fictional characters feel just as real in this wonderfully engaging tale of a love that cannot be lost."
  -- *Ken Steinke, retired IT professional*

"Scott Macfarlane's Bone Shrine is a well-paced murder mystery that examines its protagonist's addiction honestly and still honors the humanity in the addict, scratching well below the surface of his monkey. Circumstance, drugs, greed, death, spirituality, love and birth and a well-paced murder trial keep the reader turning pages to the end. Nods to local sports figures who battled injury and brought the spiritual combination of Christianity and Buddhism are weaved into this wonderful, painful, clever, and in the end, excellent story."
  --*Bill Segesser*

"The courtroom scenes were engrossing and compelling. I liked the way the story fits "pieces" into a mosaic of feelings and memories that many readers will relate to their own lives. Seamlessly flows through a complex narrative."
  --*A.L. Zuvers*, author, *Looking Back Toward Tomorrow*

"A well written mystery, Great plot and characters woven together in an intricate story that keeps the reader engaged. The ending screams for a sequel, which I hope is ready soon. Would make a very good mini series in the spirit of Mare of Easton." (five stars)

—Lee Bedell, Storm Lake Literary Critic

"Impressive. Loved all the twists and turns of the story. The character development was right on and the dialogue for these diverse characters very believable."
    —Colette Ward, author of *Strange Crossroads*

"I grew up in the eastern Oregon town of LaGrande and later worked in Portland for many years with the Trailblazers. As a lifelong Northwesterner, I came away very impressed with *The Bone Shrine*. This richly layered novel weaves the fascinating history of the Columbia River into a riveting crime drama, one featuring a contemporary and ill-fated teen couple. The Oregon Trail, flooding of Celilo Falls, a Stonehenge peace replica, the creation of the first atomic bomb, and even the Columbia Basin pothole ponds become seamless parts of this coming-of-age story. I thoroughly enjoyed the realism of *The Bone Shrine* and read it cover-to-cover in a few days. Set against the rich history of the interior Pacific Northwest, the novel never shies away from pressing modern social concerns."
    —Bucky Buckwalter, Retired VP-General Manager, Portland Trailblazers

Darkness, mystery, intrigue, and murder fill the pages of MacFarlane's page-turning crime drama. Troubled and lost, eighteen-year-old Joe finds himself into the middle of a murder investigation after his teen sweetheart Mary dies of drowning. While Joe is adamant he has nothing to do with Mary's death, the first responder police officer Deputy Zach Riggleman has another idea. Joe's past juvenile record and his drug habits further add to the police's conviction. But Rochelle, Joe's mother, is determined to get him out. MacFarlane's authoritative prose stretches out with rich imagination, and his characterization shines. The troubled Joe is endearing with his incredibly flawed personality. Readers will find it easy to sympathize with him and identify with his all-too-young adult fragilities. The driven, sympathetic Rochelle is an absolute darling. Between Joe's coming-of-age journey and the hard-hitting crime drama, A sense of mystery and doom prevails throughout the narrative. MacFarlane skillfully incorporates elements of horror and young adult drama to craft an inspiring tale. With its engrossing storyline, morally ambiguous theme, and convincing, real-life characters, fans of dark crime fiction will have plenty to enjoy. This is an inspired effort from a very talented author.

--*Bookview Review* (Gold Medallion award)

"This novel should be a movie, or even a mini-series."
--*Nick Mattson, Baker River Hotshots*

NOTE: If you've finished the story, we welcome your comments at info@ nicheeco.com or wherever you obtained the novel. Thank you!

Made in the USA
Middletown, DE
21 November 2022

15431633R00184